*Thank...*

**Killing Hope** is the first of three Amazon #1 Best Selling Gabe Quinn Thrillers, including the follow-on novels **Crossing Lines** and **Taking Liberty**.

Some background events in this novel are continued into the next two Gabe Quinn Thrillers, therefore it is recommended to read all three in the correct sequence – **Killing Hope, Crossing Lines** and **Taking Liberty** – to ensure the best reading experience. *Thanks!*

Keith Houghton

## Killing Hope
### (Gabe Quinn Thriller #1)

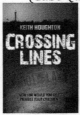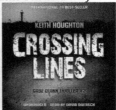

Also available in eBook and Audiobook formats

## Crossing Lines
### (Gabe Quinn Thriller #2)

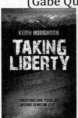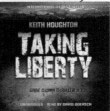

## Taking Liberty
### (Gabe Quinn Thriller #3)

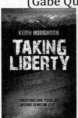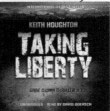

# KILLING HOPE

*GABE QUINN THRILLER #1*

## KEITH HOUGHTON

SCRIPTACULAR

ISBN: 1490413669

## For more information

Web
**www.keithhoughton.com**

Twitter
**https://twitter.com/KeithHoughton**

Facebook
**http://www.facebook.com/KeithHoughtonAuthor**

### Piracy

# ~ For Lynn, my Wife ~

*Whose endless love, faith and
encouragement is my guiding light*

Keith Houghton

# KILLING HOPE

*"If you could save a million lives by taking one ...
would you?"*

Keith Houghton

# PROLOGUE

*Revenge was a dish best served cold . . .*

He thought about the saying as he stood silently among the summer dresses and the skirt-suits hanging in the closet. He'd waited years for this moment, patiently counting down the days while adding up her sins.

The long wait had made him hungry for retribution, eager to take his fill, to thank her personally for screwing with his head. Now that he was here, all he wanted to do was gorge himself on the gory and the glory of vengeance. These final few minutes were killing him.

The confines of the closet were claustrophobic. He could smell her sweet sickly scent indelibly interwoven in the department store fabrics. One of those trendy homogenous perfumes promoted by a passing starlet and soon forgotten. It was as if she were in here with him. It made him gag.

At precisely six-thirty-five, he heard the front door to the house open and close. He heard a woman's voice complaining to herself about the inclement Philadelphia weather as she shucked off her raincoat and kicked off her pumps.

Unconsciously, he flexed his gloved fingers.

Next came the sound of paper ripping as she went through her mail. He heard bleeps followed by monotonic messages as she listened to the calls left on her answerphone. Everybody wanted a piece of the psychiatrist. But only he would eat the whole pie.

His pulse was thrumming in his throat.

Then he heard heavy feet working their way up the stair treads. The light came on in the bedroom. Any lesser intruder would have shied away from the sudden incandescence slanting through the slats. Not him. His purpose was his resolve.

She slung her suit jacket onto the bed, dragged the ponytail holder from her hair and shook out her locks.

She was oblivious to his presence in among her clothes.

No idea that she was about to be paid back, in full and then some.

He felt a rising tide of revulsion surge within him as he watched her pull off pearl earrings and discard them on the dressing table. She looked younger than he remembered – but then again he was just a boy the last time she'd meddled with his mind. A little wider in the love handles area, but otherwise in good health.

Not for long.

He sensed his muscles tighten as she peeled off her shirt and then shimmied out of her skirt.

Something primeval was moving around inside of him.

Something animalistic.

Something needful and desperate to break loose.

He waited until she had shrugged her silky black slip halfway over her head before bursting into the bedroom.

She didn't see it coming.

He struck her with a balled fist, hard, and she crumpled to the bed without making a single sound.

Then she was all his – for the weekend.

And it was time to feast.

# 1

This was the part of the job I hated the most.

No matter how many times I hauled myself through the process it never got any easier.

Some things are like that.

We are told, as children, that fear comes from not knowing. On this particular occasion I knew exactly what to expect: I knew the horror that awaited me – and yet fear was gripping my stomach in a cold fist. The rationalist within me argued it was my old ulcer in need of lubrication, when really, if I were brutally honest, I was chilled to the core at the thought of what was to come.

Being a father does that, I guess.

*   *   *

It was 3 a.m. on a cool January morning in Los Angeles – the kind that sucks the warmth right out of the skin. I should have been in bed, oblivious to all that is terrible. Instead, I was attending a murder scene.

There are three things you should know about me. The first is, I used to look after myself. Keep in some kind of a shape. One of those guys you see sweating down the street first thing on a Sunday morning, working his way toward his first heart attack at thirty-five. I used to do a lot of things. Not anymore. The second is, I don't believe in coincidences. And the third? Trust me, you don't need to know about my obsessions just yet.

The Union Pacific rail yard is an eerie place after dark. Littered with the corpses of rusting freight cars and skeletal cranes. Through the murk, I could see six or seven police units parked alongside the train tracks, deep in the impenetrable shadow of the 7th Street Bridge. Two plainclothed automobiles, and a Crime Lab van. Flashing neon casting luminous specters. Not the kind of place you bring the kids for a picnic.

I watched my step as I crossed oily shingle. Made my way toward a willowy officer standing on her own in the middle of the tracks. She looked lost. Indecisive. Fear had carved the words *scared shitless* into her face. I wondered if mine looked the same.

"They think it's your boy," she called as I approached.

No meet and greet. No ID request. No polite pleasantries on what an unusually cold morning it was. Just straight for the kill.

Diesel clawed at my throat.

"This your first homicide?" I called back.

The willowy officer offered a stiff nod and hugged herself for warmth. "I think they put me up here for a joke. Do *you* think they put me up here for a joke?"

She was probably right, but I shook my head all the same. She was a week out of the Academy and shy of street seasoning by twenty years. Somebody was enjoying a laugh at her expense. Not me; I would have run a three minute mile if only my legs were game.

"Where is everybody?"

She pointed with a flashlight. "Under the bridge." The beam struck riveted stanchions, lost itself in the darker cavities. "Down by the river. You get there through a gap in the chain-link. That's where they found the body. Down there. I've never seen nothing like that before. Want me to show you?"

She wanted to. Desperately. I could sense it. *Feel* it. Anything to get out of this godforsaken rail yard and back among the living.

"I know the way," I said to her dismay.

The crime scene lay under the dark, ribbed underbelly of the bridge. Down along the manmade river channel: where the missing showed up – either drugged or dead and sometimes both.

Let's make no bones about this: ordinarily, I am unfazed by the process. Dead bodies don't give me the creeps. I have seen enough of evil to know it exists and there isn't a damned thing you can do about it. But tonight was different. Tonight I was on tenterhooks. Wound up and as jumpy as a kid on his first date. The location, its significance and the fact I was working my first homicide case in twelve months were all conspiring to jar my nerves and throw me off balance.

Sometimes staying in bed isn't a bad idea.

"You took your time."

I nodded a *fashionably late* nod to my fledgling partner of the last three weeks, Jamie Garcia. She was holding open a flap in the chain-link fence. Even at this late hour her whole demeanor spoke business.

I ducked through the gap.

She handed me a patrolman's flashlight. "What took you so long?"

"Age, mostly." I shook the dead lamp. "This thing work?" I banged it with my fist. The light sputtered, then stayed lit. I played the beam across Jamie's face. "Sure you're up for this, Jamie?"

Jamie gave me one of those glances that women do when they want a man to know they have all their bases covered.

"I'm not the one who looks like they've seen a ghost," she said.

*   *   *

13

The first attending officers had rigged a gaudy yellow-and-black tape cordon around the crime scene. Given our isolation, it was more window dressing than functional.

We worked our way down the steep concrete slope. Sending loose grit skittering ahead of us as we went.

Behind the flimsy tape, Forensics was cataloguing potential bits of evidence in the glare of portable lamps. Scrupulously. Like archaeologists. Nothing like you see in the movies. In real life, death is far from glamorous. No Gucci sunglasses or Jimmy Choos here. These boys and girls from the Crime Scene Unit wore surgeon's slippers and hairnets. Here to collect evidence, not compliments.

Captain De La Hoya of our neighboring Hollenbeck Division acknowledged our arrival with a wave, broke off his conversation with one of his detectives and met us at the tape. I hadn't seen Miguel De La Hoya in over half a year. There was a time we'd meet socially, at least once a week. Those days were long gone.

"Gabe," he grabbed my hand and squeezed it, hard enough to show he meant business. "Good to see you, mi amigo. It's been too long. I keep meaning to call. But you know how it is. How are you? I heard you were back. Missed you, bro." The handshake turned into a brotherly hug. I let it go its course.

Miguel and I have history. Good history. I'd been neglectful.

I felt him pat me out. "You feel thin. Here, let me look at you." He held me at arms' length and looked me over like a parent examining a muddy child. "Holy shit, Gabe. You look like shit. Real shit. None of that cotton candy shit these kids call shit. Can't be easy for you being back here. How you holding up?"

"Fine." A fib. A little white lie. Call it what you will. No one wants to hear a moan. It felt like someone was playing a bad Scott Joplin rendition in my stomach. Everything jangling discordantly. "So what we got here, Miguel?"

My old friend from Hollenbeck backed off a little. He looked older than I remembered. Tired. Like he had the weight of the world on his shoulders. "Damned weird is what. Your boy's freaked out half my men. Some of the hardest, too."

Make no mistakes; Miguel is a bulldog of a man. Like the canine in comparison, he is short and stocky in a sturdy kind of way. As such, it takes a bulldozer to move him.

We ducked under the tape.

"You sure it's our boy?"

Miguel let out a shaky breath. "He got a fetish for funerals?"

I glanced at Jamie. She was looking directly at me. Had been all the while. Both our faces told the same horrified story. "Maybe."

A girl from the CSU handed us each a pair of plastic slippers to go over our day shoes.

*   *   *

The victim was a little girl. No older than nine, or maybe ten. I am not good with ages. She was lying face-up on a small plaid blanket – the kind they sell in automobile accessory stores for protecting the velour against pet hair. She had a blaze of fiery-red hair. Porcelain skin. An ankle-length denim skirt with matching jacket. Barbie-pink sneakers over stripy socks. Plastic kiddie jewelry – all intact. Nothing to show she'd been murdered or that she was even dead at all.

My stomach curled into a ball.

"Who found her?"

"Night patrol acting on an anonymous tip-off. Looks like the call came from a disposable cell somewhere in North Hollywood. No traceable number."

I inched my way forward over loose gravel.

The child might have been sleeping, had it not been for the positioning of her limbs: her legs were dead straight, feet angled up on their heels, with hands clasped tight across the chest in the customary pose of interment. It was an uncomfortable posture for the living to hold. Fake. Added post-mortem. I'd seen it before – in the home of the killer's previous victim, less than twenty-four hours earlier. At both scenes, the killer had sprinkled red rose petals around the body, smeared a rough cross of ash on the brow, and arranged the scene like a mock burial.

I caught sight of a patrolman quietly parting with his evening meal down by the water's edge. That had been me, twelve months ago – back when Miguel and I had last stood on this unholy ground.

"This place is pretty isolated," I heard Jamie say. "Our killer could be local."

Fact: killers tend to dump bodies in convenient places: in a dirt ditch down the side of a desolate country road; in the backyard under three feet of topsoil; at the bottom of a reedy lake. Jamie was right: the killer must have known about this location, beforehand. Known how to slip through the gap in the chain-link fence. Known to avoid the slippery, deadly drainage gratings spewing runoff into the river.

In the magnesium light coming from the portable lamps everything looked like the surface of the Moon: dead, bleached. But I knew it was pitch black here normally at this hour. The killer would have known that too. Known he could spend as much time down here as he liked, arranging the scene without the risk of being interrupted. Or caught.

I looked closer.

As with the previous victim, the child had no defensive wounds. No obvious signs of trauma. No ligature marks. Everything neat and tidy. No outward sign of an attack of any kind.

Even in death she was tragically pretty, but her lips were the color of her denim.

Now I could see why half of Miguel's men were spooked: it felt like we were intruding on a funeral, and in clumsy plastic slippers.

I forced cool air into my lungs.

"How long's she been down here?"

"The Medical Examiner thinks less than a couple of hours. First responders got here within five minutes of the call."

Still warm. Blood pooling. Suicidal cells.

I slipped my hand out of its glove and picked up one of the rose petals. It was a damp slice of black velvet between my fingertips. I rubbed at it, crumbling it up.

Jamie came close. "What about sexual assault?"

We all looked at her. Every eye beneath the bridge. I saw a shiver run through Miguel's tense expression; he was a father too. Most here were. It was one of those subjects everybody was thinking but nobody wanted to broach.

Miguel rocked on his feet. "The ME doesn't think so. Sweet Jesus, I hope not. But you'll have to confirm it with him, later."

Jamie went down on her haunches. She didn't seem fazed at all. Not one bit. Still new to all this. Still in practical mode. I watched her place a rubberized thumb against the girl's blue lips, apply a little pressure. But the child's mouth remained defiantly closed.

Miguel touched my arm. "This was tucked under her hands when we found her."

It was a transparent evidence bag. I peered at the contents through the cloudy plastic. Inside was a torn photograph – half of a larger print, ripped right down the middle. I could just make out the image of a man in a tuxedo. He was smiling, looked happy.

I recognized his face.

"Thanks," I said, and slid it in my pocket.

# 2

I should have gone straight home. I didn't. I headed north instead – through deserted streets crowded with shuttered stores. I was too pumped to think about sleep and had been for months.

The ripped photograph was burning a hole in my pocket.

I jumped on and off Highway 101, following illuminated signs for Dodger Stadium. Traffic was light; a few garbage trucks doing the rounds. Shift workers and the usual insomniacs. I passed a billboard advertising courses at USC – a man and woman with Colgate smiles – then left the highway and crossed quiet intersections until I came to Carroll Avenue. I wasn't exactly sure what I hoped to find here. The neighborhood looked asleep. No surprise at this hour. I slowed the car to a crawl, passing darkened homes, then pulled up behind a black SUV parked under a streetlight.

In the dark, the house wasn't much to look at: a Victorian-style two-floor clapboard affair with a porch and pitched roofs. A long flight of stone steps. All of it leaning back from the roadside on a slight elevation of grass and azalea. It looked like the Norman Bates house. A little rain and some lightning and you'd expect to hear a few screams coming from that tiny attic window. I hadn't noticed the similarity yesterday, in broad daylight.

Darkness has a way of making the mundane look monstrous.

I took out the photograph and peered at it in the wan street lighting.

The man's face looked suddenly less happy, like he was wearing the smile for somebody else's benefit. Not mine. Maybe it was the poor illumination. I turned on the interior light for a better look, took out my reading glasses and peered closer.

The picture had been taken in a TV studio; I could see big TV cameras and boom microphones in the background. There was a guy just over his shoulder. A gray-haired guy with a short gray beard and a pointy face. He was looking at our man in the tux, at the back of his head to be precise, and not at the camera taking the shot.

Pointy Face was wearing a frown from ear to ear.

My cell phone shrilled. I rummaged it out before it woke neighbors and every dog in the vicinity.

A text message:

*'Meet me at Winston's at five-thirty. You're buying.'*

I switched off the light and got out of the car. There was no sign of the crowd that had jostled in this street less than a day earlier. No curtains twitching. No morbid fascinations behind zoom lenses. Everything ordinary. But police tape still crisscrossed the front door of the Norman Bates house. In just a few plain words it announced that something terrible had happened here, and recently.

I ventured up the stoop, used a pocketknife to break the black-and-yellow seal. I paused to made sure no one was watching before I cracked open the door and slipped inside.

The place was dark, quiet. There was a smell of musk or damp wood. A pine forest after rainfall. The gentle, hypnotic heartbeat of a clock somewhere deeper inside. Could be an ordinary home anywhere, with the family tucked up tight upstairs. A faithful hound curled at the foot of the master bed. Sweet dreams. No idea that an intruder was standing with his back pressed against their front door. Slowly, my eyes adjusted to the gloom. I didn't put on lights. I don't know why. Respect, maybe. Privacy? I stayed there for long seconds, heart pounding, listening, wondering what thoughts had coursed through another man's mind as he'd stood in this same spot early Sunday morning.

Finally, I got out my Maglite and ran the narrow beam across the hallway. Dust motes danced. Mahogany stair rods popped in and out of view. A handrail with traces of fingerprint powder. Ivy green walls. Some of those painted wooden African facemasks, made in China. More chalky dust around a brass light switch. Traces of it all the way up the stairs.

Nothing had changed since yesterday. If you disregarded the latent dust on the doorjambs and the handles, it didn't look like a crime scene at all. An ordinary home. Yours or mine. No real clue pointing to the fatal events that had played themselves out here. No evidence that the place had been swarming with cops, the CSU, the clean-up crew.

But I could still detect a scent of death that no amount of detergent can erase.

\* \* \*

Don't get me wrong; I don't make a habit of creeping around in the dead of night – especially in other peoples' houses. I have my job like you have yours. It's just that mine involves that kind of thing.

I snapped hands inside Latex gloves and followed the Maglite into the living room. It knew the way. The wooden floor complained about my weight. Heels clacked, then turned to soft thuds as I crossed onto thick carpeting.

This was the home of the killer's first victim: Professor Jeffrey Samuels – a singleton in his late fifties – found dead as a doorknob by his cleaning lady early Sunday morning. So far, I knew three definite facts about Professor Jeffrey Samuels of Carroll Avenue:

One, he'd had an ear for Mozart.

And two, he'd had a taste for fancy French wine.

To my unrefined ear, the classics all sounded the same. But I could tell the difference between a merlot and a chardonnay, mainly by their color.

The third fact I was still thinking over. Still tinkering with. Samuels' sexuality probably had no bearing on the case whatsoever, but I wasn't sure. Not yet.

I moved deeper into the living area and scanned the flashlight over everyday bric-a-brac. Shadows scurried to hide themselves in alcoves and behind furniture. There were books on shelves: leather-bounds mixed with softbacks. A few trinkets: souvenirs from vacations outside of the States. More wooden carvings of African witch doctors, droopy-breasted Ethiopian women and genderless figurines entwined in dance, all carved from mahogany or some other dwindling rainforest resource. I kept scanning. I knew what I was looking for. Light glinted off glass, reflecting from framed photographs hung above the fireplace.

The pictures were mainly of him: Samuels. They showed him accepting awards at glitzy ceremonies or posing with celebrities at charity galas. The professor looked uncomfortable with his popularity. A square peg in a round hole. In most of the shots he was wearing the same tuxedo and the same forced smile. Same as the photo heating up my pocket.

There are two reasons why people plaster their living spaces with photographs of themselves: vanity or validation. Judging by Samuels' strained expression, these pictures were more about self-confirmation than narcissism.

One of the frames was slightly tilted on its nail.

You wouldn't notice unless you were looking for it.

And I was looking for it.

There was a sliver of an image in the center of the mount, torn vertically along both edges. It was barely the width of my little finger. I hadn't noticed it yesterday, wasn't exactly sure if the discrepancy had even been there yesterday.

I took the ripped photograph from my pocket and held it against the left edge of the sliver.

They were an exact fit.

\*   \*   \*

Coincidences are for people who think the universe is cute. It isn't.

Something *clunked* upstairs.

For the record, I have this thing I call my *Uh-Oh Radar*. It comes from deep down in the gut and can pick up ley lines better than any dowser. Most of the time it goes about its business without demanding too much attention. But every now and then it screams like a banshee.

I tipped my best ear toward the ceiling, *listened*.

Nobody was home, right? As far as I knew, Samuels had no pets. No tenants. No skeletons in the closet I didn't already know about. No reason why anything should be clunking around upstairs.

All the same, I slid out my firearm.

Something made a *shuffling* sound directly above my head.

Something with weight and purpose.

Instinctively, I started toward the hallway.

Then it sounded like somebody was running. Thudding across the ceiling. Right above me. Moving faster.

I rattled around furniture, rushing to the foot of the staircase. I hollered a police warning and ran the powerful Maglite up the stairs.

On the landing, a drape was fluttering in an open window – a window that hadn't been open a second or two earlier.

*Somebody was in the house!*

I went to take a cautious step up the stairway, and then heard the rumble of an engine kick into life outside. I turned and threw open the front door, clattered down the stone steps – just in time to see a dark SUV tear away from the curbside and go screeching down the street at a breakneck speed.

I got out my phone and snapped a picture of the fleeing vehicle before it was swallowed by the night.

# 3

Recently, more out of convenience than conviction, the all-night bar known as *Winston's* has become my regular haunt of late – and I do mean of *late*. Close enough to my place on Valencia to get me out of the house whenever I'm home.

I squinted at the harsh glare of the strip lights illuminating the sidewalk. A bell tinkled against glass as I went inside.

*Winston's* is actually a 24-hour drugstore with a bar in back. The place has seen easier days, but it does what it says on the sign. The bar itself is comprised of a handful of Formica-covered tables, collapsible chairs, a few rickety stools along the bar and a few rickety regulars propping it up.

I dropped onto a seat.

There was only one other patron in here tonight: a young bearded guy with bushy dreadlocks and a distrusting face. He was seated at a table in the far corner, his usual, with his back to the wall. There was a laptop on the tabletop in front of him. He gave me a nod without looking up from the screen.

Dreads virtually lived here. But then again so did I.

"The usual, Mr. Q?"

Winston Young, the proprietor – seven feet dead in his stocking feet – poured a cup of black coffee, added three sugars, then pushed it across the countertop toward me.

"Thanks."

Distantly, I heard the bell chime against the door. Somebody had entered the store. I knew who that somebody was. The plastic *Lakers* clock on the wall said it was precisely five-thirty. She was right on time. I saw Winston sink into the shadows, like a vampire shrinking from the approaching dawn.

"Of all the bars in all of the world," I heard her call, "isn't it a little early for coffee?"

Whenever my life is in crisis, Eleanor Zimmerman turns up like a bad penny. Stick around long enough and she'll convince you she's my guardian angel.

She perched herself on the stool next to mine and gave me the once over. Eleanor is the white Grace Jones. She has a silvery, box-cut hairdo and impossibly-sharp cheek bones. A dress sense that swings between sixties hippie and eighties disco. Somehow, it works.

"What hole in the ground have you been sleeping in?" she asked. "You look like shit gone bad."

"So the story goes. What do you want, Eleanor?"

"Whisky, for starters." She flapped a hand at Winston.

He leaned out of the shadows, poured her drink at arm's length, and then quickly receded again.

Eleanor downed it in one.

"Isn't it a little early for hard liquor?" I countered.

"What do you care, detective? Moreover, what do I care? It's medicinal. Prescribed, sweetie. If you've got a problem with it, take it up with my shrink." She scooped up a handful of pistachios from a little dish on the bar and started skinning them alive.

I said nothing.

Eleanor detests silence.

I do it on purpose.

She threw the doomed nuts into her mouth and cracked them apart with big white teeth. Then she stared at me, like I had transparent skin and she could see all the darkness churning away inside. "I hear you've been back to the scene of the crime."

She emphasized the last four words, as if they were something to be hallowed. I didn't like it. I made a face to show it. Making faces is one of my fortes. You'll see. Sometimes they get me out of trouble. Mostly, they land me in it.

"Have you been following me?"

"Why, are you on Twitter?"

I shook my head. "Eleanor, it's the best part of a year; I don't need mothering."

"Is that a fact? Have you looked at yourself in the mirror lately? You're a mess, darling. You make Columbo look like the height of fashion. And what is it with those sneakers?"

"They're comfortable."

"With dress pants?"

I sighed; Eleanor never misses a trick.

"When you get to my age you don't do style. You do practical. Besides, you're wearing pajamas underneath your coat, aren't you?"

"That's because it's the middle of the night and I live round the corner." She got out a slender silver tube and hooked it between her lips.

"I thought you quit."

"I did," she said. "But what do you care?" She blew fake smoke in my direction. "Would you like a drag? Oh, that's right: I forget; you quit. Along with everything else."

I unfolded a twenty and a few ones out on the counter, got to my feet. "Sarcasm is the lowest form of wit."

"Who said I was trying to be funny?"

I turned and walked away. "Goodnight, Eleanor."

*     *     *

In my line of work you need patience and cunning. Plus the gumption to know when to use which.

I waited in the shadowy alleyway down the side of *Winston's* for fifteen long minutes until Eleanor decided to call it a night and go home. I made sure she was out of sight before venturing back inside.

Dreads looked up as I approached. "I don't know how you cope with her, man. She's pheromonal."

I frowned. "Is that even a real word?"

"It is in my world."

I pointed to his laptop. "How's the exposé shaping up?"

I saw him loop a defensive arm around the computer. Dreads is a conspiracy theorist, or so he claims.

He hunched over it, protecting it. "That's classified, man. Why are you pushing me? I'm not ready to go public yet. I don't ask about your business – so stop pushing me, man."

"I thought we were buddies."

"Yeah. For sure. Buddies. And that's fine in here. In here we're in the neutral zone. Kind of like lawyer confidentiality. But out there it's a dog eat dog world, man. You're a cop and you're okay. But that don't make us interfaced."

I dug out my phone and brought up the snapshot of the SUV racing away from the Samuels crime scene. It looked like a black smudge in a murky yellow fog. A few blurry lights here and there. Shapes that could be anything. Pathetic, really. I was never any good with cameras. I pushed it across the Formica-covered table.

"Can you do anything with this?"

"Guess I could call my mom. Haven't phoned her in like a month. Too much pressure, man."

"What about the photo?"

He uncoiled himself from the computer, partially tilted its lid away from me before picking up the phone. I watched him turn it around in his hand as if it were a hand grenade. "What's this supposed to be?"

"An SUV."

"No kidding."

"I need the license plate number."

"What you need is a miracle."

"Can you do anything with it?"

"Sure. We're talking *me*, right? But don't you have police tech dudes for this kind of thing?"

I smiled. Over the last ten months or so I'd gotten to know Dreads just about as well as anyone was allowed to get to know Dreads. In a strange kind of way I trusted him. Not the kind of way needed to house-sit or come feed the dog twice a day while you're out at work, but the kind that keeps lips zippered. In some ways it's a deeper kind of trust.

I unfolded a fifty-dollar bill and hooked it over the top of his laptop screen. "You're faster," I said. "By about a week."

# 4

Sometimes I am my own worst enemy.

I still didn't go home. I stayed in my car outside *Winston's* for long minutes, thinking about the missing half of the Samuels photograph and the part still burning a hole in my pocket. The picture had been taken in a TV studio. But which network? And where? More importantly, why had the killer vandalized the photograph in the first place? Why leave one half with the murdered little girl and take the other with him? What did it mean?

I drove, west then south, on automatic pilot. Driving helps me think. I thought about the nature of the two murders, both committed within a small twenty-four hour window. The rose petals. The crosses of ash. The glued lips and the meticulous staging of each scene. You didn't need a degree in psychology to know that the killer was making a statement. My job was to figure it out in time to prevent more innocent lives from being lost.

Is that what I believed: that the killer would kill again?

I had no reason to believe he wouldn't. Neither homicide had the characteristics of a knee-jerk reactive killing. Both had been planned beforehand. Staged. I wondered why.

As for a connection, I needed more information.

Road signs blurred. Intersections. Traffic signals.

I was distracted. Something was bugging me: I was undecided if the location of the child's body was coincidence or contrivance. There was that word again. Try as I might, I couldn't get the image of the little girl out of my head. Some things indelibly etch themselves in our brains. I remember a photograph taken in Vietnam during the American insurgence. A simple monochrome composition of a naked, scrawny fleck of a child screaming as he she fled advancing US Marines. Behind her, sprawled on the street, was her slain father, his brains blown out across the pavement. I'd spent thirty years trying to shake it off. Never had. The events of this morning had bled color into that picture.

I pulled over and killed the engine, then realized with a start that my subconscious had brought me back to where I'd started: the rail yard, deep in the shadow of the 7th Street Bridge.

For some reason I got out.

The numerous city vehicles had disappeared, and with them the flashing lights and the distorted radio chatter.

It was like nothing terrible had even happened here.


I started walking. I passed silent freight cars, snuggled up tail to tail for the night like snoozing mastodons. This place had an old factory smell about it. Decades of grime and hard labor. I had an inkling why the killer had chosen this spot, but I didn't want to confront it. Not yet. I was hoping I was wrong.

I hunched into my coat and worked my way over the shingle to the gap in the chain-link fence, used the Maglite to lead the way down the steep concrete slope.

I shouldn't be back here so soon. No choice.

The Maglite picked out the black-and-yellow police tape. I ducked under it, moving deeper into the gloom. The bright beam lit up the ribbed underbelly of the bridge, played across concrete pillars covered in graffiti. City Hall had given up painting it out a long time ago; the voice of freedom was too costly to stifle.

I moved to the closest pillar and placed a palm against its rough skin. I could feel the weight of the bridge bearing down. A thousand tons pressing me into the river basin. Above my head I could see the shape of a musical staff scraped onto the rendering. Five scrawled lines with accompanying notes, painted onto the graffiti. I'd seen them before. Knew the score. Played it over and over in my head for months until it had driven me almost mad.

Tears welled in my eyes. I closed them, letting the deathly atmosphere envelop.

I had thought I was over it, past it. I was wrong.

Some wounds never heal.

I think I heard somebody cry out for help.

It sounded like me.

# 5

The lights were out and nobody was home. No delicious smells of home cooking wafting through from the kitchen. For that matter, no food in the refrigerator at all. Same setup every time.

I dropped house keys in the dish on the reception table in the small hallway and left the house lights off. I felt unclean. I needed a shower. It could wait.

Whenever I am faced with a child homicide, I have this urgency to confirm that my own children are safe and well, even if they are all grown up and moved out.

I pressed my shoulders against the front door and speed-dialed my daughter, Grace, in Florida. I listened to the number ring out, thinking about the murdered little girl lying all alone beneath the 7th Street Bridge. Thought about how I'd feel if she were my mine, and how I'd rip the spine out of her spineless killer if she were.

Grace wasn't picking up.

Then I remembered the time difference, and dialed her office number instead. Ordinarily, I resist calling Grace at work. I know how it feels to be distracted right in the middle of something important. The number went straight to automatic voice mail.

I hung up, and rubbed the phone against the sandpaper stubble coating my jaw.

Grace would call back. As it was, she called at least three times a week. *How's my Daddy doing? Are you still taking your meds? When are you coming to Florida for a visit, or better still to live?*

Grace never gave me cause to worry. Not like her younger brother.

I took a deep breath and telephoned my son, George, in New York. I don't hide the fact that George and I lock horns. Always have. Fathers and sons, I guess.

I heard an answering machine click into life. It was going to be one of those days.

"Pick up, George," I breathed into the mouthpiece. "It's your father. Remember me? Pick up if you're there. I know you don't want to speak with me right now. And that's fine. But I need to hear your voice. Just a short hello will do. Just to know you're okay."

There was another click on the line and the answer-message was replaced by a woman's voice:

"Gabe? Hello? Is that you, Gabe? Give me a second, will you?"

The harried voice belonged to Katie, my daughter-in-law. She sounded rushed and rightly so. I could hear my one-and-only grandchild in the background. It sounded like he was giving his mom a run for her money. Ask any new parent.

"Katie, how are you? How's the baby? I've been meaning to call all weekend. You know how it is."

"Tell me about it. Connor's teething."

"He is?" I felt a surge of grandpa pride. "So soon?"

"He's nine months. In baby terms, he's a late starter."

"Like his father."

I heard her chuckle.

"I'm guessing George isn't home."

"Leaping off the El Capitan as we speak."

"In Yosemite?" I shook my head. Some children give their parents more cause for concern the older they get. "One of these days those dangerous sports of his are going to get him killed."

"That's exactly what I keep telling him. But you know how stubborn he is."

"Like his father."

Again, I heard her chuckle.

"Katie, it's been ages since George and I last spoke. I feel like we're rapidly becoming strangers. Families should stick together."

She could hear the disappointment in my voice and tried her best to compensate. "He just needs time, Gabe. He'll be okay. He's still sore."

He wasn't on his own – but I didn't say it.

"How's work?" she asked.

I sighed a little too loudly and Katie caught it.

"Don't tell me," she said, "you've been back three weeks and already straight into the thick of things, I like your style, Gabe. Is this another serial?"

"Maybe."

"Anything you can share? Do you have a nickname for him yet?"

Working under her professional name of Kate Hennessey, my daughter-in-law is a successful television news journalist. She works out of the ABC Studios in New York City. Since she and George became an item, it's been the norm for Katie to act as my official media conduit on the Eastern Seaboard.

"You know how much my viewers love Celebrity Cop updates," she added.

*The Celebrity Cop.*

Inwardly, I cowered from the title – as I always did.

# 6

Detective Bob Bales looked downhearted.

I couldn't blame him; Bales and his team were working triple overtime, but not for the extra pay or for the love of it. For the last couple of weeks they'd been chasing a killer the press had labeled *Le Diable*. So far, The Devil had killed two men of the cloth and given Bales and his team hell.

I felt bad for him. I could see a sheen of cold sweat on his balding pate and hear a tremor of despondency in his words as he addressed our small gathering. He looked like he hadn't slept in a month. I wondered if I looked the same.

We were crammed into one corner of the large open-plan office area at the station house like buddies gathered for a game. Two dozen attendees for the daily Robbery-Homicide update. Anyone within earshot and not out on the beat was invited. Some had fancy titles. Some wore police uniforms. All were attentive. No beer and no pre-match banter. Never was for this kind of party.

I was doing my best to pay attention, but my thoughts kept rolling back to the 7th Street Bridge.

"Why are they calling him Le Diable?" The question came from the fresh-faced officer I'd met earlier in the day, at the Union Pacific rail yard. She must have been the only one here who hadn't seen the weekly updates in the papers.

Bales cleared his throat. "Partly because of the disturbing nature of the crime scenes."

He held up a bunch of eight-by-ten pictures as proof. I could see images of satanic symbols drawn in the blood of clergymen. Chicken heads and other weird paraphernalia strewn about bloodied altars. I was glad it wasn't my case.

"But principally because the Media likes to Hollywoodize these kinds of things," he added.

Another word I didn't think existed. Not bad for the first day of the week.

Bales gave me the nod and suddenly it was my turn on center stage. Know this: limelight makes me look green. The only plus side is it helps hide the Saturnine rings orbiting my eyes.

I clambered to my feet, put my back to the evidence board – home to a collected array of case notes and photos – and surveyed my audience. I recognized every tense face here. Knew several like friends. They were either seated or standing, with arms folded or drinking coffee, waiting to be brought up-to-speed on the weekend killings I was tentatively thinking of as The Mortician Murders. Childish, I know, but my conversation with Katie had got me thinking.

"Over the last thirty-six hours we've had two homicides by the same hand," I began. "A professor from USC and a child as yet unidentified." I copied Bales' trick: held aloft a pair of eight-by-ten color prints. "As you can see from these, the killer arranged each crime scene just the way he wanted it. Ceremoniously. He was in complete control the whole time. Here's what we know so far:

"We believe the first victim, Professor Jeffrey Samuels, a singleton in his mid-fifties, was killed sometime early Sunday morning." I stuck photos to the board as I spoke. "His cleaning lady found him at around ten a.m. and phoned the police right away. No signs of breaking and entering. No signs of a struggle. We did find two small burn marks side by side on Samuels' neck, just here – so it looks like the killer overpowered him with a Taser."

"Home invasion?"

I shrugged my lip at Detective Janine Walters. Janine was one of our veteran detectives here at Central

Division. She and her long-time partner, Fred Phillips, were a tour de force when it came to cracking cases. My asset.

"Seems unlikely, Jan," I said. "Other than the murder itself there is no evidence of foul play of any kind whatsoever. It looks like Samuels let the perpetrator in and that's when he hit him with the stun gun."

"Burglary gone sour?" The suggestion came from one of the uniforms.

"Again, it doesn't look like it. Samuels was wearing a ten-grand Rolex when we found him. Plus, there was at least a thousand dollars in his wallet on the nightstand, together with a bunch of platinum credit cards. If anything, the Samuels' residence looked like it had been tidied post mortem."

"Hey, I could do with one of those killers at my house," one of the sergeants muttered. "It's murder keeping my place tidy."

A wave of nervous laughter rippled through my audience.

I let it die down before proceeding:

"Let's see. Samuels' blood alcohol level came back at over four times the legal limit – so he wouldn't have put up much of a fight in any case, even without the Taser. No initial signs of drug or substance abuse."

"What about the cause of death?"

"We're still waiting to hear about that. Same goes for the child. I hear the ME's had a busy weekend – so it could run through midweek before we get our answers. At this point, we can find no obvious causes. No ligature marks. No wounds. No petechial hemorrhaging, which means they weren't suffocated or strangled. For now, it's a mystery."

I pinned a photograph to the board. It showed a close-up of the ash on Samuels' forehead.

"The killer made this mark on the brow of both victims. Trace are getting back to us when they've identified the type of ash he used."

Fred Phillips leaned closer. "Looks like regular cigarette ash." Fred was the Precinct's resident smoke stack; if anyone would know, he was our man. "Is that a cross or a letter X?"

"Take your pick."

"Could be a religious nut."

"Maybe."

I pinned another eight-by-ten to the board.

"As you can see in this photograph, the killer dressed Samuels in a tuxedo and dinner shirt before lying him on his bed. Notice the details. The killer took the time to wrap Samuels in a crimson cummerbund, do up his bowtie and fasten his sleeves with fancy gold cufflinks."

"How do we know he wasn't already wearing the tux?"

"Good question, Jan. Here's why: a neighbor and the last person to see him alive – other than the killer, that is – saw Samuels putting out trash shortly after midnight, Saturday. He was wearing pajamas at the time. Those same pajamas were found neatly folded away in a drawer in Samuels' bedroom."

The willowy officer: "If you ask me it looks like a suicide."

I hiked up my brow. "And the first responders thought so too – until they came across the Taser marks. Plus, there were no signs of any pills, gunshot wounds or even a suicide note. No medication in the house to show Samuels suffered from depression or anxiety. Since the discovery this morning of the child's body we are definitely looking for a repeat killer."

Someone asked: "What was Samuels' role at the University?"

"He was Head of Genetics. But that's pretty much all we know, for now. I intend visiting the campus this afternoon to interview his colleagues."

"What about the child, Gabe? Any idea who she is?"

Jamie spoke up: "We checked CLETS. She isn't in the missing person's database."

"Plus, it's been the weekend," I added. "Which means even if she has been reported missing, there's a chance she hasn't been entered it into the system yet. The child's clothes were clean. Which is a good indication she hasn't been away from home long."

I pinned a snapshot of the little girl to the board, sensed the parents among us recoil from the image.

"As you can see in this picture, the child was found laid out in the same way as Samuels. Position added post mortem. No signs of a struggle or bondage. Together with the cross of ash, we also found these same calling cards at both crime scenes."

I added more vivid close-ups to the board. Rose petals sprinkled in a circle around the bodies. Something like superglue applied to the lips.

"They make for a pretty distinctive signature." Fred Phillips was rubbing his chin. He was thinking what everybody else here was thinking. "What do we know about those? Anyone in the system with the same MO?"

"So far we've found no similar signatures from known murderers either at large or behind bars. Other than the fact they look like regular rose petals and ordinary cigarette ash, we're waiting on the forensics results. Same goes for the glue. As yet we have no idea what they mean."

"Do we have a connection between the victims?"

The all-important question. I shook my head. I'd wrung my brain all morning trying to come up with one. Same for a motive. Right now I was looking at the killer's world through the wrong end of the telescope.

"What we do know is this killer has cast iron balls. His cooling off period – if you can call it that – is less than a day. Which means if he's on a spree we could be looking at another victim within the next twelve hours."

"So who should we be looking for?"

Again, Jamie spoke up: "Serial killers are more likely to be white males in their late twenties or early thirties." She glanced at me for approval to continue. I nodded. It was textbook stuff, gleaned straight from an Academy tutorial, but we all have to start somewhere.

"Normally, they have employment that allow them free roam. They tend to be sociopaths, which means they show no remorse. They also have a grandiose sense of self. Usually, they'll have a history of behavioral problems. Maybe even jail time. Some like to brag about their crimes."

"And that's where he could make his first mistake," I said, refocusing the group. "There's a strong likelihood he may also know his victims. Especially the child's parents. Once we get her ID, we'll need to cross-reference acquaintances with Samuels, their work colleagues, what clubs they're members of, mailing lists they're buying into, who they've upset. As always, the devil is in the details." I surveyed my grim-faced audience. Things were about to get messy. "Any more questions?"

# 7

There is something intrinsically evil about a child homicide. It defies logic and it defiles imagination. Just ask the parents.

I left Jamie manning the phone while I hit the streets. Partly, because I needed to do something, anything proactive. Mostly, to clear the death fog from clouding my brain.

I got in my car and headed southwest.

"Want me to tag along?" Jamie asked before I left.

I'd given it some thought. Jamie had a good eye for detail and a burgeoning curious nature. Someday she'd make a fine detective. But right now I needed her at base, on the phone, identifying our little Jane Doe.

"Don't look downcast, Jamie. It's important work. More important than canvassing for character testimonials."

She hadn't looked like she'd believed me.

Chasing killers was brand new to Jamie. She'd spent the last three years of her life sitting through lectures and undergoing basic training. Three weeks out on the street and she'd been bitten by the homicide bug. Wanted more. But I knew that the bite could turn nasty at any moment.

"They tell you about the NCIC at the Academy?"

"It's the National Crime Information Center. Otherwise known as the FBI's database. Do you want me to submit a search request?"

I'd nodded. "If she's in the system, that's where we'll find her."

"And if she's not in the FBI's books?"

"Then we start with the schools. Show her photo around. Make a press statement if need be. Sooner or later somebody is going to miss this child."

I'd remembered my own daughter of that age wearing pink pajamas and going to sleepovers at friends' houses, and in the care of other parents. If my own daughter had been abducted on her walk home, how soon would either set of adults have raised the alarm?

"I'll get right on it."

"Good girl. And when you're done with the FBI, start compiling employee rolls from every funeral home and mortuary parlor within a fifty-mile radius. Run the names through the database. Let's see who pops up."

"You think he's a mortician?"

"I think we need to rule it out."

It had occurred to me that our boy could work in the funeral business. Stands to reason, right? The mock interment angle was a strong indicator. It was distinctive, purposeful. There was a chance he could be a disgruntled funeral home employee. Somebody who wanted to branch out pro bono.

I rolled down the car window and let cool air scream in my ears. The day was bright and breezy. A duck egg sky scratched with condensing vapor trails. I rummaged in the glove box for a CD, found one at random and slid it into the player.

*'Life in the Fast Lane'* blasted at the incoming air.

Every police detective had informants. It's kind of an unpaid outsourcing. Some are pillars of the community: church leaders, social commentators, community workers. Most are hardened criminals: time-served lowlifes, drug dealers, gang members. In both cases, their petty indiscretions are overlooked for the sake of solid intelligence leading to sound arrests.

I spent the rest of the morning doing house calls.

It was my hope that somebody knew something. There are few secrets on the streets. It all comes down to persuasion and the lesser of two evils.

But I kept coming up against brick walls.

In fact, I started getting more blank expressions than at Lehman Brothers on the morning of the crash. Okay, so informants take exception to surprise visits. I can buy that. They prefer you to call ahead, make proper arrangements to meet on neutral turf. English tea at the Waldorf Astoria. That kind of thing. But the best returns come from catching them off-guard and unprepared. Makes for more spontaneous reactions.

But stony faces were the order of the day.

I picked up a coffee and a pint of ice cream from a gas station and continued to my next call. I was just about there when my phone buzzed.

"Yes, Fred?"

"We got Union Pacific to check the rail yard security tapes for Sunday evening through Monday morning."

"And?"

"And the cameras were offline the whole time."

"How's that happen?"

"Their technicians say the cables were cut. The last recorded footage was just after midnight. Followed by mush."

"Those cameras have to be forty feet off the ground."

"So are the cables."

"Who are we dealing with here, Fred? Spider-Man?"

"Let's hope not. He's a slippery son of a gun. Catch you later."

Psychologists will tell you that the whole of Human behavior consists of patterns. Serial killers are no exception. You just have to know how to read them.

In my experience, the patterns of killers come in all shapes and sizes: the way they leave the body; the place they leave the body; the social class of those they murder; their chosen method of murder; the calling cards they leave behind.

Every little piece of information that is the same at each crime scene becomes their fingerprint.

Patterns help law enforcement draw up a picture of predictability. Kind of like a road map to the killer's mental location.

And, yes, I was already thinking of The Mortician Murderer as a serial killer. Not because of anything other than the fact I've been around the block enough times to recognize a turkey in a chicken coop when I see one. These killings came with a message – understand the message and we'd be halfway to an arrest.

My cell buzzed.

I glanced at it.

Then I turned the car around and headed back into the city.

Full speed.

# 8

Dr. Milton Perry works out of the Humanities Department of the UCLA, but Monday through Wednesday he runs a clinic for all matters religion-based, from an office on Hope Street in the heart of the city. Think of it as a multi-faith arbitration service in conjunction with the Mayor's Office. I'd never met Perry, but I knew he promoted himself as the Californian equivalent of Nelson Mandela. A little like a lump of coal with dreams of being a diamond.

"I said absolutely no interruptions," Perry boomed as I flung open his office door on the eleventh floor of the glass-and-steel skyscraper and marched inside.

Perry's office was surprisingly sparse. I say surprisingly because I'd expected the place to be crammed with religious artifacts: walls of well-thumbed books spanning the ages; dusty bibles – that kind of thing. In the very least a signed picture of the Pope. But this was clearly rented space and minimalism ruled.

Perry's flustered secretary was fluttering on my shoulder like a bird caught in the wake of a speeding truck. I ignored him, and closed the door between us.

Perry scrambled to his feet.

"Well, well, well. If it isn't the Celebrity Cop."

I get called *Celebrity Cop* a lot. You'll see. My own fault, I guess. Call it the culmination of being in the wrong place at the right time. It also comes with high expectations. Like I'm a superhero or something. When in reality it's a ball and chain.

"What an absolute delight," he grinned. There was a hint of nerves behind his confident beam.

Fact: people get edgy around uninvited cops.

He showed me some teeth to further hide his unease.

Perry is in his late sixties. In the right light you could mistake him for an African village chief in a Hugo Boss three-piece.

He spread his hands the way priests do when blessing sinners. I didn't need Perry's blessing. But I was getting it all the same.

"What kept you, detective? I've been expecting you for weeks." He gestured to a chair, "Please, sit, sit."

I remained standing.

One thing you'll learn about me is I don't follow orders easily. Scratch that. I do. Or at least I can do. They just need to be the right orders.

My disobedience didn't faze Perry's smile. That smug, condescending, *I pay your wages* god-awful grin. He settled behind the oversized desk and clasped big hands together on its leather surface. For a moment I thought he was going to ask me to join him in prayer.

"Detective, this is fantastic news. Every parishioner in Los Angeles will be relieved to hear LA's finest is about to apprehend Le Diable."

It sounded reverent. Much like a prayer.

I made despairing a face. "We have our wires crossed," I said. "I'm not here about Le Diable. In fact, Le Diable isn't even my case. Never has been."

Perry's grin fell from his face. He tilted his ear toward me, as if he needed clarification. "Detective, I have two dead clergymen on my watch. *Decapitated* clergymen, no less. Heads missing."

"I know what decapitation is."

"I have parishioners cowering in their beds. Pews emptying faster than a triple K meet on a shakedown. If you're not here about Le Diable, why on earth are you here?"

"This."

I held up my phone with the picture of the smudged SUV.

Perry squinted and reached for the phone. I pulled it out of his grasp.

"It's your Ford Explorer," I said. "We ran the plate. It's your vehicle. Fleeing a crime scene."

Perry stared at me like a man learning for the first time he'd been walking around all day with his zipper down.

All at once he didn't look so damn pleased to see me.

# 9

Stacey Kellerman cupped a long-fingered hand over her brow, shading her cobalt-blue eyes from the hardboiled Nevada sun. Even in winter it was as bright as an atom bomb blast out here in the desert. But cold. Cold enough to carpet large expanses of the scrub in drifts of powdery snow. Christmas cacti. When people who had never visited Nevada thought about Nevada they thought about heat. The baking, unrelenting, punishing heat of Hollywood westerns. But that was a misnomer. Out here, in the no-man's land running west toward Red Rock, in the midst of winter, it was hellishly cold.

She squinted against the glare as she gazed across the dandruff desert and focused on the distant saw-tooth city skyline. Vegas had changed beyond recognition in the short twenty-seven years she'd been on the planet. The monstrous mega-resorts were now more synonymous with the city than the reason they existed in the first place. Gambling was something people did to pass the time while they waited for a show or the buffet to open. Another misnomer. Vegas was the capital of misnomers.

She lit a cigarette and blew smoke rings at the sun.

Buzzards seesawed against the glare.

In many ways, Vegas had been good to her. In many ways not. When she was four years old, her prostitute mother had left her in the hands of her alcoholic father – literally. He'd done his best. He'd done his worst. Sometimes she wondered what her life might have been like had she not killed him.

She wiped a tear from the corner of her eye – a product of the cold, not sentimentality.

She saw the car long before the man driving it saw her. It was a newish Ford Mustang. Burnt orange. A Day-Glo muscle car. Climbing the shiny black desert road like a fire ant on a burnt branch. She saw it decelerate as it came to the dirt track intersection. Hesitate. Then bump off-road. Watched it churn its way toward her over the compacted, frozen earth.

They had history; Stacey and the man driving the muscle car. Not all bad. Not all good. Some of it fantastic. Mainly the sex. Okay, *all* of the sex. But then he'd turned forty and something had changed inside of him. He'd gone soft. There was no other way of putting it. He'd started pulling gray hairs. Started examining his own mortality, like it was some damned definable thing he could assess and calculate and maybe pigeonhole. Decided to settle down. Try for a family. Some up-and-coming attorney with fried egg tits.

Stacey took a long drag on the cigarette as the car rolled up the dirt track and came to a stop.

Screw him.

The door creaked open and the man climbed out.

Stacey felt a pang in her belly.

He looked as good as ever. Better in some ways. Worse in others. He was still as tall. Still in shape. Still had the same slick, coffee-colored skin she remembered with such carnal affection. Same mischievous brown eyes. But he'd given into the gray. It peppered his temples. Made him look like one of those newspaper editors in comic books. She didn't like it.

"Goddammit, Stacey," he called as he slammed the car door. "What the hell are you doing out here?"

Both his tight expression and his gruff voice told her he was irritated. Whenever they met lately, he was irritated. She suspected sex with fried egg tits wasn't all it was cracked up to be. She watched him strut toward her like John Travolta in *Staying Alive*. The sight of him made her wish things had been different. *He* had been different.

Even after all these years he still held the title of being the only black man she'd ever slept with. The only black man she need ever sleep with. The sex had been that good. No, for real. Why spoil the memory with somebody inferior? Before they'd become an item, Stacey had heard all the tales about black men. Never believed them. She did now.

"You're looking well," she said.

"Just cut to the chase, Stacey."

"Can't we even be polite anymore?"

"We passed that a long time ago."

She watched him unfold a pair of yellow-tinted Dolce and Gabbana sunglasses and slip them on. He hadn't been into all the designer gear when they were an item. Used to ridicule her for it. Funny how people changed people.

"I got a call," she answered stiffly, blowing out smoke. "Thought you'd be interested. Good to see you, Mike."

"Yeah," he said, sounding like he didn't mean it one bit. She hated him for it. "So what's the story this time, Stacey? You lost a bobby pin and need help finding it?"

She tossed the cigarette onto the compacted dirt and ground it out with the toe of her boot. "Very funny, Mike. Actually, I'm doing you a favor."

"On the coldest Monday of the week so far?"

"You interested?"

"Not for long. You better make it quick. I'm freezing my balls off out here."

She almost said *'I know how to keep them warm'* but caught herself instead. "Okay. Do you remember when we were last up here? It was the summer before last. That weekend we camped in the canyon. Slept under the stars."

"You got stuck up a rock," he acknowledged with smirk.

"I was halfway up a cliff face."

"Yeah, sure. Ten feet off the ground, Stacey. Doesn't constitute Mount Everest. You suck at rock climbing."

"I remember sucking at other things, too, that weekend. You weren't complaining then."

They shared a smile. For a moment it felt good. Warm against the chill. But then it was gone. Sucked away. He'd remembered his sunny-side-up attorney, and so had she.

"So, tell me one more time, Stacey: why the hell are we here again?"

"I miss you, Mike."

"Seriously."

"Seriously." She took a step closer, saw the tightening in his jaw tighten a little bit more, and stopped. "Jesus, Mike. Don't deny us. We were electric."

She saw him draw a big breath. "Stacey. I mean it. Get to the point, or I swear I'm leaving."

"All right," she sighed.

She pointed to the shallow drainage channel running parallel to the trail.

"Happy birthday, detective."

\* \* \*

Michael Shakes didn't like surprises. In fact, surprises pissed him off. Especially surprises involving Stacey Kellerman. They'd had a fling. Okay? A long time ago. Three weeks, two weekends, one summer. Crammed with average sex and no depth. Get over it.

The fact it was his birthday didn't change a damn thing.

He'd spotted her from the roadway, posing in immaculate riding leathers next to her all-black custom-job

Kawasaki motorbike. Unmistakable blinding blonde locks. Angelic on any other head.

As attractive as fire to a child.

Okay, so she looked good, better than ever, like a pinup shoehorned into the latest motorcycle gear. Visibly, Stacey had changed extensively since their fling. She'd undergone plastic surgery, major reconstruction, reworked and augmented everything. He wasn't sure if it was all an attempt to get him back or get even.

He studied her through his yellow-tinted sunglasses. Gleaming locks and kissable lips. Couldn't figure out if she were colluded or deluded. He had no doubt she was still the same Stacey Kellerman on the inside: driven, ruthless, soulless.

No amount of cosmetic surgery could hide those scars.

He took a step closer to the drainage channel and peered in.

The trench was mostly filled with snow. But there were twiggy shrubs poking through. And something that shouldn't have been there.

He stuck out a lip. "How'd you find it?"

"I got a call. And before you say anything, it was anonymous."

"So what did he do, draw you a map?"

"No, he sent me GPS coordinates, by text."

"Show me."

"It's deleted."

He frowned at her. He'd never understood Stacey's rationale. Never got deeper than the hard outer shell. Wasn't entirely convinced there was anything in there, deeper – that the hard outer shell went all the way to her iron core.

"Let me get this straight," he said. "Some guy called you on your cell. Told you to come out here. Which you did – on a whim. And he even sent you GPS co-ordinates."

"That's exactly what I'm saying."

"After which you deleted the evidence."

"Screw you, Mike."

"Screw me?"

"Is that a request?"

"On the coldest Monday of the week so far? Hell no!"

Michael Shakes took another long look into the drainage channel, then dug out his phone and made the call.

# 10

I glanced in the rearview mirror at the woman on the backseat of my car; at her dark eyes staring impassively right back. She hadn't spoken a single word, not even while I'd read the Miranda warning and cuffed her. She was about to be interned into one of the toughest legal systems in the country, fingerprinted, cross-checked, information digitized and on record, forever, but she was anything but fazed. In fact she looked like she was about to get her nails done. I couldn't help wondering if Milton Perry had an army of lawyers converging on the precinct, ready to slap me with a lawsuit. He'd given her up too easily. There's always a catch when somebody does that.

I left my tight-lipped passenger with the desk sergeant and took the stairs to the large open-plan office space.

"Captain's on the war path," Jamie warned as she saw me approaching. It was a little after 2 p.m. I was hungry, thirsty, but too consumed to sate either.

"Don't tell me: Milton Perry?"

She shrugged. "No idea."

Jamie looked tired. I hadn't heard from her all morning, so I presumed she was still in the thick of it. Police work takes time. The only cases solved within the hour are those on TV.

"You should take a break," I said.

She gave me a slanted smile. "Have you any idea how many people work in the funeral business, in LA alone? I'm less than halfway through the list."

"Supply and demand, I guess. What about the Feds – any luck there?"

"No. I think the word urgent isn't in their dictionary."

When it came to helping out other law enforcement agencies, the FBI can have two gears: go-slow and reverse.

"Keep pestering them," I said. "The more you get on their case, the faster they'll want you off it."

*   *   *

Captain John Ferguson of Central Division waved me over to his office. "Gabe, what's going on?" he asked as I sealed myself inside.

Two things you need to know about John Ferguson: he's not the world's tidiest person, and when he speaks, he whispers. Even when he bawls, he whispers. The story goes he's smoked one too many imported cigars, but I reckon it's a gimmick. You see, when people whisper, people listen.

"I just got done with a call from the mayor," he said. "He claims you've been harassing Milton Perry."

Ferguson's office smells like one of those backstreet penny thrift bookstores that have more dog-ears than the pound. I squeezed into a chair stacked with files, caught some before they cascaded to the floor.

"Perry's an ass." I'd been thinking it all the way back to the station house. "Prides himself in it, too."

Ferguson seated himself behind his cluttered desk and stared at me like a father confronting his son over poor grades. "What is it with you and authority?"

"For a start, I don't answer to Perry."

"No, you answer to me. And I answer to the Police Commissioner, who in turn answers to the mayor. And whether you like it or not, Perry holds big sway with the

Mayor's Office. Right now this department is facing budget cuts. Last thing we want is City Hall on a vendetta."

I chewed some lip. "You're right, John, and I'm sorry. But I have good reason to believe Perry is involved in the Samuels homicide. Don't ask me how exactly. But he's definitely linked."

I brought up the photograph on my phone. Ferguson squinted at it.

"That's Perry's Explorer fleeing the Samuels' crime scene," I said. "We cleaned it up and ran the plate." I didn't mention Dreads and his unauthorized dip into the DMV pool.

Ferguson didn't look happy. "Where did you get the picture?"

"I went back to the Samuels house. On a hunch. Perry's PA was there. She was in one of the bedrooms. When she realized I was downstairs she made a run for it."

Now he looked even less happy. "Perry's PA?"

"She's in booking as we speak. Her name's Kim Hu. She's been with Perry the last couple of years. Fiercely loyal. Won't say a word against him."

"So what was she doing at the Samuels house?"

"They declined to say. She invoked the fifth. Perry, too, for that matter. I was thinking, maybe when she's spent a few hours in a holding cell with hookers and junkies for company she'll have a change of heart."

Ferguson was nodding. "I don't like it, but I guess I don't have much choice. While she's stewing, look into her background. See if you can link her directly with Samuels. If we can't charge her with anything concrete before evening, let her go."

"What about the mayor?"

"I'll speak with him. See if I can cool his engines. I'm not Perry's biggest fan, but I don't figure him as a murderer. Let's concentrate on the PA."

"Ideally, we need a search warrant for the Explorer."

I saw Ferguson's lips twist. "Half the judges in town play golf with the guy."

"So, the other half."

Ferguson gave me one of those *'you don't need to tell me how to do my job'* looks that he gives me on a daily basis. "I'll see what I can do. No promises. In the meantime, go over the CSU records from Saturday. See if they picked up something to tie Perry or his PA to the Samuels' murder. Perry used to be a federal employee. His prints and DNA are in the system."

I'd already thought about it. Already filed the request.

I got up to leave.

"How you coping?" Ferguson asked as I reached for the door.

I paused, turned. "Fine." Another fib; I was getting used to it. "I'm fine, John. Still finding my feet. Ten months is a long time to be out of the jungle."

Ferguson performed a slow, measured nod. I could tell by the way his eyes narrowed that he didn't believe a word of it.

"What about the shrink?"

I shrugged, "What about the shrink?"

"There was only one condition on your coming back, Gabe. I put my head on the block for you, remember? The very least you can do is keep your end of the bargain. Once you're done with the CSU, go see the shrink."

# 11

It's a universal truth that as men age they become exponentially more stubborn. I am no exception. My name's up there on that graph. But I am old enough to know which fish are worth frying and which are better thrown back.

I drove north and then east on the San Bernardino Freeway toward Lincoln Heights, going over the handful of facts I knew about the case: the rose petals, the ash, the glue, the mock funereal arrangement.

The killer had committed two homicides within a twenty-four hour period. Takes some doing. He'd left specific clues at both crime scenes. Plus, he'd arranged both bodies in the exact same way. Nothing random about any of it. Everything deliberate. As such, it was unlikely that he'd chosen his victims by chance.

But what connected a venerated university professor with an abducted little girl?

It was midafternoon. I was focused on the task ahead. Buildings slid by like crystals in a kaleidoscope. Traffic blurred. I had house calls to make. A killer to catch.

I parked on the shiny blacktop outside the Hertzberg-Davis Forensic Science Center – otherwise known as the LA Crime Lab – and signed myself in. I knew it was still too early to get a complete forensics breakdown of the Samuels crime scene, but I wanted to see if there were any dots I could connect to Perry.

The boys and girls from the CSU are particularly protective of their work, and rightly so. In the wrong hands, unprocessed evidence can be compromised in a heartbeat. Try examining the crown jewels next time you're in London and see how far you get. Just doesn't happen.

Evidence inventories are a different matter, and can be freely accessed by those detectives involved in the case without fear of corruption. I scanned the list of evidence collected from the Samuels residence. It read like Frankenstein's grocery list: fingernail clippings, hairs, fibers, a bed sheet, clothing, batches of fingerprints, photographs, a list of swabs taken for semen residue, skin epithelials, a number of chemicals sent to Trace, substances and compounds that didn't really mean much to the untrained eye.

Everything to show that a crime had been committed.

Nothing to link Perry to any of it.

But Perry's PA had been there for a reason. No social visit. No coincidence. Not at that hour. Were they covering tracks? I wondered. Maybe even planting falsified evidence after the fact? Or removing the real evidence that linked Perry to the murder?

I needed the PA's confession, I realized. Needed her to betray her boss. It wouldn't be easy; she'd already sworn allegiance to the Perry camp. I'd need leverage to make her talk. Something personal. Something she valued more than loyalty.

\* \* \*

I retraced my steps. Headed westbound on the San Bernardino and jumped off at the Charlotte Street ramp, following the road as it swung back on itself into the USC Health Sciences Campus.

Up until his murder, Professor Jeffrey Samuels had been Head of Genetics at USC. I wanted to canvass those who knew him best, while their thoughts were still fresh. I didn't know what I'd unearth. Maybe nothing. Hopefully something. Truth is, you never know until you ask the questions. Taking character testimonies can be dull work. But there's no better way to draw a picture of a person. Comments come sugarcoated or laced with cyanide. Adoration or abhorrence. You can't have it both ways. You either like somebody or you don't. Generally speaking, people avoid speaking ill of the dead. But we all have enemies – people who are itching to dish the dirt once we aren't in any position to fight back.

I spent the next hour or so interviewing both faculty staff and several of the professor's prized students. Everybody was stunned to learn of his death. Some to the point of hysterics. I kept an eye out for disgruntled colleagues or castigated students with chips on their shoulders. But no one seemed interested in grinding an ax into Samuels' memory. They all loved him and were happy to gush about it.

So much sugar made me lightheaded.

Getting nowhere, I closed up shop and walked the hundred yards over to the County Medical Center, calling by my car on the way.

The sun was moving swiftly westward. I was aware of the time. Aware I needed to be elsewhere. Chasing the killer. But duty called – if only for ten minutes.

My regular partner in crime, Harry Kelso, had been laid up here in the hospital for the last four weeks following bypass surgery. He should have been released and back home on sick leave by now, but a string of persistent complications had kept him in and under observation.

A widely-known fact about Harry: Harry likes his food. It's obvious from first glance. He's the only person I know who can gain weight on a saline drip.

"That's because they got me pinned down all day, buddy," he protested joyously as I pointed it out. "I'm not running it off, see." He fingered his bloated paunch. It wobbled under the sheet like a mound of Jell-O.

I made a face. "The only thing that runs in the Kelso family is the nose."

Harry stuck out his tongue. "What can I say? They got me flat on my back all day. They come in. They feed me. Sometimes three or four times. Well-wishers send candy. Fattening fruit. I lost a lot of blood. I need to build up my energy. Did you bring dessert?"

I put the pint of ice cream on the bed table.

His face lit up.

I watched him lever open the lid, licking his lips like a kid in a candy store. Then the glee drained from his face and he glared at me with accusing eyes.

"What's this, buddy – some kind of a joke? It's all slop."

I shrugged, "Sorry, Harry. I had the heat on in the car."

"Never mind. I'll drink it later. If it kills me, I'm in the best place, right?"

We both laughed.

No matter how dire the circumstance, Harry had an inimitable way of lightening my load. I missed him. Had done all the while I'd been out of it on compassionate grounds. His heart attack had happened just days before my return to duty. Bad timing all around.

"So, how's my replacement shaping up?" Harry asked as I pulled up a chair and dropped into it.

"Jamie? She's got the makings of a fine detective someday," I said, not for the first time. "Given time and the right input she could go all the way. I'm telling you, Harry. The kids these days are light-years ahead."

"You should bring her."

"I guess."

"I'm serious. I'm going stir crazy in here. I need female company. Something sweet and soft. Know what I mean?"

"I brought you cookie dough."

Harry let out a long, tremulous sigh. I saw his eyes roll up to the ceiling, then roll back down again. I knew Harry well enough to know he was feeling like a cat on a hot tin roof cooped up in here all day long. Harry was brought up on the streets. He lived and breathed police work. Getting healthy in here was killing him.

I told him about the Mortician Murders.

"That's a terrible title," he snorted when I was done. "Honestly, buddy, it sounds like a bad Miss Marple mystery. You need to ditch it. Pronto."

Snobbish psychologists and FBI profilers believe that giving a serial killer a pet name will, in some way, validate their actions and elevate them above their normal station in life. I disagree. In my book, removing their human name keeps them where they belong: with the other monsters.

I loosened up my shoulders. "What would you suggest?"

"The Undertaker."

"The Undertaker?" I thought it over. "I guess it fits the bill. Sounds ominous. At least Katie will like it. She's itching for an exclusive."

"Just make sure I get all the credit."

I smiled. "Drink your ice cream."

# 12

An afternoon of saccharine interviews had left me gagging.

Against ugly rush-hour traffic, I headed back into the city. I called Jamie en route. There was still no reply from the Feds, she told me. I was prickled by their lack of urgency.

"What about the mortician list?"

"A few lukewarm flags," she said. "Nothing that jumps out."

I glanced at the clock on the dash. It was 5 p.m. Technically-speaking, our shifts had ended two hours ago. I told Jamie to finish up and go home, get some rest; we'd both been up early this morning. Too early. "I'll have Fred and Jan chase them up."

"The FBI could still call," she protested.

"The Feds are on East Coast time," I countered. "We won't hear anything before morning. Not now."

It was dark by the time I got to the station house. Street lights popping on. Brake lights glowing. Traffic thickening in the city's arteries like congealing blood. I made my way to the holding cells, instructed the duty sergeant to put Perry's PA in an interview room and leave her there, handcuffed to the metal table. I didn't have anything on her. Didn't have any reason to detain her any longer. But I needed her to talk.

I got a coffee, and did some digging.

Twenty minutes later, I let myself into the interview room and seated myself opposite Kim Hu. I had a lieutenant witnessing the proceedings through the one-way glass. A camera on record.

"Made any new friends?" I asked conversationally as I opened up a file of notes and leaned it against the table. "Some of those girls are real nice once you get to know them."

"How long is this going to take?" She sounded more bored than irritated. Like she had something better to do. Maybe make up more alibis for Milton Perry.

I put on reading glasses and scanned the notes.

Kim – or Kimmi as she liked to be known – is in her late twenties. She's of Asian-American descent, with a slanted bob haircut and eyes like polished jet. She has one of those china doll faces you see on billboards advertising age-defying creams. Cute, but somehow robotic.

"Why are you keeping me here?" she demanded quietly.

"You've been arrested for breaking and entering," I reminded her.

"You have no proof that I broke into anywhere."

"As a matter of fact I have Perry's word on it. He told me you were the one driving his Explorer this morning, right when I saw it leave the Samuels crime scene. I'm sure he'll stick to that story if it means he isn't implicated in any wrongdoing."

"Just because I was driving the car doesn't mean I was actually inside the property."

Kimmi was hard to read, like her whole body language was in Mandarin.

"I heard you upstairs."

"But you didn't see me. Have you found my fingerprints? My DNA? Any little shred of evidence to suggest I was even there?"

I smiled and looked at her over the top of my readers. Despite her defensive attitude I liked Kimmi. Her motives were honorable, but she was destined to learn that men like Milton Perry rarely returned the favor.

"You're not giving up on this, are you, Kimmi?"

"I'm loyal."

"And I respect that. It's a fine quality to have. Loyalty should be rewarded. But it doesn't stop you from being disposable."

Her mouth flat-lined.

I leaned forward. "Look, Kimmi, this is a murder investigation. It goes way beyond breaking and entering. You're facing serious charges here. Loyalty is all well and good, but your boss will do everything in his power to distance himself from bad publicity. And that includes letting you take the fall."

"Never."

"You sure about that? Does this undying loyalty of yours work both ways?"

I saw her shore up her defenses; her eyes shrink into unreadable slits. "You're bluffing."

"We both know what your boss is capable of."

I looked down at my notes, sensed Kimmi lean forward in her chair, trying to get an angle on what I was reading.

"You know I have nothing to do with Jeffrey's murder," she said.

"I know you were in his house. Tampering with a crime scene. And that might be enough to exclude reasonable doubt. We're only at the beginning of gathering evidence here. There's a long way to go before we file murder charges. Right now your boss is at the top of our suspect list. Which makes you an accomplice, Kimmi. Loyalty is an admirable quality. But are you willing to do jail time for Perry?"

I could see my words bouncing off her granite expression like Ping-Pong balls. Still no hint of a crack.

"You've nothing to prove here. We're only interested in getting to the truth. If your testimony excludes Perry from being involved in Samuels' murder then why bite your tongue? You won't have a thing to worry about. We can drop the breaking and entering charge and all go home."

"I can't tell you anything," she said.

"Off the record."

"Even then."

I straightened up a little. "What kind of errand were you running, Kimmi?"

Kim Hu stared at me with her cool, shark-like eyes, folded her arms tighter across her chest. "I refuse to answer on the grounds I may incriminate myself."

I leaned back. "You sure?"

She repeated the statement.

"Okay. Don't say I didn't give you a fair chance to clear things up. It says here you attended the Harvard Business School."

"Yes."

"Left with distinctions, I see. Top of your class. You must be good."

"I am."

I took off the readers. "Never been interested in business myself. You've got to be a certain type to succeed in that kind of world." I didn't add the word *cutthroat*. Didn't need to.

"It doesn't suit everyone," she admitted.

"That why Perry hired you?"

"Among other reasons."

"Does he have you running all his errands?"

"I'm in his employ. I do as he instructs."

"Like a glorified gofer. It also says here you've been arrested before. Back in Boston. While you were in college. I'm betting you didn't include the charge in your résumé. I'm sure if you had, Perry would never have hired you."

There was a tiny fracture in Kimmi's stony expression – not so small I couldn't lever it open and expose the truth.

I closed the file and slapped it on the table.

"Now, Kimmi, are you going to tell me why you were at the Samuels house this morning or do I show your boss this arrest report and test his loyalty?"

# 13

The evening was underway. But I wasn't done yet. I got in my car and circled north toward West Hollywood.

Among the professor's personal possessions we'd found membership cards belonging to various clubs: a popular health and fitness gym, a winery in Burbank, a disco club on Santa Monica Boulevard. That's right: a discothèque. I wasn't interested in the gym or the winery. But the disco club was a different matter. It happened to be one of the raciest hangouts for homosexuals in LA.

The third fact about Professor Jeffrey Samuels was the one thing no one at USC had even mentioned.

From the outside, the discothèque looks like a bank, rather than one of the busiest nightclubs on the LA gay scene. It looks like a bank, period. A smoked-glass cube-shaped bank. No frills, at least not on the outside.

It was early Monday evening and the place was closed.

I rapped loudly on the tinted-glass door, tried to peer into the gloom inside, make out shapes. I saw movement, heard something that sounded like a muffled *'We open at eleven'*. A woman's voice. I rapped harder, louder, faster, this time with the metal edge of my police shield.

Then I stepped back as the door sucked inwards. I caught a swirl drumbeats escaping onto the sidewalk.

"Can't you read?" she said. "We open at eleven."

She was tall, rake thin, with shiny black hair down to a waspish waist. Skin as pale as a Scandinavian med student attending her first autopsy. Tight black clothing. Silver piercings in a Tim Burton face.

"Sign says eleven," she emphasized with a subtle glare.

She had intense turquoise eyes. Maybe colored contacts. Something like black razor wire tattooed on her upper arms. Black nail paint to go with her black lips.

I held up my shield. "Detective Gabriel Quinn, LAPD. I need to ask you a few questions."

"Department?"

"Robbery-Homicide."

She thought about it for a second, then stepped aside and hurriedly waved me in. I wondered what her reaction might have been had I said *Narcotics*.

It was cool inside the nightclub. I could hear dance music thudding away in the background. Unmelodic modern. Not my scene.

The girl closed the door and looked at me with her hands on hips. "Look, if you're here about Murphy, we fired him last week."

"I'm not here about Murphy."

She looked confused. "Oh, okay. Cool."

We were in a wide entrance area. Black leatherette, with silver rivets holding everything together. Concealed lighting. Framed posters of toned and tanned bodies scantily clad in leather and chains. To the left, I could see a barroom. Those tall, high-stem tables that you stand at rather than sit, sprouting from the floor like black dahlias. Cozy booths in back. To the right, a larger space, mostly shrouded in darkness. A tangle of lighting equipment barnacled to the ceiling. The insipid scent of cheap air freshener ineptly trying to mask the darker stench of musk and booze.

"Thinking of joining?" she asked.

"I'm here on official police business. Are you the owner? The manager?"

I saw the corner of her mouth curl. She was entertained by the thought. "Try general dog's body. My boyfriend owns the place. I do all the running around."

"Boyfriend? I thought . . ."

The curl turned into a smirk. "You're straight, right?"

"To the point, I guess."

"Well, there's no golden rule that says you have to be gay to run a gay club. You straights are so quick to stereotype. My boyfriend and me, we're bi, as in bi-sexual. But we could easily be straight, like you, and still run this place."

I took a photo of Samuels out of my pocket. A close-up of him taken at a university fete. "Have you seen this man before?"

She tipped her head forward to get a closer look. Her long black hair cascaded over her arms like a lace shawl. The narrow strip of skin visible in her center parting was snow white.

"Sure," she said, "that's Jeff. He's in here every weekend."

"Was he here this weekend?"

"Come to think of it, no. Jeff's cool. Is he in trouble?"

I put the photograph away. "He's cool all right: he's dead."

Pale skin going paler. Turquoise eyes widening. "Oh. Jeez. Bummer. I mean, *real* bummer. Jeff was a good guy. You sure he's gone?"

I nodded.

"Oh, Jeez. How? When?"

"Saturday morning. Not from natural causes. That's all I can tell you. How well did you know him?"

"Only as much as you get to know any of the regulars. We try and keep our relationship with our patrons strictly professional. But friendly. You know? We maintain a strict privacy code."

"How long's he been coming here?"

She looked down to the floor, then back. "About two years, I think. Yep, at least two years. Jeff was popular.

Funny. Bought plenty of drinks for everyone. As you can imagine, he had a lot of friends."

"Any enemies?"

I saw the question run through her eyes. This girl was no freshly-cut daisy. She could see where I was heading and immediately cut me off at the pass:

"Definitely not. No way. At least none here. You're thinking his sexuality had something to do with his murder?"

Until this morning, until the little girl had been discovered underneath the 7th Street Bridge, I might have thought that way. Now I wasn't so sure.

"Everybody loved Jeff," she said, shaking her head as if to help the news sink in. "He was the original nice guy. Totally wizzywig."

"Wizzy-what?"

"It's a computer term. What You See Is What You Get. I'm a gamer. Mostly MMORPG." She rolled her eyes. "There I go again."

"What about Jeff," I said, "any jealous lovers?"

She shrugged slim shoulders. "Not that I know of. But then I only saw him for a handful of hours on Saturday nights. I have no idea what he did with the rest of his week."

"Anything else? Anything at all that sticks out when you think about him?"

I saw her think some more. Eyes sank to the floor and stayed there a moment before floating back up. "Maybe this isn't relevant, but there was this one guy here, I don't know, maybe five or six weeks ago. He and Jeff were having words. It was intense. They were back there, in one of the booths. It got heated. I'd never seen Jeff lose his temper before. I swear they were on the verge of throwing punches. Weird, now that I think about it."

"What were they arguing about?"

"I was busy tending the bar; I couldn't hear. They were asked to leave and they did. As far as I know they continued to argue out on the street. Somebody called the cops and the other guy ran for it before they showed."

"This other guy, he a regular too?"

"No. I never saw him before or after that night."

"What did he look like?"

She sucked on her top lip. "Maybe six foot. Medium build. Dark hair. A nose like yours."

Unconsciously, I touched my crooked nose – the result of too many collisions with criminals.

I pointed to a CCTV camera at the back of the entrance area. "Does your security system record?"

"Yes. But we only keep the tapes for a month, and then only for insurance purposes. We reuse them. It's possible Roxy knows more."

"Roxy?"

"He interceded on the argument. Broke it up. Roxy's a cop."

"Does this Roxy have a last name?"

The girl smiled from the corner of her black lips. "Some of our clientele are sensitive. We don't ask for ID. They come here to be anonymous, let their hair down."

"Was he on duty, this cop?"

"I doubt it, unless he was undercover. You should come back Wednesday. It's theme night. If you want to question Roxy in person, that's your best chance. He never misses a theme night."

"Okay. Note taken. Now backtrack a little. You said weird. In what way was it weird?"

"Because this guy, the one starting the fight, I think he was straight. He gave off all the vibes. And straight guys don't usually come in here at two o'clock in the morning."

# 14

The message light on my answering machine was flashing when I got home. A red robotic eye winking in the dark. No message recorded. No number left on Caller ID. Like this for months. I'd put it down to a network malfunction and meant to get it fixed, along with a lot of other things around here. Never had.

I deleted the entry.

It was after 9 p.m.

I dropped house keys in the dish and switched on lights. Thought about *The Undertaker* as I gobbled up the junk food I'd started eating at 2 a.m. this morning. I hadn't had the stomach for it earlier. Wasn't sure if I had now.

And, yes, I'd already decided to adopt Harry's moniker for the killer.

There were three words that came to mind when I thought about *The Undertaker*: cool, composed and methodical. No hairs out of place. No buttons undone. Not convinced CSU would find any useable DNA. The killer had taken his time at both crime scenes. Staged everything neat and tidy. This guy was smart. Not genius smart. Scary smart. The worst kind.

My cell phone rang:

*The Mayor's Office.*

"I hope you're satisfied, detective," thundered Milton Perry's voice as I picked up.

"It's late, doctor. I'm busy."

"Now you know my secret."

"This really isn't a good time."

"I have no idea how you coerced the information out of Kimmi, but I trust you will respect my privacy and be discreet."

Fact: I didn't owe Perry a dime. He was a sanctimonious SOB who used his affiliation with the mayor for his own ill-gotten gains.

"You're lucky you're not under arrest," I said. "You instructed your PA to break into a sealed crime scene and remove incriminating evidence."

"Incriminating, yes. But not in the case of Jeffrey's murder."

He didn't get it. Like many egotists in office he thought he was above the law.

The house phone rang.

"Saved by the bell," I said, and cut the call. I reached over the couch and picked up: "Yes, Eleanor?"

"Don't sound so exasperated," she answered. "I'm the best friend you have in this world and don't you forget that. Ever."

"Somehow I don't think you'll let me. What do you want?"

"Will you be at Winston's later? We have a date, remember?"

I made a snorting sound. "I'm planning an early night."

"With your condition?"

"What condition is that, Eleanor?"

"Well, actually, you have two, sweetheart: insomnia and denial. And both are fixable – if you give it a chance. Anyway, if you change your mind, you know where to find me."

I did. But I had other plans.

# 15

Predators prowled here at night: in the residential foothills overlooking the city of angels. The nocturnal hunters had been here long before the first human settlers had traveled west to these shores in search of freedom and wealth. Long before the rolling forests had been torn down and towers of metal-and-glass thrown up in their place. But primordial compasses held true. Across this manmade terrain, silent killers still followed primeval hunting paths. Patterns etched into genes. As if the concrete topography wasn't even here at all.

Randall Fisk was garbed completely in black. Face camouflaged. Hands sheathed in skin-tight surgeon's gloves. He was standing beneath an old oak tree that leaned out over a manicured lawn the size of a football field. He was surrounded by shrubbery. Enveloped in the rich odors of rotting earth. He'd been standing here the best part of an hour. Maybe two; he wasn't keeping track. Cloaked in darkness. Observing.

There was a coyote out on the dewy grass, standing like a statue in the moonlight. It was staring at him with dark, indifferent eyes. No fear. No threat. Lithe muscles completely relaxed. It had paused its nightly trek across the velvety lawn to assess whether the man was friend or foe.

Behind it, the monolithic mansion house formed a black silhouette against the starry night.

Momentarily, Randall wondered what it would be like to live here, away from the polluted city, where the air was clean. Out here, with its grand views down over the Santa Monica foothills and across the city, out to Catalina on a clear day. Wondered what price had to be paid to own a slice of this very exclusive American pie.

Men had killed for much less.

He dug his hands in his pockets and fingered their contents through the gloves. In the left pocket, a fist of cigarettes. In the right, a sprig of syringes.

He wondered which would give him the biggest buzz.

Out on the grass the coyote was sniffing the air. He could see its hot, moist breath vent from flared nostrils. It had caught the scent of prey, somewhere beyond the walled estate. It departed with a silent skip, slipping into the shadows.

Randall checked the radioactive dial on his wristwatch.

They had something in common, he and the coyote.

They were both predators.

Both following primitive pathways imprinted into their hindbrains from generations of survival. Both existing in a limbo of instinct between one killing ground and the next.

# 16

I woke to the sound of knuckles rapping hard against glass. At first I was disoriented. Thought I was back home, in Tennessee, twenty years ago – when the Mississippi had flooded overnight and rescue crews had airlifted families from submerged homes. Ours included.

"Sir? You okay in there? Please lower the window. Sir?"

But this wasn't my bedroom of twenty years ago. I was in my car. Slumped in the driver's seat, with a bib full of broken potato chips and drool dangling pendulously from one corner of my mouth. Embarrassing. How had I got here? I vaguely remembered feeling ravenous. The actual drive down to the convenience store was absent.

"Sir, do you need medical attention?"

It was coming back to me. In slow-motion flashes.

Danielle had served me at the checkout. Danielle is in her twenties, but bands of wiry gray streak her auburn hair. A sloping chin and eyes that protrude slightly. Danielle has learning difficulties. But she smiles like an angel.

"Sir, I'm going to have to insist you open the window or step out of the vehicle."

It had taken Danielle three attempts to scan a carton of milk and a bag of sour-cream-and-chives potato chips. I'd used the time to chat with her about life and its great unsolved mysteries while she'd bagged me up.

Now I could see her standing in the safety of *Ralphs'* entranceway. Wrapped in a coat two sizes too big. A look of concern darkening her snowflake face. She threw me an uncertain wave. I smiled shakily back, waved.

The nuisance rapping on the glass was an Alhambra PD patrolman. Fortyish. A motorcycle cop with a gleaming white helmet and mirrored *Ray-Bans*. Looked like he polished both religiously. He saw me blink against bright daylight and waggled an impatient finger.

"The window, sir. Now."

Or else, what? I rolled it down. I could see my reflection in his silvery sunglasses. I looked like something not quite alive. And maybe I was.

"Can I see some identification?" he asked.

I handed over my police ID, brushed crumbs off my shirt. I waved to Danielle again while the patrolman checked me out.

He took his time reading the badge. "Gabriel Quinn, Homicide Detective, Grade Three. The great white Celebrity Cop." He looked up from the badge. "Yeah, that's right; I know all about you, detective. I've seen you on TV. I follow all your cases."

It sounded more like an accusation than an observation. Same thing every time. Only this guy sounded like a stalker.

He leaned on the rim of the open window, intruding my personal space. He thought he knew me because he'd seen me on TV. Thought he could be overly familiar. They're all the same.

"What brings you down here?"

I could smell halitosis or something that had died recently in a tooth cavity.

"You here on a case?" he asked. "If so, I can help. Show you around the neighborhood."

"Some other time," I said. "Besides, I live over on Valencia."

"That so?" The patrolman seemed interested. Like he'd come pay me a surprise visit just to see if I were telling the truth. Go in my fridge and help himself to one of the year-old beers.

I'd made a mistake letting it out.

Keith Houghton

"You're in my zone," he said. "I have a place on Kendall, which makes us practically neighbors. Maybe we can get together for drinks sometime? Crack some cases together."

"I don't think so."

Hapless street cop with high hopes. No chance. My coat tails were threadbare as it was.

The patrolman straightened himself up to his full height: six feet and a bit. His black short-sleeved shirt looked one size too small. Muscles bulging. Sleeves so tight they looked like they were cutting off the blood supply. Maybe to his brain.

He adopted a defensive posture. "Oh, I see how it is. You think you're better than me because you've been on TV."

"It's not like that."

"Yes, it is. It's exactly like that. You're out of my pay grade. You're a celebrity and I'm just a street cop. And you don't want to mix it with the ignoble."

I frowned on two counts: one, because of his misuse of the word *ignoble* and two, because he even knew it existed.

"For the record," he said as he handed back my wallet, "you look like shit in the flesh."

He turned and walked away. Leather riding boots creaking over pants as tight as his shirt.

I shook my head.

My cell phone rang. The time read: a quarter after seven in the morning. The name on the tiny screen said: *John Ferguson.* There were a dozen missed calls all queued up behind it.

"Don't you ever answer your house phone?" Ferguson demanded as I picked up.

"Only when I'm home."

"How soon can you be at St. Cloud Road?"

I thought about it. "The one out in Bel Air? At this hour of the morning, from here – fifty minutes, give or take?"

"Make it thirty," he said. "It's the big place near the old Reagan ranch. It looks like your boy just struck again."

# 17

The big place on St. Cloud Road was one of those sprawling mansion houses they use in movies as the lairs of drug barons or corrupt politicians. You know the kind: where rock stars share needles with the Hollywood jet-set over caviar and *Dynasty* reruns.

I drove along the tree-lined driveway at a crawl. New England shingle rattled around the wheel wells. I could see armies of flowerpots and nicely-tended lawns. Ivy-covered walls. Wondered if it was Perrier spurting from the marble fountains.

I parked alongside a shiny black Crime Scene Unit van and got out. There was about a dozen other vehicles snuggled in the shade of the stately oaks. Most of them city vehicles.

A chubby guy wearing a Coroner's vest lifted his chin as I passed. "Nice morning for a murder." He was perched on the hood of the mortuary car, enjoying a cigarette in the warm winter sunshine. I knew him by sight, but we'd never been formally introduced. It didn't smell like regular smoke.

Captain Ferguson caught my attention with an impatient wave. He was standing in the impressive pillared entranceway of the main house. He looked pissed. I'd made good time in spite of the morning traffic. But not quite his thirty-minute deadline. Not sure if that's why he was pissed.

"You're a hard man to get ahold of," he said. "Been sleeping in your car again?"

I smoothed down my collar. "John, you don't know the half of it."

*   *   *

It was cool inside the mansion. Mausoleum marble cool. We entered a spacious atrium decked out with a black-and-white checkerboard floor. Oversized chess pieces standing to attention on either side. Big old portraits on whitewashed walls. A black wrought iron staircase swirling upward to loftier landings. Deathly silence. For some morbid reason, I liked it.

Ferguson pointed to the painting of a young blonde-haired woman as we crossed the vestibule. It reminded me of Greta Garbo in her heyday. "That's the old gal who owns the place, when she was young. Marlene van den Berg. She was quite something, wasn't she? We met a few times. She was a sweet old thing."

"She's the victim?"

Ferguson nodded.

We worked our way down a long hallway filled with black-and-white photographs. Snapshots of happy, hard-working men leaning on shovels, mopping sweaty brows. Construction and haymaking.

"The van den Bergs were old lumber money from Québec," Ferguson explained as we headed out back. "Helped build the railroads up and down the Pacific Coast."

We stepped through a pair of French doors, out into bright sunshine. This was the back of the eastern wing. A pleasant suntrap filled with potted plants and flowering vines. It was also crawling with Crime Lab people. I nodded morning greetings to the boys and girls from Forensics as we climbed terracotta steps toward a tiled patio area.

A lean youngish guy in a long red bathrobe was blowing off steam down by a diamond-shaped swimming pool. He was barely in his twenties, with shaggy bleached hair and the inklings of a goatee. He had a deep Californian tan and good teeth — the kind of kid who'd look right at home in *The Partridge Family*.

"Who's the wailer?" I asked.

"Richard Schaeffer. Apparently, he's Marlene's live-in butler. Probably had a thing for the old gal, if you ask me. She was gold-plated. She could have her pick of male courtiers."

"Doesn't look like your regular Jeeves. More like a surfer dude from Huntington Beach."

"They say we get a hankering for salt as we get older."

I licked at the dry insides of my mouth.

Down by the pool, the butler was waving his arms around like a windmill. I caught glimpses of reddened wrists and reddened eyes.

"Where was he when she needed him?"

"Handcuffed to the bed — or so he claims."

"Kinky."

Marlene van den Berg was lying on her lovely, south-facing sun terrace. The killer had positioned her in the familiar funereal pose and scattered a ragged ring of rose petals around her body. Perhaps what was even weirder was the fact she was wearing a wedding gown, complete with matching gloves up and satin slippers. Everything slightly too big. Like hand-me-downs. In a sick twist her hands were clasping a faded lemon posy to her chest.

"I guess money can't buy immortality," Ferguson said.

"Depends how good your agent is."

I took a glove from one of the watching techies and snapped it on, checked to see if her mouth was glued shut. It was. "It's our boy all right."

"The kid found this on the old gal's pillow."

I looked round at Ferguson. He was holding an evidence bag.

I took it and held it up to the light. Inside was a faded clipping from an old newspaper. A cutout column of print, two by six inches.

Without my reading glasses I couldn't make out any of the words.

* * *

By default, killers don't tend to be picky creatures. Leaving eyewitnesses – especially in home invasions – is considered messy and potentially incriminating. Occasionally, you see it: where the killer is unaware of somebody in hiding. But for the most part, the rule is: leave no witnesses.

In this case, the killer had deliberately restrained the butler before killing Marlene. The irregularity stood out like a donkey at the Kentucky Derby. I was intrigued to know why the killer had left him alive. In any other situation, if there hadn't been two other homicides by the same killer, we'd be looking at the butler for her murder.

"Listen to me, please, Mr. Schaeffer," Ferguson was saying in his hushed but forceful voice, "you're doing yourself no favors. All this evasiveness just makes you look like an accomplice."

We were seated in a pleasant sun lounge with the winter sun warming our backs. The surfer dude from Huntington Beach had been giving us the runaround for the last couple of minutes and threatening us with all kinds of lawsuits. Turned out his daddy was something of a sweet-talking Fountain Valley lawyer with a smidgeon of clout with the Assistant DA. No kidding – he'd have both our shields before the day was out, promise.

We were unimpressed.

Schaeffer thrust out his wrists. "So arrest me."

They looked pretty mashed up, all right. Inflamed. He'd been curling and uncurling his fists since coming inside. He was clearly irritated and scratching at his skin. Drugs did that, I knew. There was also the fact he'd been a heartbeat away from his own death and that tended to shake a person up a little.

"I know my rights," he said for the third or fourth time. "This is harassment."

I spread my hands. "Relax, Mr. Schaeffer. We're just asking a few questions. Trying to catch Marlene's killer, fast as we can. You do want us to catch him, don't you?"

The kid made an objectionable face that can only be pulled by youthful skin.

"The fact this killer went out of his way to restrain you first and then leave you alive means something," I said. "You're our first eyewitness in three separate murders."

"It would have been much easier just to kill you," Ferguson added. "See where we're coming from?"

Something like scared incomprehension scuttled across the kid's face.

"You need to tell us everything you know," I said. "And fast. Do the calculations, son. If you're not the guy we're looking for, that means somebody else is. And that somebody else is out there on the loose, right now."

"He could even come back." Ferguson was keen to push home our advantage. "Finish the job."

There was a swollen blood vessel on the kid's forehead. One of those fun balloons at a child's birthday party.

He let loose some overheated breath. "Okay, okay. It was late."

"Eleven, twelve?"

"More like three or four. I was in bed. Asleep."

"Alone?"

The kid shot a disgusted glare at Ferguson. "I heard somebody come into my room. At first I thought it was Marlene. She gets up early."

"Marlene come into you bedroom often, does she?"

The kid snarled.

"Was it Marlene?" I asked.

"No."

"How do you know? It was dark."

"Marlene doesn't smoke."

I shuffled forward in the rattan chair. "Regular cigarette smoke?"

The kid nodded. "Whoever it was, he smelled like an ashtray. I didn't see much of anything. I reached for the light. Then something stung me." He pulled open the neck of his red silk kimono to expose a nasty-looking double-burn blistered on the side of his neck.

"Nice hickey," Ferguson said.

"So he hit you with a Taser. Then what?"

"It hurt like hell. The next thing I know it's daylight and I'm handcuffed to the bed."

"Your handcuffs?"

The kid shook his tousled head.

"Anybody else in the house?"

"No. Marlene has day maids. That's it. Just the two of us."

"What was she doing out on the sun terrace?"

The kid shrugged.

The killer had taken Marlene from her bed, frocked her up in an old wedding gown, and then carried her outside.

"What about house security?" I said. "Fancy place like this must have state-of-the-art systems. How'd he get past them?"

"Easy. We don't have any. Marlene comes from a different era. She trusts people. She believes in people."

Still thinking of her in the present tense. This kid was no killer.

Ferguson made a disagreeable sound. "So, you're telling us the killer walked right in, straight off the street?"

The kid nodded. His complexion had greened slightly.

"This guy," I said, refocusing his attention. "Big, small, white, black?"

"I told you: it was dark. I have no idea."

"What about his accent? Mannerisms? Any other smells? Think carefully," I said. "Even the smallest detail might mean something. Maybe not to you, but to us."

We waited for an answer while the kid squirmed in his seat. He had ants in his pants the size of cockroaches. I am a firm believer of the *silence is golden* routine.

Then I saw it: a spark of recognition in his swollen eyes. "What?"

"Cleaning fluid," he said. "I think I remember smelling it."

"Chloroform smells that way to some people. What else?"

"Nothing else."

"Marlene have any enemies?"

I saw him shake his head without hesitation, saw tears well up in his eyes. "I told you: everybody loved Marlene."

I was beginning to hear the same everywhere.

"What about surprise visitors? Phone calls?"

The kid was still shaking his head.

"Were you banging the old gal?"

Ferguson's question hit the kid like a sledgehammer. Me, too, for that matter. Somehow, his quiet and unexpected delivery made a greater impact.

I saw the butler suck on his own superheated breath. If he could have taken a swipe at Ferguson and gotten away with it he would have.

And that was just about as cooperative as the butler got.

# 18

General George S. Patton was once quoted as saying: *'A good plan violently executed today is far and away better than a perfect plan next week'.*

Precisely why the plan came to me as it did, I have no idea. Often the best concepts are those that come to us when we least expect them.

Let's be clear about this: I know procedure. Most of the time I stick to it. Sometimes I don't. In the wrong hands, red tape binds. The general rule is, under normal circumstances, all LAPD undertakings involving the use of public facilities must first be run past the Police Captain, the Commander, the Chief of Police and half the city Task Force (including the mayor) before getting the go-ahead – all of which takes buckets of time. I couldn't afford to wait all week for a decision. The killer wouldn't.

I hung around the Bel Air mansion only long enough for Jan and Fred to arrive, then headed south, down to the Cedars-Sinai Medical Center in West Hollywood. The morning was brightening up. I wasn't.

*The Undertaker* had killed three times in as many days.

No pressure, then.

Eric Bryce is the Chief Hospital Administrator at Cedars-Sinai. He's been there so long he's considered part of the fixtures. He's also one of those people who live their whole life in the shadow of a raincloud. Everything's' doom and gloom on his day planner. When he heard my proposal, his everyday glower turned thunderous.

"Jesus Christ." He flapped hands in the air, as if by doing so it would summon divine intervention. I wasn't expecting any. I wasn't even sure Bryce was a religious man. "Do you realize what you're asking? Nay, what you're *expecting?*"

I'd caught up to the Chief Administrator in the hospital grounds, skulking in a plastic hut designed to make a spectacle of smokers. Fish in an aquarium. He'd seen me coming and tried making a run for it. Now he was pacing back and forth like a caged animal.

"It's a good plan, Eric. Maybe it could be better. I don't know that for a fact. But right now it's all I've got."

He paused his pacing long enough to strike up another cigarette, sucked on it so hard the tip glowed white. He was glowering so intensely that his face looked like it had collapsed into his skull. "Christ on a crutch."

"I know what you're thinking, Eric," I said. "But I have this all worked out. Trust me. Nothing will go wrong."

"Bullshit!"

I made a submissive face. "You know I wouldn't ask if it weren't important. You know it's not my idea of fun being back here."

"And it's not my idea of fun you being back here either, detective. As I recall, the last time you and I were in the same room together you accused me of working for the devil."

Damn it. I'd forgotten. Eric hadn't. And he wasn't about to let me forget it either. Thing is, I couldn't blame him; I'd been battling demons head-on at the time. Blinkered and dangerous.

"Extenuating circumstances," I offered with a surrendering sigh. "I wasn't in the right frame of mind back then. Everything I knew had been torn down and crushed. I wasn't thinking straight. I was angry. Blaming everybody else but me. I'm sorry, Eric. Really, I am."

Bryce stared with steely eyes and blew out smoke.

"Just supposing I do go along with this," he said. "I'm not saying I will. But just for argument's sake. What happens if this plan of yours goes tits over ass?"

What if it did? I hadn't given myself any time to debate the negatives. Probably because I didn't want to debate the negatives.

"It won't."

He pointed with the cigarette. "The safety and security of my patients is my number one priority. If your plan puts even one member of the public in peril, this hospital could be sued for reckless endangerment."

I screwed up my face. No matter how much I tried fooling myself into believing my plan was airtight, Bryce had a way of popping the bubble.

I pulled out a photograph of the murdered little girl, lying like a sleeping angel on the plaid blanket. Red hair fanned out. Tiny hands clasped across her chest in the customary pose of interment. I saw Bryce's raincloud snatch up its britches and flee for the hills.

I didn't like doing it: using the child's vile murder as leverage. But these were far from normal circumstances.

# 19

Stacey Kellerman had a dilemma. She didn't believe in God. Or any gods for that matter. In all of her twenty-nine years, religion had never entered her life. She'd never been to church – even for her father's funeral. Never attended a friend's wedding. Never given the idea of an afterlife any serious thought whatsoever. She considered herself a realist. Pragmatic. The only faith she'd ever needed was in her own ability to succeed. But she did believe in fate. And therein lay the impasse.

She poured herself a cold merlot from the big black refrigerator dominating the kitchen space in her duplex in Winchester.

Could fate exist in a world devoid of a grand designer? she wondered, then just as quickly dismissed the thought. The fact that she was here, at this point in her life, on the cusp of a great personal transformation, was testament that it could.

The merlot made her gums tingle.

Through the doorway she could see the living room wall papered with the photographs of people she admired: Carl Bernstein and Bob Woodward, Seymour Hersh, Katherine Graham, a black-framed twelve-by-eight glossy of Stacey shaking hands with Kate Hennessey at a swanky Manhattan bash. Flashes of teeth through false smiles.

Stacey had been highly intoxicated that night. And she guessed it showed. Her hair was slightly mussed. Her make-up slightly askew. Her white Donna Karan button-down shirt buttoned up wrong. She'd given enough head that night to make a lasting impression. You could say it was networking at its peak.

She dug out her cell and hit speed-dial. After three rings Mike Shakes' voice answered:

"Stacey, I'm busy. What do you want?"

"An update," she said, crisply.

"I don't have one. I told you: I'll call when I know something. It could take days, weeks. I'll call."

"Meanwhile, we could do dinner." She waited to hear his response, then added into the silence: "Or lunch, tomorrow."

She heard him sigh. Sighs were never a good sign.

"Stacey, I said I'll call when I have news. Okay?"

"Okay," she said. "Mike?"

"Yeah?"

"What happened to us?"

Another sigh. "That's just it: nothing happened. Goodbye, Stacey."

She heard him disconnect the call.

Mike had no idea about fate – about *their* fate – and no up-and-coming junior attorney with fried egg tits could change what they had together.

Ten years ago, fate had presented Stacey with an escape from the clutches of her abusive father. She'd grabbed it by the horns and rode it out of the stadium.

Mike had no idea how powerful fate could be.

She slung the cold merlot down her neck and made plans.

# 20

Medication numbs. I'd been numb for months. I didn't want to be numb anymore.

I was in my car outside Cedars-Sinai, with the engine running. I was squinting at the evidence bag from the van den Berg crime scene, trying to make out the faded text on the newspaper clipping. The killer had left the torn photograph from the Samuels house with the little girl. Now he'd left this clipping on Marlene's pillow. If there was a pattern here, why hadn't he left something similar on Samuels himself?

I got to the NBC4 News studios in Burbank at a little before 11 a.m. I should have brought Ferguson in on my activities. I didn't.

My contact here, Kelly Carvelli, is a striking African-American woman in the leaner end of her forties. Tall even in flats. We've been friends since the *Star Strangled Banner Case* a few years back. The case that won me my coveted Celebrity Cop title.

"Be right with you," she whispered to me as I entered her office overlooking Johnny Carson Park.

She was on the phone, brokering world-breaking stories for her popular *Channel 4 News* slot. I closed the door quietly behind me and pottered around while Kelly did her thing. There was an ant farm over by one wall, away from the sunny window. It always drew my eye. I marveled at the workers scurrying up and down their tunnels, while their queen made her deals from deep within the labyrinthine setup.

"Gabe." Kelly came off the phone. "What a pleasant surprise!"

We shared a hug. It felt good. I came away smelling of *Chanel No. 5*.

"Sunlight looks good on you," I said with a smile.

She smiled back without causing a crease. "It's been a while. I heard you were back. Doesn't seem like two minutes since . . ." her words trailed off, as though she'd stumbled down an unfamiliar alleyway and sensed danger lurking in the shadows.

"And I'm still breathing," I said.

She blinked. "That's good. No, I mean, *really* good. Breathing counts. I recommend everyone does it. Regularly."

She gave me another squeeze just to be on the safe side. I let the warmth of it enclose. Then we seated ourselves on a big sofa opposite the ant farm. The sunniest side of her office. It felt a world away from the 7th Street Bridge.

Kelly patted my knee. "So, tell me: how's the crime business these days?"

I shrugged. "Busy, I guess. Dirty. Plagued with criminals. What about the news business?"

"About the same."

We shared a laugh.

"You need a favor, don't you?"

I smiled; Kelly never had any difficulty reading my moves.

"No question you've got it," she continued before I could answer. "Just don't let it cost me my job this time. Deal?"

# 21

The house was as exactly as I'd left it: doors locked, drapes closed, one person's dirty dishes in the dishwasher, and a change of clothes hanging around in the closet.

I dropped car keys on the table and shucked off my coat, deleted the silent recording on the answering machine.

We are all creatures of habit.

I went upstairs and down the short hallway, placed a hesitant hand on the doorknob of the master bedroom. I leaned my brow against the painted wood and did my best to breathe away the terrible thoughts associated with the room. But I couldn't bring myself to turn the knob and go inside any more than I had done these last twelve months.

I went back down the stairs on heavy feet.

The hidden key was exactly where I'd left it. I used it to unlock the basement door, then descended the creaking stairs into darkness. Groped around for the pull switch and pulled on lights.

I'd converted part of the basement a while back. Planned to use it as a den on the weekends. Hang out with Harry. Watch a game. Guzzle beer. All that kind of childish man stuff. I'd even installed a big plasma TV and a pair of matching La-Z-Boys. But the TV hadn't been turned on this last year and my cable subscription had expired I don't know when.

We all have our obsessions.

One whole wall of the den was plastered with photographs. Printouts. Post-its. They formed a multi-colored mosaic that spanned the last twelve months of the life of a man I'd never met. It looked disorganized. But I knew where everything was – every scribbled word, every newspaper clipping, every dead end. None of it had been here twelve months previously. Just a poster from an old movie I was trying to forget.

I opened up my laptop on the desk, got an energy drink from the little trendy refrigerator in the corner and emptied it while the computer booted up. Then I put on my readers and checked new emails. Aside from a hundred junk messages promising me youth, money, vitality or all three, there were several communications from Dreads. I filed them in my *Dreads* folder without reading them – along with the hundred other unopened emails already in there.

Something was bugging me.

I made some space on the desk next to the laptop. I placed evidence bags on the surface and illuminated the angle-poise lamp. Brought it in close. In the first bag was a photocopy of the torn photograph from the 7th Street Bridge. Bright colors within the cone of hot light. The original was logged in at the station house. In the other, the faded newspaper clipping left on Marlene's pillow – yet to be entered into Evidence. Old and yellowed.

I put on my readers and peered closer.

Samuels' strained smile was clear to see. It documented the forced participation of the obliged. He hadn't wanted to appear ungrateful or even antisocial – so he'd made the effort, when really all he'd wanted was to be at home with his Mozart and his fancy French wine. We all go through these motions. Maybe Samuels' participation was part of his University contract. Or maybe it was for somebody else's benefit. It looked like he was wearing the same tuxedo. The same get-up I'd seen in every one of the photographs displayed on Samuels' living room wall. But something was different here. Something I couldn't quite put my finger on.

I took the folder labeled *The Mortician Murders* from the tray on the desk, crossed out the title out and replaced it with *The Undertaker Case.*

Okay, so I keep copies of my case files at home; no crime in that. You'd do the same if you were in my shoes.

I examined a CSU eight-by-ten of Samuels lying on his bed. I'm no tailor, but the outfit looked the same as the one in the torn picture. Same dinner shirt. Same cufflinks. Same ten-grand Rolex. The same crimson cummerbund and blood-red bowtie.

So why was my *Uh-Oh Radar* on full alert?

I fished out a magnifying glass, slipped the photocopy out of its bag and scrutinized it.

The shot had been taken in a TV studio. I didn't know which one. Maybe Samuels had been interviewed on a chat show. There were big TV cameras and boom microphones in the background. The gray-haired guy with the short gray beard I thought of as Pointy Face was just over Samuels' shoulder. The foot of the person who Samuels was standing next to was visible at the bottom of the picture. A woman's foot, wearing a fashionable open-toed pump.

What was I missing?

I leaned back and chewed some cheek.

Distantly, I heard the house phone ring. I put everything down and went to the foot of the stairs, waiting to hear if it was my anonymous caller leaving another silent message. But the caller hung up before the answering machine stepped in.

Back in the den, my cell phone chirped.

I picked up: *Detective Fred Phillips.*

"Yes, Fred?"

"Gabe, we need you here, ASAP." He sounded excited. Slightly breathless.

"Okay," I began curiously. "Where you at, Fred? And why?"

"A place on Folsom street in Brooklyn Heights. We need you here ASAP," he repeated. "We think we've found your boy."

# 22

I made my way there with a flashing-red light on the dash. No sirens. No time to detour and pick up Jamie. No time to grab that change of clothes, or even that shower that I desperately needed.

A handful of patrol cars had closed off access to the eastern end of Folsom Street. Men and women in blue were checking their firearms and handing out bulletproof vests. A makeshift perimeter was holding back nosy onlookers. I caught sight of a big black SWAT van parked around the corner. Black-armored professionals locking and loading.

A uniform waved me down. Then a big-shouldered Watch Commander with a flushed face pulled me over. I lowered the window and flashed ID. He nodded, looking nervy. He made hurried hand signals to his men manning the barricade. A black-and-white squad car reversed out of the way. Tires screeched. I was waved through. The barricade closed behind me, sealing my fate.

Folsom Street looked rundown. An undulating road of bleached asphalt and single-floor dwellings in dire need of upkeep. Rusting chain-links and sorry-looking palm trees.

I could see tense cops crouching behind overflowing trashcans. Weapons drawn. More cops, six or seven houses down. Straight-backed behind wilting trees, sucking in paunches, guns held prayer-like.

Jan and Fred must have hit the mother lode, I thought.

I scraped the curb and jumped out, went around to the trunk and sprang the lock. I ducked into my bulletproof vest, spotted the shotgun hooked to the insides of the lid, thought about it, then closed the trunk. These houses looked small. Cramped. No one wanted to get caught by a discharging shotgun at close quarters and by mistake.

Besides, I wanted to take *The Undertaker* alive.

Fred and Jan and a couple of no-nonsense detectives from Central were gathered in the shade of a wheel-less camper van. I joined them. Everybody had their dark blue body armor on. Everybody looking serious and pumped. Ready to take down a serial killer.

"We were running checks on the flags thrown up on the mortician screening," Fred explained. "This guy, Walden Coombs, spent six months in juvenile detention ten years ago for illegal vivisection."

It had been the last thing I'd expected to hear on a sunny Tuesday afternoon. But not surprising. My life is like that.

"Neighbors' cats," he added. "And even a pet iguana."

"So what's the connection?"

"Jeffrey Samuels." Jan said. "Coombs spent a semester under his tutelage before being booted out for stealing lab equipment."

It was a weak strike. But I'd seen flimsier ones hitting a home run.

"Okay. Which house are we looking at?"

"Across the street. The pale blue door."

I glanced around the hood of the van. The house in question looked dilapidated. Flaky paintwork. Filthy windows. Junk forming an obstacle course in the yard.

"What do we know about this Walden Coombs character?"

"Mid-twenties." Jan said. "So far as we know, unmarried. This is his parents' place. The father had his own veterinary practice until the recession hit. Blew his brains out in the kitchen about a year ago. As far as we know, the mother is still alive."

"Neighbors down the street say he's a bit of a loner." Fred added. "Spends most nights up and about."

It sounded like me. "What's Coombs do for a living?"

"He works part-time as the clean-up over at the County Medical Center. Basically, he helps out in the morgue. Mostly nightshift."

"They let him back after kicking him out?"

Fred shrugged. "Someone's got to do the menial jobs."

I took out my Glock and checked it. My palms were moist. I wiped them off on my jacket. "All right. If we're sure about this, let's do it."

\* \* \*

On my mark, the helmeted boys from SWAT struck the pale blue door of the Coombs residence with a handheld ram, hard enough to make the flaky wood splinter inwards without much protest. The door went clattering into the hallway in a cloud of dust. SWAT poured in after it. Single-file. Fanning out. Weapons butted hard against shoulders. Unblinking eyes locked along their sights. Two SWAT down the hall. Two into the living room. Two heading for the bedrooms. They were followed by a stream of teeth-clenching cops with their handhelds darting this way and that. I led the way. Heart-pumping. The place was a mess. Looked like an indoor junkyard. I scrabbled my way into the living room as another bunch of SWAT guys smashed through the backdoor. I heard the word *"Clear!"* being shouted throughout the dwelling. Then everyone was holstering their weapons and the boys from SWAT were clearing out.

I met up with Jan and Fred in the kitchen.

"Looks like nobody's home," Fred said.

I shook my head. "I wouldn't go as far as to call this a home."

We were all thinking the same thing. The place was a dump. Smelled like one, too. We were knee deep in a lifetime's accumulated filth and bric-a-brac. Our stomachs were clenched.

Then somebody shouted *"Detectives!"* and we all turned toward the rear bedroom.

*"I think you're going to want to see this!"*

\* \* \*

We clambered our way to the back of the house. Slipping and sliding over hillsides of girlie magazines and sun-crisped newspapers. There was no door to the bedroom itself – just a beaded curtain with missing strands. I swept it out of the way and the three of us pushed inside.

The room was small, cluttered. No bed. No wardrobe. No drawers. Something like black sackcloth had been taped up at the window, so that the sunlight was heavily reduced but not completely blocked out. Grubby posters were stapled to peeling walls. Horror movies and porn. Some porn horrors. Shelves of old VHS tapes with handwritten labels. Something in the corner that looked like an IV stand stolen from a hospital. Rubber tubing. A battered gas bottle.

A coffin in the middle of the room.

We were all surprised by the sight of it.

It was raised off the floor on two pairs of suitcase stands – like the kind they provide in some of the nicer hotels. The casket was polished, shiny, with gleaming brass handles. Just about the cleanest thing in the whole house.

I wedged fingers under the rim of the lid. It didn't take much strength to lever it open. Everybody was holding their breath and leaning close in morbid fascination. The lid swung up and to the side on well-greased hinges.

There was a man lying on the puffed pink satin lining. A slightly chubby man in his mid-twenties, with thick, black-framed glasses and a three-day stubble. Aside from a pair of dirty-white boxers, he was otherwise naked.

"I take it this is Walden Coombs?"

His hands were clasped across his chest, funeral-style, fingers wrapped around an iPod. I could see thin white wires running up to his ears.

I reached down, placed fingers against Coombs' jugular.

And that's when Walden Coombs flung open his eyes and let out a blood-curdling scream.

Everybody jumped.

If Fred had still been holding his gun he would have shot the guy dead, then and there.

# 23

Lifestyles are a matter of taste. We might not like what the guy next door does with his house, or the way he lives in it, but that's his choice. Walden Coombs had chosen to live his life in squalor and sleep in a coffin. It was mild compared with some, I guess.

A thorough search of the Coombs residence turned up blank. Except for a few health violations, he was squeaky clean – at least on paper. There were no traces of roses. No urns filled with ash. No hint that Coombs could be *The Undertaker*. Not even a single tube of superglue in the entire house. We did find a couple of empty bell jars and several bottles of distilled vinegar. But no pickled pets.

Coombs was taken back to the station house for questioning. As a matter of courtesy we allowed him to get dressed before taking him in. Now he was seated at a bolted-down table in one of the interview rooms, wearing a grubby tee shirt with Che Guevara's face on it, and a scowl from ear to ear.

"I won't let you get away with this." Coombs promised as I pulled out a metal chair and settled into it, facing him. "You'll be hearing from my attorney, for wrecking my house."

"Your parents' house," I corrected. "Which, by the way, looked like you'd already done a pretty good job of wrecking by yourself."

Coombs glared from beneath a sweaty brow. He was trying to be cool as a cucumber, but his body language was chili pepper red.

"Don't sit in judgment of me," he said with a sneer. "You don't even know me."

"I know what you are."

"Oh, really?" Coombs had an evil twinkle in his eye.

I didn't like it; I knew what was coming.

He leaned over the table, just to intimidate. I could smell body odor mixed with something sickly sweet. Like cleaning fluid.

"Well, I guess that makes two of us," he said. "Because I know what you are, defective. You're the great, celebrity cop child-killing piece of shit I seen on the news. Surprised you still have a job. But then again, you the man. Right? Got to look out for the man." He gave me a conceited look. I wanted to wipe it off his sweaty face with the back of a hand.

"Sit back," I said.

Coombs stayed leaning over the table for another second or two. I stared him out. He gave me more of that smugness, then settled back in the chair.

"So, remind me again, Mr. Celebrity Cop: why am I being held here against my will?"

There was a video camera standing on a tall tripod behind my shoulder, taping everything. Legally, there were limitations to how long we could hold Coombs without charging him. Limitations on what I could and couldn't say, or do.

The trick to a successful interview is to stay objective. Far too many inexperienced cops let their emotions cloud their responses. Coombs had riled me up with one sentence. I was annoyed with myself. I took a moment to calm down before answering:

"Mr. Coombs, you're here as part of an on-going police investigation. This is just routine questioning. You're free to leave anytime you like." I saw his muscles tense as he was about to stand, and added: "But if you walk out that door before answering a few simple questions you will be placed under arrest."

Coombs sneered. "Fascist. Arrested for what?"

"At least a dozen health and safety violations. Then there's the matter of the stolen hospital equipment. Maybe some underage porn on one of those VHS tapes of yours."

Coombs banged both fists against the metal table hard enough to make the sound boom. He stared with his little piggy eyes and ground his teeth.

"Hit a raw nerve?" I asked.

Coombs blew out steam and shook himself like a wet dog. "No. I'm just no kiddie fiddler. Got that? Pedophiles make me sick. They're vermin. They should be exterminated. Go ahead and watch the tapes. You'll soon get the gist of what I'm into."

I'd seen the posters on his bedroom wall; I had a good idea what excited Walden Coombs.

"Where were you Saturday morning?"

"Which Saturday morning?"

"The one we just had."

"Probably at home."

"With your mother?"

"No. Not with my mother. I haven't seen that bitch in months."

"Anyone else who can corroborate your whereabouts?"

"Why? Do I need an alibi? Am I being charged with something?"

"How about Sunday morning?"

"Which Sunday?"

I made a face. Some interviews are like extracting teeth.

"This last Sunday you mean?" He pretended to think about it. "Well, I wasn't in church, that's for sure. Reading the papers? Enjoying breakfast in bed? Is this going somewhere, defective?"

"How well did you know Jeffrey Samuels?"

"Who?"

"Your old professor at USC."

"Oh, him. I don't."

"But you were under his tutelage, at one point."

"Him and about five others. I wasn't there long. But I'm betting you already know that."

"What did you think of the professor?"

"Far as I remember he was gay."

"First thing you remember about him is his sexual persuasion. Interesting. Was that a problem for you?"

"I'm not homophobic, if that's what you mean."

"Tell me about the basement."

Coombs leaned back and folded his arms. He narrowed his eyes until they almost disappeared. I could see him thinking through his reply, making sure he didn't incriminate himself.

We'd found an operating table down there in his basement. One of those large multi-bulb theater lamps. A metal trolley full of surgical tools. Stainless steel bowls. Everything you'd need to carry out minor surgical procedures. Nothing in a sterile environment. Everything contaminated.

"We all have secrets in our basements," he said. "Mine is I'm interested in anatomy. Call it a hobby."

"Mr. Coombs, you understand that carrying out unauthorized surgeries on live animals is against the law? It also contravenes umpteen housing codes. All of which means a hefty fine, in the very least. Maybe even community service. Jail time."

"So issue the damn fine." Coombs said nonchalantly. "You have nothing on me, defective. Check your facts. I'm doing nothing illegal. So I dissect dead rats I find in my yard. So what? They're dead already. There's no crime in that. I know my rights."

I wondered if he knew anything about animal rights.

Suddenly, he straightened again, animated. "The truth is, I like to see what makes them tick. It's fascinating. Biological mechanisms. So I collect samples. Slice them open. Connect muscles to batteries. Then stimulate and observe. Sometimes I swap their organs. A rat's heart in a bird's body. Different brains. It's cutting edge. You'll see. I'm the new Dr. Frankenstein."

He was licking rubbery lips, rubbing sweaty palms together.

I got up and left the room before I did something I'd regret.

"You think he's the killer?" Captain Ferguson asked as I joined him outside. We could see Coombs through a pane of one-way glass. He was rocking back and forth in the metal chair. He didn't look fazed by his incarceration. Quite blasé.

"I guess he fits the bill," I said. "A misfit, white, with questionable morals and a trade that slots him nicely in the profile."

"But?"

"But look at him, John. Everything about this guy is untidy. His appearance. His home. Probably his work. If we know one definite fact about this killer it's he's a neat freak to the point of being obsessive compulsive. Coombs and the man we're looking for couldn't be farther apart if they lived on opposite sides of the planet."

All at once Coombs got to his feet and came up to the one-way glass. He rapped knuckles sharply against it.

"Hello? Is anybody out there? Can I get a cola?"

"Cut him loose," Ferguson whispered with a sigh.

# 24

Contrary to the movies, police work does not consist solely of chasing after the bad guy down dark, forbidding alleyways. Most of the real chasing is done sitting behind a desk with a telephone glued to the ear, hunting down new leads and investigating paper trails. Thankfully, careening car chases and blazing gun battles are mostly the stuff of make-believe.

I spent the next couple of hours going over stuff with Jamie.

We went through Marlene's long list of acquaintances, seeing if anyone had a bone to pick. I'd taken her address book to help with the investigation. Her contacts read like a *Who's Who* of the rich and famous. Many were rock stars, TV personalities, movie actors. The regular Hollywood jet-set. Who would have guessed? But there were just as many less-well-known names who held respectable positions in children's charities, health foundations and research facilities. Those we did manage to speak with seemed genuinely upset by the news of her death. It was like trying to find someone with a bad word to say about Mother Theresa. Don't even try.

We contacted schools, seeing if they'd had any no-shows fitting the little girl's description. There was still no word from the FBI. Which either meant nobody had reported her missing yet or nobody was missing her. As a father, the thought of my little girl disappearing without my knowing seemed a scary place to be. Were her parents, even now, oblivious to her abduction?

A quick search came up with in excess of five hundred elementary schools in the metro area. Too many to speak with individually. After the first couple of dozen we contacted the Board of Education and had them do the legwork with a generic fax.

Truth was, we didn't even know if the little girl was from LA.

By 2 p.m., the mortician list was just about complete. A grand total of six flags out several hundred candidates – including Walden Coombs. Jan and Fred had already struck off four out of the remaining five and would be looking into number six.

I didn't want to think about Coombs and his coffin. But I did.

At 3 p.m., I called a Robbery-Homicide update. Our small team assembled around the evidence board that had been steadily filling up all day. More CSU photos had been added. More shots of death and weirdness. I recapped yesterday's meeting, introducing the ripped photo and the newspaper clipping. Then I started pinning up pictures of the van den Berg crime scene.

"So what do we know about the old doll?" one of the sergeants asked.

"Her name was Marlene van den Berg," I answered. "She was a widow in her mid-eighties. No surviving children. In fact, no surviving relatives anywhere we can find. She was the last of her kind. And, as such, the sole heir to the van den Berg family fortune."

"Money always makes for a good motive." Fred remarked. "How much we talking, Gabe?"

"We're still working on finding that one out, Fred. Right now it's with the lawyers. What I can tell you is the Van den Berg Empire started way back, when a hundred thousand bucks made you a millionaire. We guestimate close to a half billion, give or take."

Somebody whistled.

"The old doll have a hat full of enemies?"

I looked at the sergeant. "Too soon to tell. But we're not expecting too many. She was liked by all. Isn't that right, Jan?"

Jan nodded. "Fred and I canvassed her neighbors first thing this morning. Everyone we met spoke highly of her. From all accounts, Marlene was a pillar of the community, with interests in over a dozen children's charities spanning the globe."

"So, who stands to gain from her inheritance?" the sergeant asked.

"Good question," I said. "Lawyers being lawyers, we're still in the dark about that. But I very much doubt Richard Schaeffer will."

One of our fellow detectives spoke up: "Who's Schaeffer?"

I tapped a fingernail against a photo of the surfer dude from Huntington Beach. It had been taken while he was letting off steam down by the pool. He looked like a mad magician in his billowing bathrobe.

"Richard Schaeffer is Marlene's live-in butler. So far, he's the only person the killer has left alive at any of the crime scenes. Why, we're not exactly sure. But my guess is it's important. Looks like he was hit by the same Taser as Samuels."

"Is he a suspect?"

"Not at the moment. His alibis check out."

"What's with the wedding gown?"

I glanced at the snapshot of Marlene lying in the sun on her lovely terracotta terrace, surrounded by drying rose petals.

"We presume the killer dressed her up post mortem, as he did with Samuels. We need to find out why he's doing that."

Just after 4 p.m., Ferguson summoned me into his office.

The window blinds were tilted so that the late afternoon sun painted tiger stripes across the room. Ferguson was penned up behind his cluttered desk, strumming his fingernails on the worn surface. I'd known

Ferguson long enough to know that the action meant he was pissed.

"I just got off the phone with the Commander," he announced as I closed the door.

I could hear the restrained irritation in his whispered voice. I began to feel bad; I knew what was coming.

"Don't tell me; Bob Gibson called him up?"

"Did you think for one minute he wouldn't?"

Bob Gibson is the main man over at NBC, and as such Kelly Carvelli's boss. He's also one of the Commander's golfing buddies. I'd known Kelly would need to clear her story with him first, but had fooled myself into thinking Gibson wouldn't take it further.

"The Commander wants to know why your plan wasn't run past him first. I told him I'd had a busy day and hadn't gotten round to letting him know yet. Now I want to know the same."

I made a placating face.

"Never mind," Ferguson breathed before I could come up with something, anything that didn't sound like a flimsy excuse. "I expect what's done is done." He checked his watch. "Too late to back down now even if we wanted to. The important thing is, do you think he'll buy it?"

I took a deep breath. I'd learned long ago never to play out enough rope to hang myself with.

"John, I just don't know. I guess it seemed like a good idea at the time. Still does. With this Coombs guy off the hook it's all we've got."

I saw Ferguson wrestle with the pros and the cons of my hare-brained plan. I could sense lawsuits, demotions, reprimands, all floating through his mind. He strummed pissed-off fingertips on the desk for what seemed an eternity, then said: "All right. But we do this my way. Last thing we need is the mayor getting his pound of flesh."

# 25

Randall Fisk was enjoying a quiet drink in a quiet bar. No one was bothering him. He was by himself, sitting at a corner table, with a direct line-of-sight to a small TV set hoisted in the angle of the walls. He was minding his own business and had been for the last hour or so. Sipping frothy beer and watching the comings and the goings as happy patrons drifted in and happier ones staggered out.

As bars went, *The Fog Clipper* was a dive. It was a no-frills watering hole known for its home-charm karaoke. Dimly-lit. Wood-paneled. A scattering of eclectic patronage waiting turns at the dusty pool table.

Randall Fisk hadn't always been his name. At one time it had belonged to another. And he'd had somebody else's. But he'd owned it for such a long time now that it felt like his. Ought to be his. It was comfortable, like a favorite hat. Easy to wear. Anonymous. Randall Fisk was what he called an *also known as*. One of many he'd worn over the years. An also known as. Like a zucchini was also known as something he could never quite remember. He had plenty of *also known as* identities waiting in the wings. Everybody had them. Difference was, his came out into the spotlight every now and then to perform.

Today, he was Randall Fisk: killer. Tomorrow, he could be somebody else. A headstrong character like Bill Teague, FBI Super-Special Agent. Or the pedantic Carl Benedict, Medical Examiner. That was the beauty of adoptable personas: he could become anyone he chose, anytime he pleased. It all depended on which one got the job done.

At two minutes before 5 p.m. on a cooling January evening in Los Angeles, the man also known as Randall

Fisk was sluicing ice-cold beer between his perfect-white teeth, letting it fizz around his gums before slinging it down the hatch.

So far, there hadn't been any mention of him or his work on any news bulletin. Complete media silence. Nada. No mention of the 7th Street Bridge or the van den Berg house. Somebody was keeping their mouth shut about him and his activities. He wasn't surprised; he knew how the system worked. Last thing the cops wanted was to raise a public panic. It would only make their job of tracking him ten times harder.

He checked his watch.

A few more minutes.

Randall was used to waiting. He'd waited his whole life. Learned to deal with the boredom by tuning time out. By thinking linear thoughts.

Inhale, exhale, inhale, exhale . . .

On the TV, the commercials were coming to a close. News time imminent. He pushed his beer aside.

Maybe this time.

Dead on the hour, the snazzy titles of the *Channel Four News* bulletin flashed onscreen. A pair of newsreaders appeared behind the blazing titles: a young male whipping boy and his black bitch sidekick.

*"Hello, I'm Nate Niemeyer."*

*"And I'm Kelly Carvelli. This is the Channel Four News. Coming up . . ."*

For many absolutely valid reasons not fully clear to him now, Randall detested the black bitch newsreader. Partly because she reeked of capitalism – one generation up from the ghetto and already mixing drinks with the Rockefellers – but mostly because she was a good friend of the Great Celebrity Cop, who he happened to hate with a passion. Someday, somebody would have to teach that black bitch a lesson in humility. Maybe him.

To his dismay, the majority of the news bulletin was bland flannel-filling drivel. Totally expected. He began to get bored. He got bored quickly. That was one aspect of his *condition*. Did he mention he had a condition? Was it anyone else's business? Smart people had small attention spans. His was smaller than a nanosecond. Go figure.

Randall considered leaving. But the picture on the TV had changed to an overhead view of what looked like an old redbrick mansion set against football field lawns.

The caption in the corner read:

*"Breaking News: Attempted Murder of Wealthy Aristocrat at St. Cloud Rd, Los Angeles County'.*

Randall Fisk straightened his spine with piqued interest – especially on reading the word *'attempted'*.

# 26

Bandage it up any way you like, I have a healthy aversion to hospitals. Maybe it's the all-pervading odor of detergent and death. Or maybe it's something a whole lot more sinister. The unhealthy week I'd spent in Cedars-Sinai was the longest seven days of my life, and I wasn't even the one admitted. Being here again was making my flesh creep.

"Just try and leave everything in one piece." Eric Bryce warned me as he stepped into the elevator. He was wringing his hands like a dodgy accountant on his way to an IRS meeting.

"You worry too much, Eric," I said.

"It's my job. Should be yours too, dammit." The elevator doors closed on the Chief Administrator's glower. "I'm holding you personally accountable." I heard him shout as the carriage dropped away. "You hear me?"

I turned and made my way over to the nurses' station.

No doubt about it, I owed Eric. He'd rung bells to get me a nice little second floor wing with a half-dozen empty rooms. Far enough away from the rest of his patients to prevent his insurers suffering a heart attack.

The fake news bulletin expertly delivered by my good friend Kelly Carvelli had been aired without a hitch. As far as the killer was concerned, Marlene van den Berg had survived his attack and was now on life support here at Cedars-Sinai. Whether or not the killer had watched the bulletin, only time would tell.

It was my hope he'd take the bait and come sniffing.

Officer Linda Martinez snickered at me from inside the nurses' station. Ferguson had put two conditions on my plan: no Jamie – she was still too inexperienced to be exposed to a potentially dangerous stakeout – and take plenty of back up. I had two undercover cops here with me, plus about two dozen more uniforms waiting at a discreet distance outside. Waiting to pounce on my command.

Martinez looked extremely uncomfortable in her nurse's outfit. One of those girls who thought she was a better man than all her male colleagues. She was shorter than me by a head and heavier by thirty pounds. Martinez is the blunt end of a sawn-off shotgun, and just as nasty.

It was a little before 12 a.m.

No show from our boy, not yet, anyway. Truth was, I wasn't expecting anything this side of midnight. I was already thinking of *The Undertaker* as a nocturnal killer. Pre-dawn. When we are at our most vulnerable. It was part of his pattern I was slowly piecing together.

My heels clacked against the tiled floor as I walked the length of the hallway. The lighting was turned down low. A few nightlights here and there, giving off firefly glows near the ceiling. Plenty of shadows. Every door locked, bar one.

In any ambush, maintaining a low profile is the difference between success and failure. There is a lot to be said for the element of surprise – just ask General George Custer. The last thing I wanted our killer to see if he did happen to come skulking down the hallway were two thick-necked coppers bashing their batons up and down the walls. Everything had to look ordinary. Or as ordinary as it could be with Attila the Hun camped behind the counter.

I double-checked to make sure all the doors except one were locked. They were. Then I entered our trap room and sealed myself inside. It took a moment for my eyes to adjust to the dark. A bank of twinkling monitors on the other side of the bed tried their best to brighten things up, but failed. In the darkness, I could just make out a hunched human shape under the bed sheets. Marvin, the lab skeleton from the hospital's teaching facility, was staring up at me through big black holes for eyes.

"Don't give me that look," I said. "It was the best I could do at short notice."

*  *  *

I adjusted the gray wig on Marvin's bumpy cranium, and then settled into a chair in the corner of the room, to wait. Stakeouts are ninety-nine per cent patience and one per cent perspiration. The hours are unsociable and the excitement is thin on the ground.

I stretched creaking muscles.

The last protracted stakeout I'd been involved in had sent a killer to ground – or underground along with the rest of the insects. No one had seen a wink out of *The Maestro* in almost a year.

The reality is, about half of all stakeouts are no-shows. Cops on stakeouts have two enemies, besides the crooks, that is: boredom and fatigue. Any one of which can adversely affect the outcome. Together, they can be dangerous.

I rolled my shoulders and rubbed at my eyes.

Marvin the mannequin was staring at me from beneath his lopsided wig.

"What you looking at?" I said with a yawn.

Marvin was the quiet type; he just stared back and didn't say a word. We were getting along tremendously.

I checked my watch: 2 a.m.

We were now officially into Wednesday.

And it looked like my boy wasn't going to show.

# 27

Night skies in any sizeable metropolis are rarely full of stars. In their place hangs a filthy charcoal blanket, washed through with the murky yellowness of reflected city lights. It was beneath this sullen glow that Randall, also known as *The Undertaker,* now strolled, unchallenged, across the cracked concrete of the service compound.

There was very little illumination after dark at the rear of the hospital. The wire-grilled lamp above the loading dock was out. A dead bulb – overlooked by penny-pinching bureaucrats – which left just the wan overspill coming from a hundred windows rising into the night.

Through one such window at ground level he could see an old black porter in crisp green coveralls. He was stacking cartons of toiletries from the last delivery of the day. The old guy was wearing a pair of earphones. Whistling merrily to himself. Oblivious to everything beyond the task at hand.

Randall pressed a gun-shaped object against the service door. The high-compression bolt ruptured the lock mechanism with a *thunk.*

\* \* \*

He took the stairwell to the desired floor, three steps at a time.

He nodded a professional *hello* to a sleepy-looking nurse occupying the nurse's station. Turned down a long hallway lined with private rooms. The lighting was low. His heels clicked against mopped linoleum.

His disguise was *perfect*.

He could taste the starch in his luminous white lab coat. No one queried his presence. It was late; anyone with a modicum of authority was home in bed and ignorant to the fact that a killer now stalked their prestigious hospital.

He arrived at his destination: last room on the left. *The* room. He peered through the narrow glass panel set in the teak-colored door and saw semi-darkness. Just the barest multi-colored glimmers coming from a bank of electronic equipment. Just enough to outline the huddled shape of somebody lying in a bed.

The killer wrapped his fingers around the hypodermic in his pocket and slowly turned the door handle.

# 28

I must have dropped off, slumped in the corner of the walls, with no idea how long I'd been out. I blinked and got my bearings. Marvin was still staring at me from across the room. It was still dark. I checked the time. Something past three. There was a cold sheen of sweat on my brow and a metallic taste in my mouth.

My cell phone was vibrating in my pocket.

It was Harris, Martinez's partner. He sounded fired up: "Try answering your phone, numb-nuts. There's an unidentified male heading your way."

"Alert back up," I whispered back, then sprang to my feet.

I drew out my Glock and pressed damp shoulders against the cool wall next to the door.

A silhouette passed across the glass panel. The silhouette of a man, outlined against the soft amber glow in the hallway.

The breath solidified in my lungs.

The subdued lighting coming through the glass panel cast a long rectangular swathe across the floor and partly up onto the bed. I stared at that dull orange oblong, trying hard not to blink.

The silhouette came back and stayed.

Definitely, the head and shoulders of a man.

Blood banged in my throat.

I heard the handle of the door being tried, and pressed my back harder against the wall. Braced myself.

This was it.

*This was it!*

*   *   *

Everything happened in a flash. One of those explosive moments where instinct and training takes over.

As the intruder entered the room, I barked the word every criminal expects a policeman to bark in moments like this: "Freeze!" Quickly followed by the qualifier: "Police!" But it made little difference. The intruder acted how every policeman expects them to act in these moments: by completely ignoring the request and making a bolt for freedom.

I went crashing through the door right on the intruder's heels. But he was fast. He was off and hurtling back down the hallway at an increasing rate. Younger legs being fed by pure adrenaline. He was heading for the stairwell. Headed for escape. I hollered my police warning again and it had the same affect.

At the far end of the hallway, I could see a big guy in a janitor's uniform barreling toward us. It was Harris. Big as an ox. He was lumbering our way from the direction of the nurses' station, trying to cut off the intruder's intended escape. Harris is big. Not fast. Just big. He looked like a dirigible fighting against a strong head wind.

The intruder reached the stairwell door first and threw it open. I got there ahead of Harris. Don't ask me how. I pulled open the door, looked down the stairwell, heard footfalls coming from above. I looked up, saw movement several floors higher.

Then Harris barged through the door, almost knocking me off my feet.

"He's heading for the roof," I gasped.

Harris took off. It was as if the dirigible had ruptured and the sudden venting of air was catapulting him skyward.

I followed on bendy legs.

*   *   *

There is something to be said about foot chases inside of buildings. For some inexplicable reason, those being chased invariably make for the roof. Don't ask me why. Never occurs to them for one second that better odds of escape may lie below, where more exits exist. Always the roof. For me, always an effort.

Harris steamrollered his way up the switching flights like a power-lifter doing a drill. By the time I'd climbed through five floors I was wheezing like a chain-smoker. I shouldered open the roof access door, with no idea which way the suspect or Harris had gone. No idea where Martinez was either. I presumed Harris had called the cavalry. Presumed swarms of gun-toting cops were pouring into Cedars-Sinai and blocking off every chance of escape.

I swallowed down tacky saliva and followed the Glock out into the night.

A cool breeze pushed at my skin. Nighttime city squawks. Nighttime city lights. The roar of a helicopter a few miles away. The whir of venting fans echoing in their aluminum ducts. Rattling. I was at the end of a long flat roof section of the hospital complex. High up. No guardrail. Plenty of pitfalls and shadowy structures. Ideal for criminals to hide behind. Cautiously, I moved away from the stairwell door, sweeping every nook and cranny as I went.

I didn't have to go far before I spotted the intruder.

He was pounding across the narrow rooftop of a thin corridor block that connected this building to the next. Heading for the helipad on top of the adjoining structure. No signs of my undercover back-ups. I fell into a run and made it to the bridge – just in time to see the intruder do a U-turn and start tearing back in my direction. I dug in heels. Raised the Glock. There was another figure beyond the intruder: Attila the Hun in a nurse's uniform. Martinez was leaping onto the narrow connecting roof from the direction of the helipad, forcing the intruder back my way.

I stayed put. Legs astride. Gun aimed. There was nowhere for our boy to go except down to certain death.

*We had him!*

Unbelievably, his pace increased. His head went down as he plowed toward me. Collision course. I braced myself. I didn't like the thought of wrestling the guy down up here, so close to a fatal drop.

Then something flashed behind the intruder. I felt a sharp sting against my cheek. Heard the dull crack of a whip echo around the rooftops. Rebounding off the aluminum ducts.

The intruder stumbled. His momentum carried him on a little as he belly-flopped onto the narrow roof. I thought for one moment he was going to roll off the edge. Then Harris was bulldozing past me and grabbing the guy before he slid to certain death.

*We had him!*

I stowed my gun.

All at once I was feeling euphoric. Dizzied by adrenaline.

I couldn't believe we'd caught our killer so easily!

Martinez jogged up and pointed to my face. "You're bleeding, Quinn."

I touched my cheek. My fingertips came away with black blood on them.

Harris threw on the cuffs and flipped the intruder face-up.

My euphoria fell off the roof.

"You shot me, pig! You shot me!"

The surfer dude from Huntington Beach glared up at me as a dark patch of blood spread slowly across his boardwalk T-shirt.

We had the wrong guy.

# 29

The killer known as *The Undertaker* closed the door gently behind him. Job done. With the makings of a smile tugging at his lips, he strolled back along the hospital hallway and tipped his head at the nurse behind the counter. But she was too engrossed in her computer to notice.

Right now the cops were busy concentrating their efforts on another hospital on the other side of the city, with no idea that he'd even been here.

His namesake, the other Randall Fisk, had held a poorly paid position in the cerebral department. Academically, he'd been a washout. Bottom five percentile. In other words, obtuse. That's why he'd turned to the less intellectually-challenging pastime of bullying. That, and because his drunken father had mashed him to a pulp every night. That, and because his whore of a mother had encouraged his father. That, and because he liked beating the living crap out of all the other kids – especially the one with the *condition*.

When it came to brains, the killer known as *The Undertaker* was the exact opposite. An alter ego. So smart it stung.

He gave himself a congratulatory pat on the back as he climbed into the rented car. There was a *No Smoking* sticker on the dash, strategically positioned above the ashtray. He laughed at it as he lit a cigarette.

There was a photograph in his pocket. He took it out and studied it in the orange glow of the cigarette. It depicted a sunny day at the zoo. A woman and a boy, embraced and smiling happily at the camera, looking like they hadn't a care in the world.

Everything he did was for her.

A solitary star shone brightly in the east as he headed for the Hollywood Freeway. It moved smoothly against the filthy gray bowl of night. Big as a falling meteor. He watched it crawl across the heavens. Wondered if it could be the precursor to some cataclysmic event. A portent of better things to come. Was it normal to think of such things? Did regular people, mindlessly moving from A to B in their humdrum lives, imagine the end of the world and their part in it?

Randall leaned on the gas, squeezing the speedometer's needle past sixty. The rental soared up the on-ramp, loosing sparks as it leveled out. He tuned the car stereo into an all-night crooners' station and rolled down the driver's window.

Sinatra's distinctive vocal timbre pierced the night.

Up above, the magnesium star dimmed as the police chopper altered course.

# 30

At a quarter to five in the morning, the station house was all but abandoned: just the usual skeletons manning the phones and draining the coffee machines dry. I was one of them.

I touched the Band-Aid on my cheekbone and winced.

Martinez's bullet had drilled a neat hole straight through the butler's shoulder and took a nice little nick out of my face in the process. The incident had been logged and passed on to Internal Affairs. I wasn't expecting compensation or an apology.

As for our killer, he'd been a no-show.

And I was feeling disillusioned. Couldn't help it. Lack of sleep was taking its toll.

Had I really believed he'd fall for my ruse?

I kept going over the possibilities in my head. Beating myself up. Maybe the killer had missed the news. Maybe he'd been scared away by the butler's timely arrival. Maybe he was just too damn smart to trip himself up.

I thought about the wounded kid we had under armed guard in a room over at Cedars-Sinai. Richard Schaeffer had been bandaged up and then banged up for the night. In retrospect, his stupidity had been a big error in judgment on my part. He'd bought the news bulletin. He'd actually believed Marlene was critically wounded, but still alive – even after seeing her being carted away in a zipped-up body bag.

Idiot.

But no escaping the fact: my impulsiveness had gotten an innocent kid shot. Almost killed. Come morning, his bigwig daddy lawyer would be having choice words with the Commander. And I'd be listening to a wasp in my ear.

Through the glass partition of a nearby interview room I could see a pair of detectives interrogating a young Asian kid wearing street colors. The kid looked scared. He had a bloodied nose. One of the detectives caught me snooping, nodded in my direction, and then tilted the window blind closed.

I picked up the phone and called Jamie.

"Is everything okay?" she sounded sleepy. "Gabe, it's the middle of the night. What happened? Did you catch the killer?"

I told her the bad news.

"Gabe, you're lucky you didn't lose an eye. Do you want me to come in?"

"No."

"Are you sure you're okay?"

"Right now I'm not sure of anything, Jamie. Ask me again in the morning. I'm sorry for waking you."

"It's okay. I haven't been in bed long anyway. I've been running internet searches on the killer's calling cards."

"Find anything interesting?"

"Only that the religious angle looks the most promising. It's corny, I know, but it ties everything together – especially with the mock interment. The ash on their head could represent penitence. And some cultures line the routes of their funeral processions with petals."

I nodded. It made sense. I'd been thinking along the same lines. "Which means he could be marking his victims as sinner. But what about the superglue?"

"Not worked that one out yet."

I smiled. "All the same, Jamie, nice work."

"Thanks."

"One more question before I let you go back to sleep?"

I heard her stifle a yawn. "Shoot."

"Why didn't the killer kill the butler?"

*   *   *

The question had been bugging me all day. Buzzing round in my head like a trapped hornet. Worsened by the fact I'd nearly gotten our one and only witness killed.

"I'm still working on that one too," Jamie admitted after a moment's thought. "I don't know. Maybe he's an accomplice?"

"Richard Schaeffer isn't smart enough to pull it off," I said. "His only crime was seeing a meal ticket for life and pushing to the head of the line."

What were we missing?

I let Jamie go. I poured myself enough coffee to turn *Sleepy* into *Happy*, then set about poring over case notes. I am a firm believer that the devil is in the details. Look hard enough. Look long enough. Patterns will always emerge.

I wanted to find *The Undertaker's* pattern.

I wanted to predict his next move.

In my book, homicides come in two flavors: premeditated and spontaneous.

Spontaneous ones tend to lack design and lean more toward brutality: cracking an old lady over the head for her purse; snapping a man's neck in a drunken brawl; slicing open your husband's jugular with a carving knife because he's home late from the office for the fourth night running. It is the spontaneous nature of these killings which makes them hard to predict.

Premeditated ones are a whole different ball game wrapped up like a Christmas fancy. Normally, they are planned with military precision, with every single miniscule detail worked out beforehand. Premeditated murders make for a much more sophisticated kind of murderer. But they come with patterns. And these can be the killer's downfall.

Because patterns are predictable. And once we can predict behavior we can deduce possible movements.

In other words, find the pattern and you find the killer.

But sometimes even premeditative killers can be unpredictable.

I opened my cell and brought up a picture of the 7th Street Bridge crime scene. It was broad daylight. I could see the graffiti-covered concrete and a black worm of water. There was no murdered little girl in the shot. No plaid blanket. No scattered rose petals. But there was a child in the picture. A boy. Bound to one of the concrete support pillars with piano wire.

We tell our children that monsters don't exist. That they are figments of the imagination.

We are wrong.

Sometimes monsters come for our children.

# 31

Sometime later I woke to the sound of knuckles rapping hard against glass.

"Detective? You okay in there? Detective?"

At first I was disoriented and had to blink against bright daylight.

I was in my car, slumped in the driver's seat, with drool dangling pendulously from one corner of my mouth.

Déjà vu.

The car was parked in the empty lot belonging to the Church of St. Therese in Alhambra. How had I got here? I vaguely remembered feeling inconsolably lonely, guilty, getting in my car and driving through the night. Anywhere. On autopilot. Seeking salvation. The actual ride down to the church was absent.

The nuisance rapping on the glass was the motorcycle patrolman from yesterday. He was waggling a reproving finger in a circular motion: *roll the window down.*

I did.

He leaned against the door and breathed bad breath on me.

"Detective, this is becoming a bit of a habit. You on a stakeout?"

"No," I answered as I wiped away the drool.

"Anything I can help you with? Because if you are on a stakeout, I can help. This is my patch. I know everything that goes on here. You need someone like me. I'm a good asset. Coincidentally, I'm available evenings and most weekends."

I could see my reflection in his silvery sunglasses. I looked like something not quite alive. And maybe I was.

My cell phone chirped.

"Excuse me, officer."

The patrolman stayed put.

I answered the call: "Hello?"

*"Detective Gabriel."*

It sounded more of a statement than a question. A deep muffled bass of a voice. Indistinct. Drowned out by passing traffic. I shooed at the patrolman to back away from the window. He was reluctant to move. I rolled it back up, giving him no option. The patrolman retreated a yard or two and then stopped, his gloved thumbs tucked into the leather belt above his hips, watching from behind his mirrored lenses.

"Who is this?"

"Have I caught you at a bad time, Detective Gabriel?"

The voice was still indistinct. Still muffled. But deliberately so, I realized. It sounded more machine than man. Like it was coming through a filter.

"Detective Gabriel?"

"Who is this?"

"You're the Great Celebrity Cop. Do the math. You tell me."

There are only three people in the world who call me *Detective Gabriel.* And my priest doesn't phone me anymore.

I glanced at the tiny screen on the phone.

It read: *Bill Teague.*

"How many guesses do I get?"

"One," came the voice. "Just one. Make it count."

"Okay. How about . . . Bill? Or would you like the full title: Special Agent-in-Charge William Teague of the FBI?"

I listened to clotting silence, then added:

"You forgot to withhold your number, Bill. Like you did the last time you pulled this same crazy stunt."

There was a click on the line, then a familiar and more human voice said:

"Damn it, Gabriel. You got me, you slick son of a bitch. You're just too damned good for my good, that's for sure. Where's your sense of humor?"

I glanced through the window at the motorbike cop who had taken out his cell phone and was snapping pictures of me.

"Right now trying to figure out if I've just picked up a groupie."

*   *   *

I have known Bill Teague the best part of six years. I have also known Bill Teague the worst part of six years. And we've been good friends just about the same length of time.

Bill hails from my home State of Tennessee – which is just about the only thing other than gender that he and I have in common. Bill is my official FBI contact over at the National Center for the Analysis of Violent Crime in Quantico, Virginia. You might say, a vital asset in the Behavioral Science Unit. Or the *Nutcracker Suite* as some people like to call it.

"What's with the voice-changer?" I asked.

"Boredom," he replied.

I shook my head. "For the author of several acclaimed books on criminal psychology, you really do have way too much time on your hands. Take my advice, Bill: get yourself a nice young woman and a knot of pesky kids. Settle down; it'll be the making of you."

"Yeah, maybe. It's just too damned hard trying to find a woman on my intellectual level, you know what I mean?"

"I'm serious, Bill. You need to channel all that youthful energy of yours into a more constructive direction."

"Like profiling? Isn't that why I'm on the phone?"

"I don't know. Is it? I thought maybe you were just being social. We haven't talked in months."

"All right, okay. Don't go getting all heavy on me. So I heard you were back. Heard you were working a new serial case. Piqued my interest. The Funeral Director, I heard, or something equally tacky."

I smiled at his choice of words. "News travels fast. And it's The Undertaker Case, for the record. Who told you?"

"Kate."

"You've spoken with Katie?"

"Just about all the time. We used to date, remember? Before your son stole her from me. Every so often we catch up. It's a girl thing. By the way, she says thanks for the text."

I'd gotten Jamie to message my daughter-in-law with the new name for our killer – just to keep her viewers happy.

"So, Bill, to what do I owe the pleasure?"

"As a matter of fact, Gabriel, two pleasures – so consider yourself blessed. The first is we should get together over drinks. I feel the need to profile this Funeral Director guy for you. Give you some direction."

"And what's my second pleasure?"

"I have news about the murdered child, including her name and her address. Holy shit, I'm good. So when can we do this? You owe me a drink."

# 32

One of my less-favorable traits is I'm impulsive. It lands me in deep water more than I admit. But sometimes it facilitates.

The moment I got off the phone with Bill I called Airline Reservations at LAX, then the Sheriff of King County, then Captain Ferguson. In that order. Twenty minutes later, I was at Los Angeles International Airport and following signs for Departures. I ran across the enclosed bridge connecting the parking structure to the terminal, picked up the pace and ran toward Ticketing. LAX is one of the busiest airports in the world. The major West Coast hub. Turnaround for over a million passengers each month. It seemed like they were all heading my way as I zigzagged through the droves of commuters. I had my police shield held aloft. Didn't making one bit of difference. I ignored the lines of travelers waiting for boarding tickets at the check-in desks and went straight to the head of the line.

"The name's Quinn," I said breathlessly. "I called in advance."

"Sir, you'll have to get in line," the female attendant said, reinforcing it with a jab of a finger.

Someone behind me said: "Yeah, buddy. Wait your turn like the rest of us."

I showed the attendant my shield. "This is official police business. I need to be on that flight."

The attendant sucked a pink lip. She didn't like breaking protocol.

"It's a matter of life and death," I added.

Reluctantly, she checked her screen. "I'm sorry, officer, boarding has now ended for that flight. We have another outbound in two hours. I can check you in on that one. But there'll be a ninety-minute layover in Portland."

I leaned elbows on the counter, saw her pull back; my irritated countenance must have scared her.

"It's imperative I make that flight," I said. "Imperative."

I couldn't wait two hours. Couldn't bear the thought of hanging around biting nails for two minutes. I had to make the flight.

I felt a hand on my arm. "Hey, buddy. Didn't you hear?"

I spun round and shot the guy with a dark stare. "Back off, *buddy*."

He saw my fierce glower. Thought twice, then let go.

"They're already closing the doors and preparing for take-off." I heard the attendant say.

I spun back round. "Hold that flight! That's an order!"

Every pair of eyes in the immediate vicinity rotated my way. One of those moments where dropped pins crash and bang.

The attendant gawped.

I saw her supervisor rock back and to on indecisive feet.

Being hotheaded isn't my strong suit. I don't wear it well. I look like a fraud. A teddy bear pretending to be a grizzly. The attendant knew I couldn't hold the flight. Not without the proper paperwork, signed in triplicate. Or an immediate danger – like a bomb threat. But she could see my desperation. Hear it. With a shaking hand, she buzzed her colleagues at the gate and told them to stand down for two minutes.

I thanked her and ran on, fast as I could.

*   *   *

Hours later, the blue-and-white sixty-seat SkyWest Bombardier landed at Tacoma International Airport in Seattle seven minutes ahead of schedule. It had made the nine-hundred-and-fifty mile flight in exactly two-and-a-half hours. Without a tail wind. I sent my regards to the pilot for doing a fine job, then ran down the airbridge into the North Satellite Terminal.

I waited thirty long seconds for the underground transit train to breeze up to the platform. Fill. Then reverse back down the dark tunnel. Thirty seconds later, I was deposited beneath Central Terminal. I bounded up the escalator toward daylight.

There was a green-and-gold liveried King County Sheriff's Department cruiser waiting for me outside the main doors. Engine purring. Red-and-blues flashing silently. A driver wearing a dark-brown Sheriff's Department uniform, gold-tinted shades and a no-nonsense face.

I jumped in and we took off. Wordlessly. Sped away from the concourse like a getaway car. Accelerated out of the airport. Headed east on the 508 for about a mile. Then we took the cloverleaf north onto Interstate 5. Reaching eighty within seconds. The driver kept it floored.

It was raining. Sleeting against the windshield from an overcast sky. Cardboard-gray. Streaming horizontally across the side windows. Car headlights making the droplets glint like diamonds.

We passed signs for Tukwila and the Museum of Flight. Sirens sounding. Weaving in and out of slower traffic. Blinding spray being thrown up off juggernauts as they plowed through the surface water like speedboats.

I settled back and held on.

My driver was on a death wish. I wasn't.

In the far distance I could see a crowd of skyscrapers huddling against the leaden sky.

I'd only ever been to Seattle once before.
And I didn't want to think about it.

*   *   *

I met up with King County Sheriff Mandy Kasson in her
first floor Courthouse office facing the Smith Tower. I'd
met Mandy last year during the chase of another serial
killer.

She shook my hand with vim. "Gabe. Good to see
you again. Pity it's always under these kinds of
circumstances. How was your flight?"

"Too slow even at four-hundred miles an hour. Are
they here?"

"They're currently down the hall in one of the
interview rooms used by the DA's Office. Soon as you and
I got off the phone I had my men go pick them up. We've
made them as comfortable as possible."

"Do they know why they're here?"

"They do." Sheriff Kasson smoothed down her
jacket and straightened her tie. "Shall we?"

*   *   *

There were two people in the interview room at the King
County Courthouse in downtown Seattle on a rainy
Wednesday in January. One was seated at a long oval table
with a smoked-glass inlay. One was gazing out through the
rain-spattered window at Puget Sound visible between rain-
slicked buildings. The one sitting at the table was a man.
His posture spoke of defeat: slumped and slack. Face in
hands. Quietly sobbing. The one standing by the window
was a woman. Her posture spoke of stoicism: arms

dangling loosely by her sides. Fingers curled of their own accord. A thousand mile stare coming from dazed eyes. The man's name was Peter: a regular Joe with short sandy hair and a button nose. Big-boned. Probably played linebacker in his youth. The kind of guy who believed killing an ant would condemn him to hell. The woman's name was Anne: a small redhead with a boyish figure and a sallow complexion. The kind of woman who put the car in neutral at every traffic signal, even with her foot hard on the brake. Together, they were the McNamaras. A professional couple in their forties. He was a father. She was a mother. And up until Sunday morning they'd been the proud parents of a straight-A's nine-year-old daughter called Jennifer.

# 33

The sky was a malevolent gray. Rain battering the window. Three cups of untouched coffee between us. We were seated at the long wooden table. Me on one side. Anne and Peter McNamara on the other. Halfway through the toughest kind of interview a police officer is ever likely to conduct, or a father for that matter.

Peter McNamara had roughed up his face with the back of his sleeve, trying to remove overlapping tear tracks. But his eyes were still red raw. Face heavy with hurt. His wife was the chalk to his cheese: staring at me – staring *through me* – pupils focusing on something a thousand miles away.

As yet, Anne McNamara hadn't spoken a single word.

I was leaning slightly forward – showing interested body language – all the while acutely aware that I was the only thing stopping these folks from seeing their baby.

"We were in the park," the father was saying. He was trying his best to explain in words that didn't suffocate.

"On Friday?"

"Yeah. Friday."

"Just the three of you?"

"No. Annie was home. We run an online health store. Annie was adding new products to the range. For the weekend rush. Isn't that right, Annie?"

The mother said nothing. She might as well have been a mannequin. Shock affects us all differently.

"What were you doing at the park?"

I saw a tremor run through the father's face. Heard it in his clipped words. "The bastard killed Nero."

"Nero?"

"Our dog." He grabbed a big shaky breath.

"You walk him in the park?"

"Every day."

"And you think the man who abducted your daughter killed your dog?"

A tight nod, restricted by tense neck muscles.

"What kind of a dog?"

"German Shepherd. The bastard left the syringe in him. The police say it was probably poison. I don't know."

The killer had dealt with the dog by lethal injection. Took it out of the equation. Like a casualty of war.

I drew a deep breath. "Tell me exactly what happened, on Friday, in the park."

The father shuddered, pulled the tattered bits of himself together. "They were playing. Jenny and Nero. Like they do. Chasing sticks and stuff. There isn't much foliage this time of year."

"You could keep an eye on them."

"Yeah."

"Did you notice anybody else hanging around?"

"A few other people, maybe. Some with dogs. I don't remember. It's a blur."

"Anyone on their own? A man? I know it's hard, but try and think."

A tight shake of the head. "I don't remember."

"So what happened?"

"There's this bench. Where I sit. It overlooks the lake. I sit there while they play. Jenny and Nero. Same thing every day. But something wasn't right this time. They were only out of my sight for a few seconds." He looked at his wife. "I swear, Annie, it was only a few seconds . . ."

I heard his voice crack. His throat choke up. Saw Peter McNamara's complexion redden as he tried to swallow back the surging upset. But I could see fresh tears welling in his eyes.

"What wasn't right?" I asked slowly. "On Friday. When you were sitting at the bench. What wasn't right?"

"It was tacky," he said shakily. "Sticky. Like somebody had covered it in glue. I only looked away for a second . . ."

It was the final straw. The father burst into uncontrollable sobs, slamming his big hands across his puffy face.

"I shouldn't have looked away!" he bawled.

I glanced at the mother. She had focused on my face. For the first time I saw emotion in her eyes. But not like her husband's.

"Do you have children?" she asked suddenly.

"Yes," I answered.

"Do you love them?"

"Unquestionably. More than anything."

She leaned toward me. "Would you die for them?"

"Without a doubt."

"Would you kill for them?"

The question caught me off guard.

"Annie, please . . ." I heard the father begin through his tears.

"Would you kill for them?" she pressed again, this time reaching across the table and grabbing my wrist.

"I don't know. Maybe. Yes, I guess." The answer surprised me.

"Promise me something?"

I tried pulling free, tried to pull back from the searing heat suddenly burning in her eyes. But her grip was unrelenting.

"When you find the monster that did this to my daughter, will you kill him, for me? Will you kill the monster that took away the one thing in life that I loved?"

I looked into the fiery eyes of Anne McNamara and realized she didn't want solace for the murder of her child. She wanted retribution.

# 34

Arguing against a mother's logic is like stoking a fire with your finger and expecting not to get burned.

It was 5 p.m. I was back at LAX, at the end of a long return flight filled with awkward silence. I'd remained seated with Peter McNamara all the way back – while his wife had chosen another row, staring out the tiny window, as though in a daydream. There is something deeply disturbing about seeing a grown man reduced to tears. Something unholy. I couldn't imagine what these good people were going through. Confined to their own personal hell. I could only see that their whole world had been shattered with the death of their daughter and everything they knew was now drifting slowly out of their grasp.

One of the Precinct's unmarked sedans collected the parents from the airport. I followed at a respectful distance in my own jalopy. The sedan stopped at the station house to pick up one of our public relations officers: a trained counselor who was good at listening. Then they continued on to the Coroner's Office without me.

I didn't see Anne or Peter McNamara after that.

But I did see their daughter.

\* \* \*

I was still sitting in my car on the rooftop parking lot – going over the painful McNamara interview in my head – when Captain Ferguson opened the passenger door.

"Gabe, got a minute?"

"Sure."

He climbed in and pulled the door shut behind him. He had a file folder pressed against his chest. He looked shaken.

"The parents are on their way to the Coroner's Office," I said.

Ferguson looked like he'd seen a spiritual medium and his outlook was gloomy.

"You all right, John?"

"Just drive," he answered in a coarse whisper.

I didn't. Not straight away. I stared at him for a moment. Wondering what had caused him to look so spooked. Then I turned over the engine and drove down the access ramp way, bumped out onto 6th Street.

We headed north through the darkening dusk.

"John, you're getting me worried. Is everything okay?"

"No," he said tightly. "As far from okay as it can get."

# 35

Who knows why these things happen? Planes crash. Bridges collapse. Shit happens. It's the universal way of things. Happens every damn second of every damn day. You figure it out.

Now that I think about it, I don't recall the drive to the County Medical Center, with Ferguson staring into his lap on the passenger seat. Only that we somehow arrived there miraculously in one piece. Some things are like that. When the brain enters trauma mode it goes on autopilot. Doesn't matter about us and what we think. It's a case of survival.

I remember following Ferguson into the hospital, on heavy feet. Not going through Admissions or the ER. We headed straight for the underground cold store. Riding the shaking elevator down into the basement with a lump of bile rising in my throat. Remember seeing the ashen look on Ferguson's face. Remember descending into a morgue from a B movie. No frills. No polished floors and concealed lighting. Just the bare necessities: rinse-down everything.

I remember being in a dream. Scratch that: a nightmare. Dazed. I might have put it down to jetlag had my flight been intercontinental. But it hadn't. And it wasn't. I remember colliding with a gurney in the hallway. A sheet-wrapped cadaver on the top. Almost dumping it to the floor. Remember grabbing at it. Steadying it. Remember a mortuary technician appearing from a side doorway. Coming to see what all the commotion was about. A small, slightly rounded man with a receding hairline and thick black glasses. Heavy-duty green rubber gloves covering his hands and arms, all the way up to the elbows. Fingertips daubed in blood. A matching rubber apron looking like it had spent the last ten years in a butcher's shop.

"Everything all right, defective?"

I remember the question. Remembered his face. Remember I would have reached out and gladly throttled the smirking face of Walden Coombs had I not been so damn dazed. So out of whack. Remembered his little beady eyes watching me all the way to the hallway's end. Watching like the waxwork of John Christie – the famous London strangler – I'd once seen in Madame Tussauds. It had completely escaped me that he worked here.

I remember the entranceway to the cold store being screened by those long vertical rubber blinds that only let enough light through to make whatever lies on the other side look as eerie as possible. Remember grappling my way through. Light-headed. Remember the long metal slab in the middle of a dungeon-like room. The smell. The atmosphere. Ferguson with his head hung low. Shoulders slumped. Suit looking too big for his stooped frame.

The body lying on the slab.

A body covered up to the chin by a crisp white sheet.

A body with a face I recognized.

Bile loitering in my throat before surging into my mouth.

I will always remember that moment.

The moment I realized that my partner, Harry Kelso, was dead.

\*   \*   \*

In such moments, the body reacts as it does, regardless of our input. I rushed over to a porcelain sink jutting out of the wall and puked up clotted airline coffee until my eyes stung.

"You need to get that ulcer checked out." I heard Ferguson whisper.

I found a paper towel, wiped stinking goo from my lips.

"They think it was a heart attack," he said.

"He was fine yesterday." It was my voice. But it sounded someplace else. Strained.

"He had complications, Gabe. You know that. We'll know more once the ME's taken a look."

I threw the towel in a can. I couldn't think about Harry being dissected like one of Coombs' animals.

Ferguson handed me the file folder he'd been nursing all the way from the station house. "This was on his chest when the crash team tried to revive him."

I opened it up. It was full of newspaper cuttings. Magazine articles. I pulled one out at random. It was from the front page of the *LA Times*, dated almost a year ago. I'd seen it many times before. I was familiar with every letter, every line; had a copy of it on the wall in my basement.

In a bold typeface, the headline read:

*"Maestro Writes Celebrity Cop Dirge."*

Fresh acid seared my throat.

"Gabe, I have to ask: what was he doing with all this?"

I shook my head, "I don't know."

I didn't know. Not exactly. Not for sure. But I had suspicions.

"Were you and he still working the Piano Wire Murders?"

I hesitated long enough for Ferguson to anticipate my less-than-honest response.

"Gabe, for the love of sweet Jesus –"

"John, it's not like that," I said quickly. "This is my thing. Not Harry's. As far as he was concerned, I'd moved on. I have no idea why he had this file. I don't even know how he got it. He's been holed up here for weeks. I never saw it before now."

"I'm pulling you off The Undertaker Case."

I was sideswiped. Stunned. "John, I'm okay. Honest." I didn't sound it.

Truth was, I was as far away from being okay as I had been when the *LA Times* had run the story. And Ferguson knew it.

"I'm okay," I repeated quietly. "John, I'm on top of this. Making real progress. I can do this. Trust me. I need this."

"Then do us both a favor: go see the Police psychiatrist. Convince her you're okay and I'll reconsider. In the meantime, you're off the case. I'm sorry, Gabe. Walters and Phillips can take up the slack."

I remember Walden Coombs, the living waxwork of John Christie, watching us all the way to the rickety elevator as we left Harry to his fate. A bloodstained bone-cutter saw in his hands. A hint of evil delight in his beady eyes.

I couldn't wait to get out of there and breathe fresh air.

He couldn't wait to get his bloodied mitts on poor Harry.

# 36

The police came and asked him a few questions.

Randall knew it was standard procedure.

Nothing he couldn't handle; he'd learned his answers parrot-fashion beforehand: *pleasure, Saturday, Thursday, at a mall, no.* A potbellied sergeant and his apathetic sidekick. Going through the motions. Hardly making notes. Hardly interested. They should have come yesterday, but they weren't in any rush. Made that quite clear, thank you. They came and asked everyone the same questions:

*What is the purpose of your stay at the Hollywood Hotel? When did you check in? When are you expecting to check out? Where were you yesterday, on Tuesday afternoon, when the old woman died in the pool area? Did you see anything, anything at all?*

It was routine. They had to do it. No choice. Whenever a dead body was found in a public place the police had to canvass the local area for eyewitnesses – even when foul play was not suspected. The hotel management was aware of potential liabilities. Lawsuits. Uncomfortable inquiries into health and safety. Poolside etiquette. They expedited the LAPD's fishing expedition with free dips in the guest buffet – continental-style – plus as much coffee as they could stomach.

They came and asked everyone the same questions. It was standard procedure. But the one question they didn't ask was the one question they should have asked.

# 37

Harry was dead.

Any rational person would have gone home, taken the rest of the day off. I didn't. I dropped Ferguson back at the Precinct – wordlessly – then drove straight to *Winston's*. I didn't know why. I was feeling numb – an oxymoron. Truth was, I didn't know what to feel. Harry was dead. No fixing that. He'd been on the mend. Now he was gone. I didn't know what to think – another oxymoron. How could something like this just *happen?*

I shouldered through the glass door of the convenience store on Main Street and followed my feet to the bar in back. There were a few regulars here this time of day. Some I recognized. Some I didn't. I slid onto a stool. Oblivious to their glances.

Winston pushed a thimble of whiskey across the countertop toward me. "On the house," he nodded. "Looks like you need it."

I downed the bourbon in one. Waved for a top-up. The whiskey burned. I let it; it was the only thing I could feel.

I pictured the file folder sitting in the trunk of my car, containing an assortment of clippings snipped from umpteen publications. All dated a year ago, or thereabouts. If my partner had been following my tracks, why hadn't I noticed? Why hadn't Harry said something?

I was adding up zeroes and coming up blank.

"You're wanted, Mr. Q." Winston said with a nod.

I turned on the stool, saw Jamie standing on the carpeted fringe where the store became bar. There was a look in her eyes. A look I recognized. Something like a mother finding her lost child.

Damn.

"Your phone's switched off," she said as she came over. "I know what happened. The Captain's told everyone. Gabe, I'm sorry."

"How did you know where to find me?"

"Does it matter? I was worried. How are you? Are you all right?"

I drew a raggedy breath. "You joining me in a drink, Jamie?"

"No. I'll wait in the car."

"Sit down. Please. Have a drink."

"No," she repeated, this time more forcefully. "I'll wait in the car."

"Haven't you heard?" I shouted as she walked away. "I'm off the case."

* * *

I have never been any good at wallowing in grief. Or drowning my sorrows in the late afternoon. I settled my tab and followed Jamie outside.

Since my wife's passing, I can't keep up the tough guy act for very long.

"I'm really sorry about your partner," Jamie repeated as I climbed inside her car. It smelled of bubble-gum. Rosary beads dangling from the interior mirror.

"Jamie, I'm not good company right now. You should leave me to it. Call it a day."

She turned the transmission, switched on lights, swung the vehicle out onto the street. I buckled up as we made a right, then another, heading west.

"Where we going?"

"Your contact at the Coroner's Office has been trying to reach you."

"Jamie . . ."

"The autopsy results are in," she said. "For Samuels, the girl and Marlene. He wants us there right away."

Last place I wanted to be right now.

I gazed numbly through the window at blurring buildings, at the glaring streetlights. Everything looked alien. Like I'd woken up in Tokyo and all the signs were in a foreign tongue. My coordination was off. Everything askew. Shock does that.

We drove south on Interstate 5. Same highway, different State. Seemed back-to-front to me.

I didn't even try explaining.

Deputy Chief Carl Benedict is five feet tall in his heels, with a penchant for Hawaiian shirts and Roy Orbison eyewear. Ordinarily, any one of the ME's assistants could have faxed the results through to the station house, but my contact at the Forensic Science Center is thorough to the point of obsessive compulsive.

"Myocardial infarction," he announced as we met him in his ground floor office. The place smelled like one of those haunted houses in amusement parks. It even had pickled organs in bell jars up on the shelves. Magnifying the macabre.

I didn't want to be here.

"Heart attack?" I murmured.

"Artificially induced myocardial infarction." He handed me a dog-eared folder. "Don't believe me? Take a look for yourself. I also found discreet traces of chloroform suffused with the bonding agent he used to seal their mouths."

I put on my readers and scanned hand-written dictations. Coroner's notes seldom make the *New York Times Best Seller's List.* I saw the aforementioned chloroform and indecipherable doodles.

"Second page," Benedict said with a sigh. "See the list of chemicals? Sodium thiopental. Pancuronium bromide. Potassium chloride. Recognize the formula?"

He didn't wait for me to answer.

"It's the recipe for lethal injection," he said. "And your killer administered the drugs hypodermically."

I looked up from the notes. "To trigger cardiac arrest?"

"It's standard procedure in State executions."

I looked at Jamie. She was looking at me. We were both thinking the same horrified thought:

*What kind of monster executes a nine-year-old little girl?*

"Either of you familiar with the process?"

I didn't answer; I was too busy trying to get my head around the fact that the killer had killed the child the same way he had her pet dog.

"So let me enlighten," he said. "First the pancuronium bromide and the sodium thiopental are injected." He mimed the action. It was unnecessary. "Together, these render the victim paralyzed. Sometimes unconscious – depending on the dose. Then the real killer is administered: the potassium chloride. Shuts the heart down in seconds. Bam! Just like that. It's difficult to detect on a basic Tox screen, unless you know where to look. Want to see the bodies?"

* * *

Jamie levered the notes from my hand, flicked through them like a homebuyer assessing properties. I caught flashes of nightmarish photographs snapped on the ME's stainless steel slab. Things a father should never see.

I wasn't in the right frame of mind. I shouldn't have been here.

"Who kills like this?" Jamie asked.

Benedict had a ghoulish grin on his face. "We do. The American judicial system has been doing it for years. Want to see the bodies?"

"Slow down," I said. My thoughts were bouncing off the walls of my skull like those numbered balls in a lottery machine. "Let me get this straight. You're saying he copycats State executions?"

"That's what the evidence says."

"Would he need to be medically trained for that?"

"No, not necessarily. There are plenty of video tutorials on the Net. Reference books in every library. With the right drugs and the right equipment anyone can perform their own State execution. Or euthanasia for that matter."

Benedict saw our reaction and added:

"There's a fine line between State execution and euthanasia. Both use anesthetics to suppress the breathing before the final lethal dose is given. You could say execution is just State-funded euthanasia."

"A monster with a conscience," Jamie mused out loud.

"And here's another first," Benedict continued, far too enthusiastically for my palate. "Your killer used the intraperitoneal method to administer the drugs. In other words, he injected them through the peritoneum membrane, straight into the abdominal organs. It's the same method some veterinarians use to terminate sick animals."

Silence.

Deafening silence.

I could hear distant bells, but this wasn't Sunday.

Benedict slid a photograph out of the file and held it up to the light. It was an eight-by-ten snapshot of Marlene van den Berg's sunken abdomen. Right between her elongated navel and the pubic hairline I could see a small circle of violet stars surrounding a darker blue bruise in the center.

"See these faint purple markings on the lower stomach? That's erythema: blood leaked into the subcutaneous tissue. This is your point of syringe impact."

Jamie took the photo from my hand and looked it over. "Aside from hospitals and veterinary surgeries, who has access to these kinds of drugs?"

Benedict shrugged. "Any joker with a credit card and a little savoir-faire could order them over the Internet. I hear you can buy atomic bombs online if you know where to look. Now can we go see the bodies?"

# 38

The house on Valencia Street was in total darkness. Exactly the way I'd left it. No one singing in the kitchen. No one watching the TV. No rowdy kids running up and down the stairs. A deathly silence hung over everything like dust sheets in a summer retreat.

I dropped keys on the table and automatically deleted a vacuous message left on the answering machine. Thought about going upstairs and trying the doorknob leading into the master bedroom, but instead I fumbled my way down into the basement without pulling on the lights.

Harry was dead.

No changing that.

But so too were *The Undertaker's* three victims.

I had to focus beyond my pain.

Harry wouldn't want me moping around, feeling sorry for him. I owed it to him to stick with the task at hand and finish the job.

Some things are easier said than done.

Death warps perspectives.

Officially, I was off the case.

Unofficially, I didn't give a crap.

Something that Benedict had said had haunted me all the way home.

I wiped loose tears from the corners of my eyes and knocked my laptop out of hibernation. Its screen shimmied into life and illuminated the basement in swathes of bluish light. Glimpses of murdered children forming a mosaic across the walls. Young, bloodied bodies. Sliced flesh. Newspaper clippings. Same as those in Harry's folder, hung up in my basement. My obsession. Predictions that had never come to pass.

I brought up a search page on the computer.

I knew the basics of lethal injection. Death Row inmates get the needle, then die. Benedict made it sound easy. But the dosages had to be just right. Different for each person – depending on body mass, age, absorbency levels. Maybe a dozen other variables I wasn't privy to. The fact that *The Undertaker* used this method to kill his victims made little sense to me. There were far simpler, easier ways to take a life. Ones which were less refined but had the same results with less effort. Forget the fancy trimmings. Even injecting air into the bloodstream would have the same outcome.

I typed the words *lethal injection* and was immediately presented with over a half million hits.

Straight away, I could see how easy it was to get all the information needed to copycat a State execution. I'd done precisely that with the click of a mouse. Now I needed to know if it was just as easy obtaining the chemicals, and in the right quantities.

Two or three clicks further: websites dedicated to shipping prescription drugs; foreign countries willing to supply banned substances at your own risk; recipes for producing homemade versions out of household products. It seemed anyone with the right identification could purchase all kinds of chemicals online. Even the controlled ones.

My cell phone rang.

It was Eleanor.

"I heard about Harry," she said.

I let the silence cloy.

"And I just wanted to say I'm sorry, Gabe. I know it doesn't really help any, but I'm here if you need me. If you change your mind and do want to talk, that is. I'm here. Christ, I'm always here for you. Sounds pathetic, doesn't it?"

"Eleanor . . ."

"Don't, Gabe. He was my friend too. Don't take away my grief."

"I didn't mean . . ."

"We should talk. I'm serious. You need me, Gabe. I'm your only way back into this case. This is bad. Really bad. Call me, when you're ready. I'll be here."

The line went dead.

I drew a deep breath to cool the fire in my lungs, stared at the bloodied faces staring back at me from the walls of the basement, stared at them until my eyes hurt.

In many ways, losing Hope had softened me up, but her death had also hardened me too.

I had work to do.

# 39

It was one minute to midnight and I was in my car, quietly parked on Santa Monica Boulevard, thinking murder.

A spell of light rain had turned the roadway into a shiny black mirror of distorted reflections. Fractured images of streetlights and neon signs glistening on the wet surface.

Despite the late hour and the passing downpour, there was plenty of activity on the street. This was a popular area, sprinkled with lively bars and raucous nightclubs. Tipsy partygoers drifting from one gaudy venue to the next. Blasts of dance music booming across the street and lines of scantily-clad people behind velvet ropes. Everybody waiting to make an entrance.

I knew why I was here, but I didn't want to be here. I didn't want to be anywhere, including in my own skin.

I waited for a gap in the traffic before getting out of the car and crossing the street.

Despite its cloak of darkness, the disco club still looked like a bank. A big black cube with a solitary splash of neon-pink signage above the entrance. There were people milling about on the sidewalk: laughing, chatting, hooking-up. All men. Every one of them dressed up like the cop from the *Village People*. The big brute guarding the doorway looked like a London Bobby from a bad *Jack the Ripper* movie. I showed him my shield. He showed me his.

"I'm a cop," I shouted over the music blasting through the doorway.

"We're all cops here, sister," he replied.

"So do you all have one of these?" I asked, showing him my firearm.

He didn't baulk. "You can't take that inside."

"Try stopping me. I'm the real deal. Now step aside."

I saw him think about it, think better of it, then concede.

I pushed my way through the crowded entrance. Blaring music assaulted my ears. A slave-ship beat. The club was packed to the seams with fake cops. Chatting in groups. Talking in pairs. Hitting off. Looking me up and down and wondering why I was the only guy not in costume. It was like being in a gay cop convention.

The darkened dance room to my right was a sea of people. A hundred or more men dancing to an insane beat. Flickering strobe lights picking out waves of rocking heads. Opposite, the barroom looked quieter. Less crowded. But not by much.

"You made it." The Tim Burton girl from Monday. She was behind the bar, pouring drinks as I squeezed my way over. I hadn't recognized her; she had on monochrome make-up: heavy black eyelids, full black lips, Geisha-white skin. Her long black hair was wrapped around her neck like a silk scarf. Buckled. Shiny black gloves up to her armpits. A black leather bustier. She looked happy to see me. "What's your poison?" she shouted over the music.

"I'm good, thanks."

"You're on duty?"

"No. I just . . ."

What? I was off the case. It was midnight. My best buddy had died. A drink wouldn't cheer me up but it might soften the blow.

I saw one of her perfectly curved eyebrows inch up her face. "You look like you need a drink."

I conceded.

She smiled. I saw something like a diamond glinting on one of her front teeth. "You from Tennessee?"

"How'd you know?"

"The accent. I have family back there. Give me a minute?"

I leaned against the bar. Looked around at the strange assortment of make-believe cops. I felt like a fake. I should have felt right at home. I didn't.

"This one's on me."

I took the tumbler from the girl's outstretched hand. Tennessee sour mash. Four measures, easy.

"Thanks." I took a swig, then another. It tasted good, warm.

"You looking for Roxy?"

"Yes."

"He hasn't showed yet. Why don't you let your hair down? Mingle awhile. I'll send Roxy over, soon as he arrives."

Mingling isn't in my vocabulary. Never has been. But the choice was either blend in or look like a hare at a greyhound track. I mingled. Zigzagging around the barroom. Bouncing off the high-stem tables like a pinball in an arcade machine. I felt awkward. All eyes on me. The only straight guy in the show. Ironically, the only real cop not wearing a cop uniform. I supped whiskey. It helped numb the awkwardness. I returned to the bar and got a refill, again on the house. Another four measures, easy. I went back to mingling. Found it easier. Not as many suspicious eyes this time. Found myself on the overcrowded dance floor. Pounded by throbbing bass notes. Screamed at by shrill trebles. It was hot. Sweaty. Too many bodies with flailing arms. Not enough room to breathe. Strobe lights. Flickering silhouettes. Hard to see anything. Just fleeting glimpses of fake cops in tight uniforms. Flashes of blue. Dangling handcuffs. Sweaty faces. The world spinning crazily out of control.

"Hey, gorgeous. What's your name?"

The question came from a muscular, shaven-headed guy wearing a plastic police shirt so tight it looked like food wrap. He was right in my face. Smelling of sweat and making suggestive expressions.

"I'm here on police business," I shouted back.

He held up a pair of fluffy handcuffs. "So arrest me."

A hand, followed by a long arm, slid across my shoulder from behind and pushed the shaven-haired guy in the chest. He bounced off a dancer and barred his teeth.

"Back off, Cobb." I heard someone shout next to my ear. "This is my date."

The guy called Cobb snarled and slipped away.

I turned to face my rescuer. He was pressed in close. I could smell musky cologne. He was a few inches taller than me. Sounded familiar. The strobe light panned across the heaving crowd. I caught a glimpse of his face. Fortyish. Eyes too-close-together. It was the Alhambra motorcycle cop.

"Detective, are you stalking me?"

"I was about to ask you the same thing," I shouted back. "You're wearing your real police uniform."

"I'm undercover," he answered with a grin. He thrust a whiskey tumbler in my hand. Four measures, easy. "Compliments of Stevie."

"Who's Stevie?" I shouted back.

I saw him raise a beer bottle to his lips. "Bottoms up, detective," he shouted as the thunderous music rained down on us.

# 40

It tasted like something had crawled into my mouth in the night and died. I stayed motionless for a few seconds, eyes glued shut, trying to decide whether it was my brain that was banging around or somebody was beating a big bass drum next to my head. The thumping was in rhythm with my heartbeat. I winced.

Alcohol and I don't see eye to eye. Normally, out of mutual respect, we keep our distance. I should have known better. Did know better.

Grief can be a sneaky opponent.

I cracked open a crusty eye, then the other.

I was in a bedroom. Not my bedroom. I was in a bed. Not my bed. The walls had been painted black to match the carpeting. The bedding was black satin with red rose patterns stitched into the duvet cover. Matching black-and-red drapes, half closed across a single window. Diffused daylight seeping through. Characterless prints on the walls – the kind you pick up cheap at Wal-Mart.

There was somebody's clothes draped over a chair in the corner. A crinkled shirt. Creased pants. Sloppy sneakers. Looked like mine. A wristwatch, a police shield and a Glock lying on the nightstand.

I looked up at the ceiling.

The owner of the bedroom had affixed a big mirror right above the bed. In it, I could see a frightened little boy lying amid tangled black sheets. A Band-Aid on his cheek. He was gaping down at me with eyes like mine.

I pried open tacky lips and forced last night's events to the fore.

Where was I? How had I got here?

The nightclub on Santa Monica Boulevard.

The memory came back with a thud. It collided with a frontal lobe. Another wince. This time for a different reason. It was coming back to me now. Sluggishly. In dribs and drabs. Not sure if I wanted it to.

The nightclub on Santa Monica Boulevard.

The theme night.

A hundred homosexual men in tight police outfits.

*It's Raining Men'* sung by The Weather Girls.

Jack Daniels and his merry band.

Spinning round and round on the dance floor.

And that was it.

Still didn't explain how I'd got here. Or where here was.

I pushed myself up on an elbow and felt my stomach lurch.

I could hear the sound of running water coming from the bathroom. The door was slightly open. I was in somebody else's house. In somebody else's bed. And that somebody was in the bathroom brushing their teeth.

I stiffened. Blood banged in my brain.

I threw back the sheet, realized I was buck-naked.

The running water stopped.

I looked toward the bathroom.

The bathroom door opened.

I pulled the sheet across my dignity as a man came into the bedroom.

There was a fluffy pink towel wrapped around his waist, but he was otherwise naked. Eyes that seemed impossibly close together.

"Good morning sunshine," the motorbike cop said with a grin. "I bet you need an aspirin. I know I do."

\* \* \*

"So, you're Roxy," I said, trying hard not to shake my head.

"Tim Roxbury to be exact." He acknowledged it with a tip of his head. "My party friends call me Roxy. But you can call me Tim."

We were sitting in his sunny kitchenette, minutes later, either side of a tall breakfast bar. We were both dressed and drinking instant coffee. I was waiting for the aspirin to mute the jungle drums pounding in my head.

"We went over this last night," he said, "several times. Don't you remember?"

"No."

"You were drunk."

"So it seems."

"What do you remember?"

"Just the club. The flashing lights. The loud music."

The guy with the too-close-together eyes was nodding. "So you don't remember you and Stevie?"

"Me and Stevie?"

"Oh my God," he breathed. "You really don't remember. The two of you were all over each other. Bumping and grinding."

I made a face. It hurt.

He nodded at my hand nursing my coffee cup. "Check it out."

I glanced down. There was a number written in ink across the loose skin. I hadn't noticed it before.

"Stevie's private cell," he said with a wink. "Lucky guy."

"Me and Stevie?" The idea seemed completely alien.

"Yes, you and Stevie. The one with the eyes for you. She bought your drinks all night."

"Stevie's a girl?"

Tim gave me one of those looks that showed he was being patient with my numbness. "Last time I looked, she was all girl. Her name's Stephanie Hendricks. More to the point, are you going to call her?"

"Unlikely."

"Pity. The both of you really hit it off. Real chemistry there. I had to threaten her with a night in a cell just to get you out of there."

He saw the uneasy look still messing up my face, and added:

"Don't worry, detective. I know what you're thinking. Nothing happened between you and me. I rescued your ass, is all. I'm strictly a professional. I keep my work and my play completely separate."

I frowned. It hurt some more.

"Besides, I make it a rule I don't sleep with guys on our first date. And you and I didn't even date. So go figure. If you must know, I slept on the couch. All night. Didn't lay a finger on you. Well, maybe just a couple of fingertips when I got you undressed. But I did sacrifice my bed."

"I guess I owe you a thanks."

"You're welcome."

"So, how did I . . ?"

"Like I say: you were drunk. All over the place, to be exact. I don't know. Maybe somebody spiked your drink. You were picking fights and screaming blue murder. But I had your back. You weren't in any condition to drive. So I brought you back here."

"And we definitely didn't . . ."

"Relax, will you? All we did was talk and eat pizza. Mostly it was all you, grilling me about some guy fighting with Jeff Samuels a few weeks back."

"Remind me."

Tim sighed. "This guy arguing with Jeff, I told you I hadn't seen him before, then or after. I told you he didn't leave his name or his number. I told you the guy was accusing Jeff of murder."

I straightened with a jolt.

"Of course he was way off base on that one. No way could Jeff murder anyone. Specificism's his middle name."

"You mean pacifism."

"Sure I do."

"Okay. So do we know who was he supposed to have murdered?"

"Unknown. Jeff was embarrassed by it all. The guy was in his face. Looked like he was on speed or something. I told him to leave and he did."

"Did Samuels say anything to you afterwards?"

"He called a cab and went straight home. Didn't mention the incident the next time I saw him."

"What do you remember about this guy?"

"Only that he was intense. Like De Niro in Taxi Driver. That kind of smoldering intense weirdo get-up. Good-looking, but not my type. And definitely straight as a dye."

"Any distinguishing features?"

"Gabe, we went over this last night."

"Humor me."

"Okay. He was thirtyish with dark, unruly hair. Blue eyes. Nose bent slightly to the left. Sounded vaguely southern. He wasn't very talkative, at least not with me. He seemed guarded. You think he killed Jeff?"

He saw my curious expression and added: "I heard through the grapevine. Damn shame. Jeff was a nice guy."

Tim Roxbury, the Alhambra motorcycle cop, leaned over the counter and picked up my empty coffee cup.

"Here, let me get you a refill. I'm on duty in an hour. We need to go back into the city and pick up your car. Then you need to call that number on your hand and get laid."

# 41

Have you ever noticed that sometimes the sun seems too bright? I keep sunshades in the car for such occasions. An old, scratched pair I'd picked up when Grace relocated to Florida. I had them on. But the brilliance was still needling at my retinas.

I was in Long Beach, parked in a tow-zone at the back of Rainbow Harbor, wishing I hadn't had the aspirin.

I'd agreed to meet my Quantico contact and good friend, Bill Teague, over by the picture-perfect lighthouse. It sits atop a big grassy knoll built on a breakwater overlooking a marina filled with pristine white pleasure craft.

I was still getting flashbacks of sweaty male dancers. The Burton girl's hot breath against my cheek. Her sweet scent. Soft touch. Snapshot images of her dark eyes and dark lips as the strobe light had swept the dance floor. I hadn't washed her number from the back of my hand. Not yet. Not sure why.

I posted a Police permit on the dash, pulled myself together, then crossed the parking lot to the caw of foraging gulls.

It was Thursday, 9 a.m.

I had an appointment to keep.

My FBI friend from the BAU was sitting astride a concrete bench in the lee of the lighthouse. Trademark cigarette wedged in the corner of his mouth. He looked more like a character from a Quentin Tarantino movie than an acclaimed forensic psychologist.

He saw me sweating up the hill and made a gun shape with his hand, popping off an invisible round in my direction.

"You look like shit," he shouted.

"My epitaph," I called back. "I should get it printed on tee-shirts. Make myself a fortune."

We patted each other out.

"Been too long, Bill," I said.

"Nature of the job." He dropped his cigarette on the ground and stamped on it. "There's a beer shack by the water. Let's you and I walk and talk. You can buy me a drink."

We retraced my steps down the spiraling pathway, back toward the touristy Shoreline Village, catching up on old news as we went. I hadn't seen Bill in almost a year. Felt like yesterday.

"You meet the parents yet?" he asked as we walked.

"I did. Thanks again for coming through with her name."

"Least I could do. You're officially hunting a serial killer now and that means FBI involvement. I'm happy to help wherever I can."

"Did you read the case notes Jamie faxed over?"

"Sure."

"And?"

"This Funeral Director guy sounds like an arrogant prick."

I shook my head. Bill is a profiler as sharp as a scalpel, but he can also be as blunt as the backend of an oil tanker when he chooses.

"He's also a control freak," he added. "Suffers from severe emotional repression."

I was surprised by the remark. "You mean he has anger issues? There's no evidence of rage or violence."

"There never is with this type. It's all bottled up. Waiting to explode. Trust me, Gabriel; your boy is emotionally repressed. Probably with father issues. Maybe some childhood abuse. Psychological bullying. That kind of thing. More than likely he grew up in an overly-strict household. Possibly religious."

"It would explain his calling cards, I guess."

We paused while Bill dug out another cigarette. Some licorice-smelling brand he'd got hooked on oversees. Had it specially imported. He lit it from a shiny steel flick lighter. I saw him take a deep drag. Saw his eyes roll back into their sockets as he savored the nicotine rush.

"Someday, Bill, those things will kill you."

He blew out thick blue smoke. "Something's got to. Might as well be something I enjoy."

We resumed our walk.

"So, what else? Who are we looking for, Bill?"

"The usual sociopath with a history of untreated psychiatric conditions. A loner. Somebody with authority issues. The type who believes the world owes him. Basically, someone craving recognition to compensate for his own inadequacies." He smirked. "Sounds like me, don't it?"

We arrived outside a long, brown wooden building where the scent of hops was contesting with the sting of the brine. I leaned against the white balustrade while Bill finished his cigarette. To the tourists walking by, we must have looked like two buddies enjoying the view. Far from it.

"Has he contacted you yet?" Bill asked.

"No." The thought was unsettling. "Should he?"

"Come on, Gabriel. You're the Great Celebrity Cop. That's why he's singled you out. Criminals win book deals on the back of your convictions. Heck, they want you to catch them; it's their fifteen minutes. Why else would he dump the child in the same place where the Benjamin kid bled out?"

Suddenly I recoiled at the memory of the dead, staring, questioning eyes of a ten-year-old boy, killed beneath the 7th Street Bridge almost a year ago.

"He knows your history," Bill said. "He wanted you on this case. The Seventh Street Bridge was his way of saying hello."

"I don't like it."

"So suck it up. This is his play, not yours. His psychosis is a weakness. Don't you be forgetting that."

I watched Bill flick the butt of his cigarette out into the marina. Saw it fizzle and die in the black water.

\*   \*   \*

Decked out in warm woods and brown leathers, the ale parlor at Shoreline Village seemed a cheerful enough place. One of those good vibe tourist attractions monopolizing on the fine views of the Queen Mary across the water. We slid into a booth by the window. Chuck Berry's greatest hits were warbling from speakers near the raftered ceiling. Bill batted blue eyes at the long-legged waitress and ordered a beer. I stuck with the coffee. Extra black.

"Trust me, Gabriel," Bill began as he took a swig of his beer and smacked his lips, "this guy is so fucked up in the head he believes McCartney wrote better songs than Lennon. And that's a scary place to be."

"So how do we catch this guy, Bill?"

"In his old kills."

"He's killed before? What makes you say that?"

Bill let out a long sigh, "Gabriel, how many years have you and I been doing this? You and me? Having these same conversations: me sipping sweet beer while you guzzle that awful black tar."

"About six?"

"So how many more years do we do this before you stop asking the same questions you already know the answers to?"

I smiled. "He's been practicing."

"Holy fuck! And the boy hits a home run!"

Somebody cleared their throat in the booth behind Bill. I saw my friend from the Bureau stiffen and gave him the *please, not here, not now* shake of the head.

"The simple fact of the matter," Bill said, "is novices are clumsy. They make mistakes. Leave trace evidence. The vast majority of first-time killers get caught almost straight away. I'm telling you, this guy's killed before and learned from it. He's honed his craft elsewhere and maybe over a long period of time. His methods are too well-oiled, too rehearsed, too clean to be right first time. And that's where you'll catch him. Dumb fuck."

The guy in the booth behind Bill glanced around. I kept Bill's attention:

"What about his calling cards? We think they may have a religious significance."

Bill stuck out a lip as he weighed it up. "Stands to reason, I guess. But they could mean something else entirely. Killers leave signatures for two reasons: to taunt the police or to confuse the police. In both cases they form part of their message."

"Which is?"

"Something for you to decode, Gabriel."

Bill's cell phone shrilled. It sounded like a Dean Martin tune. He dug it out and stared at the screen.

"Excuse me. I need to get this."

I looked around the beer shack while Bill took the call, thinking about *The Undertaker* practicing on other victims until he'd gotten his lethal injection technique down pat.

Bill snapped his phone shut.

I could tell by the peeved glint in his eyes he wasn't a happy bunny.

"What?"

"My services are needed in Bakersfield. This afternoon. Damn it."

"Bakersfield? It's a nice drive, Bill. Take you a good couple of hours there. But the scenery will knock you dead. You shouldn't be so damned good at your job."

"Yeah, maybe. It's a temporary distraction. Trust me, I'll be back working this case before you can take a shit."

We chatted some more, mostly about work and about anything other than the stuff I didn't want to talk about. It felt good reconnecting with my old friend from the Bureau after all these months apart. Natural, easy, with no expectations. But thoughts of Harry lying on his slab kept creeping in through my hangover and darkening the mood.

Eventually we strolled back to the parking lot.

The sky was completely overcast now: battleship gray with the promise of rain. I pulled off the shades.

"One last thing," Bill said as we came to our cars. "You know I get these weird kind of feelings?"

"Yes, Bill, I do. You believe you're psychic and I don't believe a word of it. But, please, don't let that stop you from sharing."

"Something knocked on my cerebral door when I was reading the case notes," he said. "There's a survivor. Feels like a woman. You should look into it." He popped the locks on his rental and climbed inside. "It might be the one thing that ties everything together." He slammed the door and gunned the engine. "Catch you later," he said through the glass, then tore the rental out of the parking lot, leaving burned rubber behind.

I turned toward my car, hadn't gone very far when the coffee lurched in my belly, and black clotted goo came gushing out all over the pavement.

Harry and hangovers didn't mix.

# 42

I was heading north on the Long Beach Freeway – crunching antacids – when my cell phone rang: *Ferguson*.

"Gabe, where are you?"

"Driving. Just outside of Lynwood."

"What are you doing in Long Beach?"

"Meeting an old friend."

"Case-related?"

"Bill Teague," I confessed.

I heard him sigh, "You're off the case."

"I know, I know. We were playing catch-up. What gives?"

"Think you can you check something for me? You'll think this an odd request. Can you check if you have your handcuffs?"

"My handcuffs?"

"Indulge me."

I put the phone on the passenger seat and checked to see if my department-issue handcuffs were in their holder attached to my belt. They were. I picked back up.

"All present and correct, John. What's with the big mystery?"

"The handcuffs used on Richard Schaeffer are yours," he said.

Just like that.

I experienced one of those *that's impossible* moments.

"The CSU checked and double-checked," he told me over the phone. "The only fingerprints on the cuffs came back to you. How's that happen?"

"I don't know, John."

Really and honestly, I didn't. Who would?

Like all cops, I'd had numerous sets issued over the years. But I hadn't kept tabs on any of them. Who would? Loss is unavoidable.

Exactly how the surfer dude from Huntington Beach had ended up shackled to his bed by a pair of my old handcuffs was more than just a mystery. It was a problem.

"I'm coming in," I said.

Ferguson cut me off: "Don't waste your time. I can't let you anywhere near this. Not now you've been implicated."

*Implicated!*

I almost ran into the back of a truck.

"John, listen to me . . ."

"No, Gabe, you listen to me: I don't believe you're involved for one second. But I'm not Internal Affairs. If you want to do yourself a favor, go do some digging. Let me smooth things down here. Maybe the answer will turn up elsewhere."

*   *   *

I am not a great believer in happenstance. Nor am I a betting man. But I have an idea the odds of a murderer chancing on a set of my old handcuffs, then using them in a crime I was detecting, are astronomical, if not impossible.

Bill was right: the killer had targeted me. Right from the get-go. He'd purposely left the little girl at the 7th Street Bridge, knowing my history with it. Purposely used a set of my old handcuffs to get my attention, or to implicate me. I wondered what else he had purposely arranged, or planned to.

My cell phone rang before I had chance to think about it.

"Jamie?"

"Hi, Gabe. I thought you should know we have a hit on the rose petals."

I bit a lip. "Jamie, I'm off the case. You shouldn't be telling me this. You could lose your apprenticeship."

"Let me worry about that. I'm keeping you in the loop no matter what. One of the Crime Lab girls recognized the roses by their color and their perfume. She checked with her father. He's a horticulturalist."

I was still reeling from Ferguson's revelation.

"Jamie, can I call you back?"

"Just hear me out. I promise I'll be quick. These roses, they come from a variety of German tea rose called Dark Secret."

"Has the Captain told you about the handcuffs?"

"What handcuffs? Stop changing the subject. I checked. There're only a couple of nurseries that stock it in the continental US. All are based in New England."

"The ones we found on Richard Schaeffer."

"Gabe, he hasn't told me anything. It looks like the roses are originally imported from the United Kingdom."

"They're mine."

"The roses?"

"The handcuffs we found on Richard Schaefer."

"Oh."

I listened to her breathing.

"Did you check mail order?" I asked.

"For handcuffs?"

"For rose retailers. Jamie, those petals were *fresh*. Unless our killer grew them himself – which I very much doubt – he probably didn't buy them in New England."

I could hear her think it through. Cogs whirring, competing with the grind of traffic.

"Okay. I'll petition online retailers. See if we can get their customer lists. By the way, how did he come by your handcuffs?"

"Jamie, if I knew that, I'd be psychic. Maybe I should ask Bill."

"Who's Bill?"

I let out a long breath, and then explained.

# 43

Hunger scraped at Randall's stomach, driving him to the nearest diner. He'd been on the road over an hour, heading north, out of LA. The Interstate was awash with traffic and unusually heavy rain.

A road sign for *Grapevine* loomed and then passed by, disappearing into the incessant downpour. He thought about his tight bladder, gave in, and took the next off-ramp. The rental fishtailed slightly on the slick camber as it doubled-back beneath the freeway interchange. Tires whirring from wet to dry and back to wet. There was an illuminated diner sign, barely visible through the driving rain and the metronomic motion of the wiper-blades. The place looked quiet. He dumped the rental alongside a battered old pickup with a bumper sticker proclaiming: *'Heaven Is For Angels – Hell Is For Fun'*, then skipped puddles until he was inside.

The place smelled like the floor had been mopped with dirty dishwater. A stale, gym shoe stench that reminded him of bullies and beatings. He headed straight for the restroom and emptied his bladder. No soap in the dispenser. A hand dryer out of action. Cracked mirrors. Horse trough sinks. An all-pervading reek of sour urine.

He found a booth back in the restaurant farthest from the door, and brushed stale crumbs off the faded plastic bench seat before sidling over to the rain-streaked window.

The diner was more or less empty: just an old rickety guy in the corner and a pair of fat local boys draped over bar stools at the counter. The old guy was holding a conversation with his pancakes, pitching to and fro as a dribble of maple syrup worked its way down his gray-grizzled chin. The local boys were sniggering over a private joke. A nonplussed waitress was cleaning a table, one mile an hour.

Randall turned his attention to the rain-spattered window. He liked the rain. Rain had patterns. Complex groupings intersected by fractured tracks, always in a state of flux.

He saw patterns everywhere he looked. Always had. Part of his *condition*. The coarse, braided bark on the trunk of a tree; the fingerprints of hard, narrow sand ripples on a windswept beach; the crisscrossing footprints of urban birds in freshly-laid snow. Patterns with hidden meaning. Over the years he'd become quite the expert at cracking the patterns. He thought of it as deciphering God's code in the chaos.

"What's it gonna be, honey?"

He dragged his gaze back inside the diner. The plump waitress was standing over him, snapping a pink wedge of gum between her teeth like an elastic band. She was in her late fifties, sheathed in a creased cerise outfit two sizes too small for her drifting figure. A sagging face clinging pitifully to a distant breath of youth.

"Come on, honey. I haven't got all day."

He forced his face into an amenable smile.

*Haven't got all day.*

How ironic.

*"What's it gonna be?"*

Her scuffed plastic name badge read *Dorothy*.

Right now Randall wished she'd fly back to Kansas.

# 44

Michael Shakes was undecided whether to keep the information to himself or share it with Stacey Kellerman. Contact with Stacey came at a price. Potential bad side effects too. In a word, Stacey was demanding. All-consuming. Everything had to be Stacey's way or no way.

He re-read the single string of type on the computer printout – as if maybe he'd misread it the first and the second time around – but the words remained unchanged. Damn. No matter which way he diced this; the outcome would make him the bad guy. And Stacey would never let him forget it.

Like she never let him forget the day he'd told her it was over. Not that there had really been much of anything to finish. A three-week fling didn't constitute a full-blown relationship.

But she had a right to know.

As a man of the law he had a duty to tell her.

As an ex-lover he wasn't so sure.

He picked up the office phone and started dialing Stacey's number from memory, then dropped the receiver back in its cradle.

Stacey was like that. She had to blame somebody. Anybody but herself. She blamed her mother for her father abusing her. Blamed her father for driving away her mother. Probably blamed him for costing her an arm and a leg in plastic surgery.

But she had a right to know.

He had a duty to tell her.

Michael Shakes stared at the office phone, undecided whether to keep the information to himself or share it with Stacey Kellerman.

# 45

I drove through light rain. Not enough to keep the wipers happy. I was blindly following the freeway, trying to piece together the broken links in the killer's chain. I thought about his calling cards, his victims. I was trying to come up with some kind of a motive to help determine if, where and when he might strike next. I was under no illusions. As Bill had put it: the killer was yet to enjoy his fifteen minutes of fame. More deaths were inevitable.

I called Fred Phillips.

"Fred, how we doing with the background checks?"

Before being run out of town, I'd had the team compare victim acquaintances – standard procedure – to see if there were any crossovers that might indicate a connection.

Fact: serial killers like connections and loathe randomness. Good connections lead to understanding motive. And knowing a killer's motive is one step closer to predicting his movements.

I sensed Fred hunch over the phone on the other end of the line, as if hiding our conversation from other watchful eyes in the department.

"Preliminary crosschecking between the McNamaras and the professor show no matches," he told me. "The McNamaras are all Seattle born and bred. Three generations. Originally from Massachusetts. Absolutely no ties with LA."

"How about Samuels – he have any dealings in Washington State, maybe with one of the universities up there?"

"Not that we can find. Same goes for the McNamaras and Marlene van den Berg. No surface links. I'm telling you, Gabe, these victims aren't connected. The victimology is all over the place."

"Dig deeper," I said. "Go as far back as it takes. Look into their financials. Their mailing lists. Something connects these people, Fred. He chose them for a reason."

"We'll keep looking," he said. "Incidentally, the last flag on the mortician list had an alibi."

Another letdown. "Okay. Think you can run another screening?"

"Absolutely. Give me the criteria."

"There's a chance the killer may have veterinary training. Run the same checks against all animal welfare employees in the Los Angeles area."

Fred made an amused grunt. "That should keep us busy for a while."

"Fred, I appreciate it. Can I speak with Jan?"

"Absolutely."

I heard the telephone receiver change hands, then Jan's voice come through:

"Before you say anything," she said, "as far as I'm concerned, you're still running this show. No questions asked. The same goes for everyone involved. We're just taking the wheel why you take a pit stop."

"Thanks, Jan. I owe you. Do me a favor?"

"Anything."

"Interrogate the National Crime database. Look for killings with similar characteristics."

"Do you think he's killed before?"

"According to my FBI contact, it's likely. Let's just see what turns up and take it from there."

I hung up and drove on, following the Long Beach Freeway to its northerly conclusion. I thought about *The Undertaker* abducting the little girl from the park on Friday, keeping her doped up until disposing of her early Monday morning. Thought about him watching her daily routine, knowing the father used the same bench, same time every day. Knowing he'd need to distract the father and eliminate the family dog before snatching the child. Yet more examples of his military precision. But where had he kept Jenny McNamara for forty-eight hours?

I remembered the rosary beads dangling from the rearview mirror in Jamie's car.

There were clues I needed to work. I had to keep my mind focused on one thing, anything but Harry. *The Undertaker* had purposely left the same calling cards at all three crime scenes. According to Bill, they were part of his message. I wanted to know what that message was.

I jumped off the freeway a few streets south of Alhambra and headed straight to the Church of St. Therese on El Molino Street.

I should have been angry with God for taking Harry. I wasn't. I'd played that card after losing Hope and ended up losing the hand.

I had always considered Father Daniel Flannigan too handsome to be a man of the cloth. The Cary Grant of the priesthood, chiseled from hard Sardinian granite rather than soft Irish peat. I hadn't seen Father Dan in almost a year. Not sure where I stood. With him or with God.

I parked the car in an otherwise empty lot and made my way inside. No sign of Officer Tim Roxbury and his gleaming motorcycle. I hadn't been in a house of God on personal business in almost a year. I wasn't starting now.

"Detective Gabriel," Father Dan began as he saw me advancing down the aisle. "If your intention is to take a cheap swipe at me again, I must warn you I have been taking karate lessons since last we met."

"Relax, Father," I said. "I'm here to pick your brains, not a fight. What's with the sweater?"

It took a moment for my words to penetrate, then he came out from behind the safety of the altar.

"Do you like it? It's a present from my dearest niece. Personally, I have never been a huge fan of Winnie the Pooh. But such is my penance for missing her Christmastime trip to Disney World."

He gave me a *'can we be friends?'* smile. And I felt my own frame relax a little, realized I must have had the look of a bulldozer about me as I'd stormed through the church.

"Father, I need your help."

Father Dan made a gesture toward the confessional booths, but I shook my head.

"Police business."

"God's business trumps all."

I held up a manila envelope. "It does. But right now I need your help. It's a case I'm working on."

Father Dan spread his hands. "Shall I be needing holy water or a stout shot of the good stuff?"

# 46

Stacey Kellerman had made a decision to do whatever necessary to get where she wanted. She'd made the vow a long time ago and every day since. It was a product of enduring an abusive father.

Even as a small child she'd learned to use whatever means necessary in order to survive, including compliance and feigned pleasure. The beatings had molded her. The abuse had hardened her. Together they'd determined her to make something of herself other than her poppa's little whore.

There wasn't a person alive or dead she was unwilling to use to get what she wanted. No situation she wasn't eager to exploit. No heads she wouldn't roll to achieve her goal.

"You see a chance, you take it, right?" she said to herself as she recalled the old song lyric.

And she'd seen her chance.

Rather, the chance had called her up on the telephone. From out of the blue. Made her an offer she couldn't pass up.

She looked at the phone sitting in its cradle in the kitchen of her duplex in Winchester and made another decision.

She would sell her soul for a stab at stardom.

If that meant leaving everything and everyone behind, then so be it. She had no family left in Nevada to speak of. No idea in which crack den her whore mother was holed up. Only sideways promotions ahead of her if she stayed here. She had to get out of Dodge. Head east. Cut a deal that would see her name in lights and her face on every TV in the land.

Stacey Kellerman had made a decision to do whatever it took to get where she wanted, and no one would stand in her way.

# 47

I should have known it was too good to be true.

Tim was leaning against my car in the church parking lot when I got outside; arms folded, biceps bulging, eyes hidden behind his silvery sunglasses.

"I take it the aspirin didn't work?" he said as I walked over.

I gave him *the* look. "What are you doing here, Tim?"

"I'm not stalking you," he said, "if that's what you think. Just trying to be friendly, is all. Watch your back."

"Thanks. But it doesn't need watching."

"It did last night. You phoned her yet?"

"Who?"

"Stevie."

"No."

"You should."

"Tim, she's half my age."

"She's thirty-five. What are you, fifty?"

"It doesn't matter."

"Why, because she runs a gay nightclub or because she's bi-sexual?"

"Because she has a boyfriend." I sighed. "Why the hell am I explaining it to you anyway?"

I popped the locks and got in the car, closed the door.

Tim tapped gloved knuckles on the driver's window.

"What?"

He made a *roll down the window* motion.

I did – but only halfway.

"Out of curiosity," he said. "That file. Is it the case you're working on? The one involving Jeff? Anything I can help you with?"

"Goodbye, Tim."

I went to roll up the window, but he hooked gloved fingers over the glass rim.

"Come on, Gabe, give me a break. Let me help. This is good practice for me; I've put in for my detective exam."

I was surprised. And worried.

He saw it in my face.

"Hey, I have an unblemished work record," he said. "Citations coming out my ears. It's impeachable."

"You mean impeccable."

"Exactly. All I'm asking is a chance."

I rolled up the window. He kept his fingers curled over the glass to the very last second, then pulled them quickly away as the window snapped shut.

I took out my phone and pretended to check messages.

Out of the corner of one eye I saw the motorcycle cop hang around for a few seconds more, then wander back to his bike. Heard him rev the engine, hard, then peel across the parking lot and disappear down the street. There was a woman with a stroller taking a shortcut through the church grounds. A couple of youths racing down the sidewalk on skateboards. A big black guy in a hoodie crossing the street. I waited until Tim was out of sight before opening up the file on my lap.

There was a sheet of handwritten dictations inside. Notes taken during my conversation with Father Dan. I put on my readers and read them through:

*In Christianity, the rose symbolizes the union between Jesus Christ and his Church. The word rosary also comes from the word rose. In early Christendom, the rose was a symbol of the Christian faith. In particular, the red rose signified the blood of the martyrs . . .*

I wondered if the killer saw his victims as martyrs.

*In the Middle Ages, worshippers of Christ wore bracelets of beads made from rose petals. They formed a ring of rose petals around the sinner's flesh . . .*

I wondered if the killer saw his victims as sinners.

*In the Old Testament, ashes were used as a sign of humility and mortality – as a sign of sorrow and repentance for sin. The Christian use of ashes on Ash Wednesday is taken directly from this Old Testament custom. Receiving ashes on the forehead is a reminder of our own mortality and a sign of our sorrow for sin . . .*

I wondered if the killer was using the ash to mark out his victims. But why? For atonement? The thought surprised me.

I looked through the stack of glossies one by one. Looked at the rings of rose petals surrounding each victim. Looked at the ash crosses smeared on their brows. Looked at the hands folded across the chest, as if posed for relatives at a funeral home. Everything fit in with a religious connection perfectly. But there was no mention of any mouths glued shut in the Bible.

I closed my eyes and thought some more.

Then I stuffed the photos back in the file and drove across the lot toward the roadway. I didn't get far. Something stopped me dead in my tracks. Made me stamp on the brakes.

Some things do that.

The sight of a screaming nun running across the parking lot with her hands and habit soaked in blood is one of                                                                                 them.

\* \* \*

When somebody mentions the fight or flight reflex we all know what they mean. It's that hot burst of adrenaline which either compels us to action or sends us running for the hills. As a policeman, I'd had the chicken trained out of me.

I leapt out of the car and grabbed the nun before she could flee the scene.

"Let me go!" she screamed.

She struggled against my grasp. I caught her flailing hands and held her fast.

"Sister Bethany," – I recognized her from a time I'd been here every Sunday without fail – "it's me, Gabriel."

She looked up at me with terror-stricken eyes. "He's dead!" she screamed. "Slaughtered!"

There was bright crimson blood splashed across her white coif. And something like insane fear trying to claw its way out of her face.

"Who?" I demanded. "Who's dead?"

"It was the Devil," she cried. "He was here. In the church. God save us! The Devil killed Father Flannigan!"

\* \* \*

Her words hit me like a heavenly thunderbolt – *The Devil killed Father Flannigan* – catapulting me toward the church entrance on thundering feet. I was acting on impulse, driven by fear of those words burning through my skull. I crashed through the heavy vestibule doors on the heel of my Glock. Not knowing what to expect.

The church was quiet.

Exactly as I'd left it.

No horned beast trotting around the place on its cloven feet. No fiery brimstone raining from the rafters. No smell of sulfur or the screams of the condemned.

I fell into a walk, sweeping the pews with the gun for signs of the supernatural.

Then I saw him:

Father Dan.

He was lying on the liturgical altar, on his back, his head completely removed. Decapitated. Gone. Nowhere to be seen. Glistening blood pooling on the cream-colored marble. His right hand was still twitching, as if trying to sign for help.

All at once the adrenaline was sucked out of my legs and I stumbled the last few feet, almost fell as I saw the blood still pumping from both of his carotid arteries.

Even without the head I knew it was Father Dan.

No mistaking it.

Through all the blood I could see *Winnie-the-Pooh* giving me a sheepish smile.

Then lightning ricocheted around my head. It felt like the ceiling had given way and crashed down, crushing me to the floor. I heard bone crack as the lights went out. My bone. My skull. Legs buckling. Then all I could do was watch the pretty fireworks as the clammy hand of unconsciousness dragged me away.

# 48

Somebody switched the lights back on, abruptly. A blinding intensity that made it impossible to see. I heard somebody whimpering for a sedative. They had my voice. The blazing glare dimmed sufficiently for the world to swim into focus.

The parking lot of the Church of St. Therese looked like the circus had come to town. Local clowns crowding against a police cordon. Emergency services and law enforcement personnel milling about. The usual mayhem you get at every public murder scene. There was even a news crew setting up stall on the periphery of the police tape. A chopper buzzing against the gray sky like an agitated wasp. The only thing missing was the big top and Father Dan's head.

*The Devil had killed Father Dan.*

The realization made me gag.

Someone said: "Hold still; I can't do it if you keep fidgeting."

I had no idea how long I'd been out. Long enough for Sister Bethany to raise the alarm and replace her own wails with those of patrol cars. Twenty minutes, tops. I wasn't counting. I'd come round with the worst hangover in living memory.

The young female paramedic gave me the thumbs-up. "You're all done. That should hold it together, at least for a while. I've put antibiotic gel on the wound and a couple of butterfly closures. Keep this cold pack held against your head."

I did so, stiffly.

I was propped up on the back footplate of one of the ambulances. I was wrapped in a foil blanket, like a turkey at Thanksgiving. Everything looked bright but washed-out. Not very three-dimensional.

The paramedic flashed a penlight across my eyes. Everything spun. She handed me a small bottle of pills.

"These'll help with the pain." She saw my wary expression, and added, "Two every four hours."

I dropped them in a pocket. No intention to take.

I pressed the ice pack against the growing welt on the top right corner of my forehead. Right on the hairline. Missed the temple by a fraction.

I looked over the paramedic's shoulder. Sister Bethany was being given tea and sympathy on the back of another EMS unit. And most likely a handful of Diazepam to go with it. Every now and then, I could hear her wail in misery. The news crew were loving it. They had one of their cameramen up on a stepladder, training his lens in the back of the ambulance. It went without saying that a wailing nun made for good TV.

I scanned the growing crowd while the paramedic cleaned up her work area. Wondered if the guy who'd socked me over the head hard enough for me to see an early Fourth of July was standing among them. Watching. Gloating. Maybe with Father Dan's head in a bag.

I had an inkling who the perpetrator was. But it wasn't my case.

"Gabe!"

I looked round. It was Tim Roxbury. He was pushing his way through the rank and file. I could see worry in his too-close-together eyes. I flapped a hand.

"My God, Gabe. Are you okay? You look like hell. What happened?"

"I got struck off Satan's Christmas list."

"Jeez Louise. I leave you for one minute . . ."

Something nasty rose in my throat. I twisted away and let the vomit splash onto the pavement. The paramedic gave me a *take it easy* look and then some tissue to clean up.

# 49

I'd need a brain scan, to find it and to rule out anything sinister. I didn't have time.

I hitched a ride home with Tim. I didn't want to, but he insisted.

He spoke about *Le Diable* on the way. I didn't

I was tired with telling everyone it wasn't my case. All the same, it hadn't stopped the killer from killing my priest.

But I had to focus on *The Undertaker*.

I thanked Tim for the ride and sent him packing. I sensed he wanted to come in, chat some more. No chance.

I examined the welt on my forehead in the hall mirror. The paramedic's anti-inflammatory had given me a bad belly and hadn't touched the headache one bit. Beneath the weeping egg now going hardboiled on my brow, there was a right-angled indentation that creaked whenever I worked my jaw.

Damned hardest I'd been hit since my son had leveled me with a baseball bat, at age seven.

There was a knock at the front door.

I pulled it open, ready to give Tim a piece of my mind, but came face to face with Eleanor instead.

"What the hell happened to you?" she said.

"I had a run in with the Devil."

She reached out to touch the bloodied closures on my forehead. I tipped my head just outside of her reach. Her hand withdrew like a moray eel snaking back inside its hole.

She stared at me, her gaze penetrating my invisible skin, straight into churning darkness.

"Ferguson put you up to this?" I asked.

"A deal's a deal, honey."

"And if I don't comply?"

"You remain frozen out of the case."

She placed a foot on the top step. Beneath her jacket, her silver blouse was open three-buttons down. I could see a silver necklace. One of those bar pendants with something like hieroglyphs stamped into it.

"It's your choice, Gabe."

"Strange, because it doesn't sound like much of a choice. Sounds to me like the both of you have me dead to rights."

"We need to talk," she said. "For your own good. This latest thing with Harry will be compounding everything."

I spoke quietly: "Eleanor, I know your intentions are true and just. I know you believe you can fix me. But some things are just broken. And that's the way it is. No amount of talking it through will change the past."

"That isn't my goal," she said. "I want to change your future."

"You have an answer for everything."

"I'm paid to. Ferguson tells me you're still working The Piano Wire Murders."

"Ferguson's wrong. It's a cold case. Dead."

I saw her eyes narrow. "Why don't I believe you, Gabe?"

"Because you're trained to doubt. That's what psychiatry is all about, isn't it?"

"And pursuing The Maestro in your own time is an unhealthy obsession. It'll get you killed."

"Maybe."

"Invite me in. Let's talk."

"No," I said.

"We need to start from the beginning."

"Eleanor, I really don't want to do this here."

"Then where? You never come by my office. You can't keep appointments."

"Eleanor . . ."

"No, Gabe. Not this time. This time you talk to me. Lay it all bare. On the line. Once and for all. Or I'll recommend a suspension. I mean it."

My mouth worked wordlessly.

"Now let's start at the beginning," she said again.

I let out a long hot breath. "There's nothing to tell. I met up with Father Dan in connection with The Undertaker murders . . ."

"No," she said, cutting me off.

"No?"

"Not that beginning. The other beginning. Before you went on your ten-month-long compassionate sick leave. Let's start from there. From that beginning. Let's start from when Hope was killed."

\* \* \*

I felt fire rage in my gut. "This was a mistake," I said.

All at once I couldn't breathe.

I stepped back, away from Eleanor, and closed the door.

I heard Eleanor shout from the other side: "Don't do this, Gabe. They won't let you back."

My head was spinning. I stumbled down the hallway – just as the house phone rang.

I let it.

I leaned against the wall and gasped for air.

After eight rings the answering machine kicked in. I heard static, followed by the dial tone. No message left.

I reached across and deleted the entry, then retreated to the basement and dropped into one of the La-Z-Boys.

Death stared at me from the walls.

I let it.

No choice; I'd put it up there.

As personal crusades go, mine had stumbled into a desert about six months back and dried up. The official hunt for *The Maestro* had been suspended months before that. A cold case. Unresolved. Shelved until either new information emerged or he struck again.

I scanned the mosaic of images filling the wall of the basement. My eyes were greeted with pictures of murder and mayhem.

The LAPD had an official description on file: a male in his late fifties or early sixties, white, skilled with his hands, an interest in classical music (maybe). They even had a sketchy artist's impression: a ghostly rendering that looked uncannily like the country music legend Kris Kristofferson. No name – other than the one we knew him by. And that was an alias. Worthless. Officially, the LAPD had no idea who he was. But I knew who he was.

He was my nemesis.

The murderer of my wife.

The man who had taken my beloved Hope from my life.

I looked away, as I always did.

The two clear plastic evidence bags were still sitting side by side on the desk. One containing the copy of the torn photo of Samuels in the TV studio. The other, a copy of the faded newspaper clipping found on Marlene's pillow.

I brought the angle-poise lamp in close and examined the photo of Samuels for the second time. I compared it against the crime scene shot still lying on top of the open *The Undertaker Case* file folder. I saw the anomaly straight away. In the picture taken in the TV studio, Samuels had a white handkerchief tucked nicely into the breast pocket of his tux. In the one showing Samuels lying on his bed, the handkerchief was red.

There were two possibilities why *The Undertaker* had used a red handkerchief instead of white: either he was a pattern freak and the red choice went better with the crimson cummerbund, or he'd put it there for a reason.

I picked up the newspaper clipping and examined it through the fisheye of a magnifying glass.

It was from a copy of the New York Times. Dated 1961. A column of print carefully cut from the top of a larger article. A small, bold paragraph-style header which read:

*Thalidomide: One of the biggest medical tragedies of modern times'*

My cell phone buzzed.

"Yes, Jamie?"

"Do you have a moment?"

I put down the clipping. "Shoot."

"The search for similar killings is throwing up all kinds of potential links. Can you run through them with me?"

"How many flags are we talking, Jamie?"

"Over two hundred. And the results are still compiling. We have mock executions, assisted suicides, cults. You name it."

"Give me a minute."

I put down the phone and put on my glasses. I brought the laptop out of hibernation and logged into the secure LAPD access point. The authentication process deliberated for a second, then piggybacked Jamie's workstation.

"Okay," I said, picking up the phone. "I'm looking at the same thing you are."

It was a window of slowly-accumulating data directly filtering in from the FBI's National Crime Information Center database in Clarksburg. A counter in the corner incrementing steadily. Already beyond the two hundred mark.

"Okay, let's see. First off, you can eliminate the mass cult suicides and all the deaths associated with barbiturate overdose." I heard Jamie tap keys at her end and the results on the screen were reduced by over ninety per cent in one fell swoop. Better. Still over thirty to cut back.

"What about veterinarians wreaking revenge on wayward partners?"

"Seriously?" I shook my head. But I was mindful of the fact that Benedict had proposed a possible link with veterinary training and the killer. "Save them for later. We can cross-reference them against any suspicious flags thrown up on the veterinarian search Jan's running."

The counter dropped below twenty.

"Okay, good. Now let's tighten the search criteria. Keep only the reports that mention chloroform, superglue, injection through the peritoneum membrane and the three chemicals used in lethal injection."

I heard Jamie tapping keys and saw the list on the screen crumble to a handful of entries. Jamie read them out loud:

"The suicides in DC of three Med students from the George Washington University. A female psychiatrist from Philadelphia. Two women in Chicago. And one woman from New York."

"Forget the suicides," I said. "Bring up the police reports on the others."

Four separate windows opened up, each taking up an equal quarter of the screen.

I peered closer.

The two police reports from Chicago came with photos. The other two didn't. The photos attached to the Chicago reports were standard booking pictures taken against a gray height chart. A black woman and a white woman. Dolled up in trashy make-up. Bad hairdos. Risqué clothing. Both women were holding up arrest ID number boards at chest level. Priors for prostitution. Both women had been found in rented motel rooms on separate nights and on opposite sides of the city, five years ago and a month apart. Both had been overcome with chloroform, beaten to within an inch of their lives, then injected with the lethal drug combo through the peritoneum membrane. Sexual assault indeterminable. There were rafts of DNA recovered at both crime scenes – including semen, epithelial cells, hair and saliva from dozens of paying clients. Nothing that had led to a murder conviction.

Superglue had been used to seal their lips.

I looked at the third report: a murdered psychiatrist from Pennsylvania. The woman had been attacked in her home. Savagely, and beaten to a pulp. No signs of sexual assault. The Philly coroner had found traces of the lethal injection ingredients in her blood, injected through the abdomen. Again, superglue had been used post mortem to seal what remained of her lips. The report was dated seven years ago.

"They could be him." I heard Jamie say. "But there's no mention of rose petals or ash crosses."

"That's because he wasn't making a statement back then. He was honing his craft. If this is his work, there's probably more than this out there. Not all coroners are as thorough as Benedict. It's possible the chemically-induced heart failures were misdiagnosed. These are just the few that made it through."

I looked at the fourth police report, issued by the NYPD four years ago. Again, a woman had been overcome by chloroform and attacked in her own home. But this one was different than the others.

"The fourth victim wasn't killed," I realized.

"No," Jamie said. "And she wasn't assaulted either. Physically or sexually. But she did have a puncture wound on her abdomen and her blood work showed traces of Flunitrazepam."

"Rohypnol," I said. "The date-rape drug."

"But he didn't rape her."

"Flunitrazepam is a strong sedative, Jamie. He probably used it to keep her docile. Compliable. To cause amnesia after the event."

"So she couldn't ID him."

"Maybe."

I read on. Two syringes had been found at the scene: one containing sodium thiopental and pancuronium bromide, the other potassium chloride. Both full and unused. No fingerprints. No DNA.

"Perhaps something spooked him," Jamie mused out loud.

"Or he changed his mind," I said. "Says here he handcuffed her to the headboard the whole weekend. Then left empty-handed."

For a moment I wondered who the handcuffs had belonged to. Wondered if the NYPD still had them in their evidence lock-up.

"Gabe?"

"Still here."

"If she were a victim of The Undertaker, she could be his only survivor. I think this is worth looking deeper into."

I remembered Bill's premonition.

"Okay. But you'll need your wits about you, Jamie. This woman's name and contact details have been put under a protection order. Which means they're invisible, even to us."

"Witness protection?"

"Not always. Courts can conceal personal information for various reasons – including to preserve a victim's anonymity if there's a chance they may be the target of a repeat attack. Either way, it means she has relocated and maybe even changed her name. But if you think it has legs, Jamie, by all means run with it."

"I will. I'll also contact the Coroner offices in Chicago and Philadelphia. See if any more details match."

"Good. And while you're at it, let Jan and the team know what you're doing. Before you go, any luck with the rose retailers?"

"None doing mail order."

"What about online?"

"Just one. I spoke with a supervisor there. He says he'll fax a list of transactions once he's okayed it with the company lawyer."

# 50

I do not know how long I dozed in the recliner in the basement. Long enough, I guess, for the trickle of blood coming from my head wound to dry crusty on my cheek. There was a missed call on my cell: Carl Benedict from the Coroner's Office. I climbed creaking stairs and threw water over my face. I replaced the Band-Aid on my cheek and washed out my mouth with mouthwash. Then I called him back. It was just after 4 p.m.

Benedict sounded excited, but refused to go into detail over the phone. Not unusual. I met the quirky pathologist at an unmarked side door of the Coroner Facility thirty minutes later. The sun was going down. Casting long shadows under my eyes.

We made a beeline for the morgue, along a hallway lined with narrow metal gurneys pushed up against the walls. Plastic-covered cadavers. The sweet odors of disintegrating sugars pervading through the sterile smells. Blank eyes staring up through the thick, fogged plastic.

Over the years, I'd come to recognize that it wasn't death I had a problem with, it was decay. Death was sudden. Momentary. Decay went on for years.

"So what's with all the cloak and dagger, Carl?"

"Patience is a virtue," Benedict said as we entered the morgue.

More plastic-wrapped cadavers stacked high. Bodies wherever there was room. One whole wall was given over to an array of gray metal drawer fronts. Not the fancy glass-and-chrome ones you see in the movies, with their nice internal soft-glow lighting. These looked like a stack of fifty filing cabinets seen end-on. Very *Staples*. Everything well-worn.

Benedict pulled out a drawer at chest height. "She was brought in Tuesday evening. No immediate suspicious circumstances. The on-scene paramedics put the initial cause of death down to natural causes. Luckily, I noticed something iffy on the prelim exam."

Dramatically, like a magician, Benedict threw back the sheet to reveal the upper half of a near-skeletal body.

My stomach curled into a fetal position.

A woman was lying on the plinth. She was old. Late eighties, maybe early nineties. Thinning gray skin drawn loosely over fragile bones, like damp muslin draped over driftwood. Xylophone ribs. Arms as thin as gnarled rope.

"Here lies one of my screen idols." I heard Benedict breathe. "Meet Helena Margolis. She starred in a few black-and-whites back in the mid-twentieth century. Just when the horror genre was really beginning to come alive. Believe it or not, she was quite a stunner in her time. Did you ever catch Teenage Fang Club with Gustav Graves?"

"No."

He let out a long and mournful sigh. "See the purple freckling around her lips? That's what alerted me to take a closer look."

I peered at her slack face; saw a circle of indigo stars surrounding her slit of a mouth.

"See how it's darker than his other victims?"

I straightened up. "More pressure?"

"Correct. Perimortem bruising darkens with time. Becomes more distinct. Much of what you see here is heavy bruising. It's what you'd expect if she were asphyxiated."

"He suffocated her?"

"Well, yes, no and maybe." Benedict rolled back one of the woman's papery eyelids to expose a yellowy-blue eyeball. It looked like a bird's egg gone bad. "If you look closely you won't see any major signs of ruptured capillaries. Although he smothered her, asphyxiation didn't kill her. My guess is he was trying to keep her quiet." He let the lid droop back down.

"Any trace of chloroform?"

"No."

"So why is this one mine?"

"Because she had superglue in her mouth. And this . . ." he drew back the rest of the sheet to reveal the woman's lower torso.

I followed Benedict's finger down to her deeply-sunken abdomen, to a familiar ring of purple spangles surrounding a central patch. They were much darker and larger than those I'd seen on the other victims.

"It's ecchymosis," Benedict explained. "The passage of blood from ruptured blood vessels into subcutaneous tissue. It's characteristic of greater pressure. Especially in knife attacks."

"He stabbed her?"

"With a needle. Hard." He mimicked the act: pretending to stab himself in the gut. He even winced, to push the meaning home.

"Let me get this straight, Carl. You're saying he smothered her without chloroform, then stabbed her with a syringe?"

"That's exactly what I'm saying."

"It doesn't sound like our killer's pattern."

"Want to know my theory?"

"I'm all ears."

"This killing was unplanned. Spontaneous. That's why the MO's different. He had to kill her quickly, with whatever he had at hand, and without time to set up all his fancy trimmings. Something forced him – like an act of self-preservation."

"So why not snap her neck or strangle her?" It wouldn't have taken much pressure to do either.

"You're forgetting the hypodermic is his weapon of choice."

And serial killers hate deviating.

"I've sent swabs to Trace," he said. "But if he's as clean with this one as he has been with his other kills, I'm not very hopeful. Ready for the best part?"

"I guess."

"Helena's blood work came back negative for sodium thiopental and pancuronium bromide. But the potassium chloride showed up in fatal quantities."

I rocked back on my heels.

Helena Margolis had suffered a far more horrific death in real life than any she had ever acted out in her heyday.

# 51

I was in unmoving traffic, on Mission Road, a quarter mile from Benedict and the corpse of Helena Margolis. The sun had sunken fully in the west, turning the downtown skyscrapers into gravestones silhouetted against the deepening twilight. I was listening to the steady *ping-ping* of my *Uh-Oh Radar*, trying to figure out if her murder had been an act of impulsion, or even if it was truly one of our boy's.

"She was brought in late Tuesday afternoon," Benedict had told me, "from the Ramada Inn on Vermont."

I broke out my phone and got the switchboard to patch me through to the attending officer from Tuesday's call to the Hollywood Hotel. I had to wait awhile for him to come on the line. I wasn't going anywhere.

"Helena? Yeah, sure I can tell you about her," the officer said as he came through. "Helena was a well-known bag lady in that part of town. A real familiar face on the street. She's worked that stretch of Vermont for the last twenty years."

"Worked?"

"Not what you think, detective. Helena could spin a tale or two about Hollywood's Golden Age, usually in exchange for gin money. She knew all the gossip. The tourists loved her."

It was a far cry from her halcyon days.

"What happened, Tuesday?"

"We got a call around four in the afternoon. Evidently, the pool guy had found her slumped in the foliage at the back of the pool area, and raised the alarm. We checked her vitals when we arrived. Didn't see any signs of an attack or blunt force trauma. Looked like she'd been dead a couple of hours."

"And nobody noticed her?"

"Low season, I guess. Not many hotel guests using the facilities. And the foliage is quite dense toward the rear of the property."

"Did you see anything out of the ordinary?"

"Not that I recall. Anything in particular you're looking for?"

"Rose petals scattered around her body, for instance?"

"Nada." I sensed the officer's thoughts switch to my wavelength. "You think this is a homicide? I'll be damned. She was such a sweet old lady too."

The rush hour jam eased up. I drove straight to the Ramada on Vermont through mindless twilight traffic. I ran one or two reds and ignored the blasted horns. I didn't stop until I'd parked at the back of the hotel and killed the engine.

No petals. No ash. No discarded hypodermics. None of *The Undertaker's* stylized scene setup. So why was I here?

A hunch. Following my *Uh-Oh Radar*. Thinking that maybe – just maybe – if this was our boy he'd left an unintentional clue behind in his haste to dispose of Helena Margolis.

# 52

At that precise moment, the killer known only to himself as Randall Fisk was over two-hundred miles away, in another city, in another State. Any memory of Helena Margolis was long since filed away.

He was standing in a ring-shaped observation deck at the top of the tallest freestanding structure in western North America. Sweaty palms pressed against the cool glass of the window. He was gazing out across a sea of multi-colored city lights stretching out over a thousand feet below.

The original settlers had called this place *The Meadows*. But there was very little left of them here now – settlers or meadows. The city had spread far and wide in the intervening century, covering the entire Las Vegas valley in a bejeweled carpet.

Randall swiveled the peak of his cap to the back of his head and pressed a greasy brow against the toughened glass. The big window sloped inward toward his toes, so that it felt like he was suspended over the amazing drop. The view from the Stratosphere Tower was spectacular. A treasure trove of rainbow lights, glittering beneath the inky Nevada sky.

It was quiet in the doughnut-shaped observation gallery: just a few tourists going googly-eyed at the breath-taking panorama. No one paid any attention to his death-defying act. No one really cared. They were too busy snapping photographs for Facebook and pointing out the huge, illuminated hotels strung along The Strip like charms on a bracelet.

He pressed his head harder against the glass until his brain hurt. Wondered about the stress limit of the single glazed unit. It looked thick. Bulletproof. He wondered if it was.

# 53

The gated pool area at the Ramada Inn on Vermont is located at the back of the parking lot, in a corner and out of the way. It's a smallish, L-shaped area surrounded by leafy palms and those ubiquitous white plastic lawn chairs found at every hotel poolside across the country.

There was nobody about. I slipped quietly through a metal gateway. I could smell chlorine and damp vegetation. Dim bulbs illuminated the pool from within. A pair of halogen lamps on tall poles were just flickering into life up above.

I didn't know exactly where Helena's body had been found; there was no police tape strung between the palms, No chalked outline on the ground. But she had died here, in broad daylight. At the hands of our killer.

*What did I expect to find?*

I stood stock-still and soaked up the ambience.

Crime detection is one of the few cases where first impressions matter. You'd be surprised at just how much hidden information the subconscious gleans in the first few moments of entering a place of sudden death. A feeling, a mood, even a smell can shape our perceptions and help flesh out the bones of murders past.

But my subconscious wasn't for gleaning.

After several unproductive minutes I dropped into one of the plastic chairs and listened to the rumble of the traffic out on Vermont. Listened to the whirring of the air conditioning vents on the back of the hotel. Listened to the faint rustle of the palm leaves.

What was my *Uh Oh Radar* trying to say?

Then I saw it: a tiny red eye, high up in a darkening corner of the pool area.

I blinked. It didn't.
I got to my feet and ran toward the hotel.

# 54

Randall was riding one of the shiny tower elevators as it fell back to earth. A dozen excitable tourists crammed in around him. A group of boisterous young Hispanics poking fun at each other's frightened expressions on snapshots taken on one of the Tower's thrill rides.

The woman standing next to him had no idea who he was. No notion that her personal space was already invaded by the man who would later take her life. In the confines of the elevator her body odor was palpable. Not the smell of the unwashed, but rather the smell of fear. He'd seen her ride the vertical catapult rising from the summit of the Stratosphere Tower, seen the fear injected into her face. No deodorant could mask that look.

He studied her out of the corner of his eye as the carriage hurtled toward the ground:

She was as dull as a rainy day in Detroit. Small, dowdy and dumpy. Pushing forty. Fifty pounds overweight, with oily skin, lank hair, thick glasses. She reminded him of a half-baked dough dolly left out in the rain.

Destined to grow old alone.

Not if he had his way.

He'd be doing her a favor.

# 55

Sometimes the wheels of justice grind. I spent most of the night killing time at the Ramada Inn on Vermont. Firstly, waiting for the Manager to drag himself out of bed and come over. Secondly, waiting for his superiors to stop sitting on their hands and make a decision. And thirdly, waiting for the company legal department to give the thumbs-up. Sometimes twelve hours of pressure is enough to squeeze blood from a stone.

Keeping myself occupied as such helped take my thoughts away from Harry.

I got to the station house around 6:45 a.m., ahead of the morning rush. I'd called Jamie at home and told her about Helena Margolis. She'd come in early, to hook up a TV monitor and a video player in one of the interview rooms. Now we were sitting on metal chairs, intently watching the TV screen come to life as the Ramada surveillance tape whirred into action.

An image resolved out of black fog.

The camera angle was looking back toward the rear of the hotel, across the parking lot. Only the half of the pool area farthest from the camera was visible – including the little metal gate. The footage was black-and-white. Low quality. One frame snapped every ten seconds.

"We need to be looking at around two in the afternoon," I said as Jamie picked up the remote control.

The time stamp in the corner read 6 a.m. Shift change at the hotel. Jamie pressed a button and the time-lapse footage kicked up a gear as it launched into fast-forward. The time stamp accelerated through its numbers in the bottom corner of the screen. Hours of live footage flew by in minutes:

Vehicles zipping in and out of the parking lot. People blurring across the screen like day-lit specters. Clouds careening across the sky. Mostly, the footage was plain drudgery. Then, just after 1:30 p.m., something smacked me in the face and I hollered:

*"Stop the tape!"*

Jamie hit the brakes like our lives depended on it. The video player downshifted to normal speed with a whine. Then a clunk. Then another whine. Old technology. The TV screen went black. A fuzzy white line skittered around the top edge of the picture. She rewound the tape by a few seconds, pressed the play button, then paused it.

We leaned closer.

The image on the screen was a monochrome snapshot, jittering slightly on freeze-frame. It showed a parking lot with a scattering of cars. A white van in the far background, making deliveries. No one lounging at the poolside. No people at all – except for a stick-thin figure emerging from beneath our viewpoint.

"That's her," I said. "That's Helena."

Helena Margolis didn't look much healthier than the last time I'd seen her. One more winter. Maybe.

"Slow motion," I said. "And take it easy."

In jerky, time-lapse movements, Helena Margolis skittered across the parking lot, dancing like a wooden marionette being skipped along by unseen strings. The image snapped from one shaky ten-second frame to the next. The video-capture was fuzzy up close. The modern flat panel TV monitor made the VHS recording look ancient. Detail rapidly diminishing with distance. Everything in the background just big dots. Shades of gray.

In the fourth frame, a car cut across Helena's path as it parked in a handicapped bay behind the hotel. In the fifth, Helena was at the driver's door, leaning in an open window. In the sixth, she was cowering beneath a man standing next to the open door. In the seventh, she was slumped in his arms. Dead.

As quickly as that.

I leaned closer, holding my breath, trying to make out detail in the gray fog. But the man was too far away. Too smudged. A rough human figure sketched with charcoal on a grainy canvas.

Jamie hit the remote and we watched in silent horror as frame by frame the man skipped toward the camera. He grew bigger and bigger on the screen, carrying Helena over his shoulder like a sack of sand. Three frames between him knocking Helena unconscious and disappearing beneath the camera angle, into the pool area. Six uneventful frames later, he re-emerged, empty-handed, and bounced across the parking lot as if nothing had ever happened.

In those brief few moments, Helena Margolis had lost her life. Recorded like one of her movies, in black-and-white.

"Rewind to the shot where he entered the pool area," I said.

Jamie rewound the tape and put it on pause.

We leaned close enough for our noses to touch the screen.

The man's head was no bigger than my thumbnail. Tipped downward and in the shade of a palm tree. His face was hidden by what looked like a dark baseball cap and poor quality VHS.

It was our first and best glimpse of *The Undertaker*.

But it still wasn't enough to make out real features. Just impressions. A nose, a chin, a dark coat. Not much to go on. Certainly not APB material.

We were both still staring in horror when the interview room door burst open behind us.

I twisted round.

Ferguson was in the doorway, looking flustered.

"Gabe, stop what you're doing," he said.

"Captain," I began.

"Don't." He waved a dismissing hand. "There's no time to hear your excuse, Gabe. There's an FBI chopper on its way to pick you up. Should be here any minute."

I got to my feet. "FBI?"

"Agent Stubbs will fill you in en route," he explained. "As of this moment, you're back on the case. Get your act together. You're going to Vegas."

# 56

The shiny black FBI helicopter fell out of the baby-blue sky like a slab of crystallized basalt. It thudded onto the station house helipad in a swirl of dust. I shielded my eyes and leaned against the wall of wind trying to bowl me off the roof.

The hatch popped open. A sour-faced FBI agent jumped out. He was a lithe, tanned slick-dude in his early thirties. A blond, military-style crew cut. Wayfarers. The name *Stubbs* emblazoned in white on a standard-issue navy-blue FBI windbreaker. Cowboy boots.

"You Quinn?" he shouted over the roar of the rotor blades.

I nodded, stooped across the roof toward him. I had my hand outstretched.

He ignored the gesture and thumbed over his shoulder at the open hatch. "Daylight's burning."

I climbed up and in, dropped into a forward-facing seat. Agent Stubbs followed. He slammed the hatch and dropped into the rear-facing seat opposite mine.

"Buckle up," he shouted. "We have a private charter out of Van Nuys in five minutes."

He didn't seem pleased to see me. In fact, he seemed quite irritated at the whole affair of whisking a cop off the roof of a city precinct this early in the morning. I guess I wasn't much excitement for him and he had no qualms about showing it.

"Got any gum?" I yelled above the noise of the turbine. "Middle ear issues. Altitude problems. I promise, you can have it back when I'm done with it."

Stubbs twirled a finger at the pilot behind him, and the FBI helicopter leapt skywards.

* * *

My stomach sank into my feet and stayed there. Two nauseating minutes later, we thumped down on a private concourse at Van Nuys Regional Airport and my elastic belly snapped back with a *twang*. The breath-taking flight had been straight up and straight down, with total disregard for either physics or biology.

Stubbs threw open the hatch and bailed out. I followed.

We scurried toward a Gulfstream jet that was revved up and waiting on the sun-bleached apron. It was a nice little number: tinted windows and upturned wing tips. Gleaming white with red racer lines – the kind that gangster rappers leave parked in their driveways.

Another Fed, garbed in the same FBI windbreaker, was poised in the plane's narrow hatchway. He was a thickset African-American with a shaven head and the frame of a dungeon door. Wraparound sunglasses. His name patch read *Cherry*. The same irritated expression was drawing down his face.

I must have been such a letdown.

"Good morning, Agent Cherry," I said.

"Screw you," he snapped back.

He stepped aside as I climbed the trio of steps and looked down on me with the face of an executioner. I picked a seat at the back of the plane, buckled up. The cabin was cozy in a penthouse wardrobe kind of way. Cream leather couches facing one another. Plush champagne carpeting. A detectable scent of vanilla. I half expected to see Snoop Dogg hanging out at the back. I didn't.

With a *clunk*, Cherry locked down the hatch.

"Either of you boys going to fill me in on what this is all about?" I asked as the two Feds came down the aisle toward me.

"Screw you," Agent Cherry said again, and that put paid to that line of questioning.

I'd asked Ferguson on my way to the roof. But even Ferguson was being left in the dark. Just a requisition order from Washington DC. No informal chitchat. None required.

The Feds took up defensive positions facing me. No conversation. No eye contact lasting more than a second. Body language full of expletives. I heard Rolls Royce engines purr into life. The jet began to taxi toward the runway. It picked up pace, then sudden acceleration sucked me into the soft leather. The front of the cabin tilted up as the ground fell away.

The wound on my scalp began to throb.

Through the small window I saw the Los Angeles cityscape flash by. A crazy concrete jungle crumbling into patchy green and then into the hard brown ridges of the San Gabriel Mountains. I realized I was gripping the chair arms so tightly that my knuckles had turned white. Loosened them up a little. In less than a minute we left LA airspace altogether, heading due east.

I got out my phone and called Jamie.

No signal.

Both Stubbs and Cherry were sniggering.

Stubbs opened up a packet of gum and let Cherry take one.

Someone hadn't had their grits this morning.

There was a satellite phone built into the armrest. I dialed trunk and long distance to the station house.

"That's going to cost you," Cherry said with a sarcastic smile.

"So bill me."

Distantly, I heard Jamie pick up.

"Jamie, it's me. Something just occurred. Can you get together the Ramada's guest list for the last week or so? I should have thought of it last night."

"No problem. You think he's a guest there?"

"Maybe. Hopefully. And while you're at it, get that tape over to the Crime Lab. See if they can conjure up our killer's face out of all that fog."

"Will do. Anything else?"

I thought about it as I watched the Feds share a private joke on my behalf, scoffing behind their hands like schoolyard bullies.

"I'll keep you posted. In the meantime, keep the team up-to-date. I'll be in touch the second as I know what's happening."

The plane banked, sharply, sending beams of sunlight flickering around the cabin. I grabbed at the chair arms again.

Agents Cherry and Stubbs were giggling like schoolboys.

# 57

Danger came with the job. Danger came with lots of jobs. But most people got paid danger money for their troubles. To those who operated unlawfully, there was no job more dangerous than one which worked on the wrong side of the law.

Randall knew he was taking a big risk being here, playing this dicey game. He stood a high chance of being rumbled. But the adrenaline rush was worth the gamble.

The flashy Las Vegas casino was swarming with cops and security personnel. Termites in a mound. Scurrying this way and that. Seemingly purposeless. The casino boss had gone against police advice and kept the place open. Business as usual. Money over murder. Entertainingly, only the media were being kept at bay. He could see them being detained outside the glass entranceway, while a steady trickle of eager patrons was being allowed through the police cordon one at a time.

No one was being allowed out.

The casino was on a roll.

Takings on the up.

The big police presence was actually drawing in the punters.

The irony amused him.

The slot machine gurgled at his fingertips. Absently, he fed another ten-dollar bill into its mouth and sent its barrels spinning.

Randall was in his element here. Everything about the casino was patterns: the flashing lights, the rolling die, the odds for and against. Even the ubiquitous chimes of the slot machines. More patterns than he could read in a lifetime.

It was giving him a headache.

This was why he hated Vegas.

A burly numbskull from Hotel Security tapped him on the shoulder, asked to see his ID. The guy was scruffy. Food stains on his tie. Grime rings on his cuffs. One of those faces which looked out of place on a head. The killer handed over a driver's license – fake, of course – and drew an equally fake smile.

"Where you staying, Mr. Presley?"

The Hilton. A lie, of course. Sounded right.

"Personal contact number?"

Disposable cell. No trace.

"How long you plan on being in town?"

As long as it took to get his point across. What did he think? Did he want to see his pocket full of syringes?

The numbskull wrote *'available until weekend'* on his clipboard and moved on.

Randall pulled down the peak of his cap and snapped his fingers at a passing waitress. He ordered a double martini, no ice, then collected his winnings as they gushed into the slot machine's metal tray.

# 58

Thirty minutes later the Gulfstream jet belonging to the FBI rolled to a standstill at McCarran International Airport in Las Vegas. We disembarked and the Feds led the way. My legs were shaky; heights do that to me. We crossed the cracked apron to a waiting black sedan. I could smell aviation fuel and hot rubber. It was also noticeably colder here in Nevada. This was the high desert of old cowboy movies – not the sun-seared Sahara. Against the ice-blue sky, snow-peaked mountains dominated every horizon.

Cherry settled into the backseat with me. Tight fit. Cherry was big. Not flab big. Muscle big. Stubbs went up front with the driver. Cherry smelled like I'd expect a *Gillette* commercial to smell if they ever invent smell-o-vision.

Our sedan set off at a swift pace. The driver took the long curves out of the airport like a Daytona racer. We passed imported palms set in hand-picked gravel, then turned right, through a red, onto a long, straight road running north. Our driver swung the sedan around slower knots of traffic like a footballer dodging the defense. We shot past the famous diamond-shaped *Welcome to Las Vegas* sign.

"Gotta love Sin City." I heard Stubbs mutter to himself up front.

Not me. I had two very good reasons not to like this place. The first: it had been here, a few years back, where I'd been landed with the ball and chain *Celebrity Cop* moniker. The second involved Hope's murder, and I didn't want to think about that right now.

Vegas had grown bigger in the interim – like one of those crazy chemistry tricks in science class, where a few harmless chemicals suddenly turn into an expanding monster.

"You guys from around here?" I asked conversationally.

"Screw you," Cherry said with a snicker.

The first hotels came at us like a glass-and-metal tsunami. A cliff of mountainous buildings, rising up out of the desert. Each one taller, fancier and more intimidating than the last. Everything about the place looked big and pretentious, like a monumental Dali painting come to life. But dancing girls are always dancing girls, no matter how well turned out.

We passed the black-glass pyramid belonging to the *Luxor* – with its huge replica of the Egyptian Sphinx out front – followed by the blue-and-red parapets of *Excalibur*. Our driver made a right at the next set of signals, down the side of the green-glass *MGM Grand*. Seconds later, he hit the brakes as we hit traffic.

Everything was at a standstill.

There were people all over the street – swarming between unmoving vehicles. Cops barring entrance to the casino itself. Chinese tourists with their camcorders out. People pointing. A couple of news vans in the thick of it.

My *Uh-Oh Radar* was on red alert.

"Looks like one of you boys let the cat out the bag," I said.

Stubbs grunted. It sounded like *screw you*.

\* \* \*

Our driver hopped the sedan up the curb with a *thud* and we went the rest of the way on foot. It was mayhem. People all over the place. Standing on car bumpers. Snapping pictures. I saw a news reporter plowing her way toward me with a microphone in hand and a cameraman in tow. I tried to avoid. But there wasn't much room for maneuver. She anticipated my swerve and adjusted her intercept course.

"Detective Quinn!" she shouted above the chaos. "Channel Nine News!"

She was in her late twenties. Mandatory big blonde hair. Heavy make-up. Shoulder pads. Looked like she'd just stepped out of an '80s soap.

"No comment," I shouted back.

It was an automatic response. I didn't know what she wanted me to make comment on, but I was pretty sure it wasn't about the weather or the fact I looked like shit.

Stubbs and Cherry were busy bowling people out of the way, cutting a channel to the hotel entrance. The reporter slipped under Cherry's arm and grabbed my elbow. I tried to pull free, but she wrapped a leg around mine, rooting me to the spot. Cute. Then she spun us around to face her cameraman.

"The breaking story this hour is the murder of Patricia Hoagland – a conventioneer from Boise, Idaho – right behind me, here at The MGM Grand." Her leg tightened like a constrictor. "With me is Senior Detective Gabriel Quinn of the LAPD: laughably known as the Celebrity Cop. As we all know, Detective Quinn is renowned for his high profile cases, including the apprehension of the Star Strangler here in Las Vegas a couple of years ago."

She jammed the microphone under my nose. I could smell strawberry lip-gloss on the sponge muffler.

"Detective Quinn, rumor has it that the murder of Patricia Hoagland is connected to several others committed in Los Angeles over the last week by a serial killer you're calling The Undertaker. Is this the case?"

As if on cue, a deathly silence descended over the crowd. The commotion froze, all at once – as though somebody had paused time. Every eye on the street was fixed my way. Even the uniforms controlling the doors stopped and stared. One or two cameras flashed. I heard a pin drop, then realized it was my astonishment clicking in. I blinked like a damned deer caught in the headlights.

Then Cherry interceded. He stepped in and disarmed the reporter of her microphone. Without slowing, he gave her enough of a push to send her crashing to the sidewalk. She popped off her pump in the process, and laughter rippled through the watching crowd.

I caught sight of her waving the camera out of her face as Cherry dragged me into the hotel.

We took an express elevator to the nineteenth floor. The carriage was all fractured mirrors. It looked like something Alice might have seen on the other side of the Looking Glass. A pair of police detectives were hanging around the upper landing. One was a tall African-American with the physique of a basketball player. The other was a petit woman with long brown hair scooped into a ponytail. She was on her cell phone. The exchange sounded heated. The basketball player was humming soundlessly into a harmonica. He gave me a nod as we set off at a march down a ridiculously long hallway.

Movie posters lined the walls:

*Vertigo, West by Northwest, Psycho . . .*

We were in good company, it seemed.

Another two Feds were loitering outside a guest room door: a runny-nosed kid from Chinese descent and a big Nordic brute with buzz-saw hair. The kid had a pinched-face. He was the King of Siam arms-folded type. The big guy was ex-military. Sloppy hands in sloppy pockets.

"Quinn." Pinch Face remarked as we arrived. "About time."

He didn't offer his hand. I wouldn't have taken it in any case. I'm fairly good with first impressions. And this kid was all newly-promoted god complex.

"Agent Wong," he said, as if I should bow or curtsy or perform some equally demeaning act. "This is Agent Blom. Do you know why you're here?"

"Book signing?"

Wong sneered. I could smell cologne bought in one of those dollar stores. It clawed at the nose.

"Heads-up, Quinn. I know who you are. I know all about you. I know you like to sensationalize criminals. Give them household names. I know you get people killed. And I know I don't like it. This is my crime scene and you're here in an advisory capacity only. Don't compromise it, or do anything to piss me off. I need you to confirm it's the same killer and then you can go your merry way."

I decided I didn't like Wong. Not one bit. Normally, it takes a lot for me not to like somebody. He had one of those permanently malleable faces that spoilt brats like to use to embarrass their parents at family functions.

"You boys are good at spending tax dollars," I said, "flying me all the way out here just to confirm an ID. What makes you think it's my boy?"

"This." Wong held up a clear plastic evidence bag.

When I saw its contents, my blood turned to ice.

# 59

Randall waited until the FBI entourage had passed him by before exchanging his winnings at one of the mobile cashier carts. Then he sauntered, casually and inconspicuously, toward the elevator area.

A pair of grim-faced cops were turning people away. No access to the upper floors. One particularly loud black girl in an equally loud party frock was demanding to be allowed up to her room. She'd paid top dollar – or rather her parents had. She needed the bathroom. She needed a freshen-up – or rather another line of cocaine. Her daddy had influence in town. But the cops were having none of it. Her boyfriend was more passive, hanging back, encouraging her withdrawal in soft syllables.

She'd been drinking, partying all night. They didn't look twenty-one.

Randall spied his chance and shouldered open an unmarked door leading to the stairwell.

Life was all about taking risks.

And Vegas was the risk capital of the world.

With a nub of amphetamine dissolving under his tongue, the killer bounded up the stairs three at a time.

# 60

A second later, the blood thawed in my veins as hot anger surged through my system. I snatched the bag from Wong's hand and stared at its contents with disbelieving eyes. I didn't want to think about it, but knew it could only mean one thing.

"Where did you find this?"

"Strangely enough, tucked inside her underwear. Like a tip." Wong seemed to exact a degree of pleasure from the remark.

I didn't.

I was busy trying to muster up a rational explanation for what was in the evidence bag. But there is only so much blindsiding the eyes can do before the truth enlightens.

There was bile in my throat.

"Show me," I said.

The air was stuffy inside the room on the nineteenth floor of *The MGM Grand Hotel* – like an attic in the midst of summer. Both the nets and the long orange drapes were pulled right back, I saw, allowing bright daylight to sober up the proceedings.

The focus of the room was the big King bed in the middle. A pair of Crime Lab techs were circling it like buzzards: one taking pictures, the other tweezing evidence samples from the exposed flat sheet.

I floated closer.

There was a woman lying on the bed, hands dovetailed across her bosom. Skin paled into the bluish hue of rigor mortis. She was a big girl – two hundred pounds, easy – but her killer had had no trouble hoisting her onto the thick mattress. There was a cross of ash on her brow and red rose petals scattered on the white bed sheet. I knew at a glance we were dealing with the same killer.

*The Undertaker* had ditched LA and was performing in Vegas.

I didn't want to buy tickets.

But things were different here.

Unlike with his LA victims, the killer had stripped the woman down to her discolored underwear. He'd smeared her folded arms in what looked like blood. I didn't know whose. No visible signs of cuts that I could see. So much of it in fact that it looked like she was wearing red gloves up to the elbows.

Where the blood had come into contact with her bra, it had seeped into the cotton fabric to form small crimson flowers.

*The Undertaker* had tweaked his MO.

Wong cleared his throat. "Well?"

"It's him all right," I said.

But I already knew it. No other explanation, given what was inside the evidence bag.

"I'll need copies of all your case notes, Quinn," Wong said. "Everything you have. This is now an FBI investigation."

There was something leaning against the headboard. It drew me closer. It was a photograph. The picture of four people: three men, one woman, sitting in a row of red seats bolted to a white framework of tubular bars. Their features were slightly blurred by motion. One of those shots taken on a rollercoaster, I realized – where you look your least favorable. I recognized two people in the image: the dead woman lying on the bed and the guy I'd seen an hour ago on the Ramada surveillance tape. He was wearing a black baseball cap. Face tilted strategically down at his feet. But it was him. *The Undertaker.*

I turned to Wong. "This is my case. I'm already working with Quantico on this."

"Yesterdays' news," he said. "This is our operation now. You're excused."

I stood my ground. "Get me Hugh Winters on the phone, right now, and we'll settle this."

Winters is the Special Agent-in-Charge of the Las Vegas field office, and a personal enemy of mine.

Wong was unfazed. "Who do you think assigned me to take over this case? You're a joke, Quinn. Laughable. A meter maid has more jurisdiction in this town than you."

I felt the red mist rising.

Wong saw it and snapped fingers at Blom. "Get him out of here," he said.

The big brute descended on me like a falling wall, ready to manhandle me out of the room.

Then somebody finger-whistled, loudly, from the direction of the doorway. The sudden screech was so shrill that everyone froze.

"Now you're in trouble, Wong," I said. "Meet my good friend from the Bureau, Bill Teague. So happens he trumps your pay grade by about six places. Hi there, Bill."

"Hello yourself," he grinned. There was a smoldering cigarette wedged in the corner of his cocky smile, defying hotel regulations.

Wong's lips twisted in the way that lips twist when the tongue tastes something unsavory. "Who's this asshole?"

Bill stepped into the room and didn't stop until he was an inch from Wong. I saw Wong's defenses go up, sensed Blom puff out his chest. For a moment I thought they were going to lock horns like sparring rams. But Bill was the epitome of unflustered.

He pressed his ID against Wong's nose before he could back away. "I may be an asshole," he said, "but I'm also your superior, asshole. SAC William Teague, of the Violent Crimes Division." He emphasized the word *Violent* in a way that electrified the already tense atmosphere. "Which means you don't want to be trying to have sex with me without my permission." He removed his ID and pulled back.

Wong's face had pinched itself into a point where even light couldn't escape.

"Director Fuller has personally asked me to take charge of this investigation as of now," Bill continued, addressing everyone within earshot, "which overrides your authority, Wong. Detective Quinn is my right-hand man on this. Which means no one so much as farts without clearing it with me or him first. You get me? Now, any of you limp dicks have a problem with that?"

He blew a cloud of smoke at Wong.

"This is a crime scene," Pinch Face growled.

Bill broke into a laugh. "Well blow me for brunch. For a moment there I thought you were going to say it was a no-smoking room."

*　　*　　*

Fifteen minutes later, Bill and I were seated at a table outside a bar set amid narrow reconstructed New York City streets. Indoors. My head was splitting. I'd downed aspirin and was praying for a miracle. I shouldn't have been drinking. But there hadn't seemed any good alternative at the time Bill had suggested it.

"Shit, Gabriel, you need to see a doctor," Bill said, supping beer. "Or an undertaker."

I raised my bottle. "Very funny, Bill. So, what gives? Why are you in Vegas? Last I heard you were on your way to Bakersfield."

"Simple. Your boy murdered Patsy Hoagland."

I made a mystified face, unable to see the relevance.

"She's Fuller's niece," he said.

"As in the Director of the FBI?"

"As in. Happens to be his only sister's only daughter too."

"Holy crap."

"Exactly. That's why Wong and his henchmen were sucking in air at both ends."

I'd dealt with Norman Fuller on several occasions previously. Barely escaped with minor cuts and bruises each time. The FBI Director was a persnickety dreadnought of a man. Not the kind you wanted as an enemy. Not the kind to take the cold-blooded murder of his niece lightly.

*The Undertaker*, I realized, had just made his biggest mistake to date.

"You do know he's here, Bill," I said. "The Undertaker."

"No kidding."

"So why Vegas?"

"Aside from pissing on Fuller's parade, probably to have a good time. Look around you, Gabriel. This is Disneyland for adults. Who wouldn't want to come here?"

"I'm serious, Bill."

"So am I. There's a shitload of free money to be made in this town. Just listen to the tune of those slot machines: they're playing the theme song from *Goldfinger* all the way to Fort Knox."

I watched Bill tap out a cigarette and light it from a silver Zippo. Saw him draw a lungful of smoke, hold it, then release it slowly through his flared nostrils.

"There's also over a million visitors here at the weekends," he said. "Which makes great pickings for predators."

"Have we any idea how Fuller's niece ties into all this?"

"Right now your guess is as good as mine. I didn't see it coming, and I'm the psychic. How about you?"

"Nope."

"One thing I do know is we're not going anywhere else until Uncle Norman gives us the say so. As far as you and I are concerned, that man is god." He tapped ash into a bowl on the table. "And he's capitalized pissed right now. Everyone on the slippery slope down is feeling the heat."

"What do we know about her, his niece?"

"She's dead."

"Before that, Bill."

He breathed smoke. "Patsy worked as a lab tech for a small pharmaceuticals setup in Massachusetts. That's all I know so far. What I do know is your boy just got himself a prime slot on America's Most Wanted. Congratulations, Gabriel. You just hit the jackpot."

I took a swig of beer, felt it cool my belly.

I didn't feel like celebrating.

# 61

Fact: *The Undertaker* had killed in Vegas.

I was back on the case and I wanted answers. I had no way of knowing how long the killer would remain in town, or if he would kill again here or even elsewhere. He'd spent a week in LA that I knew of. If he hung around the same amount of time in Vegas, I'd need someplace to freshen-up and call home.

I needed to stay busy, keep my thoughts away from Harry.

I made arrangements to meet up with Bill later that the afternoon. I didn't tell him about the evidence bag in my pocket, the one Wong had given me and then forgotten to get back. I don't know why. Bill had offered his condolences over Harry, and hadn't pushed me to speak on the subject any further; he could sense my pain. Besides, he had an incident room to set up. A whole posse of G-Men to corral. It would take time to get the show on the road and for the local forensics lab to go through the evidence collected at the Hoagland crime scene. I figured I had a couple of hours to kill before the investigation was fully up and running in Vegas.

I caught a gas-powered cab to the *Luxor*. I'd lodged in the fake Land of the Pharaohs the last time I'd been here. I had a strange affiliation with the place. Don't ask. The hotel is full of huge reconstructions of Egyptian gods and their entourages. Chicken wire and fiberglass. But you can't help but be slightly impressed by the Cinemascope feel of it all. I bought toiletries from a kiosk decked out like a Bedouin tent, then checked into a room on the eleventh floor of the black-glass pyramid.

I was inspecting treats in the Wet Bar when my cell phone rang.

"You winning, partner?"

It was Jamie. I told her about Patricia Hoagland and what we'd found.

"Do serial killers normally change their MO like that?" she asked.

"It's known as escalation." I found a *Snickers* in the mini fridge and dug in. Cold caramel sticking to teeth. "Repeat killers tend to fine-tune their methods as they progress," I explained. "Some increase the frequency of their kill rate. Others get better at the killing itself."

"What does the blood mean, on her hands?"

"I'm not sure yet. There are two kinds of calling cards, Jamie: symbolic and literal. Blood on the hands could signify the killer thought Patricia was guilty of something."

"Like Samuels being accused of murder."

"Precisely. Or it could mean he caught her red-handed."

I heard Jamie crack a smile. "Jan's asking if you'll fax over all the details when you have them."

"Sure. Can you guys do the same for me? Send everything we have on the case through to our Vegas counterparts. I'll be staying at the Luxor Hotel. Room . . ." I couldn't remember. "It's on the eleventh floor somewhere. Bill's in the process of setting up an incident room. Until then, we're working ad hoc. Any news on the Ramada guest list?"

"Not yet. Fred's over there now. He says the Manager's a real piece of work. Lawyers dragging heels."

I'd spent half the night with the guy. Not deliberately awkward, just following protocol. Fred was about to have his patience tried to the breaking point.

"Any luck with the rose retailer?"

I heard her sigh, "Nothing so far. I'll keep on top of it. Jan's contacted the other coroner's offices."

I finished the *Snickers*. "And?"

"And they all say they'll fax the paperwork over when they have the time."

"Thanks, Jamie." I hung up, then called Captain Ferguson, explained the situation.

"This doesn't let you off the hook," he whispered down the phone line. "Soon as you get back here you see Zimmerman. No excuses, Gabe. She needs to sign you off before you come back in. In the meantime, Jan will continue running things from this end. Work with her. And keep me in the loop."

I ran a sink of cold water and splashed away dried sweat, took a cautious peep behind the Band-Aid still glued tight to my cheek. Things were healing. I decided my bullet wound needed to breathe. I levered the Band-Aid free and discarded the bloodied sticky to the sink top. It curled up like an anemic leech.

Maroon blood had crusted up the dressing above my eye where my priest's killer had hit me into the rough. I was of two minds whether to shower it off or leave it alone. I was still debating when the room phone rang. I dried off and answered.

"Gabriel, it's me."

"Bill? How did you know I was here?"

"I'm psychic, remember?"

"Sure. Nothing to do with the fact I stayed here last time round and you know it. What gives?"

"Something to consider," he said. "The blood on Patsy's hands – I've a hunch it belongs to one of his other victims. Maybe even the child."

I shuddered. The thought of *The Undertaker* siphoning off the little girl's blood made my flesh creep.

"Why would he do such a thing?"

"Because his tent is pitched deep in Psychoville. I've spoken with the Vegas Crime Lab. They're liaising with their LA counterparts. They'll send everything over –

so we can compare DNA profiles. If it helps, you can pray I'm wrong."

Fact: Bill is never wrong.

With shaking fingers, I took out the evidence bag from my jacket pocket and stared at its contents.

*The Undertaker* had set this up, I realized, from the start.

He'd planted this evidence to get me here, knew I'd come running.

But that wasn't what bothered me the most.

I looked more closely at the thin, colored, plastic rectangle sitting in the bottom of the bag. There was a thumbnail photo of a man on it. The face of a dear friend.

My stomach turned.

I got up and ran to the bathroom, retched up warm beer until the back of my nose burned.

# 62

Stacey Kellerman was down but not out. Being caught on camera crashing to the deck with her legs sprawled in the air hadn't exactly made her day. But somewhere, someone's *YouTube* account would be receiving lots of hits on the back of her mishap.

Other than that, everything had gone according to plan.

She was sore, but she'd live.

As a young girl she'd suffered much worse.

More importantly, she'd kept up her part of the bargain and delivered the message, as instructed.

Back home, she poured herself a congratulatory cold merlot from the fridge and replayed the scene in her head: the Celebrity Cop, the crowd, the camera, the unforgiving sidewalk. She just had to hope that her humiliation was ultimately worth it.

She checked her watch. Cleaned out the glass. Refilled it. Emptied it again. Felt spaced. Filled it up again.

Soon, her *YouTube* calamity would be long forgotten and overshadowed by something much more newsworthy. Soon, Stacey Kellerman would be making headlines across the planet.

She stared at the phone sitting in its cradle on the breakfast bar – willing it to ring.

How many reporters could claim to have interviewed a serial killer *before* he'd been caught?

Exclusivity.

That's what she had. The inside scoop straight from the horse's mouth. Once this was out, every agency in the country would be clamoring to offer her jobs and hiked salaries. But she already knew where she wanted to be: NYC, and the most coveted job in American TV journalism.

She sipped more wine and thought about her future.

The killer thought he was smart. But Stacey was smarter. She was the one with all the leverage. She was the one holding all the cards.

The phone rang. Dead on time.

Stacey picked up, "Hello?"

"Hello, Stacey."

The voice was male. Calm, collected. She detected a slight southern twang. He was trying to smooth it out. But it was there. It reminded her of the killer Max Cady in the movie *Cape Fear*.

The killer had called her private line a couple of days ago and invited her to his personal party. He'd told her all about his exploits in LA, and that they were merely the tip of the iceberg when it came to his plans for Vegas. He'd chosen her to tell his story. Be his voice. It would make her famous. Stacey had been happy to make her deal with the devil.

"I've done what you asked," she said. "Now I want you to do something for me."

The Max Cady voice on the other end of the line paused, then said, "Stacey, your performance today was exceptional. Show-stopping. Give yourself a round of applause. You deserve it. Better still, have another glass of merlot and let's celebrate. When will the next message air?"

"It's on the nines all day," she said. "Starting midday."

"Good girl. In that case, what would you like me to do for you, Stacey?"

"I want you to kill the opposition," she said bluntly. Her words and intentions were as cold as the wine swilling around in her belly. She hadn't needed long to think about what kind of return she wanted for granting a serial killer his fifteen minutes. She'd aimed for this all her working life. "I want you to kill the woman whose job I want. A deal's a deal, right?"

"Are you sure you're ready to move up into the big league, Stacey?"

"Don't patronize me. I've been ready all my life. Do we have a deal? I can always pull the plug if you have cold feet."

She heard him sigh, "Who do you want me to kill for you, Stacey?"

Stacey smiled to herself. Men were animals. Predictable and pathetic. Wrapped around her little finger, always.

"I want you to eliminate the whore that hosts the World News show on ABC. I want her job. That's what I want out of all this. Do you understand me? I do my part. You do yours. You get your interview. I get her job."

"I'm not sure killing her is such a good idea, Stacey."

Stacey raised herself up on the stool and loomed over the phone. "Listen to me, Max. Either you meet me halfway or we have no deal. I want you to kill Quinn's daughter-in-law Kate Hennessey. I want you to remove her from the equation. Or we can call the whole thing off."

Stacey Kellerman took a gulp of wine. Her heart was racing and the merlot was bitter on the back of her tongue.

On the other end of the connection she could sense the killer sealing her fate.

This was so easy.

# 63

The secret to keeping warm in cold weather is to layer. I picked up several souvenir T-shirts from the hotel lobby to go under my thin Californian shirt before venturing outside.

The Las Vegas Metro PD South Central Area Command is located less than a half mile from the *Luxor*, on the other side of the neighboring hotel complex. I was glad of the walk; it gave me the chance to breathe.

There were three immediate questions burning in my brain: what connected Patricia Hoagland to the LA victims; how had the reporter come by her information; and was it merely coincidental that the latest victim was related to the Director of the FBI?

The last question could possibly prove the hardest to answer.

I drew my jacket close against the chill, walked out from beneath the unmoving gaze of the giant reconstructed Sphinx.

The desert breeze was hard against my face. I should have felt wide-awake. I didn't. Vegas has the kind of subliminal buzz only found in cities that never sleep. A barely perceptible heartbeat pulsating along the arterial roadways from the heart of the city. I should have felt right at home. I didn't.

I thought about the evidence bag weighing heavily in my pocket and felt anger surge. I took a deep breath and forced a lid on my boiling blood. Nothing I could do about it. Not right now, anyway. What was done was done. But I remembered the plea of a grieving mother, and had every intention of fulfilling her demand.

I crossed an intersection and arrived at the station house. I'd called ahead, spoken with the sergeant overseeing the Homicide Bureau. I was told my Metro counterpart was a senior inspector called Sonny Maxwell.

I signed in and left my firearm with the desk sergeant. He gave me directions to Sonny Maxwell's office. Don't ask me why, but I assumed my counterpart was the lithe basketball type I'd seen earlier in the morning, outside the Hoagland crime scene, at the *MGM Grand*. I was wrong.

"Sonny Maxwell?"

She was the small woman with the brown ponytail; the one I'd seen having the heated exchange on her cell.

We shook hands. Her grip was firm but fair.

"I saw you at The Grand this morning when you arrived," she acknowledged with a warm smile. "Didn't get the opportunity to say howdy. Too busy trying to get those damned Feds off my case. *Your* case as it turns out. Mind if I call you Gabe?"

"It's my name. You okay with Sonny?"

"No." She sounded southern. Maybe one of the Carolinas. "Just yanking your chain," she laughed. "Sonny's fine. We had a wager on how long it be before you showed up."

"I hope you won."

"I'll let you into a little secret: I load the dice." She went over to a coffee machine in the corner. "Interest you in a drink? I just put a pot on."

"My addiction."

"Could be worse." She poured coffee. "Me, I used to smoke thirty a day. Damn near killed myself kicking it into touch a few years back. Now I diet. Constantly."

"You don't look the type, Sonny."

"Well, I'll take that as a compliment. But don't be misled; I can party with the best of them. Here you go." She handed me a steaming cup.

I gazed around at the neat surroundings. By the look of things, Sonny Maxwell was a meticulous worker and a stickler for tidiness. Everything looked organized. Case files color-coded and alphabetized. Pencils sharpened. Tips at attention. A row of prickly cacti on the windowsill arranged in height order.

I pointed to a group of framed photographs on her desk. "These your kids?" Two boys and a girl. Snapshots taken on a vacation. Summer sunshine. Looked like Disney or someplace equally unreal.

I sensed Sonny bristle with pride. "Sure are. The three terrors, as I call them. Love them insatiably, though. You got kids, Gabe?"

"All grown and flown the nest," I said with a nod. "Great looking family, Sonny." I had to say it. It smacked me on the chin. A happy hen and her brood. "No pictures of Mr. Maxwell?"

"That philandering dick? Nah. Roger's living in Atlanta with his new wife. Good riddance, I say."

"Oh. I'm sorry."

"Don't be. I'm not. Roger could never keep his zipper up. That silly student of his was the best thing that ever happened to us."

She perched herself on the corner of the desk and studied me like an elementary school teacher about to tell her class a gripping story.

"Okay, Gabe, this is your pie. I ain't disputing that. So how we gonna slice it?"

Sonny had gone straight for the kill shot. Steel arrow neatly severing the spinal cord from the brain stem. I decided I liked her immediately. She reminded me of the movie actress Holly Hunter in just about any of her films.

"Joint task force?" I suggested.

"Nice idea, on paper. But I've had nothing but brick walls from the Feds all morning."

"The situation's changed, Sonny. The local Feds have had their noses pushed out. The show's now being run by one of my good friends from Quantico."

Sonny nodded, but still looked wary. "Given the circumstances I expected some bigwig from Washington, not Quantico."

"Bill Teague's just about as big as they get."

"Wasn't he the guy who helped you crack the Star Strangler Case?"

"Right."

"The one who sees dead people?"

I smiled. "Not too sure about that. Bill's quirky, I admit. But I think he's just extremely intuitive and brilliant at reading hunches. He's in the process of setting up a situation room as we speak. If you agree, you and I will oversee the police investigation while Bill looks after the Bureau's interests."

Sonny was still nodding, still looking wary.

"It's worked out okay in the past," I assured her. "Don't worry about the Feds. We'll have a free reign. Plus, the unlimited resources of the FBI at our disposal."

"Then the rumor's true . . . Hoagland is related to Director Fuller."

I nodded, solemnly. "So it seems. Sonny, believe me, this killer made a big mistake killing Patricia Hoagland. There's going to be a no holds barred when it comes to catching him. We're talking a nationwide manhunt. I know Fuller; he'll throw everything at this. More manpower than we can shake a stick at."

"Sounds like your boy hasn't a cat in hell's chance."

"Hopefully."

I saw Sonny Maxwell nod. This time she didn't look as skeptical.

"Then I guess the real question is: do you think this maniac will strike again, here, in Vegas?"

I thought about it over my coffee. Long and hard. What did I think? So far, *The Undertaker* had taken five lives in LA inside of a week. What were the chances of the same happening here in Vegas?

Each way I looked at it the odds were in his favor.

# 64

Did everybody daydream about their role in the greater play?

Somewhere, Randall had heard that the world's most successful innovators, entrepreneurs and artists did exactly that.

The killer, now known to the US media network as *The Undertaker*, lit a cigarette and sucked hard. Daydreaming allowed him to decipher patterns. It was part of his condition.

Beneath the shadow of the giant Sphinx, fanny-pouched tourists gathered in little knots like mindless sheep, waiting to be whisked away to another of the ridiculously-themed hotels. They were giving him a wide berth; smokers were lepers these days.

Normally, Randall avoided detours. Planned routes were safe. The shortest path from A to B was never through C. But this distraction had presented itself as if preordained and was too tempting to pass up.

He sucked on his smoke, daydreaming about how it might all play out.

A sleek, white-and-black tram *whooshed* into the monorail station in front of the Sphinx. It looked like something out of a science-fiction movie. He buried the cigarette in a sand-filled urn and hung back while the tourists filed in. Then he found a spot near the front of the carriage and clung to a hand loop as the monorail went into reverse.

Ten minutes later, he was slipping through the rear entrance of the high-class *Bellagio Hotel*. He rode the elevator to the thirteenth floor, watching numbers increment on a little LCD screen set above the sliding doors.

The hallway on the thirteenth floor was deserted. A Housekeeping cart parked halfway down. Stacks of fluffy white towels. Fancy *Bellagio* toiletries. Tubs of pens and pads. He scooped up a bundle of towels as he passed.

Twenty strides later, he was at his destination.

He rapped briskly on the door.

A man's voice: *"Who is it?"*

He held the towels up to the spy hole.

*"Can you come back later? We're a little busy right now."*

No, he couldn't. Towels had to be changed daily. It would only take a moment.

The door clicked open.

Randall threw his weight against it. Taken by surprise, the man on the other side stumbled backward.

Randall dropped the towels and advanced like a panther.

The Meadows were about to become the killing fields.

# 65

Sonny walked me out into the parking lot – just in case I'd forgotten the way. "Have you thought about doing a press conference?" she asked as we strolled across the blacktop. "News is everything in this town. It's compulsive viewing."

In truth I had considered it. Right from the get-go, back in LA. But press conferences tended to go one of two ways: deterrence or determination.

"Let's hold off on that idea awhile," I decided. "See how this pans out. In my experience, going to the media either scares the killer off or sends him on a killing spree. Last thing you need is a city full of panicking tourists."

"It's your call. Just throwing it out there. I have a few good contacts in the local media. We can use them – when you're ready, that is. An informed public is a vigilant public."

I'd already used the media to try and snare *The Undertaker* once, and failed.

"Sonny, you familiar with this reporter who accosted me this morning?"

"What did he look like?"

"She," I said. "Blonde hair. Shoulder pads. Looked like Barbie on gasoline fumes."

Sonny smiled. "That can only be Stacey Kellerman. She's an up-and-coming name in these parts. Headed for the bright lights – or so she thinks. Has she been giving you some trouble, Gabe?"

"None that I can't handle. I'm curious, though – because she had inside knowledge about the killer's previous victims. Plus, she knew his nickname."

"Reporters have sources. I guess you could ask her. But she probably won't give hers up without a fight, or a trade."

A red-and-white jet roared by overhead, low enough to count the windows. We waited for the thunder to roll by before continuing:

"Before you say it, Gabe, I've already sent manifest requests to all the airlines. Most visitors come here by plane. All credit card reservations are stored electronically, which means we can get a rundown on everyone who flew in from LA in the last couple of days."

"Unless he drove here or paid cash for his flight."

"Got to start somewhere," she winked.

Another thought occurred: "Once these lists come in, can we cross-reference them against hotel guest lists?"

"You mean check out everybody in person? I guess it's doable, at a push. Use up heck of a lot of manpower."

"Don't worry about that; the Bureau will be shipping in agents by the container-full."

"All the same, there's over a third of a million visitors here in Vegas at any given moment. Over half a million at the weekends. And the weekend starts Friday in this neck of the woods."

Thousands of rooms to canvass – and all providing the guests were in those rooms when our knock sounded at the door.

I was beginning to understand the enormity of the task. With guests constantly checking-in and checking-out, it would make any guest list not only extremely lengthy but also in a perpetual state of flux.

We came to a shiny silver Nissan SUV. This year's model. I could see a child's doll on the backseat. A *McDonald's* foam cup in one of the holders.

Sonny popped the locks. "Give you a ride someplace?"

"The MGM Grand, thanks. I want to go over Patricia Hoagland's room one more time. See if we missed something."

We climbed into the brand new Nissan. There was a dream-catcher dangling from the interior mirror. Sonny handed me a business card.

"My numbers. Call me if you find anything. Or need anything. Anytime. Night or day."

We stared at one another. It should have been one of those awkward moments. It wasn't.

# 66

By the book, the Metro PD had posted an officer outside the sealed Hoagland crime scene. I found him straddling a chair and reading a sports magazine. He jumped to his feet when he saw me approaching, rolled his read into a tube.

I showed ID. "Clean-up crew been here yet?"

He shook his head, opened the door and let me through.

It smelled like Benedict's lair in here.

The drapes were still pulled right back. Dust motes dancing in the sobering sunshine. Through the window I could see one of the huge hotel complexes across the street. A fake Manhattan skyline. Scaled-down skyscrapers. A luminous green Statue of Liberty.

Madness.

The CSU had removed the linens from the bed. The pillows were missing too. No sign of any rose petals, or that a woman had died on this bed hours earlier. I went over to the nightstand and used a handkerchief as a glove as I pulled open the drawer. There was a Gideon copy of the Bible inside and a copy of the Koran. Both pocket-sized. Both looked like they'd never been opened.

There was a message pad and a green pen on top of the nightstand, next to the lamp. You know the kind; every hotel has them. A handful of creamy pages, each bearing the hotel's name, crest and contact numbers. Somebody had written a telephone number and the name *Bob* on the topmost page. It looked like a woman's handwriting, slightly leftward-leaning. Carefully, I tore off the sheet, folded it, picked up the green pen and put both in my pocket.

At the foot of the bed was a long set of drawers with a flat screen TV standing on the top. A small cardboard tent advertising TV stations. The latest blockbuster movies and adults-only channels. I checked the drawers: empty. I went over to the mirrored closet that stretched across the entire wall separating the bathroom from the bedroom. A tired-looking man in dire need of a shave reached toward my fingertips as I reached for the handle. He helped me slide open the big door.

Patricia Hoagland had been traveling light, it seemed: a single piece of luggage comprised of a purple crocodile-skin-effect carry-on with a pullout handle. A thick coat and scarf draped over a hanger up above. A purple blouse and what looked like a gray business skirt suit. Never to be worn again.

The built-in safe was wide open. Empty.

I picked up the carry-on and slung it onto the bare mattress, positioned it on its back and unzipped it.

Rummaging through a dead person's personal effects might excite some people. Not me. I threw back the lid and inspected the contents with sober eyes.

It was mostly underwear. Same condition as the garments Patricia had been found in. Whites washed on hot with colors that run. A knitted sweater. Bobbly. A few used toiletries. A paperback book: the latest chick-lit from somebody I'd never heard of before. A woman's wallet containing a Mayflower Bank visa card, and a couple of hundred dollars in cash, plus a return flight ticket to Boston Logan International. No driver's license.

I left everything in the carry-on and zipped it back up.

There was a writing desk and an office chair near the window. A telephone with an Internet connection point. A few colorful pamphlets arranged in a fan. Vegas shows. Vegas shopping. Vegas nightlife. One odd-one-out leaflet advertising a company dealing in pharmaceutical research.

My cell phone played its merry tune. I dug it out, then felt my face break into a big grin when I saw the caller's ID.

"Gracie!" I yelped into the microphone.

"Hi, Daddy. How are you?"

"Fine. Better for hearing your voice. I tried calling earlier this week. Then I got waylaid with other things."

I heard Grace chuckle down the line. I loved that laugh.

"I meant to return your call a couple of days ago," she said, "but things have been hectic here this week. I'm snowed-under with work."

I smiled. "Even in sunny Florida."

She laughed again. I felt my load lighten.

"What about you, Daddy? How you coping being back?"

"Keeping myself busy."

I am a firm believer that kids should never carry their parents' burdens.

"Busy is good," she agreed. "I guess it gets you out of the house. But please be careful, Daddy. Don't push yourself too hard. You hear me?"

"I hear you, Gracie."

We chatted for a while about easy-going stuff — father and daughter chitchat. How she was doing at work. What boys she'd dated, or not. How I was dealing with things, or not. Grace is my escapism. That chuckle of hers is like womb music. After a few minutes, I heard her cover the hand-piece and mumble something to somebody beyond the range of the pick-up.

"I'm sorry, Daddy," she said as she came back. "Something requires my immediate attention. Can I call you straight back?"

"No rush," I said. "Take your time. I know you're busy."

Then she was gone. Call disconnected.

Lamely, I stared at the phone for a few seconds. When it didn't ring, I went over to the window and stared out at the Dali landscape.

Bill was right: this was Disneyland for adults. Mile after mile of themed hotels. Sprouting out of the desert like enormous glass cacti. Fed by streams of never-ending traffic and gorged on greenbacks.

In the far distance I could see copper-colored mountains with snowy peaks. Feathers of white cloud. It looked serene, peaceful – a far cry from the hustle and bustle going on nineteen floors below.

The room phone rang.

I twisted my neck to look at the phone sitting on the nightstand. Its red light was flashing. It rang for maybe three seconds, then stopped.

Then the cell shook in my hand. I answered automatically, keeping an eye on the room phone.

"Gracie," I said. "Have you heard from your brother lately?"

But it wasn't Grace's sweet southern tone that answered me back.

This new voice was deep and characterless. Imagine Darth Vader swallowing a *Speak & Spell* and you might come someplace close.

"Are you enjoying the view?" it rumbled in my ear.

I glanced at the anonymous number and frowned. "Bill, if this is you and your voice changer stunt again, I swear –"

The machine-driven voice cut me off with a haunting laugh. It was the kind of din I expect a photocopying machine would make if it had a sense of humor.

"It's a great view from the nineteenth floor, isn't it? Up there in the Emerald Tower."

My blood ran cold.

I rushed over to the door and peeped through the spy-hole: nothing in the fish-eye lens. Not even the Metro uniform.

"Whatever it is you're selling," I said, "I'm not buying."

"Even redemption?"

"It's out of my price range, but send me a brochure all the same. By the way, who is this?"

"Who do you think it is?"

"Someone with way too much time on their hands? A journalist looking for a weird new angle? Somebody who wants an autograph and thinks they've got to be Ted Bundy to get it."

The inhuman voice laughed, "Don't flatter yourself. I'm not even a fan."

I threw open the door and frightened the living daylights out of the officer still straddling his chair. There was nobody else in the hallway, in either direction. I went back inside, closed the door on the uniform's astonished face.

The anonymous caller was laughing on the other end of the line.

"Why don't you go bug somebody else?" I said.

"And miss out on all this fun? Aren't you even a little bit curious to know who I am?"

"I'm more curious to know how you got this number."

"You're a public figure. Try googling yourself."

I hung up.

The last thing I needed was a stalker tailing me around Vegas. One of the pitfalls of working high-profile cases is I get crank calls regularly. It's the bane of public life. Callers offering misdirection. Callers getting off on fake confessions. Every cracked and leaking teapot this side of the Mississippi.

Three seconds later, the room phone rang.

I watched the little red light blink on and off. Let it ring, maybe a dozen times. I was thinking there was no way the stalker could know exactly which room I was in. When it didn't stop, I picked up, heard heavy mechanical breathing coming down the line.

"Stalking is a crime," I said into the hand piece.

The caller chortled and cut the connection.

*   *   *

Almost immediately, my cell started bouncing around like a June bug on a hot plate. I dropped the room phone back in its cradle, determined to put my anonymous caller in his place. Then I breathed a sigh of relief as I saw the name on the tiny screen.

"Bill?"

"The one and only. Gabriel, are you anywhere near a TV?"

I glanced at the big flat screen facing the empty bed.

"Strangely enough, yes."

"Take a look at the Channel Ten News."

"Why?"

"Trust me, Gabriel, you'll want to see this. They've been repeating it on the nines for the last hour. Be prepared to be pissed."

I hung up, found the remote control and channel-hopped until I came to the desired station. The screen filled with the close-up image of an old, weary-looking guy in a thin Californian coat and sneakers. It was the same rough-cut guy I'd seen staring back at me from the closet mirror, moments earlier. I watched myself climb out of a black sedan, outside the *MGM Grand*. Sunlight glinting off of chrome work. Tourist cameras held high like ostrich heads.

I cranked up the volume, heard a voice I recognized: Stacey Kellerman. Her nasal drone accompanied the looped footage:

"*. . . new terror now stalking our city streets. Seen here, Detective Gabriel Quinn – made famous by his capture of The Star Strangler during the Star Strangled Banner murders here in Vegas several years ago, and laughably quoted by Newsweek as being one of the most formidable homicide detectives alive in America today – unsurprisingly declined to comment.*"

A standard school-year photograph of a young boy with blond hair and blue eyes appeared in the top corner of the screen. Immediately, a pang of anger blossomed in my chest. I had the same photograph on my basement wall back home.

"*Since failing to save Leo Benjamin last year from the hands of The Maestro, Detective Quinn has deliberately remained out of the public eye. Some say both his physical and mental fitness are no longer up to par. Is this the reason we ask that he was unable to save yet another innocent life here today? Has the Great Celebrity Cop become sloppy on the job?*"

The blood in my veins started to simmer.

The footage moved on to Stacey Kellerman herself, standing across the street from the *MGM Grand* entranceway. She had her back to the furor, probably filmed while I was up here, locking horns with Pinch Face.

"*Swiftly approaching his mid-fifties, the question on everybody's lips here is whether or not Detective Quinn is overdue retirement. Is he really up to the task of protecting our children from a serial killer responsible for five other murders in Los Angeles this week, and possibly many more in other States? Or should he have been hung out to dry when he failed to protect young Leo Benjamin from a murderer still at large even today?*

"*As a sick side note, this reporter has learned that one of the latest victims, Jennifer McNamara – a ten-year-old from Seattle – was found murdered in the very same spot where poor Leo Benjamin cruelly lost his own life less than a year ago.*

*"In the pursuit of public interest, this reporter asks: when it comes to protecting our children from mortal danger, has the Great Celebrity Cop still got what it takes? Has Gabriel Quinn the capacity to stop this killer? Or should he be put out to pasture before the lives of more innocent children are lost to his incompetence?*

*"In the last few minutes, a spokesperson for Clarke County had this to say . . ."*

I muted the TV, clenched teeth.

I had hot prickles, everywhere.

In one fell swoop, Stacey Kellerman had undermined my credibility live on TV and made me look like an old imbecile. Worst still, she'd made our case public domain.

# 67

Jamie Garcia had been raised with the philosophy that if a job was worth doing, it was not only worth doing properly, it was worth doing exceptionally. But nobody had warned her that such dedication came at a price. Her eyes were seriously beginning to throb. It felt like somebody had looped a metal tourniquet around her head and was slowly tightening it with a key.

Within the last forty minutes, the Coroner's Offices in Chicago and Philadelphia had faxed over the requested pathologist's notes on the homicides flagged up on the search for similar murders. Jamie had spent the last thirty-seven minutes poring over the three sets of reports, trying to connect invisible dots.

The desk she shared with Gabe was strewn with typed documents, hand-drawn anatomy sketches and black-and-white prints of morgue photography.

Intuition told her there was a connection here. But instinct alone wasn't enough to do the job properly, and definitely not exceptionally. She was aware that her apprenticeship in Robbery-Homicide had a limited lifespan. In three weeks' time, she'd be out on the streets; doing regular policing and proving herself there before she could even apply for a Detective rank here.

Her tutors back at the Academy had stressed on the necessity to make a great first impression – because great first impressions would open doors and facilitate swifter promotions.

But Jamie didn't want to impress.

She wanted to get it *right*.

She picked up a handful of monochrome snapshots: they showed the two deceased prostitutes from

Chicago and the dead psychiatrist from Philly. The photos had been taken on the mortuary slab. Different angles. A few close-ups of blue lips, ruddy dilated eyes, injection bruising. Death had a look about it, she realized. It was more than the fact that the bodies were unmoving and the faces empty. It was almost as though death itself was a disposition. A state in which the physical body adopted a strange muscular arrangement, where light itself became deadened.

The phone on the desk rang. She brushed aside papers and picked up:

"Jamie, it's Nadine Carr from the Crime Lab. I ran those tests on the ash you submitted and compared it against our exemplar range. A cigarette's chemical composition is like a unique signature. In this case, the levels of propylene glycol, calcium carbonate and Sorbitol point to a brand of smoking tobacco called Ukraine Gold."

"I've never heard of it."

"Maybe because it's manufactured in Europe under the Senate trademark."

"The killer smokes imported cigarettes?"

"I can't say that he does with any certainty – only that the ash you submitted comes from that brand of tobacco."

Something on one of the photographs caught Jamie's eye:

It was a shot of the murdered psychiatrist from Pennsylvania.

Jamie sieved through the woman's notes. The psychiatrist's name was Jeanette Bennett. She'd been a Medical Doctor and the director of a reputable psychiatry practice on Walnut Street, Philadelphia, specializing in children with psychoses. She'd lived in the leafy suburb known as Carroll Park, a short hop to the west of the city. According to the homicide report, Jeanette had been bound to the bed with lengths of cord before being beaten and then murdered. In the photograph, the naked body of

Jeanette Bennett was spread-eagled across the top of her bed. She'd had a fairly good figure for her age. A little podgy in the love handle area, but mostly in good trim. A swimming costume suntan line from some hot vacation and the remnants of an appendectomy scar.

Jeanette Bennett had been the victim of a brutal attack.

But there was something else too.

Something that sent a shiver scurrying down Jamie's spine.

# 68

Somebody needed to put Stacey Kellerman in the picture, I decided. I needed her to retract her character assassination, or in the very least give a balanced view. Bill was busy. That left me. But I had other pressing matters to attend to first.

I finished up at the Hoagland crime scene and made my way out into fresh air. It was colder than I remembered. Deep shadows cast by towering hotels. Slices of baby blue up above. Flashing neon. Droves of tourists drifting from one sprawling complex to the next. Every other vehicle a cab advertising shows and dancing girls.

I tried waving one down. None obliged.

"Get off the street!" one of the drivers hollered as I leaned off the sidewalk. The vehicle swerved, found its grip, then sped away. The cab behind it blasted its horn and shot past. I got out my police shield and stepped into the first lane. The next cab hit its brakes and skidded toward me on blue smoke, coming to a stop inches from my legs.

The driver popped his head out of the window.

"Police," I said before he could make a smart-ass remark. I opened up the rear door and climbed inside.

I saw the driver eye me suspiciously through the interior mirror as he flicked on the meter.

"Inkriminal," I said, and we pulled out into honking traffic.

# 69

Jamie couldn't get the image of the murdered psychiatrist from Philadelphia out of her head. The only way she could describe the woman's killing was with the word *sadistic.*

During what looked like a home invasion, the killer had gone out of his way to make the psychiatrist's death as brutal, as painful and as long-lasting as possible. The police had determined her attacker had waited for Jeanette to return home after a busy day at her practice before assaulting her. He'd waited in her closet, among her clothes; they'd found a man-sized depression in the hung garments and boot prints in the carpeting. He'd bound her to the bed and then inflicted terrible wounds to her body. It was clear from the outset of the attack that the killer had had no intention of letting her go. He'd done too much damage.

Every one of the eight-by-tens showed the same dreadful picture: the unearthly tranquility of death; blue-gray skin; bruising to the thorax; multiple puncture wounds on her lower abdomen; lacerations to her face, probably made by a small blade swept to and fro like somebody painting a portrait; small, round burn marks where her nipples used to be.

At first glance, the burn marks looked like scorched bullet holes. But Jamie knew them for what they were. She had one herself: a souvenir from a gang dispute in her youth. They were deep tissue burns caused by the applied pressure of a lit cigarette against the skin.

Jeanette had them all over her body.

It looked like she'd been drilled by a branding iron. Over and over. None of the wounds post mortem.

Jamie was holding her breath and fighting back bad memories.

She knew what these scars were.

They were the tattooed trademarks of a torturer.

# 70

The telephone number left by Patricia Hoagland on the notepad in her hotel room belonged to a downtown tattoo parlor called *Inkriminal*. I had the cab deposit me on the sidewalk, paid the fare and got out.

The place was part of a strip mall of retail stores a couple of miles north along The Strip. They were mostly tacky Vegas souvenir outlets, a one-stop tee-shirt shop, a pawnbrokers – that kind of thing. Everything rundown. You couldn't miss the tattoo parlor. There must have been a dozen large signs in various colors and fonts, proclaiming its existence. A few big arrows pointing to the doors – just in case you missed them. Windows coated in big peel-off stickers advertising exotic artistry and painful-looking body piercings.

I went inside.

The place was deeper than it was wide, with walls painted vermillion and a cops-and-robbers theme that complemented the establishment's questionable name. I could see reclaimed police bric-a-brac: bar lights from the roofs of patrol cars, a few dummies wearing skunk stripes and cuffs. Everything cheaply done. There were two men deeper inside the shop: one lying in an easy chair while the other drilled ink into his unsuspecting skin.

"Hi, welcome to Inkriminal. How can I arrest you?"

It wasn't the most original greeting I'd ever heard. But ten out of ten for effort. The greeting came from a young woman. She was standing behind a chest-high reception counter. She had a shaven head and complex tattoos covering every inch of skin from the throat down.

More metal pinned in her face than the monster from *Hellraiser.*

"I'm looking for Bob," I said.

"You here on a referral?"

"Kind of. Is Bob available?"

"Piercing or tattoo?"

I showed her my shield. "Just Bob."

She raised a studded eyebrow. "Is that for real? I mean, it looks just like mine." She pointed to a plastic version pinned to her lapel.

"Bob," I repeated.

The young woman leaned on the counter. I could see ghostly images flowing around her bare arms. Demons and angels. "Are you sure I can't interest you in a tattoo?" she said. "We have some great police designs. Plus discounts for genuine cops. How about an exact reproduction of your shield?" She saw the exasperated look pulling down my face, thought about it for a second longer, then added: "Tough crowd, huh? Not really the tattoo type? Okay. So, you want Bob? Well, you're looking at her." She extended a tattooed hand. "I'm Roberta."

We shook. "You're Bob?"

"In the flesh."

"In that case I need to ask you a few questions, if that's okay?"

"Sure, shoot." She grinned pearly teeth. "And I mean that figuratively." She leaned over the counter again. "Are you sure I can't interest you in some body art? Maybe a nasal piercing? You have the face for it."

"No."

"Your loss."

"I'll take it. Do you know someone by the name of Patricia Hoagland?"

I saw her think about. "Should I? I mean I know a Patricia Franken. That's her married name. I don't know if Hoagland was her maiden name. But she's seriously whacked-out. I mean, wow, seriously."

"Unmarried and definitely Hoagland."

Roberta stuck out a lip filled with silver loops. "Look, we get a lot of people in here. Mostly on a first name basis. We're a popular tourist attraction. Our clients come from all around the world. It's hard to remember individual names. Do you have a picture of her, or even of her tattoo?"

I hadn't seen any evidence of a tattoo on Patricia Hoagland. I showed Roberta a close-up photo on my cell, taken on the nineteenth floor of the *MGM Grand*. Saw her brow pull away all by itself.

"She had your number written down," I said, "on a pad. She was staying at the MGM."

A shrug. "I don't recognize her. I guess it's possible she could have made a booking."

"Could you check?"

"Sure." She opened up a big black ledger resting on the counter, glanced down the page, turned it to another and glanced down that one too. "Can't see anyone called Patricia. She had one of our cards, did you say?"

"Just your number. Written on a hotel pad."

A shake of the head: "Nope."

"Mind if I take a look?"

I saw her think about it.

"Easier here than going down to the station house."

She swiveled the ledger around. "Go ahead. Take a look. I'm not blind. She's not here."

I looked at today's page, scanned a list of a half dozen names. Nothing jumped out. I turned the page and scanned Saturday's bookings. Same thing. I looked at Sunday's. Nothing. Turned back to today's.

I stabbed a finger at an appointment. "What's this?"

Roberta spun the book around. "It's a new appointment. Someone booked in for a Rosicrucian, with me, today, at two."

"A Rosicrucian?"

She smiled, "Has anyone ever told you you're hard work?" She hefted a large photo album from underneath the counter. She flicked through plastic-covered images until she came to the desired page, then she spun the album around and pointed.

"A Rosicrucian is a tattoo."

It was a cross with a rose in the center. An ornate crucifix, centered with a big red flower head. I could easily imagine it being filled with ash and surrounded by petals.

No such thing as coincidence.

"The person who made this appointment," I began, "do you remember anything about them?"

"Only that he was male. He made the booking over the phone."

"What did he sound like?"

I saw her lips ripple. "You mean, was he excited, worried, nervous?"

"I mean his accent."

"He sounded like you," she said. "Like Elvis."

# 71

I stood on the sidewalk outside the tattoo parlor on Las Vegas Boulevard, letting the cool Nevada breeze sober up my thoughts. It was after midday: less than two hours before the person that had made the appointment with Roberta showed up at the tattoo parlor. Or didn't.

But if he did, I'd be here waiting.

I knew Patricia hadn't made the booking. That left only one suspect: *The Undertaker.*

I thought about Stacey Kellerman. The nuisance reporter had mentioned more murders in other States. I wanted to know if that was all conjecture designed to discredit my investigation, or if she had privileged information and inadvertently let it slip. She'd also mentioned both the little girl and the killer by our nickname – which was some feat, considering we hadn't released either to the press.

Judging by the content and timing of her report, she'd been clued-up long before I'd set foot in Vegas.

I needed to know the identity of her source.

I needed to know if she was in contact with the killer.

I had two hours to kill.

I walked the short distance north to the nearest hotel – a soaring concrete column known as the *Stratosphere Tower* – and caught a cab from their busy taxi rank.

The driver looked Vietnamese. The insides of his cab smelled of incense and there were bead rugs covering the seats.

"I take you downtown?" he speculated happily as I eased onto the backseat. "We got plenty hot ladies downtown. Plenty sexy."

He seemed genuinely disappointed when I declined his offer.

He caught my eye in the rearview mirror. "You not here for hot ladies? Maybe hot boys?"

"No," I said. "Channel Ten News studios."

Smiling toothlessly, the driver notched up the volume on his stereo as we pulled out into heavy traffic. It sounded like Asian hip-hop. We bounced south on The Strip, passing more monstrous hotels. Droves of tourists. Half a dozen lanes of nose-to-tail traffic at every intersection, separated by a palm-treed median.

My phone rang.

"Yes, Bill?" I shouted above music.

"Director Fuller's had the Governor of Nevada mobilize the National Guard. They're assisting the Nevada Highway Patrol to set up roadblocks and stop checks on every route leading out of the city, but mainly screening passengers leaving through McCarran. If anyone in the least bit suspicious tries to leave town, they'll be hauled in for questioning. Just a heads-up."

"Won't that raise public alarm?"

"Yeah, maybe. But we're feeding the media with a Homeland Security cover story. The Advisory System is already at Severe. We're saying it's routine exercises."

"Which is great," I said, "but you and I both know that stop checks are only effective when those doing the checking know who they're looking for. And even then the hit rate is less than one in ten."

Fuller's angry heart might be in the right place, I thought, but simply throwing dozens of bodies at an investigation didn't necessarily guarantee a conviction. For all we knew, *The Undertaker* may have already fled the State.

"What about that base of operations, Bill? Any luck with that?"

The show was being put together and run from our newly-commissioned command center: one of the Grand Ballrooms located inside the *MGM Grand's* Conference

Center – right beneath the Hoagland crime scene. Turned out the Las Vegas Field Office was undergoing a refit of sorts and was therefore out of the equation. I didn't mind; Hugh Winters, the Special Agent-in-Charge over there, wasn't in my fan club. Then again, I wasn't in his.

Bill had also commandeered a pair of terrace suites at the hotel, one for each of us, with connecting doors. Key on the pillow. Romantic. I thanked him for his generosity, but told him I was happy with the Pharaohs.

"We're flying people in from Quantico and Washington," Bill told me. "Mainly techies. Equipment. Most of my team. We got ourselves a regular witch-hunt going on, Gabriel. If your boy's still in town, we'll catch him."

*Or kill him,* I thought.

I told Bill about Sonny's idea to screen flight manifests against hotel guest lists. I heard him whistle on the other end of the line. Even with all the FBI's formidable resources he knew it would be a mammoth undertaking. All the same, he promised to get his team on it, soon as.

The taxi pulled up outside the *Channel 10 News* studios at the back of Paradise Road. I hung up and got out my wallet.

"Fifty buck," the driver announced happily over his shoulder.

I nearly fell off the seat. "The meter says ten dollars."

"Don't matter what meter say. Meter broke." He even rapped it with his knuckles to assert his claim. "Fifty dollar, or I call cop." He gave me another one of those smug, toothless grins – like the kind Dick Turpin had gotten down to a tee.

I flashed him my shield. "You take this kind of currency?"

His smugness vanished like donuts at a police convention.

*   *   *

The sunny reception area at *Channel 10 News* had plasma screens the size of pool tables on the walls, broadcasting various newsreels – including Stacey Kellerman's character assassination. I went through tedious introductions with a cheerleader receptionist who, after a little obfuscation, buzzed me up to the second floor.

I found the Chief News Director signing off forms with his secretary in a sunlit office. He nodded an acknowledgement when he saw me, and waved me inside.

"Sign my life away if I'm not careful," he remarked as the secretary presented one sheet after another for his attention. "Be two ticks, detective."

I used the time to survey my surroundings.

The whole of one wall looked like a shrine to the *Dallas Cowboys*. Signed photographs of the Chief News Director shaking hands with individual players in their blue-and-white jerseys. *Super Bowl Champions* memorabilia. Quite a collection.

"Used to play a bit myself, back in the good old days," the Chief told me as this secretary packed up and left. "Nothing major, you understand. Could have been, if this lousy knee hadn't busted itself up."

"They couldn't fix it?"

I saw him draw a rueful smile. "Long before the days of keyhole surgery and steroid injections. This rock's older than he looks." He stuck out a hand. "Hal Beecham. I run things round here."

Hal Beecham reminded me a little of the late JFK, Jr. – had he lived another couple of decades. He had on a sky-blue shirt open at the collar, a bright red necktie and a cream-colored waistcoat to match his buff chinos.

"Interest you in a homemade lemonade?" He got up and walked over to cabinet in the corner. "My wife spikes it with nicotine. Don't ask me how. Maybe it's better not to know. It's the business, though. Got itself a real kick."

"Sure," I said. "You an ex-smoker, Hal?"

"No, just a smoker who's no longer smoking." He poured two tall lemonades from a pitcher and threw some ice in for good measure. He handed me the drink. "You look hot under the collar, detective. Vegas can do that to a man."

I tasted the lemonade. "This is good."

"Glad you like it. I take it you're here about Kellerman?"

Preamble over. Beecham was in business mode.

"I do need to speak with her."

"Don't tell me: she's pissed you off."

"I guess."

"No guessing about it, detective. Kellerman pisses everybody off."

I smiled uneasily.

"Fact is, we let it slide because she's popular with the people. And that's what counts in this game. It's all about ratings, you see. The higher the ratings, the bigger the sponsors. The bigger the sponsors, the better the money."

"She's a loose cannon."

"Now how'd I know you were going to say that?"

Hal Beecham weighed me up over the top of his lemonade like a father meeting his prospective son-in-law for the first time.

"Detective, the thing you need to know about Kellerman is, she's driven. And there's no shame in that. This is a dog eat dog business. She knows where she wants to be and she knows what needs to be done to get there.

That girl's got her sights on the big boys." He saw my frown and added: "The networks: MSNBC, CNN, CBS, ABC."

"Ah, all the acronyms."

Beecham snickered, "Hell, if the deal was right, she'd even take a job at Fox."

"I need to speak with her." I repeated.

"About her thoughts on you? She's entitled to her own opinion, you know."

"Is that the network's opinion?"

I sensed Beecham's demeanor grow prickles.

I put down my lemonade. "Besides, Beecham, it's not what she said about me. Sticks and stones and all that. It's about the killer. She mentioned certain things we haven't released to the press. Things we haven't disclosed to anyone."

"And you need to know how she came by them, right?"

"I think she's in contact with the killer."

Beecham stuck out his bottom lip. "Should I be calling the network's lawyers? Seriously, detective. You need to tell me right now if that's the case. You and I both know the source of a journalist's information is confidential."

"What about moral obligation?"

He shrugged. "The First Amendment doesn't deal with morals."

"Even if her informant is a wanted murderer?"

"Makes no difference. Unless instructed to do so by a court of law, we aren't obliged to reveal our sources. You of all people should know that, detective. It's a breach of civil liberty."

"Her life may be in danger."

Beecham cocked an eyebrow. Didn't buy it.

I was taken-aback by Beecham's sudden closed-shop attitude. I'd hit a raw nerve with him and he had no reservations about going on the defensive.

"But I will tell you what I'm prepared to do," he said as he leaned on his desk. "If her informant is indeed the killer, we can both benefit from this. Here's what we'll do: in exchange for Kellerman's cooperation into revealing the identity of her source, and providing she knows it, we get first bite of the cherry at the upcoming press conference. Now don't look so surprised, detective; Sonny Maxwell's a good friend of mine and news travels fast in this town. She's told me there'll be one – we're just waiting on your say-so. Essentially, what I'm saying is, when it does take place, my network gets exclusivity on all the visuals. First questions, too. And if you catch this killer here in Vegas, I want it caught on Channel Ten cameras."

Without this man's consent, I realized, I wasn't going to get to speak with Stacey Kellerman – at least not on my terms.

"All right," I said with a nod. "But there's a condition: Kellerman tells me everything I need to know. Today. Before we arrange any kind of a news conference. She tells me who her contact is. When he contacted her. What deal she's struck with him. Everything."

Hal Beecham's lips formed the letter S on its side. "Why do I feel like there's an *or else* coming?"

# 72

You can tell a lot about a person by the contents of their fridge.

Stacey Kellerman's was devoid of food. Just two boxes of Californian red – one opened – and a sealed pack of *Buds*. The wine was hers. The beer was just in case somebody called. The beer had gone out of date a year back.

She poured herself a glass of cold merlot and took a hearty gulp as she closed the refrigerator door. She swirled it around her mouth, then checked her watch before swallowing it down.

Any second now.

She glanced at the phone sitting in its cradle on the breakfast bar – exactly in the same moment it began to ring.

"Congratulations, Stacey," the killer with the Max Cady voice breathed down the line as she picked up. "You made an excellent delivery. All the right inflections. I couldn't have done better myself."

"Let's get this over and done with," she said, cutting to the chase. She knew she had this guy on the back foot. Knew she had him right where she wanted him. It was time to press home her advantage. "We do this interview today. This afternoon. I have everything set up. Here, at my house. I'll make you bigger than Manson."

"Your home? Are you sure that's safe, Stacey?"

Risk versus reward.

"Would you rather I invite you to the studio? Trust me on this. We have to be discreet. You come here. We do the interview. I make you a star. Then you kill Kate Hennessey for me. Do you have a pen?"

"No need, Stacey; I know where you live. But why don't you come pick me up on that shining Kawasaki of yours instead? I'm on The Strip. A tattoo parlor called Inkriminal. You'll catch me if you come right now."

# 73

Michael Shakes couldn't get Stacey Kellerman out of his thoughts. And not because he wanted to rekindle their steamy affair. Far from it. He needed to talk with her. Urgently. He wanted to do the right thing, but he was conscious of her shooting the messenger when he did.

He gazed at the printout in his hand for long, uneasy seconds. Today, yesterday and every damned day since Monday. No matter how many times he read and then re-read the words, the meaning remained the same. A single string of typeface that would impact Stacey's world like an atom bomb. And guess who'd be hit by the fallout?

He filled his lungs and made a decision.

He was uncomfortable sitting on the information.

He had to tell her.

But it was no good telling Stacey over the phone. That would be cowardly. Insensitive. He had to do this right. Which meant he had to do it in person.

He folded the printout, slipped it in his pocket, then pulled on his coat and headed outdoors.

# 74

I made it back to the tattoo parlor on Las Vegas Boulevard with time to spare. But I didn't go inside. I didn't even hang around outside. I went straight into the liquor store across the street. I showed the kid behind the counter my shield. Through balding palms lining the median, I had a good view of *Inkriminal* from here. Plus, about fifty yards of the sidewalk on either side.

If the guy from the Ramada videotape came anywhere near for the two o'clock appointment with Roberta, I'd see him.

"Hey, you're the guy from the TV," the kid pointed out.

There was a TV on the end of the counter, running *Channel 10 News* with the volume turned low. I could see Stacey Kellerman rubbing my nose in it for all the world to see.

"You doing a stakeout?"

"Something like that." I kept my eyes pinned on the street, and thought about the pesky reporter. Hal Beecham had coughed up her contact details: an address for a place in Winchester, somewhere down Desert Inn Road, and a pair of phone numbers.

"What you watching over there?"

"Police business," I said. "Go back to yours."

I watched traffic move past, both ways. Watched people drift by. One or two called into the liquor store. I kept my back to their purchases. One or two called into the tattoo parlor across the street: foreign tourists looking for long-term souvenirs of their stay in the States. No one that remotely matched the fuzzy image of *The Undertaker* I had in my head: a tall, medium-build guy in black clothes and a black baseball cap.

At five minutes before 2 p.m., a big guy in a long dark trench coat went inside the tattoo parlor. He had a burning bush of red hair. No baseball cap. But everything else seemed to fit. Training teaches us to be prepared. I unclipped the strap holding the Glock in its sling. Waited. Wondering.

At one minute before 2 p.m., a motorbike skidded to a stop outside *Inkriminal*. The rider was clad head-to-toe in close-fitting black leather. Like *Catwoman* but without the shine and the little pointy ears. I watched the rider rock the bike onto its stand, up against the curb, then go inside the tattoo parlor. There was nobody else on the sidewalk. I chewed some cheek, debating whether or not to make a move. I waited two more minutes, but no one else came close.

When neither Big Red nor the bike rider came back out, I left the liquor store at a jog. I crossed four lanes of thin traffic and shouldered open the door to the tattoo parlor. Drew out the Glock.

I didn't know what to expect. Training tells us to expect the worst scenario in any case. I found Big Red behind the counter with Roberta. He was waving a handgun around in her face.

"Police!" I shouted. "Get your hands in the air!"

Both Big Red and Roberta obliged. Big Red had a face like a kid caught sneaking through his girlfriend's window. Looked like he might have just peed himself. Roberta just stared with scalding eyes.

"What the fuck, man?" Big Red yelped.

I'd adopted the brace position: legs apart, knees slightly bent, hips loose, both hands gripping the Glock so that my upper body formed an isosceles triangle, parallel to the ground, sights trained on the big guy's chest.

"Put the gun on the counter," I told him. "And easy does it."

"Everything's cool, man," he trembled as he obediently did as he was told.

"You okay, Roberta?"

She lowered her hands. "What do you think you're doing? This is Chad. He works here. And that's a tattoo gun, Einstein."

"Yeah, it's just a tattoo gun, man." Chad squeaked.

I could hear mocking laughter coming from farther down the parlor. Female laughter. A blonde-haired woman in tight black bike leathers. I put away the Glock.

"Well done, detective." Stacey Kellerman said as she walked toward us. She had a cell phone in her outstretched hand. She was videoing my reddening face. "You just made prime time."

*   *   *

It's not very often that I see red. But right at that moment everything in the tattoo parlor had a bloodied hue to it. And it wasn't rosy.

Stacey Kellerman buried the cell phone in a pocket. She'd just recorded the guy she'd been dissing all morning – making a fool of himself in public. No wonder she looked like the cat who'd found the cream.

She scooped a shiny black motorcycle helmet from the end of the counter. "I'll catch up with you later, Bobbie." She started for the door, grinning like the infernal Cheshire Cat.

"Stop," I said.

She ignored the request.

I blocked the doorway. "Stop, I said."

Stacey Kellerman leaned a shoulder into me. "Excuse me, detective. Haven't you made a fool of yourself enough for one day?"

I grabbed her by the elbows. I don't know what came over me. Sometimes we react irrationally. I heard her squeal. She tried pulling free, but my grip was unyielding.

"I need to talk with you," I said through barred teeth. "I need to know who your contact is."

But her knee came up. Faster than I could dodge. It thudded into my groin. Pain exploded across my abdomen, followed by a geyser of nausea. Stacey Kellerman pulled free from my weakened grasp. Forcefully, she shoved me into the counter. I doubled up in agony. I heard her tear open the door, start up her bike and roar away.

"Well, that was fun." I heard Roberta say. "Will you still be going ahead with the tattoo?"

I used the counter to pull myself straight. Hauled in deep breaths.

Chad was holding back a sneer.

Roberta turned the appointments ledger around and pointed to the two o'clock entry.

"I saw you on the TV right after you left," she said. "This is you, right? You're Quinn. For the Rosicrucian. I remember the man said that was his name. It was you who made the appointment."

# 75

The cool afternoon sun was on his back as the killer known as *The Undertaker* strolled the last block to his destination. He had his hands jammed in his pockets, cap pulled down. A newly-lit cigarette jutted out from between his teeth. Behind the cheap pair of *Wal-Mart* sunglasses, his eyes darted this way and that.

He was conscious of being caught on street cameras. It was harder being stealthy in broad daylight. In a society geared more towards the loud and the wacky, bland could stand out a mile.

A female jogger was bouncing his way. Tight gray running pants under a sporty pink tank top. A pink sweatband holding blonde hair from off a flushed face. Wires running from both ears, down to a music player strapped to her trim waist.

Randall slid his fingers around the bunch of syringes in his pocket. He could needle her before she'd know anything about it. Take her back to his room. Have some fun.

"Smoking kills," the woman breathed as she breezed by.

He blew a big cloud of smoke in her wake.

She gave him the finger as she loped away.

# 76

The killer had set me up. Some kind of a sick joke.

He'd used my name as bait to get me to the tattoo parlor for two o'clock – the exact same time Stacey Kellerman happened to be there.

I had no idea if he'd planned the encounter, knowing it would go down badly – for me. If he had, it had worked out beautifully – for him.

My blood was boiling.

I caught a cab to Deuce Street and started counting down house numbers as I strode along the sidewalk. I was angry. No point hiding the fact. Stacey Kellerman had embarrassed me twice in one day. I needed to clear the air. Clear things up. She needed to know that if she were in contact with the killer then her life could be in mortal danger.

Stacey was having fun with me.

But this was no game.

I'd called Hal Beecham from the tattoo parlor, only to learn that Stacey had taken the rest of the day off. No doubt celebrating her firework popularity. I'd taken the gamble on her being home.

Home, to Stacey Kellerman, was a neat little neighborhood in Winchester consisting mostly of two-floor townhouses stuck together in pairs. They formed a quadrangle of dwellings backing up to a small park. Clay tennis courts and a community pool.

I arrived at Stacey's place.

Nothing spectacular. Looked quiet. Black vertical blinds closed at all the windows. No motorbike on the driveway.

Maybe Stacey hadn't come home after all.

I reached up to rap knuckles against the front door. I wasn't leaving until I was absolutely sure.

# 77

Randall removed a glove from his hand and pressed two fingers against Stacey Kellerman's jugular. He detected the faintest trace of a pulse.

She was still alive – for now.

Overpowering the reporter had been easy. Expertly, he'd inserted the syringe into her throat as she'd entered the house through the door connecting it to the garage. He'd taken her by surprise, caught her before she'd slumped to the floor. He'd carried her into the kitchen – where he'd placed a dining chair in the middle of the floor space – then heaved her into it. Now he was standing over her. She smelled like a whore. Looked like one, too, in her skin-tight leathers. Everything fake. The shot of homemade secobarbital had knocked her out cold. It would keep her comatose while he set the scene.

A knock sounded at the front door.

Randall turned toward the noise – in the exact same moment Stacey Kellerman's house phone began jangling on the kitchen counter. He ignored the phone, but the knocking was persistent.

Curious, he backpedaled out of the kitchen and made his way down the hall to the front door.

# 78

No answer.

I waited a few seconds before banging on the door again, this time harder, longer. Then I listened. No sounds coming from within, as far as I could tell.

I took a step back and examined Stacey Kellerman's house from the outside. The vertical blinds prevented anyone from seeing in. No signs of life anywhere. A wooden side gate that looked like it was locked and barring entry to the backyard.

A middle-aged woman – walking a Red Setter – smiled uncertainly as she passed by on the sidewalk. I flashed her my shield and a hurried smile. She returned the greeting before moving on.

Then I dialed the cell number provided by Hal Beecham and continued rapping knuckles against the painted wood.

# 79

Randall leaned his brow against the inside of Stacey Kellerman's front door and placed an eye to the peephole. He allowed himself an uncustomary smile as he spied the Great Celebrity Cop standing barely a few feet away on the other side.

*Synchronicity.*

Question: was the Great Celebrity Cop alone or was the house surrounded by dozens of trigger-happy cops? Was there a SWAT team ready to break down the door any second and smoke-grenade him into submission?

Answer: unlikely. The Great Celebrity Cop looked like he was by himself. No heavily-armed back-up. No one to come running to his assistance if Randall decided to pull open the door and take him by surprise.

Randall watched as the police detective loomed up in the fish-eye lens. He saw him reach up and bang a fist against the wood. Tremors reverberated through Randall's skull. He soaked up the energy, his thoughts going back to his childhood, to a time when his father had banged angrily against his bedroom door following a family dispute.

Back then, Randall hadn't given in.

No reason to change anything now.

He left the Great Celebrity Cop to his knocking and returned to the kitchen, picking up a metal urn from the coffee table as he went.

# 80

I was revving up to climb over the side gate and check out the backyard when a bright orange Ford Mustang rolled onto the driveway. It was a souped-up number. No muffler. A black speed stripe running up the hood and over the roof. I recognized the driver as he climbed out. He had on a tan leather jacket over a coffee-colored roll-neck sweater. Yellow-tinted sunglasses. He was Sonny's partner: the basketball player type I'd seen on the nineteenth floor of the *MGM Grand*. Imagine Will Smith with Jackson Five tailoring.

He slammed the door and strutted over. "Hey. What's going on?"

"You're Sonny's partner. Right?"

"That's right." He stuck out a hand. We shook. "Detective Michael Shakes. But most people call me Milk."

"Milk? Oh, I get it."

"Sure you do. Any damn flavor you like. So, like I say, what's going on?"

"Right now, not a great deal. I came here looking for Kellerman. I wanted to speak with her. What brings you here?"

"Same thing. I take it she's not home?"

"Doesn't look like it."

"You tried her numbers?"

"No one's answering either."

"Not like Stacey."

I heard Shakes' cell phone ring.

"Excuse me," he said.

I saw him take the call, nod once, then twice and then his face lengthen like the shadows on Deuce Street.

"We'll be right there," he said. "Don't let anyone in and don't let anyone touch a damn thing." He closed the phone with a snap. "Seems your boy's struck again, detective. And it looks like he's doubled up this time."

# 81

A heavy-lidded police detective in a tweed jacket and loafers — who introduced himself as Duane Slack, twenty years in the service — met us as we climbed out of the Day-Glo Mustang. We were at the side entrance of the swanky *Bellagio Hotel*. No signs of the circus I'd seen at the *MGM Grand* earlier in the day. No Stacey Kellerman assaulting me with her microphone and her wraparound leg.

"Who sounded the alarm?" Shakes asked Slack as we hurried in the direction of the express elevators.

"Housekeeping."

"You kept everybody out — including hotel security?"

"Like you said. But Ira isn't happy."

"Screw Ira."

We came to the elevators. Shakes pressed the *call* button.

Slack caught my eye. "Your boy needs a putting down."

I wasn't exactly sure what *'a putting down'* involved. But who was I to argue? Defending the indefensible isn't my style. After all, Duane Slack was right on the money: if I let Anne McNamara's words continue to eat away at me, *a putting down* was the least of *The Undertaker's* worries.

We rode the fancy brass-and-glass elevator to the thirteenth floor in uneasy silence. Duane Slack smelled like damp dog.

Up on the landing of the thirteenth floor, a pair of no-nonsense boys from Metro were holding back a guy in a gray suit. He looked to be in his sixties, with white hair and a golden tan.

"It's a mistake keeping me out of this," he called after us as we made our way down the hallway. "You hear me, Shakes? You're making a big mistake."

"Pipe down, Ira," Shakes called back. "The whole town can hear you. And nobody likes the sound of your voice."

\*　\*　\*

The first thing that struck me as we entered the suite on the thirteenth floor of the *Bellagio Hotel* was the sickly-sweet stench. Crime scenes seldom smell like a candy store in the heat of summer.

This one did.

Slack explained, "The air conditioning was on full heat when we got here."

We moved deeper inside.

The suite was decked out in a similar décor as the one back at *MGM Grand*. The colors varied slightly, but only slightly. There was a wheeled food cart standing in the middle of a lavish living space. Remnants of eggs over easy on white crockery and silverware.

Slack motioned with a thumb, "In the bedroom."

The gold-colored drapes in the master bedroom were hauled right back. The room faced west, looking out over the Interstate and beyond. I could see the sun sinking toward snow-capped mountains, turning the window into a block of glowing bronze.

Two bodies were lying on the big bed: a man and a woman. Side by side. Both naked.

"Jesus H. Christ," Shakes breathed as we moved closer. "Now there's something you don't see every damn day of the week. Human porcupines."

The killer had gone to great lengths to cover his victims from head to toe in finger-sized hypodermic syringes. They jutted out at every angle. Easily a hundred protruding from the victims. Some containing red fluid. Most were empty. The whole thing looked like one of those modern art exhibits that wins all the big prizes and no one knows why.

Shakes turned to me, "Detective, does this fit with your boy's MO? You ever seen anything like this before?"

"No and no."

Truth was, I was in shock – still coming to grips with the macabre scene. On the ride over, I'd been hoping this wasn't the work of my boy, hoping it was an unrelated double homicide. I'd had enough of murder for one day. Enough of his madness. I wasn't entirely convinced that this was his handiwork.

Aside from the syringes, everything else was wrong.

This was a display of purpose, of controlled rage and channeled anger. A deliberate demonstration of the killer's intent. Made with painstaking precision. Nothing like I'd seen before.

On the wall behind the bed, in big brown letters a foot tall, the killer had smeared the words:

*If you could save a million lives by taking one . . . would you?*

"It's body chocolate," Slack told us.

"How'd you know, Duane – you tasted it?"

"There's a tub of it on the nightstand."

Shakes went over. "Otherwise known as love mud." He saw the look on my face and added: "Don't give me that look, detective. I'm engaged. Her name's Karen. She's normal. I'm normal. We're both normal, dammit. We're the definition of normalcy. We have a very normal love life. Now move on. There's no story here."

I shook my head. "So, what's *their* story?"

Slack read out loud from his notes: "Their names are Mark Roe and Sarah Gillespie. They checked in yesterday for a three night stay."

"What else do we know about them?"

He glanced at his pad, "Front Desk says they're here for a seminar."

"Which one, Duane?"

Slack walked over to an open suitcase lying on the floor below the window. He picked up a couple of brochures from the top of a pile and handed one to each of us.

"Microbiological Terrorism. Run by Harland Laboratories."

I leafed through. It was a slick, glossy production, filled with technical jargon and fabulous photographs of computer-generated molecules. I saw résumé pictures of Mark and Sarah, together with another guy with blond locks and trendy eyewear. I had a feeling I'd seen him somewhere before. The front cover showed a computer-generated DNA double helix floating against a nebulous background. The title above it read:

*Homeopathic Security - Fighting Microbiological Terrorism, Cell by Cell.*

"Your guy interested in saving the planet?" Shakes asked.

"Aren't we all?"

I rolled up the brochure and stuffed it in a pocket. I moved along the side of the bed. The surface of the nightstand looked like a miniature cityscape dusted in snow, strewn with sex toys and various kinds of lubricants. A pair of straws made out of fifty-dollar bills.

"Somebody was enjoying a party," I said.

Shakes was busy leafing through the brochure, "It's that kind of town. You'll get used to it. But stay here too long and it'll suck you dry."

Mark and Sarah were good-looking kids. Mid-to-late twenties. The kind of well-toned bodies borne through hours of daily exercise and strict dieting. Both had unruly dark hair, cut shoulder-length. The same roundish face and general head shape. They might have passed as brother and sister had it not been for the sex angle.

Then again, nothing surprised me these days.

I looked at Detective Duane Slack. "The only things here that match my killer's MO are the syringes. But even that's grossly out of character. There's no ash. No petals. No pose of interment. These two are holding hands. What convinced you it's my guy?"

"The toilet," he said bluntly.

"The toilet?"

"It's in the bathroom."

Shakes looked up from the brochure he was reading, "You don't say, Duane. Just show the man."

I followed Slack into the bathroom. He popped on the light.

There was a big mirror above a cluttered sink top. In words formed by bright pink lipstick, the killer had written the same message:

*If you could save a million lives by taking one . . . would you?*

But here he'd signed it: *'The Undertaker'*.

Slack pointed to the lavatory. "Take a look in the pan."

There was a pocket-sized hardback book jammed into the porcelain bowl. It was tilted face-up, just above the water line. I bent at the waist and peered closer. It was a book I'd seen before; I had one just like it on a bookshelf back home. A signed first, in fact. I recognized the cover. Recognized the author.

I got on my haunches and levered it free.

# 82

"I don't give a shiny shit about your protocols, Ira," Shakes was saying to the gray-suited guy still being restrained on the elevator landing. "We need access to the surveillance system. Now."

His name was Ira Rosenthal. He was the head of hotel security, I learned. He was ranting and raving and looked like he was about to pop a blood vessel or maybe two.

"You have no right keeping me out of that room, Shakes. I'll be filing a formal complaint, and personally taking it up with the Sheriff."

Shakes was having none of it. "I said cool those pipes, Ira. As of now, that room is a controlled crime scene. It's under our jurisdiction. You can have it back when we're through with it. Now show us the damned tapes or I'll bust you for obstruction."

Ira thrust out his wrists. "Do your worst, Shakes. See how far it gets you. You ain't seeing nothing without a subpoena."

Three minutes later, a livid-faced Ira Rosenthal led us to one of the soundproofed vaults squirreled away deep in the bowels of the *Bellagio*. While Shakes had continued to argue the toss with Ira, I'd phoned Bill. Bill had called Director Fuller, who in turn had contacted Ira's bosses. No casino wanted to make an enemy of the FBI – and especially not of Norman Fuller on a manhunt.

I had a feeling Ira wouldn't let us hear the last of it.

"You got a fallout shelter down here too?" Shakes commented as we walked along a wide hallway lined with big steel doors. "I bet this place could take a direct hit from a bunker-buster and come through unscathed."

Ira wasn't in a talkative frame of mind. He swiped a keycard into a slot next to one of the big doors. He closed one eye and placed the other against a small funnel poking out of the swipe machine.

"Look at Ethan Hunt here," Shakes snickered.

Behind the bombproofed door, the small, dimly-lit vault was a hive of electronic activity. Three walls covered floor-to-ceiling with flat panel monitors. Most of the screens showed overhead views of blackjack tables, casino thoroughfares, slot machines. A semi-circular control desk was in the middle of the room, manned by four eagle-eyed techies wearing pin microphones. It looked like we were in Mission Control, Houston.

I looked at Ira. "We need to see all the elevator footage from midday."

Ira tapped one of the techies on the shoulder. "Run snapshots of the thirteenth floor. South wing elevators. Midday until three."

The techie began hitting keys on a flat keypad.

"The system records a linear stream of all elevator activity," Ira explained tightly. "It's also set up to take hi-definition photographs of everyone entering and leaving the elevators."

"Long live Big Brother," Shakes said.

One of the big panels in front of us lit up in a colorful mosaic of tiny pictures. I put on my readers and peered closer. There must have been over a couple hundred thumbnail images. Each viewpoint was from the upper rear of an elevator carriage. Doors open. Showing either guests entering or leaving. Sometimes both.

"We're looking for single white males," I said.

The techie touched a control and the mosaic shuffled itself. Most of the thumbnails dropped off the bottom of the screen like shards of broken glass. We were left with sixteen larger pictures.

"That's some crazy shit software you got there," Shakes said.

I scanned the images, two standing out straight away. Both showed the same man in a long dark coat and black baseball cap, leaving the elevator. Slightly different shots.

I pointed, "That's him."

The techie discarded the other fourteen frames so that the pair in question filled half the screen each. The images were much crisper than the one on the Ramada tape. Hi-res. Full color. Japanese tech.

Shakes came in for a closer look.

The suspect was wearing a knee-length black coat. Black jeans and sneakers. I could see wispy blond hair sprouting from underneath his black cap, collar-length. His back was to us. Everything else was guesswork.

"Why does it show him leaving twice?"

The techie pointed to the time stamp in the corner of each window. "There's forty minutes between both these frames. The first shows him arriving on floor thirteen. The second shows him leaving."

"Can we see the video for that?"

The techie expanded the second image to fully fill the screen, then switched it over to the video feed. He fast-rewound from the time of the snapshot and we watched as the empty elevator ascended to the thirteenth floor. The doors parted. Our suspect was standing on the elevator landing, with his back to the camera. He walked backwards into the carriage and pressed for the lobby.

"Son of a bitch," Shakes breathed. "He knew we'd be watching."

"He touched the floor button," Ira said.

"Sure, but he's wearing gloves."

Then the suspect did something totally unexpected. Keeping his back to the camera and his face tilted toward the floor, he turned his head, raised his hand and gave us the finger.

*The Undertaker* actually gave us the finger.

I heard Ira Rosenthal say, "I'll be damned."

"Freeze it," I told the techie.

The image froze. There was writing stitched into the black cotton of the killer's baseball cap. A white stylized font – like jagged lightning.

"Zoom in on the hat."

The techie hit keys. Now the front of the killer's cap filled the screen.

Ira read the words out loud: "Black Death. What the hell is that?"

"It's a European rock band," Shakes said with a snort. "What the hell do you think it is?"

# 83

Jamie had been staring at the blank laptop screen for fifteen unproductive minutes before Captain Ferguson came over and joined her at the desk she shared with Gabe. She still had a humungous headache and waiting for people to return her calls was starting to fray at the edges of her nerves.

"How's it going?" he asked.

She blinked. "Good. Thank you, Captain."

Jamie had learned to keep her answers short. There was no room for fluff in real police work. Not like her Academy assignments.

The Captain nodded. "I just want you to know I appreciate the hours you've been putting in. I also appreciate we threw you in at the deep end, and I know it can't have been easy for you."

She managed a tired smile. "Best way to learn, Captain."

"It's also the best way to come unstuck. I'm wondering if we're putting you under too much pressure, expecting too much of you too soon."

He must have been watching her for some time, she realized. Seen her staring into space, rubbing tired eyes and drinking too much coffee.

"Nothing I can't handle," she said with a brief smile.

She saw him study her for a second or two. Felt like he could see right through her façade.

"Gabe speaks very highly of you, Jamie."

Jamie felt her cheeks prickle.

"He thinks you're excellent detective material."

"It's certainly a privileged position to be in," she said. "This apprenticeship. I consider myself extremely lucky. I've really enjoyed everything so far. Feel like I've really been able to contribute."

"Good. You have. What about the case, though? Have you made any headway today?"

Jamie leaned back in the chair. She reeled off the day's small discoveries to her attentive captain. No major breakthroughs. No correlation that she could figure between the Coroner's reports other than what they'd already discovered. She was still waiting on information coming from the online rose retailer. No word on the whereabouts of the possible survivor. She was waiting for the post office near Prospect Park in New York to get back to her, hopefully with a forwarding address. But tomorrow was Saturday and it wasn't looking too promising.

"Always waiting for something," the Captain said in his soft, measured way. "Where's this rose retailer based?"

"Maine."

"I'll get the local PD up there to put some pressure on them. In the meantime, I want you to take the weekend off. You have an appraisal first thing Monday."

The statement came as a surprise. She tried to hide it, unsuccessfully.

"Walters and Phillips have everything under control here," he added. "You've done more than your fair share. We've had you doing long shifts all week. It's time you went home and got yourself geared up for Monday. Come to the appraisal fresh."

Jamie was dumbstruck.

There it was – in a nutshell. Officially, she was off the case until Tuesday, at the soonest.

The Captain slid a sheet of paper across the desk. "Before you sign off for the night. Do with this as you see fit."

He got up and walked away.

# 84

In eight short hours, the FBI task force operating under Bill Teague's direction had converted a humdrum hotel ballroom into a *James Bond* movie set. Busy as the stock exchange. Big projection screens all over the place, broadcasting real-time views of The Strip, streamed from sidewalk cameras. There were two rows of tables running the full length of the cavernous room, down the middle. Pushed back-to-back. Cluttered with computers, flat panel monitors, coiling cables. Coffee machines on overdrive at either end. Techies working keyboards, comparing notes on clipboards and spooling off printouts.

The hunt for *The Undertaker* was in full swing here at the *MGM Grand* in Las Vegas.

We were seated in a side room: me, Shakes, Bill and eight other serious-looking Feds. Black leather chairs around a long teak conference table. This was Bill's handpicked team of highly-specialized profilers shipped in from Quantico. Not really here to do my bidding. The murders in California were incidental to their prime objective – which was to nail the son of a bitch that had slain their Director's niece. I was here as a matter of courtesy. I knew my place. Never stopped me. There was a trestle table with stacks of white cups and several metallic canisters against one wall. No one was drinking the coffee. And none of the cookies had been nibbled at either.

Everyone in the conference room had a sheaf of eight-by-tens on the table in front of them. Full color images of the *Bellagio* crime scene. Only one or two had them fanned out.

"We've issued an All-Points Bulletin," Shakes was telling our FBI audience. We'd spent the last ten minutes going over our findings. "It's not much of a description, but it's the best we have to date."

Before leaving the *Bellagio*, I'd had Ira's techie burn to disk the recording of the killer. Make duplicates. Then print out some color stills for ID purposes. Copies had been sent to the Metro PD, to the Nevada Highway Patrol camped out on the edges of town and to the National Guard at McCarran International.

"Pretty soon every roadblock and city cruiser will have photos to back up the APB," Shakes concluded. "If this dude tries leaving town, or even so much as moves around in public, we'll catch him."

"Providing that is he doesn't change his appearance," one of the Feds said.

I leaned forward. "How far have we got with the hotel guest lists and the flight manifests?"

Another Fed spoke up. He was a sweaty-browed type with a receding hairline and sunken eyes. His name badge read *SSA Miles Tomlin*:

"Some of the highbrow establishments are refusing to play ball without a court order." He opened a file, glanced at it. "So far, we have fifty returns. Mainly the more popular hotels. All check-ins made this last week. Almost one-quarter-million names."

Somebody whistled. It sounded like me.

I turned to Shakes, "Exactly how many hotels are there in Vegas?"

I could see him adding it up, "Now there's a good question. Within the city limits and counting motels too, you're looking at somewhere approaching three hundred. Give or take."

"As for the flight manifests," Tomlin continued, "all but two carriers are accounted for. All being well, we should have the complete passenger lists by no later than midday tomorrow. Again, it's a judicial issue."

"Can we get subpoenas?" I said. "For these highbrows?"

Bill cut in, "Already on it, folks. I spoke with the DA personally about thirty minutes ago. She's sweet-talking a Justice of the Nevada Supreme Court as we speak."

"We also have agents working door-to-door." Tomlin added. "Checking out known criminals. There's a chance somebody may be harboring him."

I held up a photo of the love mud scrawling we'd found on the bedroom wall back at the *Bellagio*. "What are we making of this message?"

"Could be a threat," someone suggested. "Or a warning."

I looked around the room. One of the Feds – a slender blonde with Himalayan cheekbones, whose name badge read *SSA Glenda Hoyt* – spoke up: "It reminds me of something Luke Chapter mentioned in one of his papers."

I pushed myself a little straighter. "Please explain."

"Luke Chapter was an eminent Princeton psychologist. He authored several venerated books and papers about parapsychology."

I nodded. "The investigation of psychic abilities. That's right up your street, Bill."

"Not even in the same city," he said and followed it with a wink.

"Where's the connection, Agent Hoyt?"

She cleared her throat. "Luke Chapter specialized in studying people who claimed to have predictive powers. One particular paper was titled The Hitler Dilemma."

"It's pulp fiction," Bill said dismissively. "Full of open-ended questions and answerless arguments." He turned to me. "Chapter really let himself down by aiming at a mass market with that one. I'm surprised they didn't make a movie out of it and had Tom Hanks play the lead."

I smiled. "Maybe it's in the pipeline."

"Yeah, maybe."

I looked back at Glenda Hoyt. "What else?"

"In the paper, Luke Chapter posed a morality question: if you could predict the future, would you try and prevent disaster?"

"Whoa," someone breathed. "That's way too heavy for a Friday evening."

She smiled, "It gets heavier. Luke Chapter cited Adolf Hitler as his prime example. He postulated the question: if you knew in advance what the baby Adolf was to become, would you kill him when he was still a child?"

I saw Mike Shakes look a little uncomfortable. "Isn't that paradoxical?" he said. "I mean, come on people, I've seen those movies and they never end well, either for the villain or the protagonist."

I saw Glenda Hoyt frown mountain ridges.

"Does our killer's words actually appear in Chapter's paper?" I asked.

"I can't say for definite without referencing it," she answered. "But to me, your killer's message – if you could save a million lives by taking one, would you? – sounds a lot like Luke Chapter to me."

My brain hit a brick wall and bounced back. "Okay. Let's rewind. You say Chapter used to teach at Princeton. What happened to him?"

"He found religion," Bill said. "Inevitable, I suppose – with a name like that. The last we heard, he'd shacked up with a New Age commune out in sunny California."

"Could Chapter be the killer?" Shakes asked.

Bill shook his head. "He'd be in his seventies by now."

"All the same," I said, "we should find out if he's still in that commune. Check if he has alibis. Maybe even see if he's brainwashing anyone who might carry his torch. And while we're at it, get names of everyone who ever attended one of Chapter's lectures. See if any of them pop up on the hotel guest lists." I looked around the room. "Anything else?"

Glenda Hoyt was strumming manicured nails on the table. "Maybe we have this the wrong way round. What if this killer is the voyeur – the baby killer? It makes sense if you think about it that way. It would mean he's the one trying to prevent genocide. Taking one life to save millions."

We all looked at each other.

Everyone was thinking the same damning thought.

Then the room exploded into a noisy brainstorming debate.

I leaned back and let it take its course.

Theories and speculative ideas rolled around the table. I heard words like *paranormal, savior, psychotic* and *delusional* being freely tossed about. It was like sitting at a tennis match as fantastical concepts were slammed back and forth across the room.

After a couple of minutes, I banged on the table and the noise subsided. "Agent Tomlin?"

"I agree. The argument makes sense – especially if this killer believes he has predictive capabilities."

"Agent Hoyt?"

"I know it sounds far-fetched. And I don't believe he can do it for one minute. But if we're right and he believes it, then we can't ignore it."

"In other words," I began, "it's not important what we believe. It's important what *he* believes."

"In any case," Bill said, "we need to think like him. If he believes he's saving millions by killing a few, then so should we, no matter how erroneous his logic is, or if it's all just a self-serving prophesy."

I was out of my depth. Maybe you would be too. My thoughts swimming round in circles, barely treading water. I couldn't understand how anyone could kill an innocent child on the whim she might grow up to be a killer. Bible study had taught me about an eye for an eye, but for the life of me I couldn't see any godliness in us all ending up blind.

# 85

Rochelle Lewis lives twenty miles southeast of Las Vegas. On an edge-of-town circular in a newish housing development in Boulder City. I'd never been to Rochelle's place. Never quite gotten round to it. I didn't even know if she'd be home, or even if she still lived there. Listings had no telephone number registered to the property.

I commandeered a cab out of the city and watched the eye-watering Las Vegas Strip sail past, with its Christmas tree hotels and its flashing neon billboards.

My mind was mangled up like a pound of spaghetti.

The conclusion of our task force debrief had left me in a spin and shooting off on a new tangent. Up until an hour ago, we hadn't a motive for *The Undertaker's* killings. Then he'd left us a message and the writing had been on the wall:

*If you could save a million lives by taking one . . . would you?*

The FBI's interpretation of this message boiled down to a killer taking lives to prevent a future where millions more would die – unless he acted with deadly conviction.

I didn't know how I felt about our new theory.

I am not good with paradoxes. I don't hide the fact. The thought of time travel has me jumping backward through hoops. In my black-and-white world, I deal with facts, not fantasy.

But I couldn't ignore the possibility of it being his motive – no matter how insane it sounded to me. I have learned to keep an open mind. You'd be surprised what flimsy reasons incite people to kill.

Understanding this killer's motive would help us predict his pattern.

I couldn't ignore it.

Up until ten months ago, Rochelle Lewis had lived in Los Angeles. She'd lived there all her forty-five years. No reason to change that. She'd been an elementary school teacher with a good pension to look forward to. Not much in the way of family, but enough to keep her rooted. Then something had happened to make her up sticks and seek solitude in another State. I had no idea if she were still teaching, or if she were still alive. Last time I'd spoken with Rochelle she'd tried clawing my eyes out.

We passed McCarran airport and took the cloverleaf interchange onto Interstate 215. Headed east through the darkened desert toward Henderson at a breezy fifty-five.

Two years ago, Rochelle Lewis had made three mistakes. The first mistake was she'd met a man one night. It had been an ordinary meeting in an ordinary bar. A chance encounter. Just a few friendly drinks. A few expertly-aimed compliments. The second mistake was she'd moved him in the very next day. He'd led her to believe he was a traveling salesman, supplying piano accessories to outlets along the West Coast. He'd even had a van full of piano parts and pedals to prove it. He'd used Rochelle's place as somewhere to crash for a few weeks whenever he was in LA. Used Rochelle in more ways than that, I guess. The third mistake had ruined her life.

Rochelle had known her part-time boyfriend as Travis Kimball.

But I knew him by another name.

# 86

None of the names on the sheet of paper given to Jamie by Captain Ferguson looked remotely like that of a killer. No Charles Manson or Jeffrey Dahmer. No red circles highlighting suspicious entries. Nothing that stood out like Hannibal Lecter at a Sunday barbecue. Just sixty or so innocent-looking Ramada guests with partial credit card numbers attached.

Jamie screwed up her face until it hurt.

She knew a similar list was being compiled in Vegas. But without it to cross-reference against, these sixty or so ever-so-ordinary-looking names might as well have been her own Christmas card list.

She was about to call it a night when her laptop announced she had new emails. She maximized the mail screen and scanned the new arrivals. Only one had a red flag against it. High priority. She clicked the message. The sender information said it was from the online rose vendor. Her heart rate quickened. There was a text document attached. The title read: *'Requested Buyer's List'*.

With jumping beans in her belly, Jamie printed the document out to hard copy.

# 87

The cab scuffed the curb and came to a quiet stop five or six houses down the street from Rochelle's place. I gave the driver a fifty and asked him to stay put, then walked the rest of the way on tentative toes. If Rochelle was home I didn't want her spooked and out the backdoor before I'd rung the bell.

It was a clear, crisp night in Nevada – the kind that causes Californian coats to let in the cold. I ignored it. Breath smoked from my lips as I walked beneath a black velvet sky sprinkled with diamonds. I could hear the wound on my scalp complaining with each step. I ignored that too. I kept my gaze locked on Rochelle's place as I moved in and out of shadows. The house looked exactly like its neighbors: single-floor, side awnings, shingle and shrubbery out front. Nothing special. Good place to stay hidden, I thought.

There was a pickup parked underneath the sunshade, down the side of the house. A dark-painted Ford with Alabama plates. In good condition. But not even last year's model.

I stopped at the threshold, suddenly wary about speaking with Rochelle again, face to face. Our last get-together hadn't exactly gone down well.

I looked up and down the quiet street and drew a deep breath before venturing through the open gates.

There were lights on inside the house. The muffled sounds of a TV coming from within. Sounded like somebody was watching a sports game. I peered through the glass in the front door, looking for signs of Rochelle. Nothing. Just coats on hooks and scatterings of shoes. I grabbed a peek through the large front window; saw a small untidy living room with blue upholstery and green carpeting. Magazine skyscrapers. Hillsides of clothes. There was a TV in one corner, showing a rerun of a game between the *Cowboys* and the *Colts*. Nobody watching. An opened bottle of *Coors* standing lookout on the arm of a chair.

The side gate wasn't locked. I popped the latch and snuck through. It creaked, but no one noticed.

The backyard was dark; I went slowly, letting my eyes adjust. The area was mostly rough-cut gravel and Yuccas – worn-down bristles on a balding brush. There was a large plastic hopper pushed up against the rear wall, probably for housing outdoor stuff. I could taste gasoline. An old rotary clothes dryer was stooped in one corner, looking like a broken satellite antenna. An uncoiled hose snaking across the yard. Random pots of paint and a pair of workman's boots near the backdoor.

I realized I was holding my breath and slowly let it out.

What was I expecting from Rochelle? She hadn't been co-operative the first time round. In fact, she'd gone out of her way to be obstructive and dumb. Was I hoping she'd mellowed during the last twelve months – that she'd help fill in the gaping holes in a case I wasn't supposed to be working? Why should she? I'd helped ruin her life and sent the man she loved into hiding.

I shouldn't have even been here. I should have been in the situation room, watching Bill and his team process data. I didn't care.

For now, all thoughts of *The Undertaker* were far behind me in Vegas. I had to get this out of my system.

There were two windows at the rear of Rochelle's place: one deep in darkness, the other glowing with pinkish light. I snatched a glance into the illuminated window, saw a master bedroom with red-painted walls and red bedding on an unmade bed. A red bulb glowed behind a red shade. It looked like a boudoir. To one side, I could see a brighter light coming from a bathroom. I detected movement and pulled back a little from the window as a woman came out of the bathroom. She was an African-American, in her forties. A shaven head and a nose-piercing. She hadn't had the shaven head a year ago. She'd had the nose-piercing. Rochelle Lewis. Slightly heavier than I remembered. She was in her underwear. I pulled back some more.

Then my cell phone sang as loud as a siren.

And her eyes flicked my way.

I jammed a hand in my pocket, fumbling for the off switch. Finally I found it and stopped the infernal thing from ringing.

Rochelle was looking directly at me.

I receded into shadow, heart pounding.

She came to the window, trying to see out into the darkness. Her brow creased, eyes narrowed.

I took another step back onto loose shingle.

Rochelle looked right at me.

I held my breath.

She cupped a hand against the glass and peered through.

I saw her eyes widen.

Then something like a freight train hit me from behind.

It catapulted me into the stucco wall. The air whooshed from my lungs. Stars spangled behind my eyelids. I felt something hard dig into the back of my neck, forcing my face into the rough rendering. I felt skin scuff off. Heard my nose creak, then crack.

"Fucking peeping Tom."

It was a man's voice: booming in my ear, angry, gravelly. Hot breath that reeked of beer. The guy fisted me in the right kidney, hard. The pain was excruciating. I couldn't blame him; I'd have done the same had I found someone skulking around my backyard in the dead of night. I tried to yelp as the pain exploded across my back, but my lungs were still pancaked. And I wasn't going anywhere.

Another punch. Lightning bolts zigzagged in my eyes.

The pain was immense.

Instinctively, I swung an arm around. I felt my elbow connect with my attacker's ribs. Heard foul breath loose from lips. For a split second his weight eased off. I took advantage. Swung my arm again – this time higher, harder, aiming for the face. My elbow struck bone. Pain ricocheted up my arm. My attacker stumbled backward, groaning, clutching at his busted nose.

I spun round and sucked in air.

"I'm the police," I gasped.

I couldn't make out his features in the darkness. He was heavier than me by thirty pounds, easy. A few inches taller. Probably in better shape too.

"I know," he growled back, snorting out blood.

I went for my weapon.

He came at me like a charging bull.

The air went out of me a second time as his head plunged into my stomach. My shoulders crunched the wall. More scuffed skin. I tried bringing up a knee. Anything to dislodge him. Missed. He punched me in the groin for my efforts. Tears sprang in my eyes. I brought both hands in, flat, toward the sides of his neck. It was a move I'd seen in a Steven Segal movie. It ought to have knocked him out cold. It didn't. So much for my years of martial arts training in front of the TV. The guy pummeled me some more for my troubles. I couldn't breathe. My whole body was aflame with pain. I tried stamping on his foot. Dig my fingers into his face. Anything to get the Doberman off. This wasn't Queensbury Rules. This was survival. I used the wall as leverage and managed to heave him back onto the gravel bed.

He slugged me right between the eyes.

I saw the elbow come up, the fist curl into a wrecking ball, the arm straighten like a piston. Nothing I could do about it.

My head rocked back like a punching ball. It rebounded off the wall with a *crack*. I heard vertebrae pop in my neck.

The son of a bitch went for the early knockout. The elbow came up again. The fist curled. But somehow I managed to twist as the arm straightened like a piston. And my attacker's fist hit the wall right next to my ear. The shock to his system was enough to let me throw my full weight into him.

We locked antlers like competing stags.

Then we were spinning around the gravel yard. Engaged. Embraced. Alternating leads. Fred and Ginger would have been proud. Neither of us could let go. Round and round we went, struggling for dominancy. Kicking up gravel. Sparks flying.

Our energies were sapping. Mine quicker, it seemed.

I had a tiger by the tail. We both knew it.

Let go and I was a dead man.

Round and round we went. Grappling for eyeballs. Soft flesh. Stamping at feet. Anything to get the upper hand.

The blood in my muscles had become battery acid.

My foot snagged the water hose. The guy leaned into me. I stumbled. He tried a head butt. Missed. We collided with a stand of Yuccas. I went over, backwards. Took on needles. My attacker came with me. Coming down like a brick wall. Knees digging into my shoulders. Pinning me to the broken stone. Then he started hitting me in the face: *bam, bam, bam*. Like a baker pummeling dough. Each blow sending sparks crackling through my brain

In the movies, this is where the good guy would normally catapult the bad guy off. Reverse roles, overcome him, then throw on the cuffs. March him back to the Precinct for processing. But this was real life and I was beat. I was out of breath, out of shape, and out of moves. Worst of all, my attacker knew it. He socked me in the mouth one last time and I gagged on blood.

"You don't know when to leave well alone, do you?"

He had a southern drawl. The Alabama plates made sense. A mixture of spittle and blood drizzled my face. Some of it spluttering up from my own busted lips.

Lamely, I gazed up at my attacker through dazed eyes, trying to make out his features in the swirling darkness. All I could see was a mop of unruly hair blocking out stars.

I felt him rummage under my coat. Weakly, I tried to stop him. He knocked my hands aside. He took out my Glock. I was powerless. At his mercy. I had a sudden thought that this was it: I was going to die here in the backyard of Rochelle's place, on a freezing Nevada night, at the hands of a drunken brawler.

The muzzle pressed against my cheek. Cold. Hard. My attacker brought his face down next to mine. He was gasping, bleeding, wheezing.

"Stop looking for me. You hear me, Quinn? I said stop looking for me. It's over. Don't come after me. I know where your children live."

My strength was gone. I was a dead fish. Flapping around on deck. Landed. I couldn't compute his words. Couldn't do a damned thing even if I could. I was numb with pain. Muscles on fire. Beat.

Through my daze I saw him clamber to his feet. Step back. Catch his breath. Look down at my pathetic broken body. Heard my Glock hit the floor as he dropped it on the gravel near my head. Then he walked away.

Through ringing ears, I heard him argue with Rochelle out of sight. Somewhere down the side of the house. Heard the pickup rumble into life. Heard it reverse at speed out of the driveway. Then tear down the street on screeching tires.

I stared at the star-spattered sky, breathing blood.

I was sore, but I was alive.

I still couldn't move, but that would return.

I was bruised and sore, but that would pass.

Then a woman's silhouette appeared above me.

"Rochelle?" I gasped. "Call nine-one-one."

"Fuck you, Quinn," she said as she stamped on my face.

# 88

The theater was packed out to bursting. This was obviously a popular show despite the extortionate entrance fee. The killer known only to himself as Randall Fisk was slouching in his seat, trying to look inconspicuous.

An expectant hush was settling over the excitable audience. Dry ice seeping in from the edges of the stage as the lights went down. One or two people murmuring in awe.

He could see patterns in the mist, but was in no mood to decipher them. Tonight was all about fun.

A barely-audible undulation sounded from the in-house speaker system, slowly gaining volume.

It sounded like somebody breathing.

A single funnel of brilliant blue light pierced the packed auditorium, radiating from the back of the stage. It roamed across the glassy-eyed audience like the beam from a lighthouse. Faster and faster it went, sweeping to and fro, flickering to the quickening pulse of the soundtrack.

The audience was mesmerized.

*Sheep.*

A few flashing lights and some fancy music and *hey presto* they were all spellbound by the low-budget lightshow.

Not Randall.

A deafening thunderclap exploded through the theater. The stage lit up in blinding blue light. The hypnotized audience erupted into crazy applause.

Randall shook his head.

Onstage, a world-famous magician and illusionist had appeared as if by magic in a cone of light. His pristine white suit and cape shone like freshly-laid snow. A blonde-haired woman dressed in a long, white skin-tight dress, split at the side from ankle to hip, was standing at his side.

Behind them, glistening against a backdrop of twinkling stars, was a glass box as big as a *Greyhound* bus. It hadn't been there a moment earlier. Smoke and mirrors.

The soundtrack kicked back in. It sounded like computerized rain. Broken glass falling against sheet metal.

The world-famous illusionist and his lovely assistant started cavorting around the big glass box. They stirred up eddies in the dry ice. Look: nothing inside. No mirrors. No hidden trapdoors. Nothing but fresh air. Aren't we special?

A large Stars-and-Stripes flag began to descend from the dark rafters above. It was *big*. Bigger than the glass box.

Throughout the theater, people were *ooh*ing and *ahh*ing with patriotic fervor.

Then, as the flag completely covered the stage, the music stopped, abruptly, plunging the auditorium back into expectant silence.

Randall could hear his or someone else's heart thudding.

Every unblinking eye was on the world-famous illusionist.

Like a master craftsman he played his part to perfection.

In unison, the illusionist and his girl grabbed the flag at either end and dramatically ripped it down to the stage.

A wave of stunned amazement swept through the theater.

No one could believe their eyes.

A great white shark had materialized inside the glass box, suspended within a thousand gallons of cold salt water.

The audience went ecstatic – many standing to cheer and clap and holler their appreciation at the breathtaking feat.

The air was electric.

Onstage, the world-famous magician was fisting the air, reveling in his own egocentric glory.

The crowd was going wild.

The killer known as *The Undertaker* realized he was clapping, and stopped.

As the opening chords to the 1980's rock anthem *'The Final Countdown'* started blasting out across the theater, he got to his feet and made his way outside.

# 89

Rochelle and the darkness were gone. In her place was an angel, framed in brilliance. Her features were veiled by blinding light. She was stroking my cheek. Speaking a foreign tongue. I tried to move. Tried to reach up and touch her radiance. But I was frozen. Encased within the essence of her magnificent aura. She touched a finger to my forehead and everything faded to black.

I had no idea how much time had passed since Rochelle's boot had floored me cold. I couldn't remember dreaming. When I cracked open sticky eyes everything was blurry. It stayed that way for a few seconds until the world swam back into focus.

I was no longer lying prone and vulnerable in Rochelle's backyard. I was in a hospital bed. Starched linens. A claustrophobic cubicle with the plain green curtain drawn all the way around. An Emergency Room someplace. I could hear movement beyond. People talking. I pushed my head into the pillow and groaned; I told you: I have a healthy aversion to hospitals. The realization was softened only by something I hoped wasn't morphine, but was glad that it might be.

The blurriness returned and I succumbed to sleep.

When I came to a second time, there was a woman leaning over me. She was outlined against a soft bluish glow. Her hair was scraped back into a ponytail. Little dream-catcher earrings swinging pendulously from her earlobes.

"Sonny?"

It was someone else's voice. An old guy's. Crackly and wheezy.

"Gabe," she acknowledged.

Everything was slightly out of phase. Colors filtered. Like I'd woken up in a Martin Scorsese movie.

"You had me worried for a moment," she said. "What were you doing out there? It's the middle of the night."

It took a second to make the connection.

"Taking care of business."

"Don't you believe in back-up?"

Sonny sounded concerned. I couldn't feel it, but I knew my face was all busted up. I must have looked a mess.

"Where is this?"

"Boulder City Hospital. They brought you in about two hours ago. I've been here the last hour. You're lucky the cab driver came looking for you — otherwise you could be in the morgue right now."

"I'll be okay," I lied.

I could see she didn't believe me. I didn't believe me either.

Sonny snapped her fingers in front of my nose. "Stay with me, Gabe; you keep fading out."

"Woozy."

"I'm not surprised. They shot you full of analgesics. They thought you'd cracked some ribs, but the X-rays show they're just badly bruised. You've taken a real good hammering to the head, though. Be concussed for some time." She leaned closer, blocking out the light. "Gabe, listen to me. This is important. Did you see who attacked you? Was it him? Was it The Undertaker?"

"No." It was a half-truth. But it was also a half-lie. And it didn't sit well with me lying to Sonny.

"Did Rochelle Lewis do this to you?"

The thought was interesting. I might have smiled if my face hadn't been so tied up doing an impression of a pumpkin. "Maybe the broken nose," I said. "I don't remember after that."

Sonny nodded and pulled back. "We have Rochelle in custody. I'm charging her with assaulting a police officer. Anything else you want to add?"

Harboring a fugitive?

"No," I said. "That should do it."

"So I'll ask again: what were you doing out there?"

It was just Sonny and me in the room. A uniform standing guard on the other side of the wraparound curtain, out of earshot.

"Rochelle's connected to a cold case," I confessed. "She used to live in LA. I'd heard she'd relocated here. Thought I'd catch up with her. See if she had any new information."

Sonny still looked circumspect.

"You should have called me. I would have come with you."

"You have a family, Sonny. I didn't want to inconvenience you."

"Too late for that now," she smirked.

A nurse came in and gave me a tetanus jab.

I think I blacked out.

# 90

I examined my busted-up face in the passenger mirror and wondered what the hell I'd been thinking. Or maybe I hadn't been thinking at all, and that was the root of all my woes.

There was antiseptic salve all over my face: cold and tacky. Busted lips. Blackened eyes. Everything swollen. New stitches in my right eyebrow and in the wound inflicted by Father Dan's killer. I looked like I'd just done five rounds with Mike Tyson.

But it was all superficial. Cuts and bruises heal within days. It's the internal scarring that never goes away.

We were riding back to Vegas in Sonny's SUV. I had another bottle of pills to add to my collection. Instructions to basically sit still and do nothing for the next twenty-four hours – as if I could.

Sonny was upset. Damn it. Not visibly, emotionally, teary upset like Peter McNamara had been over the murder of his beloved daughter. But she was upset all the same. I've been around women long enough to recognize it. She was upset with the thought I'd been an inch from death. Under her watch and in a situation of my own doing. One she could have prevented, had I included her.

Her hands were wrapped around the steering wheel like a child riding a rollercoaster for the first time.

I felt compelled to say something. Anything. It wasn't her fault.

"You know, you're right, Sonny," I began a little tentatively, "it was a stupid move. I could have gotten myself killed."

Her eyes stayed on the road. "Next time, call."

"I'm hoping there won't be a next time."

It was a lie, of course. I had no intention of not pursuing Rochelle's part-time boyfriend to the bitter end. Even if that end was mine.

"Really, Sonny, I am sorry for dragging you away from your family like this. It was inconsiderate."

This time, the truth.

"Don't dwell on it," she said. "I have understanding neighbors. They're retired and never seem to sleep much anyways. They love the kids and they're happy to watch them at short notice. But I don't take advantage of it."

We drove through darkened desert. Great swathes of nothingness pricked by distant lights. All of it watched over by a million twinkling stars. I touched a hand to an aching cheek and winced. I could see an unearthly glow to the northwest where Vegas blazed, occluding stars and pretty much everything else. It looked like the whole city was ablaze.

"What were you hoping to get from the Lewis woman?" Sonny asked at length.

"I don't know."

Truthfully, I didn't, Not exactly. I thought about it. What had I hoped to achieve by visiting Rochelle's place? A lead? Some indication pointing to a killer's whereabouts? Certainly not a good pummeling. At some point I would have to talk with Rochelle. Preferably in an interrogation room, with her under pressure. Force her to confess everything she knew about her part-time boyfriend Travis Kimball.

I kept quiet for a few minutes. I was angry with myself. I could feel it bubbling away inside of me like an indigestible nob of gristle.

"Is Rochelle connected to The Undertaker Case?" Sonny probed suddenly.

"No. A cold case," I confessed before realizing it. "The Piano Wire Murders." I tried to catch the words as they escaped, but my busted-up lips had other ideas. I saw Sonny glance my way, renewed worry in her brown eyes. "It's a long story," I said. "The short version is, chasing The Maestro has become an unhealthy obsession of mine."

"The Maestro?"

I hadn't even mentioned the killer's name to anyone other than Harry in over ten months. Not even to Eleanor – especially not Eleanor. Why was I confiding in a woman I'd known for less than a day? I looked at Sonny. There was an assuredness about her that felt safe. An invisible aura keeping the bad at bay. Then again, Sonny didn't know me like Eleanor knew me. She didn't know my history – which meant she wasn't so damned judgmental.

"It's the last case I worked before this one," I explained. "A year ago now. The Maestro is a serial killer. He abducted his victims and kept them bound with piano wires. Kept them alive and tortured for days before they bled to death. I couldn't catch him, Sonny. No matter what I did he was always one step ahead."

"That's who attacked you: The Maestro?"

I didn't have to say anything; Sonny knew the answer.

Despite the fact that Travis Kimball knew we'd keep tabs on Rochelle, he'd still had the balls to hole up with her in her new Nevada digs. I had no idea of how long he'd been here, shacked up with Rochelle, while I had undertaken my private crusade to catch him. What I did know was that he wasn't there now.

We drove on, following red taillights, heading for the glowing jewel in the middle of the desert night.

My cell phone rang. I glanced at the illuminated screen. I had several missed calls – including the incoming one – all from Jamie.

"Gabe, thank God!" she said as I answered. "I've been trying to get hold of you for hours. I have good news."

"You got an address for the survivor?"

"No. Something better than that. I have his name, Gabe. I have The Undertaker's name."

\* \* \*

No such thing as coincidence, right?

Only one name had turned up on both the Ramada guest list and the rose buyer's list. And it was bouncing around in my head like a firecracker:

*Ethan Davey Copes.*

"You sure on this, Jamie?"

"Absolutely," she said. "Ethan Davey Copes is the only name that appears on both lists."

Not a common name like John Smith – one that could get mistaken for a match.

*Ethan Davey Copes.*

The name felt strangely familiar – like a name from my past. It prodded at the farthest edges of my memory: *Hey, remember me?* I tried to recollect, but couldn't quite pin it.

John Wilkes Booth, James Earl Ray, John Wayne Gacy, Lee Harvey Oswald . . . *Ethan Davey Copes.*

Sounds like a killer's name, doesn't it?

"And here's the double whammy," Jamie said. "The rose retailer delivered a cool-pack of Dark Secret roses to the Ramada on Vermont last Friday."

"Just in time for the killings," I breathed. "Seriously, Jamie, this is great work. Looks like you've gone and unmasked our boy. The next question is: do we have a billing address?"

Jamie didn't disappoint.

It was a place just outside of Jackson, Tennessee. Back in my home State. Closer to Bill's neck of the woods than mine. Was this where I'd heard the name before? I wondered.

"Text me the address, Jamie. And while you're at it, forward copies of both lists through to the situation room here, in Vegas."

"Already on top of it."

I hung up and looked at Sonny. "We have his name. Plus a Tennessee billing address."

"Wow. Nice work. What now?"

"We find out everything we can about Ethan Davey Copes."

# 91

Adopting identities sometimes meant adopting personality traits. Not only did it add to the realism of the role, it also made Randall's actions seem somehow more excusable.

Let's face it; you couldn't pretend to be Joe Soap the Bank Manager if all you did was talk street lingo and wear gang colors.

The real Randall Fisk had dabbled with hookers. Therefore, so did he. But unlike his namesake, he'd used them as guinea pigs – mainly to test out his homemade chemical concoctions. These days, he didn't need to. He'd long since perfected the formulations. These days, he used hookers as stress relief.

Randall, the killer now being hunted throughout Nevada, wasn't familiar with this part of town. But every town had one. They were all the same, the world over. Not hard to find. The scent of the working girls gave it away.

The radioactive dial on his wristwatch told him it was long after 2 a.m., and yet here they were: the gutter flowers – in full bloom and waiting to be plucked.

He picked her out of the daisy-chain line-up: the one with the tiny plastic skirt and the leopard-print tank top. High black heels. Long bleached hair extensions. Eyes caked in black mascara. Anything but his type. This was role-play, remember?

He showed her the money, through the open car window. She feigned delight. She let him check out the merchandise. She even knew of a cozy backstreet motel where they could hang out and have fun together. Maybe snort some cocaine if her dealer was home.

Randall gave her a hundred dollar bill.

And the hooker climbed eagerly into the rental.

# 92

It was almost four in the morning by the time we got back to Sin City. But you wouldn't know it; the place looked just as busy as it had done in daylight hours, if not busier.

Sonny dropped me off outside the *Luxor*.

"Get some rest," she ordered as I placed stiff legs on the sidewalk. "Seriously, Gabe. I mean it. You need it. I need it. Let the Feds do the legwork tonight."

"Thanks for the ride home. I'll catch up with you in the morning."

I waited until the SUV had disappeared down the glittery Strip before going straight to the hotel registration and checking out. Then I made my way to the situation room at the *MGM Grand*. You see, I am not the world's best at taking advice, either.

The FBI and I had something in common: we were both insomniacs. The situation room was buzzing with overnight personnel. Collating information. Inputting data. Processing. Then distributing it to a hundred agents out in the field.

I searched for Bill.

"Detective Quinn? Can I help you out in any way?"

He was a middle-aged G-Man with a gray goatee and salt-and-pepper hair. A checkered waistcoat holding in a middle-age paunch. Dark circles under puppy dog eyes.

"The name's Marty Gunner," he announced as he grasped my hand and shook it. "Assistant Director of the Critical Incident Response Group. I just flew in from Washington. Got here a couple of hours ago."

"Taking over from Bill?"

"Assisting. The Director feels two heads are better than one. My team will integrate seamlessly with the boys and girls already here from the BAU."

"Fuller's pulling out all the stops."

"Who wouldn't if they were in his position?" He made a nod toward my facial wounds, at the blood still damp on my shirt and tie. "Can I ask what happened?"

"Old habits," I said. "Have you seen Bill Teague anywhere?"

"I'm afraid he's retired for the night. And I wouldn't risk waking him either – unless it's a life or death emergency. Is it, detective, a life or death emergency?"

"Maybe something even better."

I told Marty about the killer's name and his home address and gave him the task of unveiling Ethan Davey Copes.

"Leave this with me. I'll get my people straight onto this," he assured me. "We'll cross-reference it against hotel guest lists. I'll also scramble a tactical unit to Jackson. See if we can shake this guy down."

"Thanks, Marty."

"Happy to oblige. Go get some rest for a while; I'll call you the second we have something."

I left the situation room and sniffed out an all-night deli. My tussle with *The Maestro* had left me ravenous. I picked up a hefty coffee and a pastrami on rye and located an empty table overlooking a bank of screens showing horseraces from around the world.

Now it was all a waiting game.

It would take time for Marty's tactical unit to deploy to the address in Jackson, to check out the property and to report back. Plenty of time in which the FBI's powerful computer system could regurgitate every scrap of information it had on Ethan Davey Copes. Then it was a matter of fitting all the data pieces together to form a digital picture of *The Undertaker*.

The two evidence bags in my jacket pocket had survived the fistfight better than me. I put them on the table. The smaller of the two held the credit-card-sized piece of plastic found at the Hoagland crime scene. I couldn't look at it without white-hot rage pluming inside of me. The larger bag contained the pocket-sized book retrieved from the toilet at the *Bellagio* crime scene.

I used a napkin to handle the book out of the clear plastic wallet.

The world is full of people who reckon they know best. Black when it should be white. Left when it should be right. These days, everybody's a social commentator. The killer had defaced the book. Every page was crossed out with a bold red marker pen, the single world TRASH scrawled across, on the diagonal, in capitals.

The killer's handwriting had a slight leftward-lean. I wondered if we had an expert on hand who could read between the lines. Give us a new slant on *The Undertaker's* character.

But the real question burning in my mind was: why had *The Undertaker* defaced one of Bill's books?

# 93

Randall believed that God was a chemist.

It was there. In black and white. Biology 101. Anyone who didn't think so didn't know squat about anything.

Randall's love affair with chemicals had come about purely by chance, one summer break, when he was just a kid and not using the Randall Fisk pseudonym. His grandparents had bought him a chemistry set for his birthday. Nothing extraordinary. Nothing that would cause him to overturn medical science or win a Nobel. Just a simple kit of test tubes, litmus papers and packets of sugar-like compounds. But it would be enough to spark curiosity in his young, probative mind.

The set had remained boxed-up for months, gathering dust on a shelf. Then he'd broken his leg falling from a tree. A stupid mistake; too busy watching cloud patterns and daydreaming of future happenings to notice how high he'd climbed, or how thin the branches had become. The doctor had confined him to his room, with a prescription for plenty of medication and bed rest. The whole of the summer long.

Boredom had soon set in. There was only so much TV to watch, only so many books to read. He'd opened the chemistry set after the fourth day of imprisonment, and wondered why he'd never done so before.

Within the first week, he'd produced a substance that killed flies the moment it touched them. Burned them to a crisp. *Smoking.* He'd had to raid his grandparents' kitchen and the garden shed to achieve it. Do lots of experimenting, testing, until he'd mastered it, tamed it. The following week he'd created a chemical that made his skin go numb. A week later, he'd devised a solution capable of enhancing the effects of his painkillers.

He'd soon discovered that chemicals were all-powerful. They were capable of great healing and of great harm. In the wrong hands they were dangerous. But in the right hands they were godlike.

Chemistry was fundamentally simple.

Atoms made elements made molecules made substances.

It was the whole of everything.

A universe in a drop of water.

The trick was knowing what chemicals worked well together, which could enhance life and which could snuff out life.

That's why he was convinced God was a chemist.

# 94

Tennessee lay under an inch of snow, kept crisp by the freezing nightly temperatures. It was as if the entire State had been sprinkled with icing sugar.

Special Weapons and Tactics Agent Gary Cornsilk was so keyed-up he could gladly puke. But he held it in. The FBI helicopter was cramped. In attack-mode blackout. The puke would ruin everything if he let it out: equipment, armor, his credibility.

Reputation was golden in this game.

Under the cover of darkness, the dark gray military-style Bell chopper was heading west out of Jackson. Skimming along the icy South Fork tributary of the Forked Deer River system. Out toward the cold Mississippi River. Every now and then, the helicopter banked steeply to avoid a skeletal bridge or frost-furred power lines, or swerved around an out-branching of snow-crusted trees. The pilot was good. Kept it tight against the deck. On this moonless night, Cornsilk could barely make out the trees, let alone the black snake of freezing water they were following.

*"You better hit the ground running or the ground will come up and kick you in the face."*

With his mouth pressed into a grim line, Cornsilk recalled the barked words of his Training Officer. He'd almost baulked when the command had come through from the Memphis Field Office. Heights unnerved him. Always had. But he dared not show it.

In this game, weakness meant ridicule.

The pilot was piping music into their earpieces: *Ride of the Valkyries*. Totally unapt. This wasn't Vietnam. None of these boys had seen real action. They were all wet behind the ears; like him. All out to prove something. Him too.

The chopper skewed on its side for a few seconds as it tracked a river bend. Cornsilk tasted bile rise in his throat. Didn't show it. One of his colleagues pulled a comical face. Cornsilk laughed along with the rest of the six-man SWAT team.

*Fuck you, White Man*, he thought.

Over the sound of soaring violins, Watch Commander Nielsen hollered a few reminders into his microphone, into their ears:

*Investigate the suspected home location of a serial killer presently terrorizing the West Coast.*

*No bloodshed.*

*Reconnaissance mission only.*

*In and out.*

*Round up any residents for questioning.*

*Secure the premises and await back-up.*

*Clean and sweet.*

*Textbook.*

Sure.

Weren't they always?

*Here we go . . .*

The chopper made a stiff bank to the right.

Cornsilk clung to a hand loop. Clung to his puke.

One or two of his colleagues whooped with glee.

Then they were landing with a thud in a snowy field. The hatch was pulled back. Icy air blasted their faces. They bailed out into ankle-deep snow. A frozen top layer. Like walking on broken glass. The helicopter sprang back into the night as the team waded through stiff grass toward a black copse of trees, leaving claw-mark furrows behind them.

Nielsen quickly fingered out instructions.

Adrenaline flashed through Cornsilk's chest when he saw he was tasked with taking the front entrance along with the Watch Commander.

This was it. The real deal. Here was his chance to make his mark. Leave all these cretins speechless once and for all.

They separated into three groups of two and fanned out. They worked their way through the frozen undergrowth in the direction of what appeared to be a farmhouse. No lights. No sounds of human inhabitancy. No cooking smells. A dark, ominous structure. Could be anything. A big black lump of nothing in a bitch of a backwater.

They crept closer across hardened earth.

Cornsilk had his Heckler and Koch UMP butted up against his shoulder. Night-vision powered up. He could see his breath form a freezing fog, billowing like glitter dust in his goggles.

It was a big building all right. A few ramshackle outer structures. A tall silo out back. It all looked long abandoned. Overgrown. Covered in a thin sheet of snow. The broken carcass of a tractor lay off to one side, half buried by brambles. Smashed windows. Discarded farm machinery. Scrub invading everything. No Christmas card scene.

Cornsilk began to feel a little disappointed.

Nielsen shook his fist.

Cornsilk was to go in first.

What an honor!

Deep breath, now.

No stalling.

He flipped off the safety and inched his way across the icy ground.

A kettledrum boomed in his chest.

The front door was the only thing about the whole place that didn't look decrepit. In fact, it didn't look that old at all.

Cornsilk reached out with a gloved hand and tentatively tried the handle.

Unlocked.

The door clicked open.

He glanced over his shoulder at the Watch Commander lingering a yard or so behind.

Nielsen was an impatient man. Didn't take delays kindly. He gave Cornsilk a curt nod.

*Get inside! Move it!*

Cornsilk threw open the door.

Pitch-blackness.

It took a moment for his infrareds to adapt. Green-washed patterns of a hallway and stairs shimmied into view.

Then something caught his eye.

Something blindingly-white in the edge of his enhanced night-vision.

*What was that?*

He took a cautious step forward. Caught a whiff of benzene.

It was a small flower of radiance. Mushrooming toward him from underneath the staircase.

His eyes widened in disbelief.

"Fall back!" he screamed into the pin microphone. "It's a trap!"

# 95

The call came through at around five in the morning, Pacific Standard Time. I'd retired to my new terrace suite at the *Grand* after beating myself up about letting *The Maestro* beat me up. I'd tried catnapping, but slipped in and out of a fugue state instead. Truth was, I couldn't sleep knowing that Harry was dead and that *The Undertaker* had killed multiple times in Los Angeles and in Las Vegas.

The 5 a.m. call came with bad news:

Disaster had struck in Jackson, Tennessee.

Two SWAT agents were dead. Three more were seriously injured. One in a critical condition. That made six innocent families torn to pieces overnight. And all the responsibility of *The Undertaker.*

I felt sick to the pit of my stomach.

"We think he may have used some kind of a liquid explosive," Assistant Director Marty Gunner was telling me over the phone. He sounded shaken. His words were like thorns against an elephant's hide. "We're thinking maybe hydrazine nitrate. Too early to say for sure at this stage. Preliminary reports say the place is a mess. We're in the process of sending in a recovery and evaluation team as we speak. It's going to be daylight and then some before we crack the lid on this one."

"Marty, I'm sorry."

*The Undertaker* had booby-trapped the address in Jackson. He'd rigged a bomb in advance to stop us digging deeper. Knew we might trace him back to the farmhouse. Knew as soon as anyone came snooping the place would be blown to smithereens.

"What about our prime suspect, Marty?"

I heard the Assistant Director let out a tremulous sigh.

"So far, we have his IRS records, social security details, driver license, that kind of thing. We're still pulling information in from Clarksburg. Once we have his financial records we can track his credit trail. We're expecting a full breakdown within the next couple of hours."

I lingered on the rim of the mattress and rubbed tired eyes. Computers processed data at the speed of light. But people didn't.

"So what do we know about him?"

Copes was thirty-two. Born and raised in Jackson, TN. The FBI had a copy of his birth certificate. But no marriage license. It looked like he'd worked on the family farm up until the recession had hit. No record of gainful employment thereafter.

"What about hotel guest lists, Marty?"

"So far, he's a no-show. But we're still checking."

The driver's license had come with a photograph. But it was an old picture, taken when Copes was a spotty teenager.

"Why no up-to-date photo?"

"Because when it comes to updating information," Marty said, "some people are lazy. They re-use their original photograph for renewals until someone says otherwise. In any case, I'll get the picture blown up and sent out to all our checkpoints. Maybe get one of our boys to artificially age it."

I thanked Marty and left him to it. Nothing I could do to speed up the process.

I flopped back onto the bed and stared up at the ceiling. It was dark in the room, but I could still see stars. I licked at the dried antiseptic salve coating my lips and thought about the mess we were in. Thought about the premeditated nature of everything this killer did. Thought about the Feds blown to bits in Jackson. Thought about

Mark and Sarah – the human porcupines – lying in a display of controlled rage on their bed in the *Bellagio*. Thought about Patricia Hoagland with the possibility of the little girl's blood on her hands. Thought about Helena Margolis with her lethal stab wound. Thought about Marlene and Samuels lying in their rings of rose petals. Thought about little Jenny McNamara who would never grow up to become anything other than a sad statistic.

Then I thought about Harry and of never hearing his self-induced laughter again. Thought about Father Dan slain by the devil himself. Came to the conclusion I was through with thinking.

I went into the bathroom and stared at the horror show face loitering in the bathroom mirror.

In one fell swoop our investigation had escalated from a statewide manhunt to a nationwide witch-hunt.

Things were about to hot up.

# 96

The faint wail of police sirens came to him over the motel roof. It sounded like the cry of a prehistoric beast as it roved through the pre-dawn night. Studiously, he listened to the sound. Swaying in tempo to its long, sinuous undulations.

Randall was standing on a narrow balcony-cum-walkway. He was outside of a motel room somewhere in downtown Vegas. Not exactly sure where. He was leaning against a rusty railing. Buck-naked and lacquered in sweat. Pulling long drags on a hot cigarette.

As far as cheap backstreet accommodations went, this had to be one of the worst he'd ever seen. Everything threadbare. Not seen a lick of paint in twenty years and then some. Not even any water in the communal pool, just a thick grime ring and broken tiles.

Through the grubby ground-floor window of the room opposite, he could see a couple making out. The man was a greasy punk. Likely a drug user. He had his larger-than-life girlfriend pinned up against the wall and was hammering her from behind.

The killer known as *The Undertaker* breathed through his cigarette.

His work here in Sin City was done. His grand finale complete. While the cops had been chasing their tails, he'd been busy putting the finishing touches to a plan he'd been working on for months. Now, he had a flight booked and an exit strategy. He had business elsewhere.

Later today Elvis would be leaving the building, but not for good.

Randall flicked the cigarette into the filthy pool basin.

Behind him, on the bed inside the motel room, the hooker was still out of it, curled in a fetal position on the tatty mattress. He'd injected her with enough of his creative chemistry to keep her compliant for hours. When she woke, she'd have no memory of him or what had transpired here. Probably for the better.

He returned to the room and threw on his clothes. He studied the hooker while her dressed, admiring the patterns of sweat-streaked make-up. The whorls of tangled hair. The leopard print of her skin where her fake tan had worn away. So many patterns, so little meaning. He tore a crisp one-hundred dollar bill from his wallet and tossed it onto the bed. Then he went into the bathroom and took a leak in the cracked toilet bowl.

A previous tenant had scrawled the words '*time to check out*' across the paint-peeling wall where a mirror had once hung. It was either written in old blood or old feces. Hard to tell against all the years of accumulated grime.

The killer known as *The Undertaker* closed the door quietly on his way out.

# 97

My second wake-up call came less than an hour after the first: an urgent message to meet with agents Stubbs and Cherry, downstairs at the hotel taxi rank. I'd spent the interim going over the killer's kill patterns in my head, trying to figure everything out. Seeing if the FBI's theory of him killing the few to save the many held water. But all thoughts of the killer believing he was psychic had left me dry.

I threw on clothes, raked back my unkempt hair, and made my way outside.

The first rays of dawn were glimmering off the highest floors of the mountainous hotels, turning the streets into chasms and the buildings into sheer cliff faces.

Agent Cherry was waiting at a long black limousine, with the door opened and the engine running.

"You should see the other guy," I said as I saw him scowl at my blackened eyes.

Roughly, he bundled me onto the backseat and slid in after me. Agent Stubbs was up front. We careened out onto the roadway and headed north along The Strip at a lightning's pace.

I buckled up. "One of you boys mind telling me what all the excitement's about?"

"Screw you," they said in unison.

We ran a stoplight. Then another. And the next. Raced on to the sound of honked consternation. Two minutes later, alloys scraped against the curb hard enough to rattle teeth and we jumped out onto a wood-decked sidewalk.

We were outside the *Treasure Island Hotel*, looking like we'd emerged into an outdoor set belonging to a swashbuckling musical. I followed Stubbs and Cherry across a large wooden jetty onto the hotel property. There was a large replica of a Spanish galleon out front, moored in a smallish waterfront of fake cliffs and caves. More of the same inside: columns shaped like palm trees, holding up a ceiling of checkerboard rafters. Wordlessly, we made our way through all the petty pirate paraphernalia to the sixth floor.

The upper landing was crowded with law enforcement personnel. Heavy-lidded Metro officers rubbing shoulders with waxy-haired Feds with lapel microphones. Jackets that looked like hotel management and security, wringing hands and worrying about lawsuits.

Whatever it was that was going on here, it was big.

The air had a palpable taste of dread.

We made our way down one of those never-ending hallways – more solemn-faced uniforms standing guard at regular intervals – until we arrived at an open doorway leading to one of the guest suites. Cherry waved me in. I left my FBI escorts out in the hallway and entered the room.

Aside from an unmade bed and a random scattering of clothing, nothing looked out of place. No corpse on the bed. No Agent Wong fouling the air. No Jolly Roger. It was yet another one of those cloned hotel accommodations. Same style of drapes. Same generic furniture. Same everything as everywhere else. In a town famous for its variety, there wasn't a whole lot of it on show.

"Gabe!"

I back-peddled, looked through an open connective doorway leading to the adjoining guest room. Sonny was waving from about three rooms down. All the connecting doors between us were wide open.

She held out a pair of Latex gloves as I approached. "Did you hear about Jackson?"

"I did."

"Well, brace yourself, because it's nothing compared to this." She handed me a pair of elasticized slippers.

Hopping, I slipped them on.

* * *

Have you ever disliked someone so much that you wished them dead?

This time round, *The Undertaker* had gone to town and painted it blood red. The abrupt scale and escalation of his kill pattern was hard to take in all at once. Unthinkable. He'd accelerated from zero to a hundred and broke the sound barrier in the process.

All told, there were five new victims on the sixth floor of the *Treasure Island Hotel* in Las Vegas: three boys and two girls. Five. I couldn't believe it. The oldest was barely out of his mid-twenties, the youngest barely out of her teens.

More dead kids.

My stomach was sinking faster than a shipwreck in high seas.

I advanced slowly. Feet finding their own firm footing.

The killer had pushed the twin beds apart, so that one was tucked underneath the window and the other tight against the mirrored closet. The arrangement had opened up a large rectangular space about five feet wide. And all of the five victims were in this gap.

*Five.*

The number was yet to snag on any of my cognitive hooks.

*Five dead kids.*

"This is exactly as they were found," Sonny was saying.

346

The kids were all sitting cross-legged on the plush hotel carpeting, naked as the day they were born and holding each other's blood-soaked hands. The killer had leaned them against one another, like a macabre balancing act, so that they formed a circle, facing inward. On the floor in the middle of the group was a mound of unused hypodermics. It looked like a glassy campfire. The composition reminded me of young adults engaged in an innocent childhood game: *spin the bottle*. A snapshot at a party. Or something one of those trendy but grisly artists do these days with the willing but deceased.

I moved closer, carefully avoiding the ring of rose petals on the carpet. I felt like a sneak– as if I were invading a private séance. These kids looked like they were meditating. That maybe the crackling of my plastic slippers would disturb them at any moment and our worst fears would be for nothing.

But these kids were all as dead as doorknobs. Smudged ash crosses on their foreheads and their lips blued. Just children. Away from home. Maybe for the first time. Trying their luck in the casinos, or maybe at a convention. Youthful bodies hardening with rigor. Destined to return home in black plastic body bags.

I had fire in my belly.

Up until this moment, I had thought the killer's arrangement of Mark and Sarah back at the *Bellagio* as the pinnacle of his MO evolution. I was woefully wrong.

"Your boy's got some balls." I heard Sonny say. "Why do you think he did this?"

"For impact." Realizing it for myself as I formed the words. "To show he means business and that he's in total control. Sonny, you and I both know that overpowering and then killing five young and healthy people like this, singlehandedly, and in one fell swoop, takes precision, timing and a whole lot of effort. You're right: it takes balls. But to arrange them like this takes more than that. It takes madness."

"All the same . . ."

I knew what she was thinking. "He uses a quick-acting anesthetic. Chiefly, secobarbital. That's why there's no signs of a struggle." I pointed out fingertip burn marks on one or two of the male victims. "He's also handy with a Taser."

I looked around the room. There was a collection of liquor bottles on a table. Drinking glasses. Bags of potato chips and candy bars. Empty beer bottles crowding the nightstand.

"Looks like they were partying. No doubt making plenty of noise. Intoxicated. Probably didn't realize what was happening until it was too late."

Sonny pointed. "The connecting doors were all open when we got here. I'm thinking he made his way from one room to the next."

"They stood no chance."

"Fortunately, there is some good news."

I looked at her, disbelieving that there could be anything good about this whole terrible situation.

"This was originally a party of six."

"You mean he missed one?"

"Purely by chance, it seems. His name's Brandon Chu. He was down in the casino all night from around eleven. In the poker lounge with a few regulars. When he came back to his room around five-thirty he walked smack-bang into this."

"Where is he now?"

"Down the hall. White as a sheet. See this one?" Sonny pointed to one of the female victims. The girl had shoulder-length, vinyl-black hair and slight oriental features. She was painfully thin; ribs like slats on a blind. "They were an item, she and Chu. As you can imagine, he's pretty torn up."

"I bet he is. Did he see anything, Sonny, anything at all – other than this?"

"No. The killer was long gone by the time he got here. The ME believes they were all killed sometime between one and two. Give or take."

While Brandon was losing chips, his buddies were losing a whole lot more.

Sonny held out a clear plastic evidence bag. "The killer also left this."

Why wasn't I surprised?

I took it with a shaky hand.

Agent Cherry poked his head around the door: "Word up: CSU's here."

We were all set to leave when the room phone rang.

I looked at Sonny.

She looked at me.

We both wore the same puzzled expression.

"Expecting any calls, Sonny?"

"Not on a weekend. You?"

"Not me. I'm not even from round here."

"Maybe it's Housekeeping."

"I guess."

I let the phone ring several times more, wondering how long it would go on for and if it would ever end. When it didn't, Sonny picked up.

Immediately, I saw by her reaction that it wasn't the Front Desk offering a complementary upgrade.

"It's for you," she said, holding out the receiver. "It's                                            *him*."

\*    \*    \*

"How do you like your wake-up call?" came a menacing voice down the line as I pressed my ear to the hand-piece. It was the same inhuman *Speak & Spell* monotone from yesterday – my anonymous caller from the *Luxor*.

"Who is this?"

"You know who I am. We've already been introduced."

"The crackpot stalker."

"Is that the best you can do? I much prefer our working title. The one Harry gave you."

My blood ran cold.

I made *the signal* to Sonny. She nodded and rushed out the room.

"You're probably wondering how I know about that," the monster with the synthesized voice said. "Would you believe me if I said I heard it from the horse's mouth?"

I sank a hand in a pocket, fingered the credit-card piece of plastic in the evidence bag found at the Hoagland crime scene.

"You killed Harry," I breathed.

"Consider it a personal favor," the voice grated, shredding nerves and bone. "Now do you know who I am?"

\* \* \*

I don't believe things turn out the way they do because of random chance. I believe purpose and planning play their part.

As I heard *The Undertaker's* synthesized tone coming down the line, I knew he'd seen me arrive at the hotel and knew he'd murdered my best friend and partner, Harry Kelso.

"You killed Harry," I breathed again.

I was having difficulty computing. *Believing.* All this time I'd been ignoring the truth – since the moment Agent Wong had handed me the evidence bag with Harry's driver's license inside. Ignoring the obvious – like I had done the whole time, simply because the obvious was a clammy claw squeezing my heart.

"Why?"

"To get your attention. To focus you. It worked, didn't it?"

While I'd been chasing down the surfer dude from Huntington Beach in my Cedars-Sinai trap, *The Undertaker* had been killing Harry over at the County Medical Center.

My impetuosity had got my best buddy killed.

"Consider it your invitation to the circus," the voice said.

Through eyes misting over with red hate I saw Sonny come back into the room. She gestured to her ear. She'd gotten the Feds onto tracing the call. I didn't know how. Maybe it was just a matter of throwing a switch at Washington and they could triangulate from over a thousand miles away. I had to keep him talking. Didn't want to keep him talking. Didn't even want to hear his mechanical breathing. All I could think about was how badly I wanted to rip his head off, verbally, but most of all physically.

I saw Sonny making hand gestures: keep calm, put personal anger aside, keep the upper hand and above all else stay in control.

Easier said than done.

"Congratulations," I managed through clenched teeth. "Your booby-trap bomb killed federal agents in Jackson. That's put you at the top of the FBI's Most Wanted list. There's no way out of this for you now. Nowhere to hide. The Feds won't stop until they catch you or kill you. Me either, for that matter."

"I'm flattered."

I looked at the five dead kids posed in a circle.

"Don't be. Killing a bunch of drunken and defenseless kids in their sleep makes you a coward. They were just kids, dammit. Kids with the world at their feet."

"Spare me the melodramatics," the voice thundered back. "In this world, no one is innocent. We are all flawed. We are all sinners."

"Is that where the ash comes into it?"

"You can't even begin to imagine."

The mist was congealing into a veil of blood.

"Let me tell you my theory: you're a psychopath. You probably hear voices and believe it's God telling you to do his bidding. You think by killing a few innocent people you can prevent a greater loss of life somewhere down the line. In any dictionary, that's the definition of a nut job."

I heard the killer breathe. It sounded like Darth Vader. "Even if you're right, you wouldn't understand."

"Indulge me."

"Why, so you can keep me on the line long enough to trace the call? I don't think so, defective."

The line went dead.

I stared at the hand piece, ears buzzing in the sudden silence. Then my cell phone warbled. I saw Sonny dart back out of the room.

I let it squawk. Waited until she returned, with Agent Cherry, before answering. Set it to speakerphone.

"Do you think the killing of one man is justifiable if it stops him committing mass murder?" the Darth Vader wannabe rumbled from the tiny speaker.

"You mean The Hitler Dilemma?"

Another moment of mechanical breathing.

I stepped into the gap: "See, I've been doing my homework too. Any which way you dice this, Chapter's got you on plagiarism. Besides, I'd let the authorities handle it. I wouldn't resort to vigilantism."

"And if your repeated warnings fell on deaf ears?"

*The Undertaker* had already warned the authorities, I realized. Somewhere in the system, there was a series of filed reports about impending doom, with Ethan Davey Copes' name attached.

"You tried it, didn't you?" I said. "They thought you were a crackpot, didn't they? You warned them but they ignored you. So you decided to take matters into your own hands. Kill innocent people. Did it ever occur to you that the voices in your head could be wrong?"

"You know nothing about me."

"And there lies another mistake," I said. "We know where you live, and that's just the start. I know your name's Ethan Davey Copes, and soon I'll know everything about you. Then I'll be coming to get you, Ethan. You hear me, you sick psycho son of a bitch? I'm coming to get you!"

*The Undertaker* cut the connection.

*   *   *

The cardinal rule when chasing killers is never to reveal how much you know to the killers themselves. I should have known better. *I did know better.* But I wanted to unsettle the smug bastard just as much as he had done me.

"Gabe . . ."

"Sonny," I began, waggling the receiver, "he'll call back. Trust me, this type can't resist."

Agent Cherry pressed a finger to his ear: listening to a techie in his earpiece. "He disconnected before we got a fix. If he does come back online, you need to keep him talking. At least one more minute."

It was the most I'd ever heard Cherry say in one mouthful.

"He'll call back," I assured them both, unsure if the statement was for their benefit or for mine.

I stared at my cell phone, willing it to ring, willing *The Undertaker* to take the bait. Then . . . it sprang into life in my hand.

I let it ring a dozen times before accepting the call. Burning away precious seconds, invaluable in any trace.

"A name and an address do not constitute a relationship," the killer's disguised voice rumbled from the speaker.

"It doesn't matter," I said, pressing home the advantage. I spoke slowly, reigning in my anger, while the precious seconds ticked away. "Pretty soon we'll know everything about you. Where you went to school. Which teachers gave you a thumbs-down on your report card. Where you work. What jobs you got fired from, and why. Which girlfriends shunned you, and why. What the doctors thought about your psychosis. Which medications you should be taking, but aren't. Soon we'll know you better than you do yourself.

"You can't hide behind your anonymity anymore. We know who you are, Ethan. And I'm coming to get you. You hear me? I'm going to make it my life's mission to hunt you down and make you pay for what you did to little Jenny, to Harry, and to all the other innocent people you've murdered along the way. You hear me, you sick bastard? *I'm coming to get you!*"

Cherry was holding up both hands. The Feds needed just ten more seconds. Ten crucial seconds to catch a killer. I had to keep this psychopath distracted – anything to guarantee we had a fix. There was a government satellite somewhere over the Mid-West realigning itself, triangulating on the killer's signal. Suddenly, sweat was coursing down my sides.

I heard *The Undertaker* laugh like a wood chipper.

"While you're at it," he whispered back, "get your sniffer dogs to check out the earth under the seed silo back in Jackson. I left something there especially for you, defective. Appreciate. Enjoy your wake-up call. Catch me later."

With a click, the line went dead.

Desperately, I stared at Agent Cherry.

Sonny was doing the same.

The tension in the room of the *Treasure Island* could be sliced with a cutlass.

The Fed was listening intently to the voice in his earpiece.

My gut was holding my throat hostage.

I saw Cherry shake his head and our shoulders sagged.

"We need to close this place down right now," I said. "He's here. In this building. I'm convinced of it."

*   *   *

Sonny barked orders into her police radio and rumbled all available law enforcement personnel within a ten-block radius to converge on *Treasure Island*. Even as we were running out of the room I could hear the wails of sirens careening our way in the distance.

I had no idea where we were heading or what we'd do once we got there. But I was convinced *The Undertaker* was somewhere near. He was close to home. I could *feel* it.

Within seconds, Sonny had the entire complex shored up. Tighter than a rope around a pirate's neck. No one allowed in or out without having their IDs checked and double-checked. If *The Undertaker* was here, he was about to get marooned by his own ego.

We fell into an elevator and hit the ground floor button. Sonny got out her firearm. Checked it. Automatically, I did the same. The adrenaline was pumping and there was a steely determination in Sonny's eye I found oddly reassuring.

"We don't want to underestimate him, Sonny," I said as the floor numbers dropped away. "He's dangerous and smart. And that makes for a lethal combination."

"Then it's a good thing we're smarter," she said.

Sonny's radio bleeped as we emerged into a throng of conventioneers aiming for the breakfast buffet.

"We have a male fitting the APB outside the main entrance," she announced as we worked our way through the stampede. "Gabe, I think we got him."

*     *     *

Bongos were banging behind my ribs as we barged across the busy lobby toward the main entrance.

I didn't know what to expect.

Was I about to meet *The Undertaker*, at last – facedown on the wooden sidewalk, bound and cuffed? Would that face fit that of the monster I had lurking in the back of my mind? Would I carry out the wishes of a grieving mother?

Up ahead, through smoked-glass doors, I could see a guy in a long dark coat and baseball cap shrugging off a pair of Metro police officers. They were halfway down the gangplank connecting *Treasure Island* to the mainland.

Blood surged in my brain.

"Hold that man!" Sonny shouted as we flew through the doors.

It was like putting a match to a fuse.

The guy in the cap snatched a quick glance in our direction, and then shot off like a firework on New Year's Eve.

The stunned patrolmen immediately launched into hot pursuit.

And so did we.

*     *     *

We clattered down the gangplank, scattering tourists like spooked geese. Late nights, early mornings, fast food, cold-blooded killers: they were all conspiring against me now, pushing my blood pressure through the roof.

But I wasn't the only one with a death wish.

The guy in the cap leapt straight for the eight-lane roadway and nose-dived into traffic speeding south, without slowing. The air came alive with screeching tires and blasted horns. Puffs of vaporized rubber. Flashing lights. He almost got sideswiped by a taxi. A bang. A spin. He hit the hood and rolled over it. But, as crazies do, he picked himself up and pounded on across the street. Long coat trailing behind him like the cape of a cartoon superhero. The two cops were hot on his heels, waving down traffic and banging on hoods. The guy in the cap reached the tree-lined median and hurdled it clean. Started causing the same mayhem in the northbound lane.

I hit the pavement on creaking ankles; saw our suspect miss being mown down by a fraction of a heartbeat. Brake smoke billowing. I heard a thundering crash as a vehicle tailgated another. Then another.

Foot chases can be dangerous things. I'd been rolled by a vehicle once or twice in my time. Cars have no conscience. Even at this early hour, Las Vegas Boulevard was flush with traffic.

We zigzagged through slowing vehicles, reached the opposite sidewalk the same time as the cops. The race leader was easily forty yards ahead. Young legs and adrenaline. Sonny accelerated past the patrolmen, widening the gap between us. A second later, I was past them too.

It wasn't hard to figure that Sonny worked out. She made a fine runner, I thought. Clean gait and straight spine. Elbows tucked nicely in. Legs pumping like pistons. Everything moving in harmony. Nice technique. Nice fluidity. All round nice.

*What was I thinking?*

I plowed on. Years of muscle memory taking over. Forcing blood into thighs and calves. Forcing air in and out of my lungs at a steady rate.

The guy in the cap was bowling people off the sidewalk like pins. More screeching tires. Angry yelps. At this rate he was going to get somebody killed. I saw him leap across a parking garage entranceway and race through the deep shadow cast by an elevated crosswalk connecting one huge hotel to its neighbor. Sonny was still accelerating. Closing the gap. The cops were keeping pace with me, about five yards behind. I dodged a taxi exiting the parking structure. Almost got myself clipped. Heard the driver holler an obscenity. The guy in the cap veered left, into the big open piazza outside *The Venetian* resort complex. I made the left about twenty seconds after Sonny did. Saw her drilling across a large ornate footbridge curving over a wide turquoise canal. Saw the guy in the cap disappear through the main doors of *The Venetian*, about twenty yards ahead of Sonny.

I sprinted across the piazza, sending pigeons aloft.

"They're headed for the mall," a geeky-looking kid manning the door announced as I burst my way through.

I caught sight of Sonny making a left at the end of the long vaulted lobby. Ran on. I had my breathing under control now. But my legs were setting like wet cement. I got to the entrance of the *Grand Canal Shoppes* with the cops on my shoulder.

I looked around, desperately searching for Sonny.

The mall was a miniature version of Venice; complete with a canal and fake gas lamps on cobbled streets. At this hour, most of the boutiques were closed up – just one or two coffee vendors open for breakfast business. A handful of yawning tourists and businessmen milling aimlessly about.

I spotted the pursuit about fifty yards away. The guy in the cap had taken a convex footbridge to cross the canal and was sprinting parallel to the waterway, on the other bank. Away from our position.

"Split up!" I yelled at the cops.

They cut across the nearest footbridge, following Sonny's course. I picked up the pace, staying on this side of the canal. I closed the gap as the suspect bulldozed through a gaggle of Japanese tourists, lost his footing and slid on his knees across the cobbles. That must have hurt. Then he was picking himself up and plowing on. Sonny was less than ten paces behind him.

Now we were running exactly parallel with one another, but on opposite sides of the waterway.

I could see a larger footbridge coming up. Beyond that, the street of specialty shops dead-ended about a hundred yards later. The guy in the cap was heading straight into a cul-de-sac. He'd have no choice but to double-back. Making a U-turn was out of the question – because that would leave him facing Sonny and the advancing cops. His only avenue of escape was the bridge spanning the widest point. But between him and the bridge was an open-air café. Nothing between me and the bridge. And at this point it was level pegging.

I notched it up a gear. Capitalized on those muscle memories and squeezed battery acid blood to spark and fire one last time. I saw the suspect clatter through tables, sending chairs flying. Sonny ducked as one flew her way. I made it to the humpbacked crossover seconds ahead of the suspect, slipped and slid over shiny cobbles as I clambered to the apex of the bridge. I drew out my Glock and adopted a two-handed defensive stance:

"Stop! Police!"

The guy in the cap leapt onto the bridge and charged my way, head down. No intention of stopping. No intention of being caught. I holstered the firearm. Dipped my shoulder like a cornerback about to intercept a wide receiver. Braced myself for impact. He tried to swerve in the last moment. Dodge past. But I'd anticipated the move.

Keith Houghton

I threw my weight into him, sideways. Our shoulders locked. The combined momentum lifted us off the cobbled bridge and tipped us over the small ornate wall. The world flipped upside-down and we hit the cold canal water like two sacks of sand.

# 98

Our melancholy was tangible.

His name was Kevin Boone. But his clients knew him as *Repo*. He was twenty-eight and from Henderson, with a rap sheet that read like a comedy of errors. Turned out he was nothing more than a smalltime dealer – of drugs, not cards – peddling low-grade PCP to any teenager with an allowance. Presently, Boone was serving a two-year probation under State law. So when he'd been pulled aside outside *Treasure Island* he'd decided to make a bolt for it rather than risk violating his parole.

But he hadn't bargained on Sonny's athleticism.

Then again, neither had I.

Damn it: he wasn't *The Undertaker*.

"What now?" Sonny asked as we watched the handcuffed kid being marched away for processing.

I was conscious of the fact we may have let the real killer slip away in our haste to apprehend Boone.

"We go back to where we were at. We put together everything we know about Ethan Davey Copes. Apply it to the evidence we already have. Get Bill's team of profilers to work out where he might be holed up or even where he might strike next."

Sonny was nodding. "But first we need to get you fixed up with some dry clothes."

We were in *The Venetian* security suite. I was sipping hot Italian coffee from one of the street vendors, soaked to the bone and trying to clear chlorine from my sinuses.

Five minutes later we were in Sonny's SUV, heading west away from The Strip.

"There's still a chance he'll turn up on one of the hotel lists," she said as she drove.

I stared through the windshield as the burgeoning sunrise painted the distant mountains in swathes of gold. She was trying to console me, I knew. See the bright side of a very dark morning. But lately all of my silver linings had turned out leaden.

My cell phone rang. It was a miracle it still functioned after its dip in the canal.

There was a text message, from an anonymous caller:

*"If you had to take one life to save another, could you?"*

Sonny glanced my way. "Sure you still want to hold back on that press conference?"

I buried the phone back in a pocket. "Arrange it for tomorrow morning."

"Why tomorrow? I can set it up sooner. This afternoon."

"Tomorrow's fine."

"Any particular reason why?"

I thought about it. Why was I stalling?

"Sonny, I want to make sure we've done everything we can to catch this guy first before we go live. I don't want any of those news sharks sensing blood and sinking the investigation."

"You're worried Stacey will grill you in public."

"No. I just don't want her whitewashing the whole affair and turn our manhunt into a personal crusade."

We drove beneath the Interstate overpass and out the other side.

"Who's Harry?" Sonny asked all of a sudden.

The unexpected question blindsided me. "My partner," I stuttered. "Former partner."

"I didn't realize he was one of the victims."

"That's because officially he isn't. He's collateral damage. Harry was in the hospital, back in LA. Some minor complications following surgery. Infections, I think. The Undertaker murdered him Tuesday night."

Four days ago. It seemed like yesterday.

"And you're sure it was The Undertaker?"

I glanced at her for the first time. "Sonny, I know he killed him. He left Harry's driver's license at the Hoagland crime scene."

She could hear the contained rage bubbling away behind my words. So could I.

"I don't get it. Why leave his license?"

"As bait to get me here. Bill said the killer had picked me out on purpose. That it was only a matter of time before he made contact. He left Jennifer McNamara at the 7th Street Bridge because that's the same place where The Maestro dumped his last victim."

"The killer knows your history."

I rubbed molars together. "Sonny, there's no hiding it: my history is public domain. Trying googling me. My life's been an open book ever since the press labeled me with the Celebrity Cop moniker. Now there's no going back from it. Every cuckoo with a grub to chew on comes knocking at my door."

"Gabe, I'm sorry."

"Don't be."

"I mean about Harry."

More molars mashed.

She let them grind, then said: "Mike told me he found you over at Stacey's place."

I let out a long breath. "I wanted to speak with her. She mentioned a few things in her news report that only we knew."

"You're thinking the killer contacted her?"

"I do. Maybe even coached her on what to say to the camera."

She nodded. "He's playing with you, isn't he? Sounds like he's on a personal vendetta. So how do we catch him, Gabe?"

The huge bronze mountains gleamed in the early morning sunlight. I pulled down the visor.

"We find the link that connects all the victims together. Once we've done that, we'll know who he's going after and catch him before he gets there."

# 99

The fat man in the long white coat was with his mother and father, over by the big desk with the big Earth globe on the top. They were talking about him. Trying to keep their voices low. He had his face pressed against the cool glass of the window. Picking out patterns in the parking lot. Listening to every word they said.

It was a memory the killer also known as Ethan Davey Copes had from being a small child. The visit to the clinic had been the first of many. The beginning of a long journey of psychological reprogramming that would travel through his entire childhood and go absolutely nowhere.

At that age he hadn't fully understood terms such as *Einstein Syndrome*, *high-spectrum learner* or *top percentile achiever*. To him, the fact that he had chosen not to speak very much meant he could dedicate more brainpower to absorbing the world around him. In more ways than one, boys weren't like girls. Boys soaked up facts. Gobbled up general knowledge. Made patterns out of the chaos.

God's wonderful blueprint – foretelling of things not yet come to pass.

Randall replayed the memory as he gazed through the airplane window at the baggage handlers nonchalantly tossing luggage into the cargo hold.

"It's a problem," his mother kept saying in the memory. Over and over. She sounded upset. Teary. "People think our son is retarded. They won't give him a chance. It's a problem."

The fat man in the long white coat nodded. "Let me assure you, your son is quite the opposite. His introversion is just a symptom of his condition."

There it was: the *C* word.

His father sounded more annoyed than upset. His father had been angry for some time, he recalled. Angry at God for giving them a child with . . .

"A condition? What are you saying exactly? My boy has a *condition*?"

"Yes, sir, he does. But it isn't a life-threatening condition, if that's what worries you. All it means is your son's mental functions have developed differently than ours. Better, in some ways. Here, take a look at these test results. They're off the charts. Look at this curve. He's a smart kid. But the wires in his brain are plugged into the wrong sockets."

"So, what's his prognosis?"

"With the proper behavioral program there's no reason he shouldn't become a fully functioning member of society."

He remembered a note of hope rising in his mother's voice: "You mean he'll be normal? He'll fit in? He'll be *okay*?"

"Better than okay, in some ways. Your boy's one in a million. If we get this right now, today, no one will ever know your son's different. With the right medication he'll blend right in. Excel, in fact. He'll be able to hold down a good job. Form relationships. Indeed, he'll fit right in."

Randall closed his eyes as the plane's engines throbbed into life. He could feel the patterns of their vibrations course through him. For a moment he reveled in it. Lost himself in the repetitive resonations.

There was a clunk as the airbridge disengaged.

He'd fit right in, all right; he'd become adept at hiding the big *C*. In fact, he'd breezed through the extra security checks here at the airport without a hitch. Smiled on cue to the granite-faced officials. Acted bored. Disinterested. Better things to do. Said all the right things. No concealed weapons. No sharp implements. No, he wasn't an international terrorist. No, he wasn't hiding C4 in his shoe. No one to guess his true identity. No one smart enough to see right through his disguise.

They were all too busy looking for a blond-haired guy in a baseball cap. Had paid no interest whatsoever to his dark hair and newly-adopted alias.

Randall smiled to himself as the Boeing 757 began taxiing out of the departure gate at McCarran International.

# 100

Sonny lived in a pleasant gated community south of Spring Valley. The subdivision formed several concentric circles of pretty Spanish-style villas with terracotta tiles and palm trees. A perfect picture of suburban tranquility. I was envious.

"You won't be intruding," she assured me as she pulled her family SUV onto the driveway. "Just be prepared to be mobbed. You have no idea how much you being here will be a treat for the kids."

I had every intention of making it a quick turnaround. A pit stop to grab some food, clean up, get out, hit the streets, and hunt down *The Undertaker* before he took away more innocent lives. But Sonny's kids had other ideas.

They were polite, charming and interested – which is a rare combination these days. Full of early morning energy, fuelled with curiosity and not caffeine. Clearly, working long shifts and making ends meet hadn't affected Sonny's ability to raise fine children. I was impressed. They were a real credit to her. I mean it.

"What's it like being on TV?"

"How many movie stars do you know?"

"Do you live in Hollywood?"

"What's it like catching bad guys?"

"Have you ever shot someone?"

"Can I hold your gun?"

Five minutes into introductions and interrogations, Sonny clapped her hands and shooed her kids away.

"Y'all got chores to get to. So go and get to."

I was happy to watch from the sidelines as Sonny handed out instructions to her three shiny-eyed offspring:

tidy bedrooms; feed pets; put laundry in the utility room; get washed, dressed; eat breakfast. It reminded me of my own family life back in Tennessee when my own kids were this age. It was endearing. The normalcy smacked you on the nose. But things never stay the same.

A little while later, I was scanning more vacation photographs on the walls when Sonny came downstairs with a bundle of folded clothes.

She handed them over. "I hope you don't mind; these were Roger's. They're new and never been worn. You're about the same build."

"Sure?"

"Absolutely."

I took them from her.

"The bathroom's at the top of the landing. There's a razor and cream in the cabinet. Take your time. Let me know when you're done with the shower and I'll redress that head wound. In the meantime, your sneakers are going in the dryer."

"Thanks, Sonny."

"You're welcome. Now go and get to."

* * *

Roger's clothes were a good fit. Expensive. I decided I liked his tailoring, but not his style.

Ninety minutes later, Detective Michael Shakes teamed up with Sonny Maxwell and me – together with our FBI counterparts – in the boardroom attached to the situation room at the *MGM Grand*. In light of new developments, we'd called the emergency meeting to discuss where we were at and where we were going with The Undertaker Case. We all needed to be on the same page, pulling out all the stops to catch this killer, and fast.

Bill wasn't attending. He'd sent me a simple text, saying he was otherwise tied up and would be busy coordinating the National Guard at the airport for most of the day. The quite capable Marty Gunner would oversee things in his absence.

So far, the killer we knew as *The Undertaker* – aka Ethan Davey Copes – had taken eight lives in Vegas within a twenty-four-hour period. A monumental undertaking in anyone's book. All told, that made sixteen homicides – including FBI and incidentals – over the course of one week. It read like a *Rambo* movie script.

"We reverse-traced the call you took at the Treasure Island," Agent Glenda Hoyt was telling me. She looked a little brighter-eyed than yesterday, but not by much. "He's definitely using a pre-paid disposable cell."

"He knows exactly how long it takes us to trace a call." Agent Miles Tomlin added. He looked uncomfortable – like he'd slept in his clothes. I knew that feeling. "Which means he could have a technical background or be connected to law enforcement."

I heard Sonny make a snorting sound: "Anyone who's ever seen a procedural cop show knows how long it takes to trace a call." Sonny had little patience with the FBI, and it showed.

We were seated around the conference table; Feds on one side, cops on the other – like opposing counsels. We were all working as one big task force with the same objectives, but somehow it didn't feel that way.

"What else do we know about Ethan Davey Copes?" I asked, refocusing the group.

Marty Gunner had a handful of printouts on the table in front of him. He looked like he'd been up all night too. I'd mastered that look a long time ago. He slid them across the table to each of us in turn.

"This is just about everything our computers at Clarksburg have on him."

I spun the sheet around. There was a list of dates, facts, a photocopy of the DMV driver's license. My first real look at the killer's face, as it had been when he was a spotty teenager. He looked like a bully. One of those soulless, square-faced kids who play baseball with frogs. I scanned the sheet. I'd seen more information on a milk carton.

"He was born thirty-two years ago in Jackson, Tennessee," Marty continued. "The only child of Graham and Belinda Copes. Grew up on the family farm."

"The one that got blown to pieces?"

"Correct."

"Copes dropped out of the education system at the age of thirteen and started home schooling."

I was staring at the kid's face, detesting every pore. "What do we know about the parents?"

"Both deceased. Graham and Belinda inherited the farm from the grandfather, Nathan Copes, when Ethan was nine. Records indicate they both died in a farming accident about ten years back."

"So, he lost his parents in his early twenties," Shakes mused with a nod. "And you said the farmstead was abandoned, right? So where'd he go for the last ten years?"

"We have no idea."

"You mean he just disappeared for ten whole years, then turned up in LA on a killing spree? What about his work records?"

Shakes sounded unhappy with the FBI's lack of specifics. Truth was, I'd expected more too. We all had.

Glenda Hoyt leaned forward. "He slipped under the radar. These things happen. We have no record of any gainful employment."

"How about ungainful?" Shakes asked.

"There's no such word."

"You know what I mean, sister. Did he serve time anywhere?"

I saw Glenda glance toward her colleague, Miles Tomlin.

Tomlin cleared his throat. "Not that we're aware of. The likelihood is that when his parents died and he could no longer support himself or the farm, he drifted. Maybe he did manual labor for cash in hand. Everything under the counter."

"So we have no current tax records?" I said.

"No IRS returns filed in his name."

Shakes wasn't letting it go: "What about the credit card he used with the online rose retailer?"

Marty dealt another set of sheets across the table. "The card belongs to the First Tennessee Bank. Issued just after Copes turned twenty-one. He also holds an account with Citibank. But that's just a savings. As you can see, the card is rarely used."

I scanned the paper. Previous to the last couple of weeks, the First Tennessee card hadn't been used since last summer, and then only on grocery purchases from a Wal-Mart in Fresno. Again, six months prior to that; another Wal-Mart in Colorado Springs. Then another six months before that; a Wal-Mart in Sioux Falls. The Feds had a list of Wal-Mart transactions going back ten years. One every six months.

"Why only twice each year?" Sonny wondered out loud.

"To keep the card activated," I said. "Otherwise the bank would have closed the account. The transactions show he's mobile and able to move freely around the country. According to this list, the card hasn't been used in the same city twice in ten years. That's twenty separate locations."

"Why Wal-Mart?"

"Because it's inconspicuous."

Sonny asked: "How does he pay the balance on the card?"

Marty answered: "That's where the Citibank savings account comes into it. Copes keeps the balance at around one hundred dollars. Tops it up annually to cover the Wal-Mart purchases."

"So this is a checking account?"

"No. It looks like all the transactions are done electronically, online, from Wi-Fi hotspots."

"Copes have any other family?" Shakes asked.

Marty shrugged. "None that we can ascertain. We're still leafing through the family tree. But it looks like Copes is the last in his direct bloodline."

"So let's get this straight," Shakes began, "Copes is a drifter, uneducated and bumming odd jobs for loose change. Does that sound like the guy we're after?"

I had to hand it to Mike Shakes for saying out loud something that my *Uh Oh Radar* had been screaming about for the last minute or two.

Something didn't quite add up. *The Undertaker* was articulate. Educated. I'd spoken with him on the phone. He didn't sound like he'd dropped out of the school system. Didn't sound like a hobo scraping by on handouts. Plus, he was mobile – which meant he had access to funds or a gainful employment that saw him traveling the nation. Something that didn't pop up on the FBI's radar. Copes' profile didn't sound like our killer.

"He mentioned something buried under the silo in Jackson," I said.

Marty nodded. "We've got people looking into it."

Shakes leaned forward in her chair. "Okay. We know who he is but not where he is. So where do *we* go from here?"

Marty looked at his colleagues, who looked blankly back at him. I knew the answer, but delayed answering.

"We have Nevada Highway Patrol troopers manning checkpoints on every major artery out of the city," Marty told our group. "Everyone's IDs are being checked and double-checked. We have National Guard in force at the airport. About a hundred federal agents are canvassing hotel staff and casino employees. When it comes to legwork, we're doing all we can. If he's here, sooner or later we'll find him."

"What about the off roads?" Sonny asked.

Marty looked blank.

Shakes spread his hands on the table. "Get with the program, guys. There are dozens of dirt trails leading out into the desert."

Marty still looked blank.

"We close down Vegas," I said.

Every jaw in the room dropped a little. One or two more than others.

"Gabe's right," Sonny agreed, searching the table for support. "We're working from a fifteen-year-old photograph. It's pathetic. What's the point of stop checks if we don't know what this guy looks like today?"

Tomlin shrugged. "We're checking IDs."

"Which is great if he's using his real name," she countered. "For God's sake, don't you people think outside the box once in a while?"

I was nodding. "Using an alias explains why he hasn't shown up on any hotel lists. We may have to rethink our whole stop and search strategy."

We were no nearer to catching *The Undertaker* today than we were a week ago, I realized.

\* \* \*

It was a tall ask.

Completely closing down Vegas would soak up more manpower than even the FBI could muster. It would also cause enough political unrest back in Washington to put pressure on Fuller into pulling the whole plug. Right now, there were over a half million tourists in town. Come tomorrow and Monday, half of them would be headed off home, with more on the way to take their places. A constant influx and efflux. Closing down Vegas would mean keeping all those people here, in hotel rooms booked out to newcomers. Closing down Vegas would mean keeping all the newcomers out. The operation would cause chaos on a scale equivalent to a national disaster. I wasn't sure the casino-hotels would go down without a fight. Wasn't even sure closing down a major city was viable or even doable. Was it any wonder that Assistant Director Marty Gunner looked like he'd just learned he had a communicable disease?

He excused himself and left the room.

We waited on the outcome of his phone call to the Bureau's director, whose one and only niece was lying on a mortuary slab here in Vegas.

If Norman Fuller believed we'd catch his niece's killer by closing down Vegas, I had a feeling he'd give the green light. I knew I would.

The ramifications were enormous.

Everyone was looking nervy.

I broke the uneasy silence, "Let's see if we can hammer out a connection while we're waiting. Any theories, anyone?"

Shakes grunted. "Are we still working on the assumption he believes he can see the future?"

I nodded. "For now, at least. It's all we have – until we have something better to work with. When we spoke on the phone, he didn't refute it. In fact, he knew exactly what I was referring to when I mentioned the Hitler Dilemma."

"Then that's the connection," Shakes said. "He believes all of his victims are connected to some future heinous act. All we need to do now is determine what that act is."

We stewed in silence, deafened by the din of mental gears grinding.

I still wasn't comfortable with the tenuous science fiction aspect behind our killer's possible motive. Give me Westerns any day of the week. At least some degree of fact is involved.

"Mark Roe and Sarah Gillespie were here for a company seminar," Shakes said, breaking up our brainstorming. He was wearing a *'bear with me, I'm just figuring this out on the fly'* kind of face.

"Microbiological Terrorism," I remembered.

"Has anyone checked which convention Patricia Hoagland was attending, or if those kids at Treasure Island were in town for a conference?"

I looked at Glenda Hoyt and Miles Tomlin. They were looking at each other. Why hadn't any of us asked this question before now?

"Check," I said.

Glenda opened her cell phone and spoke quickly to one of her colleagues out in the situation room.

"Mark and Sarah worked for a company called Harland Labs," I told our group while we waited on the outcome. "They're a biotech outfit based in Boston."

"And Patricia Hoagland was employed by Waldo Parker," Glenda announced as she nodded at the voice in her ear.

"What about the kids at Treasure Island?"

Glenda was holding up a hand, listening to the voice on her phone. "They were all employed by a company called Quasitrone. Here for their biennial convention."

Three separate employers.

No connection through their employment, then.

I was about to probe further when the door opened and Marty Gunner returned looking like a man who had just learned his communicable disease was in fact fatal.

"As of five this afternoon —" Marty checked his watch, "— in about three hours and thirty-six minutes' time, all routes out of Vegas will be closed for a twenty-four hour period."

Sonny slapped a hand on the table. "Hot damn. We're actually closing Vegas. I don't believe it. That's like closing down Disneyland. It's unheard of."

"Actually, they did," Glenda Hoyt said. "Back in ninety-nine, during Hurricane Floyd. I was there with my folks. We cowered in a bathtub for two whole hours."

Fuller had given the okay on the impossible.

Now it was our turn to realize his instructions.

That gave us one day to catch a killer hiding in a city of millions.

I got up and went over to the water cooler, poured a long shot for Marty. It wasn't whiskey. He looked like he needed whiskey. I handed it to him all the same. He guzzled it down.

"Thanks," he said.

I felt bad for Marty. If we messed up, his head would be on the chopping block. Fuller took no prisoners.

"Give us the details when you're ready, Marty," I said.

"Yeah, we don't want to rush you unduly." Mike Shakes sniffed. "But we do have a killer to catch."

# 101

Jamie Garcia spent the morning the same way she'd spent every Saturday morning since her older brother had been gunned down in a drive-by shooting when she was fifteen: at the Rainbow Project on East 3rd Street in El Este de Los Ángeles, talking with kids.

The scheme was in its tenth year. It had been conceived by the Residents Association and was housed in a small reclaimed building that used to be the 3rd Street market, on the corner opposite Our Lady of Lourdes Church. Its goal was to help steer youngsters away from a life of gang crime, by using a combination of positive teachings and community workshops. So far, it had an immaculate record of achievement.

Most of the morning had been taken up giving a brief talk about knife crime to a group of attentive youngsters ranging between the ages of seven and eleven. They'd listened to Jamie's talk with pinned-back ears. Eyes wide, like baby birds being fed a juicy stream of maggots. Jamie loved her work here. She couldn't think of any better way to volunteer her free time to the community she loved so much. But all the time she'd been speaking, her mind had been on something else. Something that didn't belong inside the four walls of this cheery building.

She'd made up her mind.

Despite the Captain's orders, she didn't want to sit on her hands until her appraisal on Monday. She wanted to be productive. *Needed* to be productive – especially while Gabe was out of town. Sitting around doing nothing wasn't her. She wanted to work what bits of the case she could work outside of the Division building on 6th Street, in her own time, off her own back.

Most of all, she wanted to put the killer of Jennifer McNamara behind bars. Not just for the little girl's parents, but for the kids sitting here listening to her words, here, right now.

Like the song lyric, she believed that children were the future. They were the world's hope for something better.

By taking little Jenny's life, *The Undertaker* had killed that hope.

Jamie Garcia was determined to make up for it.

# 102

The unbelievable was playing out.

A noose was to be drawn around Las Vegas, effectively strangling the circulation of traffic, aircraft and the flow of people out of the city. In effect, no one was leaving town before five o'clock, Sunday evening. That gave us twenty-four hours to catch *The Undertaker*. It meant all hands on deck.

The situation was unprecedented. As such, we were all thinking on our feet and dealing with each crisis as it happened.

Assistant Director Marty Gunner gathered his point men together and delegated duties. He stressed that no one – and he meant *no one* – was to be allowed out through the checkpoints unless they met the exceptions criteria. Those exceptions included single females, families with young children here on vacation, the elderly over seventy, emergency services personnel, and delivery truck drivers carrying the correct paperwork. And even then, their vehicles would be checked thoroughly with sniffer dogs for stowaways. Plus, their IDs scrutinized under a microscope.

No passenger flights were allowed to leave McCarran without the same checks in place. The airlines would be up in arms.

No one cared.

Once the Feds had their strategies organized, Marty got on the phone to his counterpart with the Nevada Highway Patrol and confirmed that everyone knew the script. The Chief of the NHP was coordinating State troopers from a temporary command post located just off Route 95. Already doing a fine job by all accounts. His new orders were to apprehend any male even loosely fitting our APB description, no matter what his ID said. If in doubt, detain. That was Marty's instruction. Handcuff and hold until the FBI had run credentials through their system and given the green light to release.

My first worry was that *The Undertaker* might be happy where he was, in Vegas, and not even try to run a roadblock until after the noose had been withdrawn.

My second worry was that he'd already left.

No plan is fool proof. But many are proven false by fools.

Provision was being put into place on the city periphery to provide temporary turnarounds and stopovers for vehicles being checked. Diverting traffic back into the city would prove a logistics nightmare. But Marty was one step ahead. He'd already dispatched city personnel to help co-ordinate road signals – to do everything they could to prevent the city's main arteries from seizing up.

Every hotel in Vegas with rooms not currently reserved for the weekend was being instructed to keep them aside for tourists and commuters stuck in town. They didn't argue. Keeping visitors in town meant more guests to charm in the casinos.

Meanwhile, Federal Agents would be canvassing hotel guests on the ground and running checks.

Five o'clock came and went. The roadblocks started living up to their name. Turnpikes turned into turnarounds. Traffic started tailing back for miles. The airport turned into a hotel. Even with a heavy law enforcement and National Guard presence, there was widespread restlessness across the city, almost immediately. That tension would mount as the evening wore on, I knew. Within ten minutes of the lockdown of Las Vegas coming into effect, we had reports of more than a dozen outbreaks of civil disorder, resulting in arrests and red faces caught on local TV cameras.

This was going to get icky.

I called Bill on his cell, but the call went straight to voicemail. I collared Marty, signing off commands in the situation room:

"Marty, you heard from Bill lately?"

"Not since midday."

"Is that normal?"

He gave me a *we're talking about Bill here* look. And we left it there.

Thirty minutes into lockdown, the situation room fell under siege to the irrepressible press as they set up camp in the hotel thoroughfare outside. I kept my distance; I was in no mood for another showdown with Stacey Kellerman or any of her clones.

We were already making headlines across the nation and possibly internationally.

My third worry was that *The Undertaker* could be holed up in a private residence somewhere, and that all our valiant efforts would be in vain. All officers patrolling the city were told to be extra vigilant, and to check out any suspicious circumstances across the city neighborhoods.

All police leave was canceled for the weekend. Every officer capable of working was brought in. In an unprecedented move, Uncle Sam agreed to pick up the tab. It was anyone's guess how many millions *The Undertaker* was going to cost the taxpayer over the next twenty-four hours of delays and disruption.

Already this had become the biggest manhunt in Nevada history.

Forty-five minutes into the proceedings, I telephoned Ferguson back in Los Angeles and brought him up to speed. News of the Vegas lockdown had already reached LA. In fact, the networks were running the hastily-put-together FBI press release like the world was ending. It was spreading across the country like wildfire. An hour into the lockdown, the news had gone global. Viral on the Internet. Eyes worldwide were suddenly watching Vegas and examining our every move.

The pressure was intense.

By 6:30 p.m., *The Undertaker's* face was lighting up TVs across the land. The media had been provided with a digitally-aged version of his Tennessee driver's license. Even if Ethan Davey Copes had already left the State, he'd have nowhere to hide. The whole planet was on the lookout.

Two hours into lockdown, Marty Gunner pulled me over to one side:

"What is it, Marty? You heard from Bill?"

"Jackson," he answered, and I could tell from his tone that the news wasn't good.

A body – or the skeletal remains of one – had been exhumed from beneath the silo on the Copes' farm. It didn't sound good. Pelvic width told us it was male. Joint development indicated a young adult, possibly late teens. Decay told us it had been in the earth for at least a decade. The remains were being shipped out for dental analysis. Top priority. No point running DNA comparisons; the body had been buried prior to our new genetic age. But providing the boy had undergone dentistry work, we'd have an ID soon enough.

"They also found two items buried with the remains," Marty told me. "One was this:"

He handed me a sheet of paper. It was a printout from an email attachment. It showed the picture of an old-fashioned glass and steel syringe. I hadn't seen one like it in years.

"It's a medical-grade hypodermic," he said.

"Which points to our killer."

"Correct. The other was this:"

The second sheet had a picture of a small object on it, photographed beside an angled ruler for sizing purposes. The object was about the size of a thumbnail. Silver in color with what appeared to be a square black enamel inlay. Somebody had brushed off dirt and ten years of grime, but not very well.

Something grabbed my gut and squeezed it.

I stared at the photograph, mind suddenly whirling. It was one of those dumbfounding moments where the universe flips on its head and everything you thought you knew suddenly doesn't add up any more. Marty must have seen my thunderstruck expression, because he immediately asked:

"Does it mean something to you, detective?"

I swallowed over a gritty tongue, shook my head.

Marty nodded slowly. He gave me a *you don't look so sure* frown. I wasn't sure if he believed me. I knew I didn't.

"All right," he said. "I'll give you a shout when the dental results come through."

He left me with the printouts.

My hands were shaking.

I looked again at the second photograph and experienced the same gut-clutching nausea that sent me rushing to the restroom.

# 103

Michael Shakes didn't believe in goblins and fairies. But he did believe in the spiritual realm. In fact, he had what he considered a pretty good handle on the life thereafter. He'd seen enough of death to know that something inexplicable happened at the moment life left a body. It also helped that he'd grown up with a spiritual medium in the family. His mother's sister, his aunt, considered eccentric and probably insane by most of the people who came into her life. His aunt had been born blind. But she'd had vision. Able to see things beyond this worldly plane. He'd had a solid bond with his aunt, fascinated by her insights throughout his childhood. So it had come as no surprise that she'd visited him after her passing, in a dream still vivid today. She'd told him she'd send signs whenever he needed her help.

Michael Shakes believed in the spiritual realm. But he'd never believed his aunt could actually contact him from the other side.

Until now.

# 104

We all need somebody we can confide in. How does the saying go — a problem shared is a problem halved? Trouble is, I believe a problem shared is more often a problem doubled. Stands to reason, right? There are things I keep inside. Demons I don't dare let loose. But talking helps. *Right?*

Presently, there was only one person I could count on with my life here in Vegas and we were staring at each other across a copying machine in a small antechamber attached to the situation room. We were alone, looking like we'd both just realized we'd eaten bad eggs for breakfast.

"Call me numb," Sonny was saying as she glanced at the printout given to me by Marty Gunner, "but I don't get it. You say this is *yours* and the Feds found it with skeletal remains on the Copes farm?"

I nodded, stiffly.

I saw Sonny's brow furrow as she tried to work it out. Wondered if mine looked the same.

"And you're absolutely certain about this? No way you could be mistaken? There must be hundreds of these things with the same design."

"No, Sonny." I was deadly serious. "It's mine all right. They're unique. My wife had them handmade for our wedding day. See the engraving?"

Somebody had tried to brush away soil and made a bad job of it. Still, you could see the letter G engraved into the black enamel, down to the silver.

"We had matching pairs," I said. "I had the cufflinks. Hope had the earrings. We had our initials G and H engraved specially into the onyx. G on one. H on the other."

"And you told Marty it wasn't yours?"

I didn't know why I'd lied. Impulsiveness, I guess. We've all been there. Heat of the moment.

Sonny was shaking her head and biting a lip. "Gabe, I don't know what to say. How is this possible?"

"The same way it was possible the killer used my handcuffs on Marlene van den Berg's live-in butler back in LA. This creep's been setting this up for a long time. Maybe for years. Collecting Celebrity Cop memorabilia and waiting for a time to use it."

"Gabe, that's not just weird, it's scary."

I saw her reexamine the photograph, as if trying to find some small, previously missed detail to convince me otherwise. But there was no disguising it. It was what it was.

"And you're absolutely certain?" she asked again.

I lifted up my left wrist and showed her the solitary cufflink I'd worn every day for almost a year, since my wife's death – even on another man's dress shirt. You could just make out the silver letter H against the black onyx.

*H for Hope.*

"I'm still not seeing it," she said. "How could your cufflink come into his possession?"

I thought about it. Heard retired synapses spark back to life as an old memory emerged.

"Last time I wore them both we were at an awards dinner in Memphis," I began.

"We?"

"The whole family. Must be going on twenty years ago. Some loony tune posing as a waiter tried killing the mayor with an ice pick. Right there in front of fifty top law enforcement personnel. A scuffle broke out. It took a few of us to apprehend him. Bring him down. Turned out he was a member of the Aryan Brotherhood with an ax to grind against our newly-appointed black mayor."

"And the cufflink?"

"Lost during the scrap."

"So where's this guy now – the white supremacist?"

"No idea, Sonny. He got twenty years for attempted second degree. Plus, he had outstanding warrants. Mainly in assault and battery, unsurprisingly. I guess he might have made parole by now."

"Was his name Ethan Davey Copes?"

I smiled loosely. "You know, Sonny, I don't recall exactly. Like I say, it was twenty years ago. Either way, Ethan would have been just a boy at the time."

"We could be looking at a friend of the Copes family. Or a distant relative. Somebody who had a bad influence on Ethan."

Was that where I'd heard the name before? I wondered. We'd have to look into it. See if the Aryan Brother had made parole. Rule him either in or out of the investigation.

Sonny made a face. "I guess the next question is: why did The Undertaker bury it with a ten-year-old corpse?"

Again, I thought about it. "I don't know." But I had my suspicions. I just wasn't prepared to deal with them yet.

The door opened. Michael Shakes appeared. He looked like a man who had just won a sizeable amount on the spin of a roulette wheel.

His big grin was filled with brilliant white teeth.

"High fives, people," he grinned. "This dog just uncovered the killer's connection. For real."

# 105

In retrospect, being diagnosed with a condition hadn't necessarily been a bad thing for Randall. Certainly, it had had its drawbacks. He'd been bullied in school. Bullied out of school. Ostracized and left to his own devises most of the time. But solitude had brought focus.

While the other kids had played with their bats and their balls, he'd been high in a treetop. Or on a roof. Watching clouds skate across the sky. Spying all kinds of weird and wonderful things going on:

An elephant.

A rocket ship.

The American President with his face blown off . . .

The more he'd studied the world around him, the more he'd come to understand there were hidden meanings within the patterns. Nature's hieroglyphs. Deciphering them had been like a blind man learning a foreign language by lip-reading alone. But he'd stuck with it and finally mastered it.

By the time puberty had opened up a whole new world of experiences to him, he'd started thinking of his condition as a gift instead of a hindrance.

But nothing in life was free. Everything came at a price. Relationships had become distractions. Schooling unable to keep up with his probative mind. People became playthings.

After all, you couldn't trade away your mortal veil without losing a little of your humanity, could you?

In retrospect, the killer also known as Ethan Davey Copes, had turned a curse into a blessing.

And everything happened for a reason.

# 106

"It's a strange thing." Mike Shakes was telling us in excited words of all one syllable. "So bear with me."

His grin was gone but he still looked pumped. He sounded like a child who had witnessed an automobile crash for the first time and wanted his friends to come along and see the grisly wreckage for themselves.

"Something drew me back to the Treasure Island crime scene. Don't ask me what. Let's say a hunch. I didn't know what I'd find – if anything. When I got there, the place was still sealed up. The CSU had pretty much cleared out the digs. Everything was waiting for the cleansing crew to come and make the place habitable again. So I moseyed around. Opening drawers. Looking under beds. That kind of thing. Anyway, I was in the first guest room when something strange happened."

"You realized you were crap at story-telling," Sonny said with a smile.

Shakes grinned back. "The clock radio turned on all by itself."

Sonny's smile turned dismissive. "Milk, those things have timers. It's a known prank. The leaving guest sets the radio alarm to come on at full volume in the middle of the night, just to freak out the next occupants."

"So they do, Sonny. But this was early evening," Shakes countered. "And exactly the moment I was in the room. What are the chances of that? Scared the living daylights out of me. That's all I know. But the point I'm making is, the song on the radio was My Way by Sinatra."

I saw Sonny roll her eyes like women do when rationalizing the supernatural. "Milk, that's astounding – considering we're in Vegas."

"It's even more astounding when you understand it was my aunt's favorite song. Played at her funeral."

"Sentimentality aside," I said, "how did you come by the connection?"

"Because, tucked under the radio was a pamphlet. The CSU must have thought it was one of those flashy brochures advertising Vegas nightlife. Only it wasn't. It was the same pamphlet you and I saw at the Bellagio crime scene. The one with the double helix on the front cover."

"Harland Labs," I said.

"Wait a minute," Sonny started, "we've already established each group has different employers."

"The killer must have left the pamphlet there for us to find," I said. "He took it from the Bellagio crime scene."

But Shakes was shaking his head. "And that's what I thought too, at first – until I did some digging. Remember the company the kids worked for?"

"Someplace called Quasitrone."

"Correct. It's an IT firm based in Connecticut."

"And the connection?"

"They're the hi-tech arm of Harland Labs."

Our astonishment was visible.

Shakes flashed his teeth. "And it gets better from there."

*See the lovely car wreckage, isn't it sweet?*

"You remember Glenda Hoyt told us Patricia Hoagland worked for Waldo Parker? Well, Waldo Parker is in fact a specialized chemical manufacturer supplying bespoke products to the pharmaceutical industry. And guess who their number one customer is?"

"Harland Labs," Sonny and I said as one.

"And that's the killer's connection, folks. They're all linked to this biotech outfit in Boston."

Our astonishment turned to a sense of urgency.

"Harland Labs is in town for a seminar. We need to round up the rest of their employees." I said.

Shakes nodded. "Gabe, I'm already ahead of you. I called their head office on the way over. The place is shut down for the week, but I managed to speak with a secretary. Not counting the deceased, there are eleven other employees here for the weekend. Aside from Brandon Chu, they all returned home yesterday evening on the advisement of the company's CEO – who, by the way, is still in town."

"What's his name?"

"Harland Candlewood. Remember the good-looking dude in the Harland Labs pamphlet, the guy standing side-by-side with Mark and Sarah?"

"Sure. The guy with the trendy eyewear." Automatically, I reached for the rolled-up copy I'd stuffed in my jacket pocket back at the *Bellagio* crime scene, then realized I'd left it in my hotel suite.

"The company secretary says he's staying at Caesar's Palace. I checked. He is. I got put through to his suite. He wasn't home."

"Do we have any idea where he is?"

"Your guess is as good as mine."

Sonny was chewing her cheek. "What shall we do with Chu?"

I shrugged. "Where is he right now?"

"In a holding cell back at Area Command."

"Keep him there. It's safer. At least until this whole thing blows over. If the killer is killing everyone connected with Harland Labs, Chu's life is still in danger. We need to tell Marty and get the Feds on this straight away."

I went for the door.

"Wait." Shakes grabbed my arm. "I saved the best for last. Out of curiosity, I did a little digging into Candlewood himself. Get this: before forming Harland Labs he captained a company supplying euthanasia drugs to veterinary surgeries."

Which meant he had access to each of the drugs our killer had been using.

Suddenly, we had a new person of interest.

"We need to find this Harland Candlewood," I said. "And fast."

# 107

There are times when the swell of an event carries us along with it. This was one such occasion. Our investigation had suddenly changed tack. We all had new wind gusting in our sails and a new current to follow. We all wanted to know who Harland Candlewood was and whether he was capable of murder.

Could Harland Candlewood be Ethan Davey Copes?

The change in identity would help explain the disappearance of Copes from the records shortly after the death of his parents. But what it didn't explain was how a country bumpkin like Copes could blossom into the figurehead of a hi-tech company up in Boston.

One of Marty's techies brought up a photograph of Harland Candlewood on his computer screen, garnered from a simple Google search. We all peered at it – as if by doing so we could determine guilt. It was the same guy from the Harland Laboratories brochure. A dazzling smile and a mop of wavy blonde hair. Sky-blue eyes behind black Versace glasses. A likeness to the younger image of Copes we had from his driver's license, but maybe with some facial surgery, maybe, at a push and with a little imagination. The photo had been taken at an exclusive function. Dated twelve months ago. Black ties and ball gowns. He was shaking hands with a gray-bearded African-American who looked like the movie actor Morgan Freeman, but was in fact the retired Secretary General of the UN, Kofi Annan.

Candlewood had celebrated contacts.

The techie twiddled keys and came up with Candlewood's most recent DMV driver's license photo.

No obscuring eyewear this time. No Academy Award winning grin. Same face shape as Copes. Same piercing blue eyes.

"Get copies out to our field agents," Marty Gunner instructed his techie. "Let's get this guy found ASAP."

We left the Feds to it.

"Is it possible Candlewood's our killer?" Sonny asked as she, Shakes and I headed out.

I grabbed a deep breath and mulled it over. I didn't know what to think. Everything was up in the air again. Just when I thought we were closing in, a few detours had been thrown in our way. All at once we had a pick of suspects.

"Let's see how Candlewood pans out," I said. "We still have other leads to check. I don't want to jump the gun on this one, Sonny. Although right now Candlewood measures up, we have a finite time window to get this right." I turned to Mike, "Milk, can you get a breakdown of Candlewood's movements over the last week or so?"

"Sure."

"Sonny?"

"Yep?"

"I know it's not your favorite pastime, but work with the Feds on this, will you? Find out as much as you can about Harland Candlewood. If he is involved in these killings, now's our best chance of questioning him while he's still in town."

"Anything for the cause. What about you?"

"I'm going to track down that white supremacist. See how he factors into all this."

*   *   *

I made some calls. I have a good charge plan. I spoke with old contacts back in the Memphis PD and the Attorney's

Office there. It was Saturday evening. No one likes to answer business calls at the weekend. It took time. Precious time. I was asking a lot. Favors had to be called in. Big favors. Memories jogged. Eventually, I found the name of the Aryan Brother: Chad Judd. Coincidentally – there's that word again – he'd made parole three months ago, then disappeared into the backwoods. Unsurprisingly, he hadn't kept to any of his agreed PO appointments.

I passed the information on to some of Marty's geeky colleagues manning the computers in our situation room, and asked them to dredge up anything they could on the ex-convict. If he had snatched my cufflink that night and kept it all those years, I wanted to know who he'd passed it on to, and why.

We were four hours into lockdown when the fiery-faced mayor of Las Vegas turned up with his official entourage. The city outskirts were undergoing a dress-down. Desperate people trying to get around the roadblocks by going off-road. Taking their chances on the desert terrain. Some four-wheel-drives had managed to make it through before being forced back by police choppers. Many more less powerful vehicles were now bogged down in sand and scrub lining the roadsides. It was dark out there. Pitch black in the desert. Cold and getting colder by the minute. Hundreds of private vehicles parked on the shoulder. People out of cars. Getting restless, hungry, angry. Already, the city's emergency services were being stretched to snapping point.

Assistant Director Marty Gunner dealt with the mayor, politely but directly. Marty had the political weight and the federal clout to sucker punch any move the mayor tried to pull. The sheriff turned up a minute later, championing the mayor's corner. A heated exchange ensued. Marty dug in his heels and delivered a verbal right hook and floored them both. The mayor and the sheriff left the ring. But not before making some very dark promises.

We were making enemies, fast.

I kept glancing at my watch like a man on Death Row. I was conscious of the time. Things were getting uncomfortable. Rapidly reaching boiling point. We needed to find our man before Vegas exploded.

At a quarter after 10 p.m., Sonny came through with news on Candlewood's background:

According to the official records, Candlewood was Massachusetts born and bred. Came from old colonial money. He was a trained molecular biologist with a Master's in Genetics from Harvard. No wife. No kids. A few parking violations, but no police record to speak of. He'd worked for daddy's pharmaceuticals business before going solo five years ago – when he'd started up the biotech outfit in Boston, geared toward vaccine development. By all accounts, Candlewood was a clean-cut guy with a company going places. No warning bells other than the one thing that stood out from the sugary accolades sweetening his résumé: Candlewood had undergone psychotherapy in his teens.

"What's with that?" I asked Sonny.

"He had an argument with a neighbor. The dispute resulted in Candlewood poisoning the guy's dog. It was either therapy or juvenile detention."

Marty Gunner nodded. "Typical pre-serial behavior."

Shakes came over, "How much we betting he used potassium chloride on the dog?" He handed me a printout. "It looks like Candlewood was in California up until Thursday. Which puts him there during the LA homicides. That's a list of Candlewood's company credit card transactions spanning the last two weeks. Take a look at the highlighted entries."

I put on my reading glasses. "He had a reservation at the Ramada on Vermont?"

"Same time as Ethan Davey Copes."

Another shocker.

Both Copes and Candlewood had lodged at the Hollywood Hotel when Helena Margolis was brutally slain. Were they a team? I wondered. Was that it? Were we dealing with two *Undertakers*? It had never occurred to me before now that there could be more than one killer involved. It was one explanation for the amount of kills and the changes in MO. I looked at the highlighted entries again. Had the pair agreed that Copes carry out the LA murders while Candlewood killed off his own employees here in Vegas? If so, why?

Marty broke the silence, "So which one's the killer?"

"Maybe they both are," I said. "Maybe they're working together, as a kill team."

I ran my eyes over the photograph of Harland Candlewood, trying to imagine what he'd look like wearing a black baseball cap. Captured on the *Bellagio* surveillance footage, we'd seen the same wavy blonde hair sprouting out the back of *The Undertaker's* hat. It didn't take a wizard with Photoshop to see the similarities.

Miles Tomlin joined us, "We got word back on the dental IDs." He pushed between Sonny and Shakes, slapped a sheet of paper on the table in front of us and stabbed a finger at a line of text marked up in bold. "Tests show the remains belong to –"

"Damn it," I said as I read the words: "Ethan Davey Copes."

His were the skeletal remains underneath the silo in Jackson.

"Copes is a smokescreen," I said. "The killer's using an alias."

We were all processing the revelation when Glenda Hoyt rushed over, "Candlewood's keycard has just been used at Caesar's Palace. He's back in his room. This is our chance."

# 108

We went through the rear entrance of *Caesar's Palace*, weapons drawn and intentions steely. Shakes, Sonny, Marty and me – together with about a dozen geed-up cops and G-Men. We tried keeping it as low-key as we could. Sure. A SWAT unit was three minutes away. We didn't wait. Couldn't. We commandeered all of the elevators and let the uniforms take control of the stairwells. More Metro PD covering the exits.

According to the Front Desk, Candlewood's keycard had been active within the last ten minutes – which meant there was a strong likelihood he was still here, in the building, hopefully still holed up in his room. It was a Senators Suite near the top of the Palace Tower, overlooking the hotel's lavish pool area.

We grouped at the foot of the Tower elevators. Cops and Feds. We were all flak-jacketed and buzzing. Sonny had a map of the suite's floor plan opened out. We gathered around like a football team working on game strategies.

"The suite is split into three sections," she told us, pointing them out. "Two bedrooms with bathrooms either side of the main living room. There's a small reception hall as we go in, with a toilet to the right and a walk-in closet to the left."

"So we split into three teams of four," I said. "Miles, your team take the left-hand bedroom. Glenda, your team take the right. Marty, you're with Sonny, Milk and me in the main living area. The rest of you cover the hallway and the adjoining suites."

A gong sounded from the elevators. Doors parted.

"Everyone know what they're doing?"

I got fifteen sharp nods.

Sonny waved everyone inside. "Okay, people. Let's do this."

I watched floor numbers increment, my shoulders pressed against the mirrored insides of the carriage. I could taste testosterone in the close confines, mixed with deodorant and determination.

Then we were pouring out of the elevators. Fists wrapped around gun grips. Hours of tactical training kicking in. We ran in silence down the hallway toward the target room. Keeping to the edges. Shooing surprised guests back into their rooms. Cops peeling off before we got there; securing the suites either side. We pressed backs against walls as a handful of hotel guests were cleared out of harm's way and rushed down the hall to the waiting elevators. Everyone was running on a tank full of adrenaline. We waited for the cops to give the all-clear hand signals. Then Sonny swiped the master keycard through the lock on the double-doors belonging to the Senator Suite and we piled in, one after the other. Fast and slick like hot oil poured over cold water. The suite was in total darkness. We fanned out, following white Maglite beams. Some of us spreading into the bedrooms and bathrooms, as planned.

I followed Shakes into the main living area, sweeping the Maglite left and right as I went. The beam struck furniture, paintings. There was a conference table surrounded by eight comfy chairs. A pleasant sitting area. A huge window with the drapes pulled back, revealing a nighttime view of a neon-glitter cityscape.

Miles: *"Clear!"*

Glenda: *"Clear!"*

Sonny: *"Clear!*

No one home. Candlewood had come and gone. We holstered weapons as our adrenaline fizzled and died.

"Somebody get the lights," I shouted.

They came on throughout the suite.

"Search the rest of the hotel," I instructed Miles Tomlin as he joined us in the main living area. "He could still be on the premises. No one leaves without our say-so."

He nodded, quickly, waved to his team, and they piled out the way we'd come in.

Sonny got on her police radio and ordered the troops downstairs to man the barricades.

If Candlewood were anywhere close, we'd nab him.

I scanned the opulent Senators Suite on the upper floor of the Palace Tower, looking for anything that would give us a lead on Candlewood's location.

There was a metallic carry-on piece of luggage standing in the middle of the conference table, telescopic handle closed up. A handful of loose change on a writing desk. A return ticket to Boston on the lounge table, next to a Harland Labs brochure.

"Anyone else smell that?" I asked.

I saw cops and Feds wrinkle noses, received several shakes of the head. There was a strange smell in here, I thought. Something not quite right.

"Detectives!"

We converged on the master bedroom.

Glenda Hoyt was standing alongside a King-sized bed. On top of the fancy quilted comforter was a long black raincoat and a black baseball cap. The words *Black Death* were embroidered into the fabric of the hat, just above the peak.

We were all astounded. Flushed with renewed hope.

"There's our proof," Sonny said. "Candlewood's the killer."

Somebody shouted: "In here!"

We backed out of the bedroom, into the reception hall. A Fed was waving us toward a walk-in closet. It was too narrow for everyone to fit in all at once. Shakes stayed in the bedroom with Glenda while Sonny and I went in to investigate.

Inside, on an otherwise empty shelf, was a handful of hypodermics and several vials of what appeared to be clear liquid. I snapped on Latex gloves and picked up the nearest. The label read *potassium chloride*.

Jackpot!

"Check the carry-on!" I shouted to Shakes.

We heard Marty call out from back in the main part of the suite: "I'm already on it!"

And that's when the world blew up in my face.

# 109

I have no idea how long I was out of things. Seconds, maybe. Hard to tell – my internal clock was spinning. When I came to, I could hear people coughing, moaning, groaning. Somebody crying. It was dark. I was flat on my back. Disoriented. It took a moment to realize what had happened and where I was. I could hear bells ringing. Not sure if they were in my head or if it was a fire alarm. I spluttered out bits of gritty chalk. Eyes and throat caked in dust. I could smell smoke and cooking fat. Could hear what sounded like things falling, randomly crashing. Metal creaking. Sparks crackling. A stiff breeze swirling dust. It was cold. I coughed. Choked. I tried sitting up, but there was something big and flat pinning me down, slantwise, about six inches above my face. Heavy.

"Gabe?"

"Sonny?"

She sounded in a tight spot. Flat on her back, like me, jammed. I felt a hand fumble into mine.

"You okay, Sonny?"

"I think so. Not sure. But I think so. What happened?"

"Must have been a bomb," I said, working it out there and then. "In the carry-on. Triggered to go off the moment somebody opened it."

I coughed out more chalky dust, realized it was wall plaster.

We were lying in the remnants of the walk-in closet. The lights were out. Everything was displaced. Shattered. We were underneath the remains of the interior wall and maybe some of the ceiling. It was anyone's guess what the rest of the suite looked like.

I could still hear people moaning. Somebody sobbing. Blast victims fumbling around in the debris like blind people after an earthquake.

I managed to twist onto a side. Just. Difficult in the confined space. "Sure you're okay, Sonny?" It was a crazy question, given our circumstances.

"Everything feels attached." I heard her shuffle, felt her grip tighten as she pulled herself closer across the gritty carpeting. "You?"

"I think so."

Truth was, my head was splitting. Fireflies zigzagging in my vision. One cheek wet; blood coming from the wound where my priest's killer had walloped me with a candlestick. You can only crash a car so many times before it's wreckage.

Sonny released my hand. I heard her try and push upward against the collapsed partition. Heard loose rubble fall. Dust billow. Then she was right next to me in the darkness. Churning up dust. She coughed. I could just make out the shape of her face in the flashes of electrical arcing coming from exposed cabling in the shattered wall. Her face was close. I could feel warm breath on my lips. She grabbed my hand again. I squeezed it.

"Damn room's on top of us," she breathed. "You claustrophobic, Gabe?"

"Yep." But I was too worried about other things to let the fear take control.

"Same here. Anyone else with us?"

I remembered the cop showing us *The Undertaker's* stash in the walk-in closet right before everything collapsed. Shakes had been out in the master bedroom, with Glenda Hoyt, over the other end of the suite. Maybe a few other cops here and there. Some Feds. I couldn't swear on it.

"Anyone else in here?" Sonny asked, this time louder.

No one answered.

I could hear people moving around in the bedroom and maybe out in the main part of the suite itself. More debris crashing. People crawling over rubble. People coughing. Somebody still crying. Distantly, I could make out an alarm squawking – maybe sirens too. It sounded outside the hotel. Maybe the Fire Department.

"Oh my God," Sonny breathed against my face.

I sensed sudden infectious panic. "What?"

"Marty," she said. "Marty opened the case."

"Crap."

Now I remembered. Marty would have taken the full brunt of the blast. My stomach clenched. I shouted out his name.

Nothing.

I started to think the worst.

Sonny asked, "Can you move?"

I pushed at the sheet of wood or wall that angled over us like a tomb lid. It gave a few inches, but I didn't have the leverage to move it more.

"Anyone out there?" I shouted. "Hello? We're trapped over here."

"Quinn?"

The voice was male. Out in the main part of the suite. Sounded shaky.

"Who's that?"

"It's Miles. Miles Tomlin. Jesus, this is a mess." He was stuttering. He sounded shocked. We all were.

I heard him clambering over rubble toward the bedroom – or what was left of it.

"Half the room's been blown out the hotel." I heard him say. "Oh, Jesus."

"We're in here," Sonny shouted. "In what's left of the closet. Can you get to us?"

"I don't know. Maybe. I'll try."

Miles sounded scared. He was mostly used to office work and pen-pushing. Certainly not a day out in Baghdad.

I saw glints from a flashlight illuminate the swirling dust. Heard debris groan and moan as whatever it was that was pinning us down lifted a little. Then all at once it slid off to one side and chalky dust billowed again. The beam of a Maglite dazzled us.

I squinted, belching out dust.

Miles Tomlin fell to his knees and started brushing away debris with his free hand.

The sprinkler system kicked in, drenching us in icy water.

"I can't find Marty," Tomlin said through the hammering rain. I could hear panic rising in his voice. "I can't find him anywhere."

# 110

No question, we were lucky to be alive and in one piece. How many people can say they've survived a bomb blast relatively unscathed?

Things like that didn't happen every day of the week – at least not on mainland USA. For a brief, explosive second we'd experienced a taste of what some peoples' lives are like on a daily basis. I have no desire to trade places.

All told, there were five police officers and four Federal Agents in the Senator Suite at *Caesar's Palace* when the killer's booby-trap device exploded. Miraculously, most of the injuries turned out to be superficial. Some third degree burns. A few scrapes and bruises and minor lacerations. One broken arm. Four fractured ribs. No lost limbs, thankfully. Mostly shock and sooty lungs.

All told, five police officers and three Federal Agents had survived relatively unscathed.

We were lucky.

There was only one fatality:

Assistant Director of the FBI's Critical Incident Response Group, Marty Gunner.

\* \* \*

I couldn't get Marty off my mind as I shivered on the back plate of yet another ambulance. The private access road leading into the pool area at the rear of the hotel was crammed with fire trucks, police cars and EMS vehicles. Plenty of flashing neon – but still no match for our flashier surroundings. The Palace Tower had been evacuated, together with the conference and business centers situated in the floors beneath. We couldn't risk debris falling on unsuspecting guests. Fire crews were assessing the extent of the damage, including the integrity of the surrounding floors and suites. I could hear crowds of displaced patrons and gathering onlookers stirring out on the street. Camera-phones flashing. A news helicopter hovering nearby. Multiple videos already uploading to *YouTube*.

Mike Shakes was huddled in a foil blanket on the back plate of another ambulance. A bandage was wrapped around his head, just above eye level. A bloody patch spreading near his right temple. He looked like he'd been down a coal mine. Chalked with soot. Clothes blackened. I knew that I looked the same. When he saw me, he closed his eyes for a second and nodded.

I looked across the illuminated pool area, up to the Palace Tower. There was a black gaping hole torn out of its side about three-quarters of the way up. A ragged bullet wound in a flank of flesh. The surrounding windows in a twenty-yard radius were either shattered or cracked.

The blast had blown Marty and most of the living room furniture clean through the window – where he and the fiery ejecta had plummeted through a dozen or more floors before plunging into one of the hotel's pools. Traces of smoke curled lazily out of the hole, up into the black sky. Rivulets of blackened water sobbing down the hotel fascia where the sprinkler system had washed out blast detritus. It was a mess.

The cops had cordoned off the expansive pool area. The once tranquil oasis of palms and lawn chairs looked like a bomb had dropped on it – which, in a way, it had. The fancy tiles and Romanesque fountains were peppered with blackened debris and broken glass. Forensics were on their way. There was a lot of cleaning up to do. A great deal of figuring things out. All the while, Marty's body was lying facedown in a pool of filthy water, scorched and torn, gently bobbing on the stiff January breeze.

Somebody was going to have to fish him out.

Not me.

# 111

The passenger jet hit a pocket of turbulence and jiggled her teeth.

Jamie shielded her eyes from the glaring cabin light and pressed her nose against the cold plastic windowpane. Somewhere down in that nighttime world of inky blackness, the unseen snowy peaks of the Rockies drifted past beneath the plane. Every now and then, she spied clusters of tiny lights: dwellings and small communities separated by great troughs of nothingness.

Night flights were hard work. She wasn't one of those people who could sleep on a plane. To her, the whole thing was too noisy, too jumpy and too claustrophobic.

She'd spent the last hour or so deep in thought about Jeanette Bennett, the murdered psychiatrist from Philly. There was something more than just the fact she'd been brutally branded by cigarettes that gnawed away at her unconscious mind. The whole vicious attack seemed personal, as though the killer had been releasing pent-up rage. It had occurred to her that there was a strong chance the killer had known Jeanette. Maybe he'd been one of her patients. As far as she knew, the psychiatrist had specialized in the treatment of children with mental conditions. Could the entire attack have been the product of payback? she wondered. Could her killing be all about revenge?

Even serial killers were children once.

And some might view the meddling of their mind as a mortal sin.

"Excuse me. Is this seat taken?"

Jamie brought her gaze back inside the cabin, blinked to refocus.

A gray-haired woman was standing in the aisle, leaning toward her. She looked like a retiree, sounded British. She was dressed in a fitted tweed suit, with one of those Victorian-style blouses that have a small ruff rather than a collar.

"May I?" she smiled, indicating the vacant seat next to Jamie.

"Sure."

The woman seated herself and pressed wrinkles from her skirt. "I couldn't help noticing," she continued in a hushed voice. Some passengers were sleeping, despite the turbulence. "The photographs." She nodded at the spread of glossies covering Jamie's tray table. "Are you with the police?"

Jamie realized the case photos were on view, for all to see, and she quickly gathered them up. "I'm sorry. I didn't mean for anyone to see these. I'm LAPD."

The woman smiled, "No worries, my dear. I work with the boys and girls in blue all the time." She held out her hand. "I'm Doctor Margaret Dovecote. Professor of Pathology at the Rockefeller University in New York City."

"Jamie Garcia."

"Pleasure, Jamie." They shook hands. "To be perfectly honest, I'm not very good with these overnight flights. If God had intended us to fly I'm certain he would have had the foresight to give us wings." She nodded once more at the photos in Jamie's hands. "I do hate being nosy, but since disease is my labor of love, I'm compelled to ask: did all of the victims die from the same virus?"

Jamie felt her face form a frown. "These are all homicides," she said. "What makes you think it's a virus?"

"The rings of roses, for a start. As in the nursery rhyme: ring-a-ring o' roses, a pocket full o' poses." She leaned a little closer, whispered: "You see, viruses are a bit of an obsession of mine. You could say, I find the study infectious."

Jamie smiled. Not sure why.

She watched the British woman pop a pair of bifocals onto the tip of her nose. "May I?" she asked, holding out an open palm. "I assure you I have seen plenty of death in my time and am quite immune to it."

Jamie handed her the stack of glosses, and watched the woman peer down her nose at each photograph in turn. It was against protocols to let anyone outside of law enforcement see the images. But for some reason it felt okay.

"You see, my dear," the woman said as she examined the pictures, "traditionally, rings of roses and ash crosses have been used throughout the ages as icons to denote mass infections. The most well-known of which is the mark of the Bubonic plague in Europe during the Fourteenth Century." She glanced Jamie's way, over the top of her spectacles. "I take it you've heard of the Black Death?"

It took several long seconds for Jamie's sluggish mind to catch up.

*Ring-a-round a rosie . . . the Black Death . . . the mark of the plague.*

She saw the woman's silky brow crinkle like tissue paper. "My dear, are you all right? Did I speak out of place? You look like you've just seen a ghost."

No ghost, Jamie thought. Just a very real monster.

# 112

This time round, there was no time for showers and a change of clothes. No time to mourn Marty's death or try figuring out the craziness behind it all. Events were sweeping us along.

Harland Candlewood had been identified on Fremont Street, downtown at the *Golden Nugget,* and the Feds had beaten us to him.

Sonny and I jumped in an unmarked police car and took off at full whack. Several black-and-whites in tow. There was no keeping to the speed limit. Everyone's adrenaline level was back in the stratosphere. We careened through slower traffic heading north along The Strip, almost knocking off wing mirrors as we went.

Police sirens soared through the night.

The heads-up had come through from one of Sonny's contacts working security at the downtown casino. A posse of Feds had grabbed Candlewood about five minutes ago and hustled him into a private poker lounge. They'd booted out the resident poker players and put armed men on the door. It sounded like retribution was being dealt out at the *Golden Nugget.* Somebody was going to pay for Marty's death and right now that somebody was Harland Candlewood. Guilty until proven otherwise.

I was conscious that we had to get there and get him, before there was nothing left of him to question.

If Candlewood was part of a killer duo, we needed him alive.

We needed him to identify his partner.

Our procession charged through red lights like bulls at the Pamplona run. Sonny drove like a Daytona veteran. We zigzagged through standing traffic fast enough to make it blur. More black-and-whites fell in behind, converging at intersections. By the time we'd arrived at the touristy Fremont Street, there must have been over thirty sets of flashing roof lights in our wake.

"Out of the way!" Sonny hollered as we leapt out of our cars and headed into the casino. "Police!"

Puzzled tourists parted. Lips gossiped. Camera-phones flashed. Fifty or so cops barging into the swanky premises (some of us still blackened and damp and looking like miners after a cave-in) must have looked like we were about to collar America's Most Wanted. And maybe we were.

We ran across the marble lobby, leaving dirty footprints. We crashed through the casino. And vaulted the spiraling stairs leading up to the high-roller rooms.

A pair of fierce-faced Feds were standing either side of the frosted-glass door leading into the private poker lounge. They looked edgy. Had every right to be. When they saw our arsenal of cops spilling out onto the landing, that edginess turned to something close to distress. They held up hands as we advanced, trying to get us to back off. But nothing was going to stop us. Not even the threat of violence. We were a tsunami of law enforcement, sweeping everything out of our way.

"What's the deal here?" Sonny barked as we burst through the glass doors, very nearly knocking them off their hinges.

I counted seven G-Men standing around an oval-shaped poker table – four of which I recognized instantly: Agents Stubbs, Cherry, Blom and Wong. The other three were meathead lackeys with all the charm of dungeon torturers. They all had their jackets off, except for Wong. Shirtsleeves rolled up. Faces hard and sweaty in the unforgiving light coming from the overhead strip lamp. It looked like we'd walked in on a Mafia tea party.

A blond-haired guy was sprawled on the poker table itself. His fancy silk shirt was ripped around the collar. Blood coated his face and neck. One shoe was missing. His fingers looked mashed by the heels of guns. Bloodied and curled like bird claws. I could hear him whimpering, sobbing.

I'd never walked in on this kind of FBI lynch mob before.

I was shocked. We all were.

Old-time Vegas, alive and kicking.

"Stay out of this." Wong spat with the charisma of a rattlesnake. "This is Bureau business. The suspect has just admitted to murder."

"Looks like he would have admitted his mother's from Mars if you'd asked him," I said.

"Screw you, Quinn."

In a flash, Sonny had her gun out. It was a dangerous move. Like throwing gasoline on a fire. But we all copied – even the Feds. A clatter of firearms being cocked. Twenty or more weapons aimed across the poker table with bullets ready to fly.

Face-off.

It was unreal.

"I think you're forgetting this is my jurisdiction," Sonny said with real grit in her teeth. "Now step away from Mr. Candlewood. I'm not going to say please, or ask twice."

Wong sneered. Wong was good at sneering. A lifetime of practice had perfected the technique. "Or what, Inspector Maxwell? You'll shoot me? Give me a break."

Sonny took a step forward, aimed the muzzle of her gun at the dip between Wong's snake eyes.

"If I have to waste a good bullet on your weasel face," she said, "I will. Same goes for every last one of you boys. You should all know I'm premenstrual right now – which means I won't be taking prisoners. So it would really be in your best interests not to piss off my itchy trigger finger any more than you already have done."

I saw the posse think about it, collectively. I could smell rusty cogs whirring – or maybe that was Wong's cheap cologne. They were undecided if Sonny meant the threat. But couldn't take the chance she wasn't bluffing.

She sounded genuine to me.

The tension was as thick as London fog.

Then the cornered Feds lowered their weapons and started backing away from the poker table.

I felt the relief pour from lungs.

As if on cue, cops swarmed in around us – enough to clear us a direct path to Candlewood.

"You think this is over?" Wong snarled as the Feds were manhandled out of the poker lounge. "Think again. You'll pay for this, Quinn. This isn't over."

I had a bad feeling it wasn't.

# 113

Gaining an authentic admission of guilt takes art and finesse. It's easy to beat a confession out of a suspect. Harder to make it genuine. Harder still to make it stick. Wong and his Bureau bullies had beaten Harland Candlewood to a pulp. Under extreme duress he'd blurted out a confession inadmissible in every court in the land.

"Doctors think it's touch and go," Detective Michael Shakes was saying as we peered through the glass partition into the hospital room where Harland Candlewood was hooked up to monitors. His face was hidden by bandages. He looked like the Invisible Man without the hat and the glasses. I could see the colored pulse lines fluctuate on the monitor displays next to his bed. He'd slipped into a coma on the way in and his rates were up and down like the Dow.

We were at Sunrise Hospital: just Shakes and me. It was after midnight. I'd persuaded Sonny to go home to her kids and leave us to it. Sonny had argued the point; all fired up and ready to shakedown the Feds. But I'd insisted. One of us needed to be bright and fresh for the press conference scheduled for the morning. And, besides, Candlewood wasn't going anywhere; comas aren't day trips to the coast. We had a handful of cops guarding him, checking IDs at the nurse's station on the way in. More uniforms downstairs, preventing the media from overrunning the hospital. No one even remotely related to a federal agent was being allowed within a half mile of Harland Candlewood.

"The Feds fucked us over," Shakes lamented as we gazed through the glass at the unmoving patient. "Even if

Candlewood makes it, the doctors say there's a good chance he'll be brain damaged."

Candlewood's outlook was gloomy, for sure. The next twenty-four hours were critical. His doctors were fifty-fifty. If Candlewood pulled through, we had a chance of finding out what role, if any, the head of the biotech outfit played in *The Undertaker* murders. If Candlewood didn't pull through, there were going to be tough questions asked all round at Washington.

Understandably, I was angry with Wong and his posse. We all were. Their lynch mob mentality had ruined any chances we'd had of interviewing Candlewood and of finding out the real identity behind the Ethan Davey Copes character. As yet, we weren't pressing charges; it all depended on what happened next and whether the DA buckled under federal pressure.

Just when we'd found our legs, the Feds had come along and crippled us.

No wonder Shakes was grinding teeth. So was I.

I heard his cell phone sing. He answered it.

I thought about the possibility of the head of the biotech company actually being *The Undertaker*. Did all the pieces fit? According to his credit card transactions, he'd had a room at the Ramada on Vermont in Hollywood the day Helena Margolis had met her death. Physically, he was a good match for our APB photo fit. We'd found the coat and cap, together with syringes and controlled chemicals, in his hotel room before it had been blown to kingdom come. Half his employees had been murdered here in Vegas.

Enough evidence to send him to his own execution by lethal injection.

But something was niggling away at me.

Was this bruised and battered man lying here really the monster I'd been chasing all the way from LA? Looking him over, I wasn't so sure. Couldn't be sure.

Something didn't feel right. My *Uh Oh Radar* was making noises.

"Get this," Shakes said as he came off the phone. "That was Duane. Seems that our friends the Feds have fucked us over twice in one night. The lockdown's been lifted. They're letting everyone leave town. The Feds are closing up shop and moving out."

*   *   *

We were screwed.

In the power vacuum created by Marty Gunner's untimely death, the Special Agent-in-Charge of the Las Vegas Field Office had assumed control of the case. My case, remember. His name was Hugh Winters. And he didn't consider me his best buddy – not for a long time, anyway.

Shakes and I arrived at the situation room to find techies uncoupling computers and stowing away screens into boxes filled with packing peanuts. It looked like backstage after a music gig. Go home: show's over. Most of the FBI personnel were nowhere to be seen – probably already on their way back to Virginia or DC. Just one or two Feds left to oversee the clean-up. Hugh Winters wasn't one of them.

"I'm going to see Winters," I told Shakes as we marched out of the *MGM Grand*.

Shakes had to run to keep up. "Gabe, wait. It's the middle of the night. Listen to me. He'll be at home. Tucked up in his bed with Mrs. Winters and their two-year-old Shih Tzu."

I didn't ask.

"You sure this is a good idea?"

My teeth were clenched. "It's the best one I have right now."

"What about your friend from Quantico?"

I'd called Bill the moment I'd heard Winters was hijacking the investigation. But the connection had gone straight to voicemail – as it had when I'd called him about Candlewood before that. I was worried. No one had heard from Bill since my text message earlier in the day.

"Bill's out of the loop," I said as we crossed the taxi rank. "It's down to us to rescue this case now, before the Feds box it up and throw away the key."

We got in Shakes' car and headed west toward Spring Valley, pedal to the metal, as they say.

A showdown with the resident SAC wouldn't go down well. I knew I'd be treading on toes by confronting Winters face to face. But I was through pussyfooting around. Good people had died these last few days. The Bureau thought that by pinning all of the murders on Candlewood's head they could simply make everything go away. They thought that by hijacking my case I'd go away too. They were wrong.

After a couple of miles, we turned off Tropicana into the brightly-lit entranceway leading into a gated community. The place looked asleep. Darkened homes retreating from vanilla streetlights.

"We're here to see Hugh Winters," Shakes said through the driver's window to a bored-looking security guard leaning out of his hut.

"You got an invitation?"

"Best kind." Shakes showed his police shield.

The barrier lifted and we passed through the checkpoint.

We took a left, following a crescent. Another left and we arrived at the Winters residence. It was located at the end of a quiet cul-de-sac of big fancy six-bedroom dwellings, on a slight north-leaning rise and overlooking a private golf club. Trimmed lawns and imported pines. Swimming pools out back. All of it in darkness. I asked

Shakes to stay in the car, then stormed up the Winters' driveway.

It took three persistent rings of the doorbell and a lot of knuckles against wood before lights blinked on in the house. I could hear somebody lumbering down wooden stairs. A light came on in the hall. Bolts scraped back.

"What the hell is your problem, detective?" Hugh Winters demanded as he swung open the heavy front door and glared in my direction.

Hugh Winters is a jowly sixty-something with a balding pate, a stubby little nose and gold-wire spectacles. Sounds juvenile, I know, but he reminds me of one of the little pigs from the Grimm fairy tale. I saw him pull his heavy housecoat around his paunch as he gave me a *get the hell out of Dodge* nod.

"It's after one o'clock in the morning," he continued before I could speak. "Are you insane? Make an appointment in business hours like everybody else. Goodnight."

He went to shut the door, to slam it in my face. I put a foot in the closing gap. He pulled it open again, though not as wide this time. He gave me a malevolent glare.

"This is my investigation," I said.

"Was," he answered, coolly. "As in past tense, detective. We allowed you in as a matter of courtesy. That invitation has now been rescinded."

"You've lifted the lockdown."

"We caught the suspect. The FBI nailed him in one day. More than you could do in a week. We'll be taking full credit for the capture. Now get your damned foot out of my door and go back to wherever you came from."

He tried closing it on my foot again. Didn't happen.

"You didn't just nail him," I growled, raising myself a little taller, "you crucified him."

"I hear he resisted arrest."

"Bullshit."

Winters' piggy little eyebrows lifted halfway up his domed brow.

"Your boys worked him over so good he'll need spoon-feeding for the rest of his life. And that's providing he pulls through."

"Not my problem, detective."

"You don't get it, Winters. I needed him to talk. Your goons had no right roughing him up like that. Marty wouldn't have okayed that kind of retribution. For all we know, Candlewood isn't the killer."

Winters' face was doing its best not to break into a snarl. "Go home, detective. You've got your man. Do the paperwork and get the hell out of my State."

My fists were balled. Red mist descending. Muscles tensing, ready to propel me into an imminent brawl.

Beyond Winters, I could hear somebody else shuffling down the wooden stairs. I caught sight of fluffy slippers and a pearlescent silken kimono. A scent of primrose.

"Darling, who is it?"

"Nobody." Winters answered, keeping his little piggy eyes on mine. "Go back to bed, dear."

More shuffling. Then a blonde-haired woman appeared in the gap next to Winters. She was in her early fifties, but looked ten years younger. *God, she was beautiful.* Eyes like sapphires. Lips like ruby.

"Gabe?"

"Angela."

"What are you doing here?"

"To pick a fight with Hugh." I'd never been able to lie to Angela.

She poked Winters in his fleshy ribs with an elbow. "Has my grumpy husband been misbehaving again?"

"You could say that. I'm sorry I woke you."

She flapped a dismissive hand. "I was still counting sheep. We haven't seen you since the funeral. How are you, Gabe?"

"Pissed."

She smiled. No need to say it. I felt the heat go out of my rage. Angela had always been a calming influence.

I saw her nudge her hubby again. "Hugh, you didn't tell me it was Gabe. Stop being a complete asshole and show him in. It's rude leaving him on the stoop."

Winters made as if to open the door fully. I took my foot out of the frame. Then he reversed his decision and slammed the door in my face.

I heard the two of them burst into argument. I backed up a little. I didn't want to cause a fight. Didn't want to upset Angela. Then the light in the hall went out and heavy feet trudged back up the wooden stairs.

I took a deep breath, let it escape slowly through pursed lips.

The remainder of the house lights winked out one by one as I made my way back to the car.

# 114

I'd never subscribed to sulking or skulking, but right now I was considering an annual subscription. I got Shakes to drop me off at the *MGM Grand*. It was after two in the morning. For the first time in a relentless week of chasing *The Undertaker* a sense of the directionless had settled over me. Dark clouds against the dark of night. I needed to regroup, refocus and rethink what I thought I already knew. Caffeine always helped.

I picked up a thick black Americano from the all-night deli in the hotel and drained it dry before I reached my terrace suite.

I ran a sink.

Called Bill.

He didn't pick up.

I left another message, this time voicing my worry.

Then I shed Roger's blackened clothes. Washed. Shaved. Examined the fresh butterfly closures on the bony corner of my temple. Wondered if they were waterproof. No traces of blood, as yet; always a good sign.

I popped a couple of aspirins and swilled them down with tepid water.

Then I showered. Scrubbed filthy plaster out of hair and eyes. Worked soap into skin creases. Watched gray water drain down the plughole. It felt indecent washing away the remnants of the bomb blast – like I didn't give a damn about Marty's death. But I did. I blamed myself for it. Anyone would.

I rinsed off, climbed out, rubbed down.

The butterfly closures were intact.

Sonny had laundered my LA attire. I pulled on clean clothes, musing over the evening's tragic events.

Something felt hinky about the whole affair.

If you ask me: it was all a little too contrived – like one of those movies where the plot conveniently intersects unrelated characters just to add an otherwise implausible twist.

Despite the evidence, I wasn't convinced Candlewood was the only killer – if at all a killer in his own right. I could no longer think of *The Undertaker* in terms of being Ethan Davey Copes either; not since the boy's body had been exhumed back in Jackson.

That left three possibilities:

Candlewood was the killer. He worked alone. He'd thrown up smokescreen after smokescreen to obscure his true identity, which meant the Feds were right. They had their man and it was game over. I could go home, close the case and move on. Or . . .

Candlewood had an accomplice. They'd lodged together at the Ramada on Vermont back in LA. Maybe the guy who liked to mask his voice, which meant there was still a killer on the loose. And I couldn't allow the Feds to close the investigation until he was in custody or dead. Or . . .

Candlewood was a stooge. The real killer, *The Undertaker,* was an unidentified subject (an Unsub as the Feds liked to say), still at large. He'd used Candlewood as a decoy to throw us off track. Planted the incriminating evidence in Candlewood's Tower suite and framed him for the murders. In which case, the Feds were wrong. And it was game on.

I thought about the implications of all three scenarios. We had a connection: Harland Labs. I still didn't know how the LA victims factored into it. But I knew they must, somehow. We also had the working theory that the killings were a means to prevent a future calamity from happening. Bizarre just thinking about it, I know. But potentially fatal to ignore.

If the killer believed it, we had to believe it too.

I thought about the biotech outfit up in Boston – which had become the primary connection in our investigation.

If Candlewood was the killer, why systematically kill his employees and those connected to his firm? Why not simply terminate their contracts instead of their lives? It didn't make any sense. Unless Candlewood's only involvement was as a scapegoat for the real killer.

I slid open the glass door leading out onto the terrace, recoiled from the icy wind.

When push came to shove, I could only be certain of one thing: if Candlewood wasn't the killer then *The Undertaker* was still out there. And the biggest manhunt in Nevada history had just been called off. For nothing.

I left the sliding door ajar and curled up on the bed, finally shivering my way into a tortured sleep.

# 115

New York City was snowbound and had been for weeks. Old gray slush was compacted on the ground. Hard as granite. Jamie could feel the chill of it eating into her face as she watched their shaky descent through the gunmetal cloud deck. The Boeing 737 landed in a squall of hail and slithered its way down the salted apron. One or two people cheered and clapped, mostly with relief.

Jamie said her goodbyes to the British woman and made her way to the car rentals counter. She opted for a two-door intermediate then took the courtesy bus out to the rental pick-up point. It was winter-muffler weather. Far too cold for her thin Californian coat. The sun had risen an hour ago, but it looked more like eight in the evening than eight in the morning. She found her allocated car and warmed her hands against the blowers before setting off. She debated telephoning Gabe, but remembered the time difference. She sent him a text message instead. Then she punched a zip code into the GPS navigator and followed its monosyllabic directions out of the airport.

Bullets of sleet rained from an ashen sky.

She turned on the wipers.

Traffic was heavy heading south – slowed by the inclement weather. The drive was long, monotonous. Lack of sleep dimmed the edges of her vision. She should have grabbed a coffee at the airport, maybe some breakfast, maybe even a nap. Too late now.

She thought about her destination as she drove, not knowing what or who she'd find once she got there.

An hour and twenty-five miles later, she crossed a bridge with an impressively long span. Cold, gray waters stretching to a slate-colored horizon. The sleet began to ease off as she left the city behind. Up ahead, the sky was brightening to an aluminum gray. She left the expressway after the first toll station and continued south. After a couple of miles, the navigator told her to take a sharp left down a sloping lane. The backend of the rental fishtailed on the slippery corner. She corrected it. Now she could see the Atlantic Ocean coming toward her. A wedge of steel seen through the skeletons of leafless trees.

*"You have arrived at your destination."*

Jamie slotted the rental behind a black SUV and climbed out of the car. It couldn't have been more than a degree or two above freezing. She pulled her flimsy coat close, braced herself against the bracing breeze. She could hear gulls cawing in the distance. Taste salt in the back of her throat.

There was only one house at the end of the lane: a redbrick construction with colonial undertones. White-rimmed windows with Georgian-style panes. A wisp of white smoke curling from a terracotta smoke stack.

She climbed the stone stoop leading to a large front door, took a deep breath before pressing the bronze doorbell. She'd already decided that if nobody was home she'd wait for their return – probably freeze to death in the process.

No answer.

She skipped from foot to foot; trying to stay warm. She rapped a fist against the white-painted wood. The cold impact stung her knuckles. She knocked again, harder with the heel of her hand.

Jamie detected movement from within. She backtracked a little as the door creaked open.

It was a man in his early thirties. Tousled dark hair and the makings of a five o'clock shadow. He reminded Jamie of Robert De Niro in *Taxi Driver*. The same smoldering smile. Same broody eyes.

"Can I help you?"

There was a bundle in his arms, she noticed. A baby, she realized. Wrapped up snug in baby-blue woolen blankets.

With cold fingers, Jamie held up her ID. "I'm sorry to disturb you, sir. I'm with the police department."

He glanced at her badge, nodded. "You're a long way from home, Jamie Garcia," he whispered, drawing the baby bundle closer to his chest. "How can I be of assistance to the LAPD?"

He had a thick southern accent. An infectious smile. For some inexplicable reason, Jamie had always thought there was something strangely attractive about a good-looking man nursing a helpless baby.

"I believe Katherine Dufresne lives here."

"You mean my wife? Yes, in fact she does. Least, I hope she does. Is she in some kind of trouble? She collects parking tickets like they're postage stamps."

"Is your wife home, sir?"

"Actually, no. Well, in a manner of speaking, yes." He glanced over Jamie's head, as if to peer down the road toward the open ocean. "Kate likes to run, you see. Come rain or shine. Up and down the beach she goes. Incessantly."

"When will she be back?"

"Soon, soon." He looked back and smiled the same cinematic smile. "You're more than welcome to come inside and wait. I'm sure she won't be long. Warmer than catching your death out here."

\*   \*   \*

The large entrance hall had a timber floor and a chandelier made from an old ship's wheel hung from a vaulted ceiling. A theme that complemented its nautical setting.

"Your coat?"

Jamie shucked it off. "Thanks."

The man draped it over a peg on the wall. "Not used to this kind of weather, I guess — you being from California and all. Got to have rhinoceros skin for this climate." He nodded toward an open doorway. "The living room's right through there. Just make yourself at home while I put this little critter in his crib. Coffee?"

"Yes, thanks. One sugar."

The man flashed another one of those infectious smiles and disappeared up the hall.

Distantly, Jamie could hear music tinkling away in another part of the house. It sounded like Dean Martin lamenting a fallen love.

The living room was a treasure trove of antique furniture. Maritime collectables. A real log fire burning merrily away in one corner. Yellowy walls with oil paintings of sail ships and steam packets.

She went over to the large bay window and gazed out. It was a picture-postcard view of the wintry ocean. Gulls swooping in the distance like white stitches in a gray blanket. A snowy garden sloping down to a shale beach and a small wooden jetty. Something that looked like a cruise liner creeping across the horizon.

She picked up a framed photograph from the window ledge. The picture had been taken aboard a small fishing boat on a bright summer's day. It depicted her host standing next to a captured shark. The shark was dangling by its tail from a hook and pulley, bleeding onto the boat's white wooden decking. The man in the picture was beaming.

"That's a long-fin Mako. All seven feet and five hundred pounds of pure killing machine."

Jamie turned.

Her host was walking toward her, holding two mugs of steaming coffee. "Took almost an hour to wrestle her out the water."

Jamie put the picture back on the sill and accepted one of the drinks.

"Please, officer, take a seat."

They sat, on opposite sofas, either side of the crackling log fire.

"Are you going to tell me what my wife's done?"

"It's nothing," Jamie said.

"Must be something, for you to come all this way."

"Just a few questions." Jamie sipped at the coffee, mindful that this man might not be aware of his wife's past. "Your home's lovely by the way."

The man studied her through his big dark eyes. She saw his lips part as he was about to question her further. But the wail of a crying baby drifted into the room.

He got to his feet. "I guess my wife's little secret will have to wait. Drink up, Jamie. I shall return and interrogate you further in due course."

Jamie watched her host leave the room, relieved that the microscope had been removed.

She drank more coffee. Her lips tingled as they thawed. The crackling fire was gloriously warm. She yawned, spotted a hefty leather-bound photo album sitting on a side table. She threw the remainder of the coffee down her throat. Then, using both hands, heaved the heavy book onto her lap.

The photographs were the regular type: mostly vacation snaps and family gatherings. Some in and around the beach house itself. Christmassy ones. A happy married couple down by the ocean's edge, hugging each other. Pages filled with baby pictures – from birth to present day. He was a good-looking boy. Very much like his father. But there was something vaguely familiar about the mother too. Something that fingered at the back of Jamie's mind.

Distantly, she could hear the man singing a soft lullaby.

*Ring a-round the rosie, a pocketful of posies . . .*

She let it wash over her. Soothing like a hot soak. She yawned some more.

Another page: professional-looking portraits with older family members. Several of her host and a woman she presumed to be his mother at various stages in his life. One taken when he was a boy, at a zoo on a Technicolor day. A close-up of his wife, Katherine Dufresne, all dolled-up, taken in what looked like a TV studio. TV cameras and boom microphones. She was standing next to a man in a tuxedo. A man she knew as Professor Jeffrey Samuels.

Suddenly, Jamie's heart flooded with adrenaline.

"How are we feeling?"

She looked up, startled.

Her host was advancing across the plush Persian rug. Jamie blinked, had to force her eyes to focus. All at once, her head felt too heavy for her neck to support.

He knelt down beside her and put his face close to hers. "I expect you're wondering what's happening to you."

Instinctively, she tried to jerk away, but nothing happened. She tried to answer, but nothing came out.

"Your coffee was dosed with a fast-acting paralytic," he whispered in her ear. "In about twenty seconds time you won't be able to feel a single damn thing."

Jamie could hear a gurgling sound in the back of her throat. It might have been a scream. It was the best she could do.

The man with the *Taxi Driver* face brushed a strand of hair from off her cheek, then leaned in and kissed her gently on the mouth.

She tasted mint mouthwash trying to mask tobacco.

"Is it scary knowing you're a fly caught in the spider's web?" he whispered against her numbing lips. "Is it scary, Jamie, knowing you've stepped over the abyss and there's no going back?"

# 116

The hard Nevada water had made my hair fluffy. I spent the best part of five minutes trying to flatten it down before giving it up as a bad job. Another bad hair day in a long line of bad hair days was the least of my troubles. We were fifteen minutes away from a press conference and the newshounds were baying for blood.

The news of the explosion at *Caesar's Palace* had been all over the media since sunrise. Zoomed-in shots of the blackened hole ripped out of the Palace Tower. Debris smoldering in the oasis pool area. Interviews with terrified eyewitnesses. EMS vehicles screaming from the scene. Video footage looping every ten minutes.

The press would have themselves a turkey shoot.

I'd already been on the phone to Sonny to co-ordinate strategies. Get our stories straight. I didn't like the thought of talking to the media one bit. A room full of Stacey Kellermans isn't my idea of a pajama party.

There was a text message from Jamie on my phone when I woke:

*'Gabe. The survivor's address came through, but her home number's unlisted. She's still in New York. Staten Island. On my way there now to interview her. Don't be mad! I'll be in touch. In the meantime, here's something to think about: are the killer's calling cards connected to the nursery rhyme Ring o' Roses? Or the Bubonic Plague? Jamie."*

At first I was mad, but I understood. Jamie was conscientious and probably feeling useless in my absence. If flying all the way to New York to interview a possible survivor of *The Undertaker* made her feel worthy, then who was I to put a dampener on it?

I sent her a message back, saying: *Be careful. Call me soon.*

Then breakfast arrived, brought to my room by a tip-hungry teenager. I shoveled down eggs-over-easy with French toast, breakfast muffins and waffles with maple syrup. It was the most I'd eaten in one sitting for weeks. I washed it down with lashings of hot coffee and a handful of antacids.

My cell rang:

*Bill Teague.*

"Bill? Thank God! I was worried something terrible had happened."

"It did." I heard him say. "Fuller summoned me to Washington on the last minute. Demanded an in-person account on how agents managed to get themselves killed in Jackson. No time to return your calls. Then we got the news about Marty and the place exploded."

Marty Gunner was dead. The memory thumped me in the gut. "Bill, I'm sorry."

"Me too. Marty was the best. I'm on my way back to Vegas, to help out."

"Haven't you heard? The show's over. Candlewood's hospitalized and in custody. The National Guard have all gone home for the weekend. Your colleagues have packed up and shipped out."

"Doesn't mean shit, Gabriel. I'm embarrassed to say my colleagues got it wrong. Candlewood is innocent, and I have evidence to substantiate the fact. I'm on my way back."

"But what about Fuller?"

"Fuller can go fly. Expect me later today. Later, buddy."

# 117

The press conference had been put together in one of the hotel's meeting rooms, down the hall from the abandoned situation room. A couple of dozen chairs faced a small podium with a table and two chairs up top. It was already full to popping with paparazzi.

Twenty-four hours ago, every top brass official in the State would have been here. Maybe one or two Bureau bigwigs. With the capture of Candlewood, the big cheeses had stayed home, enjoying their Sunday breakfast in bed and content to watch this play out on the TV.

I surveyed the press pool teeming with news sharks. I couldn't see Stacey Kellerman. I relaxed a fraction. No signs of Hugh Winters either. I relaxed a little more. The brick-faced sheriff was standing with two of his cohorts over in the far corner.

"You okay, Gabe?" Sonny whispered as we walked toward the raised dais.

"Press conferences are like pulling teeth."

Truth was, I wanted to be one of those guys watching this play out on the TV, letting somebody else get their tale in a spin.

We took our places in the crosshairs. A tech guy wearing headphones came over and made sure the cluster of microphones positioned in the middle of the desk were picking up. They were. Then he backed away as a general hush settled over our eagle-eyed audience.

A spotlight hit my face. I squinted at the sudden glare.

Video cameras aimed our way. One or two cameras flashed.

Sonny tapped a microphone, "Hope you ladies are here for the bingo," she said into the pick-up.

A wave of laughter rippled through the room.

I took a sip of water. It tasted like vinegar.

# 118

As the killer now known worldwide as *The Undertaker* waved farewell to his son and the fifty-bucks-an-hour nanny, he wondered what it would be like to kill someone in his own home – right here, in the house he shared with his loving wife and their brand new baby. Not just anyone's life. A police officer's life. What would that feel like? What would it feel like to kill a cop in his own family home?

He continued to grin manically and wave big daddy bye-byes to the shiny red Nissan compact as it climbed up the road and out of sight, taking away his baby boy, probably forever.

# 119

Yes, the lockdown was lifted. Yes, there had been casualties. Yes, federal agents had died both here and in Tennessee. Yes, a suspect had been detained, but was currently on life support and under armed guard. No, we didn't believe he was the killer.

Five minutes in, I saw Agent Wong enter the room. I had hoped he'd keep a low profile after beating Candlewood senseless. I was wrong. He still wore that annoyingly smarmy face of his, as if it were a flag on parade day. He made a beeline for the sheriff without even glancing our way.

I watched Wong whisper something in the sheriff's ear – a glance in my direction from the sheriff – then the two of them hurriedly left the room together.

". . . and that's just about all we have until we get the coroner's report," Sonny finished up.

"Detective Quinn?"

I searched the room. My inquisitor was a tall redhead with high cheekbones and piercing green eyes.

"Carrie Voss, Las Vegas Star."

"Yes, Carrie?"

I was halfway through sketching out a brief outline of why we'd seen fit to enforce the lockdown when I saw the sheriff return. He waved at the pair of lemon-faced officers still manning the corner, pointed in our direction.

"This looks like fun." I heard Sonny comment under her breath.

The sheriff joined his men and all three started to steamroll straight toward us. They looked like bullies spoiling for a fight.

"One moment, Carrie," I said, placing a hand over the microphone nest.

The trio climbed onto the podium. The sheriff wore an uncomfortable frown – like he'd just had a mishap in the restroom and everybody was staring at the damp patch on his crotch.

"Detective Quinn, please come with me. Inspector Maxwell will take things from here."

"Is it Candlewood?" I asked.

"Just come with me," he said, this time more firmly. "You okay with that, Sonny?"

I sensed Sonny's defenses prickle. "Not really. Unless you haven't noticed, we're slap bang in the middle of a press conference here. What's going on?"

"Just take over the show and I'll explain later." He had his back to the cameras. His tone was brusque. I didn't like it.

Sonny leaned across the desk and covered the microphones with a hand. "We're live on air. What the hell is going on?"

The sheriff gave Sonny a *your job's on the line if you don't do as I say right this minute* scowl.

I got to my feet. "It's all right, Sonny. I'll be back soon as I clear this up. Meanwhile, give them hell."

The sheriff leaned into the pick-ups. "Ladies and gentlemen, Senior Inspector Sonny Maxwell will be answering all your questions from here on in. Thank you for your time and patience. Have a good day."

Then, to the rattle of raised whispers and snapping cameras, I was escorted out of the room.

# 120

In spite of the judicial system's claims to the contrary, there is no such thing as innocent until proven guilty. Rightly or wrongly, innocence is never presumed.

"Detective Gabriel Quinn you have the right to remain silent. Anything you say can and will be used against you in a court of law."

We were out in the hallway. A little ways from the room where the press conference was still being held. Our little group was attracting inquisitive glances from nosy passersby. I had an officer on either shoulder. I could smell their unease. One was reading me my rights from a little pocket reminder. It was all bullshit.

I shot a grouchy face at the sheriff. "Do you mind explaining what this is all about?"

"You have the right to speak to an attorney," the uniform continued unabated. "If you cannot afford an attorney, one will be appointed to you."

"Why am I being arrested? This is crazy. Sheriff? Anyone?"

"Do you understand these rights as they have been read to you?"

"Will you cut the bullshit and get to the point?"

"Detective, do you understand these rights as they have been read to you?"

I glared at the officer. "Yes! Dammit! What the hell is going on here?"

"Please, step into the room." The officer opened up the door to a supply closet.

"Are you serious?"

Both uniforms placed heels of hands on butts of guns.

"If you refuse to comply you will be forcibly detained."

I was incredulous. Scratch that; I was furious. I was being treated like a wayward schoolboy facing detention. The sheriff was doing everything in his power to avoid my demanding glare. The arresting officer shrugged out his handcuffs. I gave him a scowl and backed up into the supply closet. The door closed in my face. I shook my head, baffled by the run of events and by the unorthodox procedure. After about a minute, I found a light switch and threw it on.

The room was small, cramped, and full of what looked like leftover conventions miscellanea.

I got out my cell and tried Bill's number. It went straight to voicemail.

*Damn!*

I dropped onto on a crate and chewed some cheek.

A minute and twenty questions later, the door burst open and Sonny flew into the room.

I sprang to my feet. It was the first time I'd seen Sonny looking anywhere near shaken and the sight shook me too.

"Well that was sweet," she said as she slammed the door behind her. "After you left, the shit hit the fan and everyone just got a mouthful." She started pacing back and forth – which wasn't easy, given the confines of the closet.

I grabbed her by the shoulders, made her look at me. "Sonny . . ."

"Gabe, this is seriously screwed up."

I could see she wasn't bluffing.

"I mean *seriously* screwed up. From the top all the way down to the bottom."

"Sonny . . . what's going on?"

She dragged a deep and wavy breath, composed herself. "They sold you down the river. That's what's going on."

"Who?"

"Those damn Feds. That's who! I told you we couldn't trust them. They look after their own. Always do. And screw everybody else."

"Sonny . . . will you just tell me what's happened?"

Another deep breath, "Winters came in right after you left. He threw me off the podium and took over the conference."

"He did? The son of a bitch. Why?"

"You remember Stacey Kellerman?"

I nodded. "How could I forget her? Has she got something to do with this? What's she been saying to the Feds? What lies has she been spinning this time?"

"She went and got herself murdered," Sonny said as her gaze leveled with mine. "She's dead, Gabe. And they think you killed her. The Feds think you murdered Stacey Kellerman."

\* \* \*

When you get to my age you figure you've just about heard every line there is to spin. Revelations hardly flummox. Being accused of murder is the exception. My face must have been a real picture – like Munch's *Scream,* only less animated.

"Breathe," Sonny said.

I did. But it wasn't easy; I had fire in my lungs.

"Stacey Kellerman's dead?" I couldn't believe my own words. "But how?"

"Somebody bludgeoned her to death. The Feds are all over it like a bad dose of hives."

"When did this happen?"

"No idea. But I intend to find out. Word is, the Feds got an anonymous tipoff sometime in the early hours of the morning."

"They did? Why didn't we hear about it?"

"The call came through to the situation room right before they started closing it down. It got patched through to Wong."

And Wong wasn't the sharing type.

"So while Milk and I were at the hospital . . ."

"Wong and his men went to Kellerman's."

I made a face. "Sonny, that doesn't add up. Why would the Feds go running to Stacey's place on the back of an anonymous tipoff? That's police business. *Your* business. You should have got the call."

"Unless he thought it related directly to our case."

"Which would mean the tipster had inside information." I turned up my lip. My *Uh-Oh Radar* was pinging. "Have we any idea what this tipster said?"

"No. But if it came through the nine-one-one network we can retrieve the call log."

I shook my head, trying to force the revelation through my thick skull. "And you say she was bludgeoned to death?"

"Gabe, I know what you're thinking. I'm thinking the same thing too. It doesn't fit with his MO. It's probably unrelated. Nothing to do with our case."

You know me and coincidences.

"Sonny, I still don't see how I fit into all this."

"Well, there's the cruncher," she said. "I know it's all a crock and you had nothing to do with it, but the Feds swear they found incriminating evidence at the Kellerman crime scene. Proof definitive, Gabe. Something that points the finger of blame directly at you."

Another stunner.

"Me?"

At any other time I would have been bowled over by this second accusation, but I was still flat on my back from the first.

"You do know I'm being set up?"

"Gabe, you don't need to convince me; I'm on your side. Heck, we've spent most of the weekend

443

together. I know you're innocent. What I don't understand is why the Feds would falsify evidence."

"Because they didn't," I said.

It had suddenly occurred to me that I'd played straight into the killer's hands.

"Sonny, it's not the Feds. They're just the stooges in all this. It's him. The Undertaker. He's the one setting me up."

Now it was Sonny's turn to make a face. "Candlewood killed Kellerman?"

"Forget Candlewood! Candlewood's a red herring thrown in to throw us off the scent. Candlewood isn't The Undertaker. The Undertaker's still out there. He set me up."

"But why?"

The door opened. The sheriff appeared in the doorway like the man who marches the guilty to the gallows. He waved us both out. He still had his cohorts with him. There were more boys and girls from the Metro PD holding crowds of reporters at bay down the hallway. The press conference was over; there were bigger fish to fry. Namely, me. Suddenly, the arrest of the Celebrity Cop from LA was more newsworthy than a dozen homicides.

"Sheriff, what's happening?"

The sheriff drew a troubled breath, let it slowly out. "This is no longer our call. SAC Winters is personally heading up the investigation into Ms. Kellerman's homicide."

My mouth was a hard line, "And I'm their prime suspect."

"I don't know anything more than that, detective. This is pretty much out of my hands. It's an FBI matter now."

"You do know I'm being framed?"

The sheriff didn't acknowledge it either way.

"So what happens next?" Sonny asked.

"Until further notice, Detective Quinn is under house arrest."

"And you're buying their crap?"

I saw the sheriff's face squirm. He knew he was being manipulated, but his hands might as well have been cuffed.

"Like I say, Sonny, it's not my call. They've got agents all over this. They've even commandeered the Crime Lab."

"Which means they've found something," I realized. "Do we know what?"

Again, the sheriff didn't acknowledge it either way.

"I'll look into it," Sonny assured me. "Me and Milk will get to the bottom of this. I promise."

I looked at the sheriff. "And if I refuse to go quietly?"

Another long sigh, "That wouldn't be in your best interest, detective. Winters has already been on the phone to Internal Affairs. They're sending somebody over. From LA. It won't look good if you make a fuss."

"Won't look good?" Sonny echoed. "Jesus Christ."

My whole credibility was on the line – being piped to every TV news channel on the planet – and he thought making a fuss was inappropriate?

"This is bullshit," I repeated between closed teeth.

The sheriff shrugged. "Maybe it is. But if Winters had his way you'd already be shackled in a holding cell right now. I told him there was no way I wanted my department overrun with news people. Be glad of the compromise."

"So I got house arrest as a concession. Gee, thanks." I didn't mean it.

I saw Wong swaggering his way toward us. His face was all snicker. "Hope you like prison food, Quinn."

It was as if somebody had flicked a switch in my brain. Don't ask me why I did it. I just did it. Call it impulsion – or even repulsion. I launched myself at Wong. Talons first. All I wanted to do was wring his little wiry neck. Wipe that self-righteous grin clean off his face. I took everyone by surprise – including Wong. Even managed to yank his tie hard enough to make his eyeballs bulge before the officers wrestled me off.

"Your shield is mine, old man." Wong gasped as he loosened the noose around his neck. "And your pension. You screwed up big time. Now it's time to pay the piper."

The sheriff nodded to his men and, a little red-faced, they marched me toward the elevators.

Sonny called, "Gabe, I'll shake the bugs out of this rug. Trust me."

"Thanks, Sonny. I do. In the meantime have somebody fetch me copies of all our case notes. Plus a laptop. While you clear my name I'm going to catch The Undertaker."

# 121

Randall was flexible. You had to be. You couldn't go around eliminating dozens of people from all walks of life and in all kinds of situations by being fixed to a single game plan. You had to adapt. Be creative. Be ready to initiate contingency plans. The fact that Officer Garcia had arrived unexpectedly at his family home had catapulted the cat among the pigeons, for sure. Her appearance had forced him to reschedule, to accelerate his plans.

But it hadn't shifted his focus one iota.

No one questioned him as he escorted the drugged LA cop through the airport. No one queried his fake police ID. As far as the Port Authority Police at Newark Liberty cared, he was Reno Homicide Detective Nate Westbrook – returning a mentally-ill criminal to Nevada jurisdiction. Even his fake letter of approval from the TSA legitimizing the carrying of Jamie's weapon on board was waved through unchecked. Security wasn't interested in anyone who didn't fit within the stereotypical parameters of a Middle Eastern terrorist. In fact, his passage onto the plane and out of Newark was expedited by his newly-assumed identity and the handcuffed woman in his custody.

"Officer, would you like some refreshments? Coffee? Tea?"

He hauled his gaze away from the case notes – Jamie's case notes – and gave the stewardess a wholesome grin.

She was a formulaic trolley dolly. More fake smiles than brain cells. Lacquered plastic – with six coats of make-up, baked to perfection. Smelled like a perfumery. Bright red talons. A deliberately suggestive smile. A cleavage trying desperately to break out of its tight white cotton confines.

She had no idea she was smiling down at one of the FBI's Most Wanted. No perception she was inches away from death – if he chose it that way. No awareness of her own frail mortality hanging precariously in the balance.

He allowed the stewardess a brief glimpse of the police shield hooked to his belt and the handcuffs on Jamie's wrists.

The stewardess seemed impressed. She settled on her haunches and kept her voice to a minimum, "We have an air marshal seated a few rows back if you need him. Let me know if there's anything I can help you with." She touched his knee. "Anything at all."

He thanked her for her courtesy, but assured her the restraints on his captured fugitive were purely a technicality. His prisoner was heavily sedated and could offer no resistance. The rest of the passengers were quite safe. No need to worry. No need to wake the marshal.

She blinked spider-leg lashes at him.

As a compromise, he ordered a bourbon on the rocks. She came back a minute later with his whiskey and her cell number.

"I'm in New Jersey every other day," she said. "Call me sometime. No strings."

He slipped the number in his pocket as the plane began its long descent to its layover in Denver.

# 122

I was locked in my terrace suite at the *MGM Grand*, with a guard on the door in the hallway outside, and worms squirming in my stomach. Nothing I could do about either. I was off the case and feeling sore. Scratch that; I was feeling *pissed*. Somebody had set me up and that somebody was ringing my cell phone right this minute.

"You stitched me up, you son of a bitch."

I could hear *The Undertaker* laughing down the line. It sounded like a paper-shredder gorging itself on corrugated cardboard.

Truth was, I was still freaked out by the Darth Vader monotone. Still repulsed by its inhuman drone. Some things are a spillover from childhood and will forever live under our beds.

"Oh dear," mocked the mechanical voice. "Has something happened to upset your day, defective? Are those nasty past indiscretions finally catching up with you?"

I hung up.

When it rang again I let it ring until it stopped.

# 123

Detective Michael Shakes stayed seated in his Day-Glo orange Mustang for fifteen minutes before climbing out and slamming the door. In those fifteen minutes he'd watched the boys from the Coroner's Office wheel an empty gurney into the house on Deuce Street in Winchester, then wheel the same gurney out ten minutes later. The only difference had been the direction of movement and the black body bag on top of the stretcher.

He had also spent the last couple of hours chastising himself. He should have checked up on Stacey sooner. Should have followed up on his instincts. Found out why she hadn't been answering her phone. Made a point of breaking down her door. Maybe even disturbing her killer. Saving her. A whole load of *should haves* and not one single *did do*.

Too late now.

Stacey was dead and so was a little piece of him.

He waited for the ME's van to disappear down the street before striding up the front walk and going inside the house.

He'd been here before. Once or twice during their fling. Everything looked the same as it had done back then. Everything except the arcs of blood on the crisp white walls.

He made his way toward the open-plan kitchen, across cream-colored carpeting. He nodded solemn greetings to the CSU techs still processing the scene.

By the looks of things, Forensics had worked through the night. He could see dozens of numbered hit markers stuck on walls, cupboards, windows. Post-its indicating direction of blood spatter and suspect fingerprints. Patches of white powder on darker surfaces. Yellow flags showing the locations of suspect footprints and areas where evidence had been removed for analysis.

Judging by the amount of arterial spray on the kitchen walls, Stacey had met her fate between the breakfast bar and the big black refrigerator. There was a chair standing on the tiled floor. One of those breakfast bar chairs with the extra-long legs. Basically, a tall stool with a back.

There was bright sticky blood everywhere. It looked like somebody had thrown red paint all over the place. Pooled on the floor. Smeared over the kitchen counters, utensils, appliances. Congealed blood and bits of flesh. Soufflé skin and tangled hair. A few whiter fragments jutting out of the pool on the floor that could be bone. Lumps of thicker material that could be brain matter. The only object in the kitchen devoid of blood spatter was the chair itself – the chair in which Stacey had been sitting while her killer had gone to town on her.

There was a black metal urn on the breakfast bar. It was covered in coagulated blood. He could see strips of scalp and blonde hair matted up in the gooey mess. More clots of jellied brain matter.

The killer had beaten Stacey to a pulp with the ashes of her father.

Michael Shakes tasted bile in his throat.

Stacey had been a pain in the ass, all right, but she hadn't deserved this ending. The killer had pulverized her head. Smashing her skull into a hundred pieces. He wondered for how much of it she'd been conscious. Hopefully none.

He fingered the slip of paper in his pocket. The slip of paper containing the information he had deliberated over all week. The slip of paper revealing the identity of the body that Stacey Kellerman had found in a snowy ditch out near Red Rock on the coldest Monday of the week.

Now he could never tell her that the decomposing body had belonged to her mother, and that he suspected her mother's killer was the same one who had told Stacey of its whereabouts in the first place. Probably the same killer who had taken Stacey's own life.

With tears stinging the corners of his eyes, Detective Michael Shakes screwed the paper into a ball and dropped it in the trash on his way out.

# 124

I got a call from Mike Shakes about forty minutes later. He'd visited the Kellerman crime scene while Sonny had used her leverage with the CSU to find out what incriminating evidence, if any, the Feds had uncovered.

"The place is a bloodbath," Shakes was telling me. I could hear he was rattled by what he'd seen. He kept catching his breath, gulping. "Whoever killed Stacey worked her over real good. There was blood all over the place. Never seen so much blood, dammit."

"He bludgeoned her to death."

"With an urn containing her father's ashes, no less. He mashed her head up so bad the CSU say if she'd been found anywhere else we wouldn't have been able to identify her."

I swallowed over a tacky tongue. "Did Sonny find anything out?"

"Only that the Feds recovered a bloodied Band-Aid from the crime scene. It was clutched in Stacey's hand."

"That's everything they have?"

"Gabe, they're adamant it's all they need. It's got your blood on it."

I was stunned. "They ran the DNA?"

"In record time. Your favorite agent came down heavy on the Crime Lab nightshift. Promising either big bonuses or final paychecks – depending on their co-operation. They turned around the results in less than five hours flat."

"And they're certain it's my DNA?"

"Sonny double-checked the evidence. She said the match came back positive against Gabriel Quinn, Senior Detective, Homicide Division, LAPD."

There it was: guilty as charged.

"Any idea how it got there?" Shakes asked.

"No." My voice was shaking, keeping up with the rest of my body.

"Sonny said you had a Band-Aid on your cheek when she first met you, Friday."

Shakes had to follow through. I'd have done the same.

"Sonny's right. It was helping heal a bullet nick I caught earlier in the week. I took it off in my room at the Luxor."

"So how did the killer get a hold of it?"

"He must have been in my room," I realized out loud. "Maybe when Housekeeping were making up the bed."

"Wow, Gabe. That's some smart premeditation. Your boy's either seriously deranged or seriously dangerous."

"Both," I said, "which is much worse. Do we have a time of death for Stacey?"

"The ME puts the TOD at late Friday afternoon. Give or take." I heard him pause. Pauses mean trouble. "Remember where you were, Friday afternoon?"

I mulled it over. "With you, I guess. At the place with the fountains out front."

"That's right. The Bellagio crime scene, with Mark and Sarah. How about before that?"

"With Hal Beecham, at the Channel Ten Studios."

"Who's already made a statement to the Feds saying you paid him a visit after seeing Stacey's report, by the way. Says you were all fired up and wanted to grind an ax."

I could feel anger surging again. "He's right, Milk. At least in one sense. I wanted to speak with Kellerman. But only to find out the identity of her source."

"Which led you where?"

"A tattoo parlor on Las Vegas Boulevard."

"Where two more witnesses saw you assault Stacey."

It sounded bad. First Beecham had seen me all wired-up, then Roberta and her pals over at *Inkriminal* had watched me manhandle the reporter. Not only did it sound bad, it looked bad. On that evidence alone I would have arrested me too.

"To make matters worse," Shakes continued, "one of the girls at the tattoo parlor is Hugh Winters' daughter."

I gaped like a fish. "Roberta?"

I had no idea. I'd known Winters' daughter had the same name, but the last time I'd seen her she'd been a baby. I hadn't made the connection.

"Milk, you know I was just trying to speak with Kellerman."

"I do. So where did you go next?"

A fiery lance seared my chest. "To Stacey's place."

"Now do you see how this thing looks? You were at Stacey's place round about the right time she was killed. Even I saw you there. And the Feds know it. Together with the DNA evidence, they have an eyewitness putting you at the scene. That's why they've got you locked up. Gabe. You were there the same time she was murdered."

\*   \*   \*

As a general rule, I leave conspiracy theories to those who know best. People like Dreads. I believe we stepped foot on the Moon and I don't buy there was a shooter on the grassy knoll. Things start falling apart when conspiracies get personal. Hypocritical, I know. But being framed for murder carries that kind of weight.

The Undertaker had been in my hotel room. He'd stolen the discarded Band-Aid from the sink top, then planted it at a crime scene. Presumably to cement my guilt. And it had worked. Which meant he'd planned Stacey's murder well in advance. Planned to set me up for it all along. The fact I'd happened to be there at the same time was . . .

*Coincidence?*

"I don't get it," I said to Mike Shakes down the phone. "Why frame me? To get me off the case? Mission accomplished. So why get me on the case to begin with?"

"To set you up."

"You mean he wanted to frame me for murder all along and that's why he involved me from the get-go?"

I heard Shakes sigh. "I don't know what I'm saying, Gabe. But it's a possibility. I guess anything goes with this fruitcake."

"Damn."

"Want me to get you an attorney? I'm sleeping with the best in town."

"Are things looking that bad for me?"

"Put it this way: Hugh Winters is a weasel. You should never underestimate vermin. Think about it."

I did.

"By the way," I added, "he called my cell again, about an hour ago."

"Who?"

"The Undertaker."

"Holy shit. Which proves the Feds got the wrong man. That's great. What now?"

"You and Sonny keep working on clearing my name. In the meantime, I'll work on finding the killer's true identity."

# 125

Thousands of feet below, the snow-locked Rockies slid silently by beneath the plane. There were patterns in the vaporous clouds clinging to the shattered peaks: a train derailment in Delhi; a mining disaster in Kiev; the face of a man plotting a presidential assassination. The killer known internationally as *The Undertaker* pulled down the window blind and blinked. He waited for his eyes to adjust before refocusing on the photographs confiscated from Officer Garcia's purse.

It was strange seeing the bodies drenched in the cold light cast by the Forensics' lamps, to see the little yellow marker tents with their big black numbers, strategically placed around the bodies like flags on a map. Violating his personal creations. It hadn't occurred to him at the time, but now he could see why he'd been nailed with the mortician moniker. The way he'd arranged each scene would be important to those hunting him. But they would never figure out the truth.

The truth was personal.

He'd been no more than nine or ten at the time.

There was a ramshackle shack hidden deep in the woods. A couple of miles north of town, through dense brush and over rocky outcrops. One of those secluded places that was hard to reach without amassing plenty of scrapes and bruises. The shack was a single-roomed construction of silvered wood. An old hunter's cabin – easily a hundred years old. Dead rabbits strung from shrugging eaves. Smoke curling from a rusty pipe stack. The other kids spoke only of it in their ghost stories, nervously circulated around locker rooms on dark afternoons – like it was part of an urban legend. Nobody went anywhere near it.

An old, twisted woman lived in the remote shack. A witch – or so the other kids said. Mad as a hatter. He'd spent several weeks watching her skin rabbits with her broken teeth; collect wind-fallen branches in the hammock of her apron; stand buck-naked in the rain chanting angry incantations at the thundering skies. She was as mad as a hatter, all right. But he'd seen no evidence of her casting spells.

He had seen her patterns, though. Repeated routines – like a clockwork doll going through the motions, day in day out. He'd studied them for hours. Learned where she'd be at any given moment. Got comfortable with the structure, the predictability. Even started enjoying his time spent watching her go through the same familiar activities day after day. Then, one Sunday evening at the beginning of May, the patterns had stopped.

She should have been pulling water from the well. Cursing and sweating. But instead she was slumped in the rickety swing-seat at the corner of the porch. Eyes glazed. Mouth tugged to one side by gravity and the looseness of her jaw.

He'd seen dead people before – but not in real life.

When he'd returned the following evening she was still slumped in the swing. Only this time her feet were bloated. Yellowy-purple. And there were flies buzzing in and out of her mouth.

On the third evening he'd advanced slowly. Heart hammering. Taking small, quiet, tentative steps. Each one bringing more of the inanimate woman into view. She'd looked as dead as a doorknob. A waxwork with blue-cheese skin. Flies scuttling over her milky eyeballs.

On the fourth evening he'd crept up the old wooden steps. Wincing with each creak. Holding his breath. Wondering if anyone were watching. Courage had carried him to within a few feet before overwhelming fear had propelled him back into the woods.

On the fifth evening he'd tied a handkerchief over his mouth and nose, then hauled her bloated corpse off the swing. Pulse twanging like an elastic band in his throat. He'd forced her limbs flat against the decking by kneeling on the joints until they'd crumbled. Laid her out in the death pose he'd seen on TV: arms folded across the chest, toes angled skywards, eyelids drawn shut.

When he'd returned the sixth day he'd brought roses plucked from his grandmother's garden. Sprinkled petals around the doughy body, like they did in the movies. Brushed straggly hair out of her puffy face. Then shied away as maggots had tumbled from the black pit of her mouth.

On his seventh visit he'd brought something to fix her ghastly grin. He'd wafted away the flies. Flicked away maggots. Held his breath against the terrible smell while he'd daubed her cardboard lips with glue. Forced her jaws together until they'd stuck. Scrawled a rough cross on her dewy brow. Then stepped back and mouthed a quiet prayer. It had only seemed right.

That night, the seventh night, everything was perfect.

He left her that way, in the customary pose of interment.

Through no fault of his own, he hadn't been able to return to the shack in the woods for over a week later. When he had, he'd found the old woman gone. Just a dark stain on the splintered boards.

Had she been taken by the angels? he'd wondered.

Then he'd noticed the tracks leading into the woods.

He'd followed them. Stealthily as a predator. Curious at first, then with a ball of anger rolling around in his belly. Coyote cubs were feeding hungrily on the old woman's remains. Ripping her rotting flesh into leathery strips and cracking soft bones with needle teeth.

He'd wrung every one of their necks with his bare hands.

When the coyote mother had returned and howled for her loss he'd let her pain last awhile before clubbing her bitch head to pulp with a stone.

He'd only ever returned to the shack in the woods one more time after that: years later – armed with a canister of chemicals and a match.

# 126

By midday, my arrest and subsequent detainment was all over the TV news and Internet feeds. Top billing: Celebrity Cop arrested for the murder of a prominent, up-and-coming news reporter. Bludgeoned to death by the very person she had raised doubts about live on air. Of course, it was so much horse manure. But sometimes if enough is thrown, some of it sticks.

Speculation about my intent, motive and possible role in *The Undertaker* killings was rife.

If I didn't get off the hook soon I'd have no character left to assassinate.

Copies of our case notes arrived at my guest suite, together with a shiny new laptop. The officer guarding my door looked them over before allowing them inside. I arranged the files and photos out on the large floor space like a mosaic, in crime scene order, stepped back, rolled up sleeves and set to.

The Feds had amassed a fair wealth of information in the short space of time they'd run with the investigation. I counted five boxes of files, a skyscraper stack of eight-by-tens, plus comprehensive background histories on each victim. There were even IRS records and bank transaction particulars for Harland Laboratories.

I was in business.

I thought about Candlewood lying in his hospital bed under armed guard, hooked up to his machines, with a touch-and-go prognosis. No one was interested in rationalizing how Candlewood could be *The Undertaker*. No one was interested in theorizing his motive. As far as the FBI were concerned, Candlewood was *The Undertaker*. Fuller had his prize pig. Game over.

But I knew otherwise.

Where did that leave me?

Chasing another phantom.

I put on my readers and opened up the hefty FBI dossier on Harland Laboratories.

Except for substantial IRS receipts, most of the information turned out to be technical literature: research papers, fact sheets, charts, projections, graphs, statistics – jargon about as legible to me as Mandarin.

I phoned Room Service and had them deliver a large pot of coffee to keep me ticking over.

About ten minutes later, I came across a copy of the company's latest project and experienced what some people call a *goosy* moment:

In the fall of last year, Harland Laboratories had won a prestigious federal contract to synthesize and develop a new super-vaccine capable of warding off virtually every childhood disease known to man. What separated this new super-vaccine from its current competitors was the fact it could be administered to newborns. It was a breakthrough. Conservative estimates had the super-vaccine saving thousands of young lives every year, here in the States, with millions more worldwide. The sheer scale of the undertaking had forced Harland Labs to source-out work to their newly-acquired production facilities in California and Florida. As commissions went, it was titanic. Enough to make Harland Labs a very tempting buy for some of the bigger pharmaceutical boys having missed out on the lucrative government deal.

The project's working title was: "*Pocketful of Posies*".

It was like I'd won the Nevada sweepstakes.

\* \* \*

Strange how broken links can suddenly come together to form a chain. I thought about Jamie's text message. Thought about the stylized embroidering on *The Undertaker's* cap. Thought about the rings of roses. The ash crosses. Thought about all the syringes. Thought about Luke Chapter's cheapskate punch line.

If Harland Labs were the connection, then their current project had to be the catalyst.

I glanced at the annual report in my hands, followed my gut instinct to the page listing financial backers. Other than the Candlewood family, Harland Labs had a handful of fiscal investors scattered across the country. One or two distinguished names I'd seen with thumbs in other people's pies. Celebrities trying to make good. One that instantly leapt up off the page and punched me in the gut:

*Marlene van den Berg.*

Spurred on, I delved deeper. I came across a list of acclaimed consultants having donated their brains to the *'Pocketful of Posies'* project – if only figuratively. Most were esteemed professors in various biology-related fields belonging to colleges and universities across the US. One was based in Los Angeles. His name was *Professor J. Samuels, PhD.*

Knock out.

Simple as that.

Three minutes' worth of reading and I'd connected all the dots. No one in the FBI had even bothered to scratch deeper than the surface.

I stripped off the readers and rubbed the bridge of my nose.

*The Undertaker* had been eliminating everybody directly involved with the super-vaccine project. Add that to the killer's prophesy of a future catastrophe and *hey presto* we had ourselves a motive.

*If you could save a million lives by taking one . . .*

Okay, so it sounded like yet more fodder from a science fiction movie. But it was the only theory which fit the facts perfectly.

Here's how my reasoning was shaping up:

*The Undertaker* believed the super-vaccine project was flawed. Instead of saving thousands of lives, it would take them. In order to prevent mass murder by Harland Labs, he was systematically killing everyone with a vested interest in seeing the project to its fruition, including workers, backers, technical wizards – everyone whose future hands would be bloodied by the countless future deaths.

It suddenly occurred to me that if *The Undertaker* could really see the future then he'd be doing the nation an enormous service. And if we stopped him – if *I* stopped him – I'd be signing the death warrant on thousands of future baby lives.

But it was all nonsense, wasn't it?

*The Undertaker* was delusional. All serial killers are. I didn't believe for a second he could prophesize. Would you? But he believed it. I couldn't ignore that. It was his motive.

*If you could save a million lives by taking one . . . would you?*

Seeing thousands of dead kids makes for a good motivator, I guess.

\* \* \*

First things first, I called Sonny from my swanky prison cell and told her the news. Then I asked whether she'd cleared my name yet.

"Still working on it," she told me. "I've got men canvassing the Kellerman neighborhood – seeing if anyone saw a man fitting the killer's description loitering in the vicinity, Friday."

"And?"

"And so far we've found a further two eyewitnesses who put you at the scene."

"Great."

Our unofficial investigation was making the FBI's case against me even stronger.

"What else, Sonny?"

"Kellerman's phone records show she had calls from the same disposable cell number, starting last week. Several, Friday itself."

"You got that information fast."

"Friends in high places. It's the same number the FBI logged when the killer called you, back at the Treasure Island."

Encouraging. We were getting someplace.

"Do we know what the Feds have in store for me?"

"Far as I know they're doing everything by the book. Amassing enough evidence to make sure their case against you rock-solid before they move you someplace more secure. It wouldn't surprise me if they have you incarcerated by the end of the day. Luckily for us, it's Sunday. All the High Court Justices are out playing golf, or conveniently not answering their phones."

"Thanks, Sonny. I appreciate it."

"Sure thing. What are friends for? I'll keep you posted if anything else turns up."

I spent the next couple of hours on the Internet, referencing the Harland Labs annual report and running down lists of names connected with their current project. I had no idea how many were on *The Undertaker's* private hit list. I couldn't take the chance of missing any. His priority system was anyone's guess. All told, I gathered more than a hundred candidates. Spread far and wide. I emailed as many as I could, either through company mailboxes or private accounts. Warned them about their link to the killer and to be extra vigilant of their own safety over the coming days or weeks until we made an arrest. Then I emailed the list through to Jan and Fred back at Central Division, and asked them to keep on top of it. It was the best I could do – for now.

At three o'clock there was a knock at the door.

I padded across the thick carpeting and opened up.

"Hello, gorgeous. Am I too late for visiting time?"

*"Eleanor?"*

I let my astonishment show. It was for real. Written all over my stupefied face like street graffiti.

Eleanor Zimmerman was leaning against the doorframe, wrapped from neck to toe in a fake sable coat. She had one eyebrow raised, alluringly. She looked every bit the Hollywood starlet. All that was missing was the fake cigarette.

"What happened to your face?" she asked.

"I butted heads with an old adversary."

We stared at one another.

Finally, Eleanor smiled. "Good thing you're thick-skulled. Now you gonna let this gal in or leave her out here with this good-looking officer?"

\* \* \*

Eleanor and I go way back. Sometimes I think it's too way back. Nothing has ever happened between us – I was already happily married and committed when we first met – but I'd always had the feeling something might have happened had Eleanor had her wicked way.

I stepped aside and gave the gawking officer a *'mind your own God-damned business'* stare. Closed the door behind us.

"This is what you call one hell of a lovely hotel suite," Eleanor commented as she inspected the set up. I watched her work her way around the open-plan room, running fingertips over the heavy fabrics and the glassy surfaces. Murmuring every now and then as she made exquisite new discoveries.

"How much does a pad like this set you back for the night?" she asked. "Four, five hundred bucks?"

"Eleanor. What are you doing here?"

She turned and held up a bottle of whiskey in one hand. A pair of matching glass tumblers in the other. All previously hidden beneath her fake sable. "I heard you needed a friend. So I brought one."

She placed the glassware on a table. Shrugged off her faux fur and draped it over a lampstand. Eleanor was wearing a silvery blouse and gray business suit slacks. The outfit made her irises glow.

"Still doesn't explain why you're here," I said, keeping my distance.

"You're up to your neck in quicksand. I'm here to pull you out."

I started picking up case notes from littering the floor. "Eleanor, I appreciate the sentiments. Really, I do. And it's good to see a friendly face. But how exactly do you plan on getting me out of here?"

I saw her peer through the sliding doors, out onto the terrace, like she was weighing up offers in a store window.

"Don't tell me this place has an outside Jacuzzi?"

"Eleanor."

"Have you forgotten who I work for?"

I sighed. "No, Eleanor. You work for the Los Angeles Police Department. Same as me."

She turned and raised a finger. "Technically. But the actual office I report to is –"

"Internal Affairs." I hadn't forgotten. "I heard they were sending somebody over. I wasn't expecting the resident shrink."

She made a wounded face. "Ouch. You make me sound dirty."

"Eleanor, you don't need any help on that score."

She laughed, "You're right."

I was under no illusions. The primary reason behind Eleanor's visit was to psyche me out. Evaluate my mental health. Then report back to the Police Commissioner with her professional assessment. Her appraisal wouldn't change the fact that there were trumped-up charges against me. It would simply help explain why I might have committed murder in the first place. Right now, Eleanor was friend and foe.

I watched her seat herself on a sofa and crack open the whiskey. Saw her lick lips, unconsciously, as she unscrewed the bottle top. It was like watching a ballerina perform a perfect pirouette.

I fell into the facing chair, already deciding to play it coy.

"I can't believe you brought whiskey and glasses all the way from LA."

"I didn't," she said as she dribbled the amber liquid into the tumblers until they were two fingers full. "Vegas isn't third world, darling. I picked them up downstairs."

She held one out. I shook my head.

"Oh, come on. Live a little. Who knows, I might get lucky."

"In Vegas?"

"In my fifties."

I took the drink.

Eleanor smiled. "See. I don't bite. At least not without permission. Now drink up; we have a bottle and a whole roll of red tape to get through."

I made mine last. I couldn't say the same for Eleanor. Eleanor could soak up whiskey like it was Evian. Always could. The worst part about it was that she hardly ever got drunk. Don't you hate that? Maybe after an entire bottle. Maybe a little tipsy, a little more promiscuous – if that were possible. Never rolling round on the floor in a pool of her own vomit, drunk. We were born under different stars.

"What's Ferguson had to say?" I asked.

"Hasn't he called?"

I shook my head.

"He's probably been told to stay incommunicado until the coast clears. He hasn't called me, if that's what you're thinking."

"Who, then?"

"If you must know, it was Hugh."

"The bastard."

I could see she didn't approve of my little outburst. She pulled back from it as if it were a naked flame.

"He's not exactly the forgiving type, is he?"

"He's vindictive," I said. "That's Hugh to a tee. Even after all these years."

"You shouldn't have slept with his wife."

"I didn't! They weren't married back then. And neither was I."

I necked the whiskey.

Eleanor refilled our tumblers.

We talked. Rather, Eleanor asked questions and I avoided. It was a tango we'd danced more this last year than any year before. Practice had made us perfect. Anyone listening would think we'd been married forever.

"Why do you think the killer is setting you up?"

"To get me off the case."

"Why, when he deliberately drew you in?"

"It's a sub-plot to his master theme. Milk believes it's all been a ruse from the start. All leading up to framing me for murder."

"Milk?"

"One of the Vegas homicide detectives I'm working with."

"So, the rest of the murders are incidental to framing you for murder?"

"That's not what I said."

"It's how it sounded."

"Stop psycho-analyzing me, Eleanor."

"It's my job."

I shook my head. "I think setting me up was a bonus."

"And how does that make you feel?"

"Angry, mostly. Cheated. That son of a bitch knows every button of mine to press."

I looked at her. My whole career in law enforcement rested on this conversation. My future in Eleanor's hands. I looked at them; her hands. They were slender and white. No rings. No calluses. Something about them made me want to reach out and hold one.

"Tell me about your relationship with Inspector Maxwell," she said suddenly.

I gave Eleanor a sideways stare. "What's that got to do with this appraisal?"

"I'm establishing emotional state."

"For whose benefit – IA's or yours? There is no relationship, if that's what you're fishing for. I've only just met her. Which means there's no emotional state to establish. I've known Sonny a couple of days and it's all been above board and professional. Why are you doing this?"

"To help me determine if you've been compromised."

"I'm not a locked box full of emotional secrets."

Her brow lifted. "Honestly?"

"Sonny's been good to me. If anything, she's the one who's kept me focused. Especially after the incident at Rochelle's place."

Eleanor perked up. "Rochelle Lewis?"

Instantly, I regretted letting it slip. Disclosing sensitive information to Eleanor is like opening yourself up to an organ bank and saying *help yourselves*.

My phone rang.

"Saved by the bell," Eleanor said with a wan smile.

The number on the screen belonged to Detective Fred Phillips, back in LA.

"Fred? How's it going? What gives?"

"I thought you should be aware of the big things afoot back here. Are you by any chance near a television set?"

"Sure. Why?"

"Tune to one of the national news channels. Choose any one; they're all showing the same story."

I picked up the TV remote and did as directed, saw a big red-and-white *Breaking News* banner splashed across the screen.

"Got it, Fred."

"Okay. We're all rooting for you, Gabe."

"Appreciate it, Fred."

I put down the phone and cranked up the TV volume.

"What is it?" Eleanor asked.

"I'm not sure."

I read the text scrolling across the screen. Below the flashy banner, in smaller letters, were the words:

*'Dr. Milton Perry indicted on Le Diable killings.'*

# 127

On the gridlocked Interstate 15 in Las Vegas, an eighteen-wheeler tanker full of 2% milk had sideswiped a truck carrying plush toys and then flat-bellied into the median barrier. The big silver tanker had cracked like an egg, spilling a slurry of frothy milk all over the freeway – while the storage truck had jack-knifed and tipped over, scattering its cuddly contents right across the creamy asphalt.

The entire northbound expressway was at a standstill - right at the onset of the evening rush hour.

The killer known to himself as Randall Fisk rolled down the driver's window and turned up his nose.

Already, the stench of souring milk was pungent in the air.

He got out of the car, lit a cigarette and surveyed the dairy disaster with a frown.

It was surreal.

The whole of the five-lane Interstate had become a glossy white lake, broken by lumpy soft-toy islands. People were out of their vehicles. Churning through the milk. Salvaging soggy souvenirs. Traffic tailing back for at least a mile, deep into the growing dusk. Maybe two. Strings of brilliantly-lit pearls, lengthening by the second. Traffic crawling past on the other side of the median. All red taillights. Full of curious drivers.

Something was watching him. Something small and green, with Ping-Pong ball eyes.

*Kermit the Frog.*

It was sitting stark upright, with waves of milk lapping against its velvety green skin.

Being back in Vegas sooner than planned felt like a glove with a missing finger. Something he couldn't quite put a finger on, or *in*. But now that he was here he couldn't think of a more fitting ending to this chapter of his life.

Randall sucked hard on the cigarette. Blew out smoke rings.

Over the concrete retaining wall, he could see his destination: the impressively tall *Stratosphere Tower*. It was lighting up the sky like the Olympic flame.

He finished the cigarette and got back behind the wheel. He patted Officer Jamie Garcia on the knee. Not long now. Soon it would be all over.

When he looked back at the creamy carnage, all that was left of the plush frog was a pipe-cleaner finger poking up from its milky grave.

*Fuck you, too, Kermit.*

# 128

Have you ever had one of those moments where your synapses simply refuse to snap?

For about five very long seconds I couldn't compute the magnitude of those few words scrolling across the screen.

"Milton Perry?" Eleanor breathed as she came up beside me. "Indicted for the Le Diable killings. That's a crock of shit if ever I've seen one. I don't believe it for one second."

I didn't know what to believe; my brain was still rebounding from being whacked.

I'd forgotten all about my visit with Milton Perry in his rented office space on Hope Street in downtown LA. Forgotten about his complaining about the killer killing men of the cloth. Forgotten about *Le Diable* killing Father Dan – until now.

We both stared at the screen.

Beyond the flashy banner, the news channel was running a looped recording of what appeared to be an ordinary-looking house in an ordinary-looking street – except that this one had FBI agents and police personnel crawling all over it. Yellow-and-black police tape zigzagged between lampposts. Helicopters hovered overhead. Our viewpoint was from behind the police cordon, along with the rest of the news cameras.

"*. . . arrested less than an hour ago, charged with three counts of first degree murder.*" A man's voiceover was saying. "*Initial reports indicate the police recovered all three decapitated heads from the Milton house. Here, you can see what we believe are those heads being brought out . . .*"

Eleanor and I leaned into the screen. Morbid fascination.

The camera zoomed in on a procession of Feds in FBI windbreakers as they marched out through the front door of the house, single-file. Three agents, each carrying run-of-the-mill coolers, like the kind you can pick up cheap in any of the large grocery stores – the ones that hardly sell groceries anymore.

The newsreel switched to a shot of Milton Perry being escorted out of his office building in downtown LA by more stony-faced Feds. The office building where I'd spoken to him earlier in the week. He looked flustered. Sweaty. It was like a scene from a TV cop show – where the detainee is hustled through a crowd of camera-flashing reporters before being bundled into an FBI truck. I couldn't completely believe what I was seeing.

"Was he even on the suspect list?" Eleanor asked as we watched the footage.

"No idea," I admitted. "Wasn't my case."

The recording switched to an interview with a special agent, outside the FBI Field Office on Wilshire Boulevard. His name on the screen said Gene Devereux. He was a tall African-American with a stern face and suspicious eyes. He reminded me of Sydney Poitier in *The Heat of the Night.*

He cleared his throat and spoke:

*"After an extensive investigation, the FBI have today apprehended and arraigned Dr. Milton Perry on the count of three brutal homicides against prominent religious figures in the Los Angeles area. Overwhelming evidence was recovered this afternoon from the Milton crime scene."*

*"What led you to Dr. Perry?"* a voice asked.

*"Like all killers, Perry got sloppy. Sooner or later they all make mistakes and leave crucial evidence behind at a crime scene. Forensics obtained such evidence from the Church of St. Therese in Alhambra. Evidence which points directly toward Perry being the perpetrator of these atrocities."*

"Do you know anything about that?" Eleanor asked.

"Other than the fact the killer murdered my priest, not a jot."

Back on the TV:

*What about the heads?*

*We discovered the existence of three decapitated heads in a subsequent search of the Milton household. We have no reason to believe they do not belong to the beheaded clergymen.*

Eleanor flicked the TV off.

"What are you doing?"

"Turning off this bullshit." She held the remote control out of my reach. "Look, I know Milton. I've known him for years. Okay, so he's a cantankerous old swine. And he knows how to make enemies. But his bark is worse than his bite. He's about as capable of murder as you are."

I didn't point out that murder was the very reason she was in Vegas in the first place.

"Where do we go from here?" I asked.

"We finish the whiskey."

"I mean with your assessment."

She gave me one of those matronly nods. "Well, the way I see it, it can go one of three ways. I can write you up as suffering from PTSD –"

"Eleanor, I don't have Posttraumatic Stress Disorder."

"– or I can draw an inconclusive verdict and recommend further tests. In which case, they won't be able to use your recent history against you, but you will be suspended from all duties pending an enquiry."

"And screw the fact I'm innocent."

"Darling, I'm not the one you need to convince. You've made enemies over the years. Enemies in high places. Some of whom would love to see the fall of the Celebrity Cop."

I grimaced. "I hate that moniker."

"Oh, relax. I've heard worse. You should hear some of the names I get called. Sticks and stones."

"You said three. What's the third option?"

My cell phone vibrated on the table. I let it. Waiting for Eleanor's answer.

She picked up instead.

I saw her expression harden as she listened to the caller on the other end of the connection. Then she faced me. Held out the phone.

"It's him," she said in a whisper. "You better take it."

*   *   *

The first words I heard as I put the cell to my ear were:

"Hang up and she's dead."

I froze. What else could I do?

"I have somebody here with me who would like to talk with you," the synthesized voice rumbled on, "only I had to give her a little something to make her compliant. The downside is, she's pretty spaced-out right now and can't come to the phone."

"Go to hell," I said. And I meant it.

"In that case, I'll be sure to send Officer Garcia your love."

Fire swept through my lungs.

"Jamie's in –"

"New York? Think again, defective. She's right here with me."

"You're bluffing," I breathed. "Jamie's in –"

"My arms," the killer whispered in my ear.

"Then put her on the phone."

"I'd love nothing more. But that would mean waking her up and I have a feeling she won't be happy if I do that."

"Then stop wasting my time," I snarled and hung up.

Immediately, my cell phone buzzed in my hand.

*It was Jamie's number!*

"Hang up again and I give you my word that Officer Garcia will die. Then you'll have yet another innocent death on your conscience."

"What do you want?"

"I want you to listen very carefully to the instructions you are about to hear. If, from this moment on, you fail to do everything I say, then Jamie will die. Do you understand me?"

My thoughts were tumbling over themselves, tripping me up.

*"Do I make myself clear?"*

"Crystal," I said. "Just tell me where you are and I'll trade places with Jamie. This is between you and me. Jamie has nothing to do with this. If you want a bargaining chip, I'm worth more to you than —"

"Pay attention!"

I bit my tongue.

"If you stray from these instructions, I assure you Jamie will die. Do you understand me, defective? *Do you understand me?"*

* * *

Personal detachment. That's what police training hopes to achieve — because feelings have bias. It is drummed into us, time and again, that becoming emotionally-involved can lead to deadly mistakes in judgment. But reality isn't black and white. Sometimes it's blood red.

I listened to his demands, then dropped the phone to my lap.

"Gabe?"

I blinked at Eleanor. "He's got Jamie." My words sounded puny, like I was a foot tall and at the end of a long tunnel.

"Where?"

"Here, in Vegas. At the Stratosphere Tower. Don't ask me how. I don't know. Last time I heard she was in New York. This morning. And now . . ."

"What does he want you to do?"

"I've got thirty minutes to get there. Otherwise he'll kill her." I saw the color drain from Eleanor's face. Knew that it mirrored my own.

"Call Sonny."

"He said no cops."

"Call Sonny."

"He says he'll kill her if he so much as sees a patrol car anywhere in the vicinity."

Eleanor came over and slapped me hard across the cheek. I recoiled from the sting.

"Call Sonny," she said.

I came out of my delirium and called Sonny.

"But you're under house arrest," Sonny said as I quickly outlined the situation.

"Let me worry about that. Will you help me?"

"Without a second's hesitation. Let me scramble a SWAT team to smoke him out. I've seen things like this get messy real quick. They can be on the top of him before he knows what's hit."

"No, Sonny. No SWAT. I mean it. I appreciate what you're saying, but Jamie's life is on the line here. We can't afford to take any chances. Too many innocent lives have already been lost."

"And if this guy is as smart as he claims he is, we'll need everything in our arsenal to get her out of there alive. Besides, there's only three ways down from that tower: two sets of double elevators and the emergency stairwell. He's a sitting duck. This is our chance."

"And Jamie's safety is paramount. Which means no snipers, Sonny. I mean it. No tear gas. And especially none of Wong's henchmen spoiling the show. In fact, *don't tell anyone in the FBI*. Here's what we'll do . . ."

# 129

*"You will come to the internal observation deck of the Stratosphere Tower. You have thirty minutes. No more. No less. Thirty minutes. I'm allowing for rush-hour traffic; so try not to be late. Come alone. No shadows. No snipers on rooftops. No undercover cops dressed up as bellhops. Alone. If I get one sniff of any back up, Jamie will die. If you fail to get here in time, Jamie will die. If you try any funny business whatsoever, Jamie will die. You have thirty minutes."*

The killer's demands rang in my head.

"This was my third option," Eleanor said as we prepared to make our move.

"Breaking me out?"

"I didn't say it was legal."

I waited until she had opened the guest room door and distracted the officer on guard before making my move. I used the key that Bill had left to access his adjoining suite, then ran across the darkened room to the door. Quietly pulled it open. I could hear Eleanor flirting loudly with the uniform down the hall. I counted to three, then leapt across the hallway and slipped through the stairwell door.

*The Undertaker* had insisted I come alone. I was acutely aware – even paranoid – that he was watching my every move and had been all the while. My mortal fear was that if we came down heavy he'd snuff out Jamie's life in a heartbeat. I couldn't risk that happening. But I wasn't his puppet either.

This was Vegas; gambling was expected.

I snuck out through the hotel kitchen and waved down a passing cab. Flashed the driver my shield. He hit the gas and we elbowed our way through rush-hour traffic, heading downtown, with dusk rapidly descending

Seven minutes had passed. So far so good.

# 130

Streams of red-and-white lights crept along the city's arteries like illuminated blood cells. Mixing at intersections. Pulsing through traffic signals. Ferrying precious life through the heart of the night-washed city.

From his lofty vantage point high within the *Stratosphere Tower*, the killer known as *The Undertaker* picked out patterns in the strings of faery lights, fortifying his resolve. He ignored the incessant voice in his head pleading for chemical consolation. He had to do this final showdown raw. Uninhibited. No stimulants or suppressants to alter his experience.

He wanted to *feel* this. He wanted to *live* this.

Carefully, he aimed Officer Garcia's firearm at one corner of the big windowpane and squeezed the trigger. The weapon kicked in his hand. Thunder boomed around the empty observation deck. The bullet left a feathered hole in the toughened glass. Another expertly-placed shot had the entire pane exploding outward with a resounding crash, sending lethal shards raining down on the streets below.

# 131

I was all fired up. But I had to keep the flames under control. No good burning myself out before I got there. I could see the illuminated Tower looming bigger and bigger through the windshield as we headed north along The Strip. It looked like a giant black rosebud atop a sleek cream-colored stem, standing proud against the deepening twilight.

I was conscious of the passing seconds.

"Faster," I urged the driver.

He flung the cab around like it was bull at a rodeo. Darted in and out of traffic. Leaving the sounds of angry horns behind.

There was a growing crowd of people on the sidewalk. All eyes staring up at the skyscraping *Stratosphere Tower.*

I gave the driver a fifty and leapt out. Glanced skyward to the distant smoked-glass observation decks rising a thousand feet above the city.

*"Can you see him?"; "He's got a gun."; "Has anybody called the cops?"; "Did anyone else hear the shots?"; "Oh my God, is he a terrorist?"*

I fought my way through the massing throng.

Word had filtered through to downstairs that there was a madman on the rampage and terror had swept through the hotel like wildfire. People were pouring out through every exit, fleeing for their lives. It was pandemonium. Panic stations. Gamblers clutching their winnings to their chests like their lives depended on it.

This was bad.

No longer just my personal problem.

I held my police shield aloft and ordered people to clear the way. It was like going against a stampede.

No rational person could seriously expect a zero police presence with all this commotion going on. But, then again, I wasn't dealing with a rational person. Even with Sonny putting a stop on all law enforcement and EMS services coming within a block radius of the Tower, it was hard to see the invisible cordon holding. I heard at least a dozen terrified tourists dialing 911 as I pushed my way into the foyer. It was going to be a close call all round.

I had to make the killer's deadline. Or Jamie died.

I scanned the casino floor, saw signs for the Tower elevators. I sprinted up a flight of stairs, worked my way through a shopping mall and past storekeepers rolling down shutters. The news of a gunman stalking the property was bad for business.

I ran into a flustered security guard waving everybody out.

"Hold up! You can't go this way!" he shouted it in my face, trying to tackle me to a stop.

I showed him my shield.

He stepped aside.

"He's got a gun," he called as I ran on.

"So do I."

\* \* \*

A pair of red-jacketed elevator operators were standing in the deserted elevator area, looking like they'd jump out of their skins if so much as a fly flew past unexpectedly. One was a ginger-haired wisp of a kid. The other was a portly ringmaster type with a gray goatee. When they saw me hurtling their way, their pasty faces visibly flushed with relief.

"Told you the cavalry wouldn't be long." I heard the older of the two mutter. "The name's Ted Quayle," he said, sticking out a hand. "Head of Tower Operations. This is Kevin Lacy, my assistant."

"Elevator Tour Guide Extraordinaire," the kid announced with a lisp.

"Detective Quinn," I said. "I need to get up there, ASAP."

"I'm afraid that's out of the question." Ted said. "Your guy's locked the carriages down at the hundred-eighth floor."

"That's the internal observation level," the kid added.

"Any way we can get them down?"

"Not from here."

"This the only way up?"

"We have stairs." Ted pointed them out. "But it would take a top athlete about thirty minutes to get to the top."

Too long. Jamie would be dead by then. Probably me too.

"What's with those doors?"

There was an identical set of brushed steel doors directly above us, set back on a narrow gantry, immediately above the lower elevator doors. They looked like something out of the *Wizard of Oz*.

"They're double elevators." Ted explained, with accompanying hand gestures. "One rides piggyback on top of the other. We can transport twice as many passengers that way."

"To different floors," the kid added.

I glanced at my watch: two minutes to deadline. I felt a pang of urgency rising in my belly.

"How many people are up there right now?"

Ted looked deep in thought. "Say no more than two or three, tops. Kevin was in the Pod when your guy started ordering everybody down."

"That's right," he nodded. "He cleared the flaming decks. Then drew the elevators back up. He's deactivated all the internal cameras – so we don't know what he's doing. I was with the last group to make it out alive."

I scowled.

"I swear, if he's damaged my elevators, I'll kill him."

Ted gave the kid a shake of his head, "No you won't, Kevin."

"Yes I will, Ted." He nodded beyond my shoulder. "Here comes your girlfriend, Quinn."

I turned to see Sonny sprinting toward us.

"Sonny."

"Gabe," she gasped. "Sorry I'm late; had to come through all the darned kitchens. Pots and pans all over the place. What have I missed? Is he still up there?"

Kevin said: "As far as we know, Sonny."

I gave the kid a threatening glare.

"All eight cars are locked on the hundred-eighth floor," Ted reiterated, with more hand gestures.

"Has anyone tried summoning them?"

We exchanged uncertain glances.

Sonny shook her head and pressed the big button on the wall.

Immediately, my cell phone shrilled.

"Trying to get a rise out of me, defective?" *The Undertaker* snickered as I answered the call.

"Just send down the damned elevator."

Distantly, we heard a metallic whine as the elevator mechanism engaged.

# 132

I had no idea what to expect as the elevator rocketed to the top of the *Stratosphere Tower* with enough speed to force the blood out of my brain.

What did I think would happen once I came face to face with *The Undertaker*? A trade? Jamie in exchange for me? Why? Kidnapping was not this monster's plaything. I was going in blind. Going against everything I'd learned and being impetuous. I'd have to think on my feet. Improvise. I was going to get somebody killed. Probably me.

I shook out my Glock and checked the clip as the ground fell away.

Everything that had happened over the last week had led to this point: the 7th Street Bridge; the LA homicides; the murder of Harry; the Vegas killings; the booby-trapped bombs. And yet *The Undertaker* was as far out of reach right now as he had been a week ago.

Why take Jamie hostage? It didn't make any sense. Was it to include me in his body count? It didn't add up.

I was missing something.

Nothing the killer had done so far had indicated he'd pull a crazy stunt like this.

What did he have to gain from this situation?

Was this a trap?

If so, then was I the real target?

I knew he'd framed me for Stacey's murder. I knew he'd had me running around and chasing my tail all week.

But, then, if he wanted me dead, why not come straight after me in the first place?

I watched the digital floor numbers escalate like the jackpot accumulator on a slot machine.

The only fact I knew with any certainty was that Jamie's life hung in the balance. Everything else was wild speculation.

I glanced at the illuminated ceiling grille and visualized Sonny standing barely a few yards above me, in the upper elevator carriage. Possibly contemplating the exact same questions.

I glanced at my wristwatch: thirty seconds.

Half a minute to make *The Undertaker's* ultimatum.

I was cutting it close.

\*   \*   \*

The doors hissed open, noisily. I followed the Glock out into a short hallway that led to the wraparound observation deck. I took it easy; checking out alcoves and doorways as I went. My pulse was already elevated by the rapid ascent. I could hear it tapping out Morse code in my throat.

The whole external wall of the observation deck was composed of big glass panels. Sloping upward and outward from the carpeted floor. Beyond, was a myriad of twinkling rainbow lights. A night-washed cityscape ablaze with luminous color. For a moment my balance went askew. I pressed shoulders against the internal wall and drew a deep, uneasy breath. The view was *dizzying*.

A cold breeze snapped at my skin. I wondered where it was coming from. I headed into it. The observation deck was a huge hollow ring. I followed the natural curve. Clammy hands wrapped around the Glock. Lightning bugs dancing in the corners of my eyes. The breeze grew stronger, becoming noticeably colder. Now I could hear the distant grind of traffic and the incessant whine of wind.

Then I stopped. Dead.

Finally, after a week of relentless pursuit, I had come face to face with the killer.

*The Undertaker.*

*       *       *

But not just *The Undertaker.*

He had company: him and a woman – directly facing me.

*Jamie.*

She was still alive!

She looked worse for wear. Out of it. Drunk and immobile, but still standing. Her head was tipped forward. Arms dangling loosely by her sides. She must have been drugged, I realized. The person with her was *him*: the monster we'd been chasing all week. The child killer.

He'd blown out one of the big glass panels at floor level, creating a gaping maw about three yards wide and two yards tall. Freezing night air was blasting through it, blowing bits of refuse around the deck and ruffling hair. The drop looked perilous. *Was* perilous. One wrong move and they'd both fall through to their deaths.

I took a hesitant step forward.

Then I stopped.

The breath solidified in my throat.

I blinked at the picture of *The Undertaker* and Jamie standing barely ten yards in front of me.

I shouldn't have recognized the killer's face.

But I did.

*Bill.*

*Bill and Jamie.*

My brain buckled.

How could this be?

Only one explanation:

My good friend from the Bureau was *The Undertaker.*

\* \* \*

Things don't always make sense. This didn't. The Universe has a warped sense of humor. Get used to it.

\* \* \*

I almost dropped the gun – not the smartest move in any deadly confrontation. But shock makes us do crazy things. I once saw a woman see her husband mown down by a drunk driver. The guy had cartwheeled over the vehicle. Ten feet off the ground. Hit the pavement, hard – where his head had cracked open like an egg. Shock had caused the woman to run in the opposite direction – straight under a passing bus. Shock can be a killer. As for this epiphany, it was enough to throw every sense out of kilter.

I screwed up my eyes, vainly trying to make sense of the senseless.

My friend from the Bureau was the killer!

The air was on fire.

*Bill was The Undertaker!*

\* \* \*

It goes without saying that major quakes are followed by aftershocks. It is also the case that these aftershocks can wreak more devastation than the first unsettling tremor.

My brain was still reeling from being pulverized when I realized there was a third person standing behind Bill and Jamie. I hadn't seen him at first. He'd been obscured, hiding. But now he was stepping into view. He had a gun to Bill's head. Pressed hard enough into Bill's temple to force his head into a tilt to one side.

I squinted against the cold wind scratching tears from my eyes, not exactly sure what I was seeing. Not exactly sure what to believe. The eyes can be deceptive. Blind you from the truth.

The man wore a dark, brooding stare as though he owned it. Did own it. You know the type: one of those self-assured cocky kinds that like to be the center of attention, then sulk when they're not.

All the same, it was another face I recognized.

A face that burned into my soul.

And in that moment my whole world fell apart.

* * *

Like I say, some things don't bear thinking about. This one didn't. But I had no choice. The reality was pummeling me in the face and demanding a reaction.

"George?"

It came out a rasp, over my busted lips. Didn't sound like it came from me. Maybe a mouse cowering in a corner someplace. Certainly not from me; I was still trying to unravel the unfathomable, and failing fast.

What did I expect?

It was truly the definition of incomprehensible.

Beyond reason.

Inexplicable.

All those words we use to separate us from the truth.

How could George, *my son*, be here, now?

Had *The Undertaker* kidnapped him, too?

But George was the one holding the gun against Bill's head.

Which meant only one thing . . .

George was the killer.

The thought put my brain on ice and stopped the Earth from spinning.

*My boy . . .*

Funny how two simple, normally unassuming words can cut you clean to the core.

*My Boy.*

The killer belonged to me.

No doubt about it now. It was staring me bang in the face. Punching me in the gut. Bleeding every last ounce of logic from my whirling mind.

My son, George, was *The Undertaker.*

My child: the slayer of children.

I blinked against the weight of realization constricting my chest. But the impossible image of my son stayed put. Fixed and unmoving at the center of my collapsing universe.

* * *

There is no preparation for this kind of world-shattering event. No manual to guide our reactions. No *now here's what to do when you find out your son is a murderer* precedent to work from.

Distantly, I remembered wondering how the parents of killers must feel in the moment they learn their own offspring have sinned so evilly. Back then, I'd presumed that revulsion, embarrassment and heartbreak would vie for emotional dominance. Now that I was experiencing it firsthand, my scrabbling mind could barely cope with the bunch of conflicting emotions panel-beating my brain into submission, let alone make any rational sense of it all.

In one fell swoop, my whole belief system had come crashing to a cataclysmic end.

My son was a cold-blooded killer.

No changing that.

The proof was in the pudding.

It's not something you digest every damn day of the week.


\* \* \*


"Hello, Dad. Nice of you to pay us a visit."

He had to shout his words above the roaring wind. But it was George's voice, all right. The voice of my beloved son. Not the robotic funeral dirge I'd become accustomed to of late.

"You're just in the nick of time," he shouted. "You were always a stickler for good time-keeping."

I went to say something, anything, but nothing came out — or if it did, the wind whisked it away before anyone heard it.

"As you can see, Dad, I have two of your most favorite people in the whole wide world here with me."

I saw him tap Bill and then Jamie on the head with the muzzle of the gun. Jamie's gun.

"Of course, they're both drugged up to the eyeballs right now and really don't know what's happening. Which means they're being real nice and cooperative. Do you know what's happening, Dad? Have you connected all those dots of yours yet? Are you going to be cooperative?"

I was aware of my mouth still working wordlessly.

I must have looked like a man who'd just found out his son was a murderer.

"Cat got your tongue? Don't you want to speak to me? Heck, it's all you've wanted for months."

Truth was, I was paralyzed by disbelief. Heart on fire, stoked by the billows of my lungs. Bruised brain still playing catch-up.

"No matter," he shouted. "I guess this will all play out as it will whether you choose to participate or not."

He waggled the gun in my direction.

"You going to shoot me, Dad?"

I lowered the Glock, automatically – mainly because it had become a dead weight in my hands – but partly because pointing it at my own flesh and blood seemed somehow blasphemous.

"You had no idea, did you?" His eyes were wild. Feral.

There were tears in mine.

"I expect you'd like some answers," he shouted. "I know I would if I were in your shoes. How can this be? How can my son take the lives of others? When did he lose his mind or see the light?"

"You've stopped taking your medicine, haven't you?" I found my voice. It was as scratchy as an old vinyl record.

"It speaks! I guess it runs in the family – forgetting to take our meds, that is."

"George . . ."

"I'm speaking!" he yelled, then, softer: "God damn it, Dad. I'm speaking. You never let me speak."

"George –"

"Let me finish! *Jesus!*"

Again, he tapped Bill's head with the gun. This time harder. I saw Bill blink involuntarily. Otherwise, there was no reaction; he was a zombie, just like Jamie.

"You see, Daddy dear, all that your fancy therapists and your astute men of medicine ever did for me was diagnose a disorder. You got the bill while I got the brush-off. Those magical meds kept me walking the straight and the narrow for years. Helped me get a great education. Helped me hook a great woman and start a family. I owe them a lot. But the truth is, without them, I see things, Dad. Not dead people like Bill here. That's bullshit. I see patterns of predictability. I've seen them all my life. And your interfering muted them for a long time."

"George . . ."

"No! Listen to me for a change, dammit. Learn why we're here right now. I saw Harland Laboratories producing a faulty vaccine. They were going to kill thousands of babies. Millions across the world. I had to do something about it, Dad. Wouldn't you?"

"But taking the child's life . . ."

"She was destined to be a prime player someday. She left me no choice." He shook his head, violently. "No choice."

"But, George . . . this is all wrong. Can't you see if you prevent something from happening, no one will ever know? History will just see you as a murderer."

George threw me a narrow-eyed glare. Fierce enough to scare lions. He'd always hated me being right – as sons often do. For all his grandiose lecturing, the thought hadn't even occurred to him.

"I'm begging you, son. Just let them go. Jamie and Bill have nothing to do with this. Your fight is with me. Not with them. This is all about you and me. It always was. Please, George. I'm begging you. Just let them go."

My son's dark glower deepened – as it always had done whenever I'd put demands on him.

"The same way you let Momma go?" he roared. "The same way you allowed her to die?"

Flames scorched my chest. I knew it was coming. Knew the accusation would fly. This moment had been brewing for months. Time and again I'd tried to defuse it. But George had refused to talk it through. Here was my penance.

"You should have done better, Dad. You could have stopped it. If you had made better choices Momma would be alive today."

"All our actions have consequences," I said. "I was trying to do the right thing."

Listen to me: I sounded defeated, words hollow. Truth was, I did blame myself for Hope's death. Eleven months ago, while I had been desperately trying to save a child's life, *The Maestro* had been in my family home, in our bedroom, killing Hope with his damned piano wires. I'd arrived too late to save Leo Benjamin beneath the 7th Street Bridge. Too late again to save Hope, my mortally-wounded wife – who survived for a brief seven days in Cedars-Sinai under the care of Eric Bryce – before becoming *The Maestro's* final victim to date. But I had been trying to make the right decisions. Really, I had. George had never understood that. Never accepted some things are out of our hands.

In his eyes, I had killed his mother.

He was right.

George's expression twisted in on itself. "Your pig-headed arrogance cost them both their lives, Dad. And now it's your turn to feel what I feel."

Before I could respond, George pushed Jamie into the gaping hole.

Just like that.

Without a second thought, he heaved her through the fierce maw, out into the cold air and the thousand feet drop.

I caught a glimpse of Jamie's glazed eyes right before she slipped through the shattered pane and disappeared into the night. Then she was taken by the brutal wind. And gravity. And the insanity of my own flesh and blood. Falling to her death.

My fault.

* * *

Then everything happened in a blur. In slow motion. In surreal time.

George grabbed Bill by the scruff of his neck and proceeded to throw him after Jamie.

My pulse kicked back in and I raised the Glock. I didn't know if I was capable of shooting my own son, or if I would get a wounding shot off before he hurled Bill into the ravenous maw. But I snatched an aim at him all the same. Went to squeeze the trigger – just as a crack of thunder reverberated around the observation deck.

Blood spurted from George's shoulder.

His wild eyes slammed shut with pain.

Another bang echoed around us and another spurt of blood jetted from George's upper thigh.

Then he was twisting, falling, taking Bill down with him.

And both men tumbled into the hole!

But I was already stumbling forward on leaden legs, reaching out a hand, desperate to prevent yet more tragedy from scarring my family.

I saw George grab the metal frame as they fell through. Saw him hook fingers around the razor-edged metal. Saw Bill's suit jacket snag on a jaw of jagged glass. Hook him up. Saw the fabric start to rip, shred, ladder. Both men were within a heartbeat of certain death. Dangling in the cruel wind. I fell to my knees. Freezing wind screamed in my face. George's fingertips were white, straining, slipping. He was staring up at me with defiant eyes, challenging me as he always had.

*What now, Dad? What are you going to do now? Going to make another one of your epic decisions? Another one you're doomed to live with, but can't.*

Behind him, I could see a craze of illuminated city streets and the tiny red-and-white lights of cars far, far below.

Insanely, George started laughing.

It was the maniacal cackle of a madman.

In that terrifying moment I saw every one of his victims. Every one of the innocent lives lost. Every one of the families devastated forever by his madness. And I remembered my promise to a grieving mother. My solemn pledge to right the wrong of her murdered child.

I looked into my son's feral eyes and reacted automatically.

There was no time to think.

No time to breathe.

There was only one choice to make:

A life for a life.

I grabbed Bill by the elbows and heaved with all my might.

As I did, George's fingers finally lost their grip.

And I watched with a sword of fire slicing through my heart as my only begotten son plunged to his doom.

\* \* \*

With every last morsel of strength I could muster, I hauled my friend from the Bureau out of the jaws of death. Then Sonny was by my side, helping me drag him clear. Scooting away from the deathly drop. We backed up against the curved wall of the observation deck, buffeted by wind and disbelief.

I was shattered. Exhausted. I rolled onto my back. There was a jackhammer behind my eyeballs. Everything spinning crazily out of control.

What had I done?

*What had I done?*

I'd killed George!

I'd murdered my own son!

I felt hands couple beneath my neck. Fingers lock. I realized Sonny was resting my head in her lap. I blinked up at her shocked eyes. Felt my own spring with tears.

"God forgive me, Sonny."

She brushed at my face. Tears, I guess.

"It's going to be all right." Her voice seemed far away, lost in the howling wind. "Everything's going to be all right."

*But I couldn't breathe!*

The collapsing universe was pressing down on me, squashing me like a bug. Crushing me for my sins.

My son was dead.

And so was I.

No chance I could live with myself now.

Not after murdering my own son.

I closed my eyes and let the demons loose.

Long months I'd held them back.

Unrestrained, they rushed in from the shadows.

And stole me from one hell to another.

# 133

She reminded me of little Jenny McNamara, lying here in the familiar pose of interment. Peaceful, serene – like she was sleeping. I brushed a strand of hair from off her face and kissed her silken brow.

I wished things could have turned out different.

I asked for forgiveness.

Knew it wouldn't be forthcoming.

I was trembling like a plucked string.

There was no visible evidence of her terrible injuries.

No detectable trauma from her fatal fall.

In my opinion, the undertakers had done a fine job on Jamie.

# 134

I was alive but I was dead. Another oxymoron. I was tired with thinking and done with breathing. I drifted through the world of the living like a specter. Interacting on the surface. Numb. Swept along by events and the relentless flow of life.

I deserved to be dead. No doubt there. Any decent parent would have sacrificed their own life for that of their child. I deserved a lot of things – the least of which was eternal damnation. Being alive was my punishment.

I'd have to suck it up – for now.

# 135

A mere seven days had now passed since the face-off at the *Stratosphere Tower* in Las Vegas with the killer known globally as *The Undertaker*. It seemed like forever. As far as Norman Fuller and the FBI were concerned, they had their man: Harland Candlewood – still comatose and with a dubious outlook. As far as we were concerned, they could go rent a room and screw around until the cows came home.

Seven days of mental torture had come to pass since I'd stared Death in the eyes and looked away. Three of which I'd spent in a Vegas hospital, recovering from sheer exhaustion and the consequences of a cracked skull.

I should have seen it coming. I hadn't.

"That's what happens when you allow killers to club you over the head." My surgeon had told me brusquely.

Ironically, the bed rest had given me a whole new lease on life. I should have been happy. I wasn't.

Physically, I was patched up and medicated to the hilt.

Emotionally . . . well, emotionally I was spent.

Empty.

What more is there to say?

Seeing your own son kill somebody in cold blood – especially someone you care about – does that kind of thing, I guess.

# 136

"I'm telling you, Gabe, we searched every street and every rooftop in the vicinity," Sonny had told me once I'd come back to the living, in the hospital. "There's no sign of the killer anywhere. Looks like he vanished into thin air. I don't know how he did it."

I did. At least, I had my suspicions.

BASE-jumping the El Capitan peak in Yosemite had been good practice for a leap of faith from the tallest tower west of the Mississippi. I knew my son loved his dangerous sports. Knew he'd look before he'd leaped. I was tempted to tell Sonny to search for a parachute, but decided *The Undertaker* would have every base covered – including his escape from Nevada, even with a pair of bleeding bullet wounds.

I knew my son – as my son knew me.

"Did you check rooftop ventilators?"

"Gabe, listen to me: we checked everywhere within a square mile of the Tower. And I mean *everywhere.* Rooftops, alleyways, window ledges. It's like he sprouted wings and flew away. He's literally in the wind."

Rightly or wrongly, I'd masked the flame of hope behind my ribs. I didn't have any right to hold a candle for my killer son. I couldn't explain it. Some things are unexplainable. He was my son. I couldn't explain it. If you think you can, you try.

The lack of a body meant a strong possibility that George was still alive. Somewhere. Out there. A fugitive. On the run. Free to kill again. But *alive.*

You know what they say: where there's life . . . but I had no right even thinking it.

# 137

An awkward position. Why do we put ourselves in awkward positions? Mainly to escape criticism or judgment or truth. Sometimes all three. Your choice.

At some point during my recovery, I decided to keep the identity of the killer to myself. Don't ask. We all do it. We all keep our darkest secrets close to our hearts and our mortal fears closer still. Maybe it's selfishness. Maybe it's not.

Maybe it's self-preservation.

George had disabled all of the security cameras in the Tower – as he had done that night in the Union Pacific rail yard back in LA. No one had seen his face. No one but me.

Only I knew the true identity of Jamie's killer. For now it would stay that way. Ultimately, I was responsible. And I would be the one to make things right. I couldn't do that with the world pointing their fingers of accusation my way. I needed freedom. I needed to be able to go about my own business. Family business.

Luckily for George, Sonny hadn't glimpsed his face as he'd fallen through the window. And Bill had no recollection of his time under the influence of *The Undertaker's* mind-warping drugs. No recall of even meeting him in the lobby of the *Stratosphere Hotel*. No recollection of the urgent text message he'd received on landing back in Vegas – ostensibly coming from me via Jamie's phone – saying we'd got the killer holed up at the *Stratosphere Tower*. A needle in the neck had ensured his compliance. The rest was history.

Unsurprisingly, George hadn't returned to his family home on Staten Island after his stint in Sin City.

An inconsolable Katie had poured out her heart to me by phone. I'd listened from the grave of my hospital bed. Feeling all mangled up inside as she'd recited the note which simply told her that her husband had left. No reason given. No clue to where he was going or if he might return. Just a goodbye and kisses for the baby.

We were all left holding the *whys*.

My doting daughter, Grace, had arrived on day two. She'd already lost one parent and had no intentions of losing another. She kept me comfortable and topped up with encouragement. Have I told you Gracie is my lamplight? She's my grace in every sense of the word. It pained me to keep her from the terrible truth. But I love her too much. Knowing her brother was a serial killer would ruin her life – as it had mine. She stayed two days before work called her back to Florida, and I insisted she go.

On day seven, Jamie was buried.

# 138

Black ties never look good on me. They make me look even more morose than I normally do. The only consolation was it went well with my frame of mind. Let's leave it at that.

Everybody knows how I feel about public appearances – so being in the spotlight for the first time since our press conference in Vegas was predictably tough. No choice. Socializing of any kind rubbed against my nerves. Crawling under my bed with the rest of the demons seemed preferable.

Some things are inescapable.

The turnout for Jamie's funeral saw every available officer and civilian worker from Central Division come pay their last respects to a fallen comrade, and many that were still on duty but snuck over all the same. As is the case with most police funerals, there was a big law enforcement presence. One of our own was gone. Slain in the line of duty. Coming out in numbers was our way of showing a united front. In fact, the entire length of the driveway running through Calvary Cemetery in East Los Angeles was lined with gleaming patrol cars. Polished to perfection. I counted more than seventy, excluding the hearses and the family sedans. In a few short weeks, Jamie Garcia had made a big impression on her comrades. Enough to win her a twenty-one gun salute, and her parents their very own Stars and Stripes, courtesy of the Department. Captains Ferguson and De La Hoya, Coroner Benedict, a few mourners from the Crime Lab – everyone whose lives had been touched by Jamie Garcia – were here.

And yet all eyes were on me.

Gabriel Quinn: the father of the killer, the fraud.

No argument from me that I was to blame. No disputing that irreversible fact. I had exposed Jamie to mortal danger. Okayed her pursuit of the killer's survivor. Didn't even flinch when I'd learned she was in New York. Her death was my fault. Plain and simple. Her blood on my hands. I wondered how many of those other black-tied people shared my thoughts.

On returning to Quantico, Bill had cleared me of the trumped-up charges for the murder of Stacey Kellerman. We all agreed the evidence had been planted and I'd been framed. But it didn't make me feel any less of a monster.

Takes one to father one, I guess.

The next day I tendered my letter of resignation.

"Gabe, don't give me any of this bull crap." Ferguson's voice was as loud as a whisper could get. "Jamie's death has been hard on all of us. Especially you, I know. You're not thinking straight right now. Go away and take time out. Don't make hasty decisions you'll later regret."

We were in his office, with the window blinds closed. We were still wearing black ties. They were still choking our voices.

"The Department doesn't hold grudges," he said. "No one's blaming you."

No one except me.

He tossed my badge back across the desk.

"Take a leave of absence if you have to. Take as long as you need. Go clear your head. Visit your daughter in Florida. Kick some sand. Now's the worst time to make this kind of long-term decision. We're all mourning, Gabe. Don't forget your boy's still out there. You're our best chance of nailing this son of a bitch."

What could I say?

He was right.

I was.

# 139

Thinking back, I don't know what prompted me to drive down the Hollywood Freeway and visit the Metropolitan Detention Center on Alameda Street. Perhaps I wanted closure. Or maybe unconsciously I was following my *Uh-Oh Radar*. It was a gloomy day with makings of rain. I didn't notice. It had been the same hellish weather in my head all week.

On demand, I presented an ID at the gray-on-gray reception desk. Signed the dog-eared logbook. Handed over my firearm, then passed through the metal detector screen. Got frisked. Followed the officer-in-charge down another gray-on-gray hallway to the Visiting Room, where another granite-faced attendant took over and ushered me to a private interview area.

Dr. Milton Perry was seated at a metal table bolted to the floor. He was wearing a standard orange jumpsuit over a white undershirt. And the look of a man on death row. Same look I was wearing. He looked too big for the flimsy plastic chair. He got to his feet as I entered – or as much as his chains would allow. Gave me a shaky smile. I could smell his unease. He smelled like me.

"Detective! Thank God." He reached for my hand but his restraints yanked him back.

I kept it out of his reach.

"Eleanor promised you'd come," he said as we seated ourselves. "I can't thank you enough. I know you and I didn't exactly part on favorable terms. I do hope it won't influence your decision. '

"What do you want, Perry?"

I let my irritation show. I was hiding the fact that my son was *The Undertaker*; I couldn't keep everything in.

If the FBI were right about Perry being *Le Diable*, then the man sitting before me now had clubbed me over the head with a candlestick before slaying my friend, Father Dan, together with two other men of the cloth. And to think I was worried about my own eternal damnation. I was in no mood for pleasantries. No mood for anything.

Perry's eyes scanned my stoic face. I could see fear behind his gaze. He was doing his best to appear happy with his imprisonment. As if. But I could see it, sweating through – like a trapped animal. This place scared him. The thought of spending the rest of his life behind bars had shaken him up real good. As it would me.

"I heard about your partner," he began tentatively. "May I offer condolences?"

I feigned a glance at my watch. "Just get to the point, Perry."

"First off, I want to clear up the confusion about my PA being in Jeff's house."

"We've been over this."

I saw more of the fear leak out of his eyes.

"I need your help to clear my name."

Can't say I was surprised.

"And why would I do that?"

He spread his hands. "Because I am innocent."

"Haven't you heard the cliché? That's what they all say."

I got up to leave.

"Like you and Stacey Kellerman?"

I paused.

"Your situation isn't anything like the same."

Truth was, I didn't want it to be. Didn't want to share anything with Perry. Even murder.

"I have an alibi," he said.

I had familiarized myself with Perry's arrest statements before coming here. There was no mention of an alibi for any of the murders he was being accused of.

They'd found decapitated heads in his basement. No alibis. Everything cut and dry. Case closed.

"Detective, do you believe Le Diable murdered Father Flannigan?"

Instinctively, I touched the healing wound on my scalp. I'd been there. Seen it with my own eyes. Had the scar to prove it.

"Yes."

"What if I said I wasn't even in town that day?"

"I'd say prove it."

Perry shifted his weight and glanced nervously around us. All at once he seemed edgy, like the walls had ears. His stress was palpable.

"I am being framed."

"Why? By who?"

He spread his big hands again. "Why, because I have many enemies. Just like you. People who would like nothing more than to see me fall. As for who . . . let me ask you, detective. Who stands to gain from my incarceration?"

I pouted.

Ordinarily, I wouldn't have given Perry the time of day. But I'd promised a pleading Eleanor to at least listen.

Perry leaned across the table, as far as the chains would allow. "Le Diable," he whispered – as though its very utterance would invoke evil to rise around us.

I got to my feet. I was through with Perry's bull. "I shouldn't have come here. This was a mistake."

"Wait," Perry pleaded, standing. "Please, wait. Please. I'm begging you. I know you and I have our differences. Please don't allow them to cloud your judgment. I assure you I am innocent."

"So give me something solid. Anything."

I waited. Saw him weigh up his options. He didn't have many. When you're caught between a rock and a hard place everything's gritty.

He whispered, "Promise me what I am about to tell you will remain off the public record."

"No."

Milton Perry closed his eyes and let out a long tremulous breath. "All right. I give in. I was with Abe Oswald."

"The mayor? When were you with the mayor?"

"Each time there was a murder."

I looked at Perry suspiciously. "Come on, Perry. I said no bull. That's just about the best alibi you can get in this town. If it's the truth, why didn't you say this before?"

"I couldn't."

"What do you mean you couldn't?"

He rubbed at his face. All at once he was acting like a man who was about to throw off the weight of the world before going to the gallows.

"Because we were in a motel at Laguna Beach," he confessed slowly. "Abe and me. We were . . . together."

I already knew about Perry's romantic affair with Professor Jeffrey Samuels. Already knew that he'd gotten his PA to remove incriminating evidence of their sexual encounters from the house on Carroll Avenue: condoms, sex toys, lubricants . . .

"We're married men," Perry added. "If this ever gets out . . ."

"You think the mayor will back up your story?"

I saw the air go out of Perry's lungs. He looked resigned to his fate. We both knew the answer.

"Orange suits you," I said as I turned to leave.

Perry just stared into his manacled hands.

I should have felt sorry for him, being innocent and all. But the truth was, I didn't feel a thing. Not a damned thing.

I just walked away and left him to it.

# EPILOGUE

I should have gone straight home. I didn't. I headed south instead – following Alameda Street across two busy intersections before making a left onto 7th Street, going east. I didn't stop until I came to the Union Pacific rail yard. It looked different in daylight. In some respects, less eerie. Less the scene of several terrible killings.

I knew better.

I parked my car away from the engineers attending to the decommissioned locomotives and watched my step as I crossed oily shingle. Diesel clawed at my throat. I stepped over rusty rail tracks. Made my way through the gap in the chain-link fence. Took it easy negotiating the steep concrete incline as I headed down into the broad manmade trench that masquerades as the LA River.

Several kids were skateboarding the graffiti-covered incline. Their whoops of laughter echoing around the vaulted carapace of the 7th Street Bridge.

I came to the gritty concrete where the slope leveled out. Stopped. Dug in heels. I could see the supporting pillars from here; I didn't need to go any closer.

I watched the kids playing. Let the smell of sewage and rotting refuse blow across my face. I thought about the events of the last few weeks that had led me to this moment. Thought about all the senseless deaths – some too close to home. Realized I wasn't ready to deal with the brutal reality of it all – not just yet. I'd spent the last eleven months refusing to deal with the murder of my wife. Maybe I'd spend the next eleven refusing to deal with my murderous son.

It was only a matter of time before *The Undertaker* struck again, I knew. If not for this blood prophecy, then another. Some new mindless prediction that needed intervention. And when he did, it would be down to me to catch him.

*Or kill him.*

The thought scared me silly.

No matter how many times I'd hauled myself mentally through the process it never got any easier.

Some things are like that.

We are told, as children, that fear comes from not knowing. On this particular occasion I knew exactly what to expect; I knew the horror that awaited me somewhere down the line – and yet fear was gripping my stomach in a cold fist. The rationalist within me argued it was my old ulcer in need of lubrication, when really, if I were completely honest, I was chilled to the core at the thought of what was to come.

Being a father does that, I guess.

# Words from Keith

*Thank you for reading my novel!*

If you liked it, you'll love the follow-ons

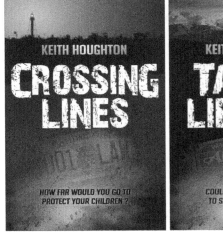

**And if you did enjoy this book, please consider writing a quick review on Amazon for me.**

**Great reviews help other readers decide on my books and hopefully enjoy them as much as you have!**

Simply go to the book's Amazon page, scroll down to the review section and click on **Write a Review**. Or log into your Amazon account and add it from there.

You don't need to write a long and rambling review, a few short words will do the trick.

***Thanks!***

Also, I really appreciate feedback about my books, and love hearing from readers.

Please stay in touch and be the first to hear about my new releases by leaving your email on my website or by dropping me a quick 'hello' to:

**contact@keithhoughton.com**

Once you subscribe you will be entered into my exclusive **Reader Competitions** (such as winning signed copies of my books, or even having your name as a character in a future novel), all by just adding your email address to my spam-free Murder Group mailing list at:

**www.keithhoughton.com**

Simply look for the **Murder Group** popup box and add your email.

You will qualify for all **Reader Competitions**, plus you'll receive a very occasional email update from me about upcoming projects and new releases.

# Titles by Keith Houghton

## Standalone Psychological Thrillers

*Before You Leap*

*No Coming Back*

*Crash*

## Maggie Novak Thrillers

*Don't Even Breathe*

*A Place Called Fear*

*The Other Child*

*Her Only Regret*

## Gabe Quinn Thrillers

*Killing Hope*

*Crossing Lines*

*Taking Liberty*

*Chasing Fame*

## Say Hello!

Join me on social media at

Twitter
**https://twitter.com/KeithHoughton**

Facebook:
**http://www.facebook.com/KeithHoughtonAuthor**

Gabe Quinn Fan Group
**https://www.facebook.com/groups/gabequinn**

*Thanks for all Your support!!*

*Keith*

Keith Houghton

Made in the USA
Monee, IL
17 March 2021